AMBER Road

A Novel of Love and Betrayal on the Roman Frontier

Book 2 in the *Roma Amor* saga by
Sherry Christie

Bexley House Books

Sherry Christie

AMBER ROAD. Copyright © 2020 by Sherry Christie. All rights reserved.

The BHB colophon is a trademark of Bexley House Books.

For information, please write to Bexley House Books, 117 Kelley Point Rd., Jonesport, ME 04649 USA.

Bexley House Books
www.roma-amor.com

ISBN: 978-0-578-45592-1

Library of Congress Control Number: 2020906276

Bexley House Books, Jonesport, Maine

Cover design by Bespoke Book Covers, Ltd.

Maps by Inge Herzog Rice

Printed in the United States of America

*To my mother, who loved English, and
my father, who loved history.*

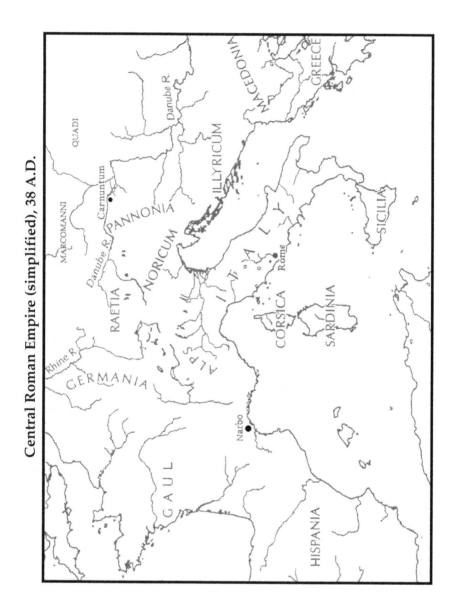

Central Roman Empire (simplified), 38 A.D.

The Danube Frontier and the Mark (simplified), 38 A.D.

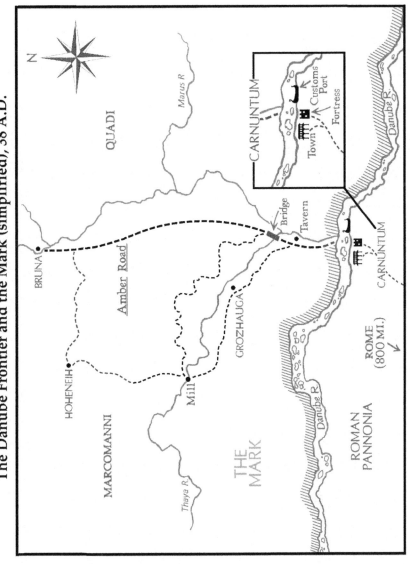

WHO'S WHO IN AMBER ROAD

Romans

AQUILO, MARCUS LICINIUS Formerly Marcus Licinius Carinna; once broad-stripe tribune of the Fifteenth Legion; son of the late Senator Titus Licinius Carinna
Antonia TERENTIA Marcus's mother
NINA Marcus's twin sister
PUBLIUS Marcus's older brother, a suicide
DIO His secretary, a freedman born in the family
CLEON Marcus's chief bodyguard, a onetime gladiator
OLLIUS His other bodyguard, also a former gladiator
RUFUS His horse-boy, a mute Thracian slave
PHORMIO Marcus's late body-slave and companion

LEONNATUS of Narbo A wealthy Gallic trader in Carnuntum

POPPAEUS Legate commanding the Fifteenth Legion
L. Verginius PLACIDUS Senior surgeon of the legion
Valerius SECUNDUS A narrow-stripe legion tribune

SAXA Commander of the Praetorian Guard's Special Cohort in Rome
Aelius LAMIA Acting Special Cohort prefect for the Northeast
Vatia GLABRIO A Special Cohort agent in Carnuntum

*****Gaius CAESAR (CALIGULA)** Princeps of Rome
*****AGRIPPINA** Oldest of his three sisters
*****DRUSILLA** Caligula's favorite sister
*****LIVILLA** Youngest of Caligula's sisters
*****M. Aemilius LEPIDUS** Drusilla's husband; patron of Marcus's family
*****GERMANICUS Caesar** Late father of Caligula and his sisters, a famous general

*****G. Calvisius SABINUS** Governor of the province of Pannonia and its legions
*****Cornelia GALLA** His wife, a cousin of Marcus's father
*****Quinctilius VARUS** Late governor of Germania, whose army was massacred by Germanic rebels

Germans

AURIMA A junior priestess of Austro; recently a hostage in Rome
FRIDURIC Aurima's brother
HELLE (Helewidis) Friduric's wife
THANCMAR A miller; older half brother of Friduric and Aurima

AMMISIA A priestess of Austro; mother of Aurima, Friduric, and Thancmar; murdered six years earlier
INGIOMAR Ironhand (to Romans: Inguiomerus) Widower of Ammisia; Aurima's and Friduric's father; war chieftain of the eastern Marcomanni and lord of the stronghold of Hoheneih
MAELO Ammisia's brother; Ingiomar's right-hand man
ODO Maelo's adolescent son

***VANNAZ (to Romans: Vannius)** King of the Marcomanni and Quadi
***VANGIO** Vannius's nephew

GISILA Vannius's mother; chief priestess of Austro
HROSWITHA Grandmother of Aurima and her siblings; a senior priestess of Austro
MARBODO (to Romans: Maroboduus): late king of the Marcomanni, Hroswitha's brother

BERINHARD Lord of Grozhauga, a Quadi stronghold
CHLOTHAR Brother of Berinhard

*Historical figures

WHAT'S IN THE BOOK

1: OATH-BREAKER'S SON

Nearly three months, and still she had not returned.

If not for that brave, passionate, unpredictable girl, I would have been a State official appointed by my bosom friend Caligula Caesar, getting fat from bribes and lavish dinner parties. I would have been the cosseted young heir of my noble family, sharing our old house on the Palatine with overfamiliar slaves, an influential and autocratic father, a mother who acquired factories and olive-oil mills as other matrons collect jewels, a twin sister ignominiously divorced for childlessness, and an urnful of ashes that had been my brother, who killed himself to escape dishonor.

I would have been Marcus Licinius Carinna, rich and popular, with my feet set on the path to the Senate and perhaps, one day, a consulship.

Now I was none of these things. Instead I was an ex-Army officer with a traitor's name, drinking away the wait for my beloved in a squalid *taberna* in a dusty little outpost in a province hundreds of miles from Rome.

And at the moment, I might be in trouble.

When off duty, soldiers usually head for the nearest brothel or swillhole. Why these legionaries from the Fifteenth had wandered to the most distant edge of town was a mystery. But even out of uniform, there was no mistaking the boast in their swagger: *We are the heroes protecting you ungrateful rabble from the barbarian hordes. Kiss our stinking feet.*

The first of them loomed up in the alley outside. Enough of the spring twilight was left to show mosquitoes hovering around his close-cropped hair. He rapped a coin on the open counter of the *taberna.* "Jug o' wine. Best you got."

"Aye, pour us the forty-year Falernian," added another man behind him. They cackled.

The *tabernarius* hastily uncapped one of the countertop wells and ladled wine into a jug. No one around here wanted to rile a soldier.

I turned back to my own cup. They were unlikely to recognize me slouched over a table inside the darkening wineshop. Unless they came in.

"Move, you two," said another voice. "I need to fix this buggering boot nail."

And the third one came in.

He bumped against a customer, swore, and upended the man's bench, dumping him on the dirt floor. "And I'll have this table, thanks." He yanked it toward himself, spilling a partly full cup. The dispossessed drinker slunk away without complaint. "Here, brothers!"

The other two stumbled in, cursing. "Stinks like Hades' bunghole in here."

The small *taberna* was already so crowded there was hardly room to swat a fly. The soldiers choked it like six toes in a boot.

I hunched over, shielding my face with a hand. With luck I would be ignored.

"You! Get up. I want your seat."

I pretended not to hear. Seven months earlier I had been a hero, rallying ambushed troops to end a Germanic uprising. I did not want to find out what the legion thought of me now.

"Are you deaf? Get up, I said!"

I lifted my head slowly. Saw the man's hairy calves and second-best boots, laces knotted where they had broken. Then the patched tunic, faded but recognizably reddish. Ropy arms blotched with tattoos and grime. A sneer on an ill-shaven face that I did not think I knew. It is hard, though, to recall one face out of several thousand.

"A German!" His hand shot out to grab me by the beard. "Get out, you filthy barbarian!"

I lunged to my feet. Before I could force my way past, one of his comrades loomed up beside him, trapping me in the corner. And where was Ollius? Still emptying his bladder, the useless oaf.

"No trouble now, men," the *tabernarius* bleated. "No one wants trouble."

Trouble was the last thing I needed. But without warning some sort of furnace door burst open within me and I was engulfed in rage—at being unable to claim my own authority, at squandering my life in this dog's crotch of a settlement, at waiting for a woman who did not come.

"Let me pass, you idiot," I snapped. It came out in educated Latin, not the slum-garble I had trained myself to speak.

"Who do you think—" The soldier's bleary eyes widened. "Tribune?" Shock gave way to fury that contorted his sunburned face. "What are you doing here?"

I hit him in the jaw so hard his teeth cracked together. He stumbled back. A bench toppled as other customers scrambled away. I hurled the table into the second soldier, then grabbed the third by his neck-cloth and drove my fist into his face.

Ollius blundered in, now that I did not need him. He snatched up a stool and swung it around, and men thrashed and sprawled in all directions. I yelled for him to stop. He was ruining my fight.

He seized my arm and shouted something. I kicked his knee out from under him.

The next I knew, I was being dragged by the belt through clumps of filthy straw in the alley outside the *taberna*. Children booting a ball hooted in glee. Chickens squawked and flapped away.

When Ollius let go, I scrambled up to pitch myself into the brawl again. He pushed me back. "That's enough."

"Hands off me!" I gave a mighty heave to knock him off his feet. Though shorter, he was strong and stocky. It would have been easier to tumble Augustus's obelisk.

"I'm your bodyguard, you fool!"

"You're dish— dismissed! Guard somebody else."

"Marcus, stop," he snapped.

It was like a slap of cold water. I shoved him again, but my madness was fading.

"Gods above." He bent to massage his kneecap. "After all this time!" Blood speckled his shaved head.

One of the soldiers plunged through the tavern doorway with a broken table leg. Ollius swept his sword from its scabbard and smacked the club out of the man's hand. "Get back inside, sonny boy. I've put better men than you in the sand."

The soldier's mouth twisted above a goat's-beard of gore. Then something at the end of the alley caught his eye. "Fuck you, oath-breaker's son!" He spat into the dirt. Retreating into the *taberna*, he called out, "Stand down, brothers. We'll get him later."

A hooded man was riding toward us, flanked by four guards. They tramped in a heavy cadence, clinking martially, past a slave with a water jar who shrank against the wall. A man wealthy enough to have an armed escort was a rare sight in this seedy quarter, where the drink was bitter and the whores were vicious. Even the boys who had shouted insults in Pannonian paused their ball game to watch.

The little troop had already seen us. I rotated my head to loosen my neck muscles. Ollius sucked in a breath and squared himself.

Lamplight bloomed in the *taberna* as the rider reined in by a dingy fox and grapes painted on the outside wall. Someone blocking the light moved out of the way, and it spilled across the counter onto Ollius and me.

The rider let out an exclamation. He dismounted awkwardly, favoring a stiff leg, and stumped toward us.

Of all the blasted luck! I moved a few steps away. Back toward the stifling attic I shared with all four of my men, two dusty flights above a stonecutter's yard.

Too late. The uneven scuff of footsteps halted, and the newcomer said, "Marcus Carinna?"

I turned. My heart still thumped hard from the fight. "Leonnatus."

Leonnatus pushed back his hood. Thick brows like snow cornices met over his long nose; his shovel chin jutted like a disgruntled schoolmaster's. Perhaps the dome of his brow was a little higher, the wreath of white hair a little farther in retreat, but he had not otherwise changed since the previous autumn.

"You are back in Carnuntum, yet you have not visited me," he said.

In truth, I had been here since the great snowfalls of February. But I had hidden behind my beard and long hair, and had avoided places where I was known.

"I was shocked to hear of your father's death," Leonnatus went on. His small bright eyes were steady on mine. "Your lady mother wrote me that you had left Rome."

I inclined my head.

For a moment neither of us spoke. Women farther down the alley called in their children. Someone spattered slops from a balcony.

Then we both spoke at once. I overrode him discourteously: "When you write her next, tell her I am in good health."

"I have some of your favorite Baeterran, nicely chilled," he said. "Come and join me in a cup."

It caught me off guard. My skin and clothes were stained and reeking with sweat and the unholy muck Ollius had dragged me through. "Another time," I said gruffly, meaning never.

"Carinna." He lowered his voice. "Humor an old man you once called a friend."

"I am not fit company." A few paces away I added without turning, "And I no longer use that name."

2: SIMMER

The flimsy outside stair groaned with every footfall. At the top, the door hung wide open in the night.

I stepped over Dio, splayed on the floor with arms outflung. No breath of air stirred the oven heat. Stooping under the rafters, I unbuckled my knife belt and let it fall.

The whack as it hit the floorboards startled him awake. "Marcus?" He sat up. "Phew! Did you fall into a dung heap?"

"Near enough." I peeled off my tunic and let it drop. "Anything left to drink?"

"A bit." A gurgle, a splash, the thump of a jug set down in the darkness. "Nothing to eat with it, I fear. Unless you like gnats." He held out the cup.

My swelling knuckles twinged when I grasped it. "What happened?" he asked.

"Accident." I tipped the cup to my lips. The wine was immeasurably worse than Leonnatus's Baeterran, hardly fit to rinse a chamber pot.

Dio hunched cross-legged on the floor, busying himself with flint and steel. A spark flared and was coaxed to ignite a lamp wick. "Were you recognized?"

I was too angry at my loss of control to admit to the brawl. "I saw Leonnatus."

"What did he say?" Dio tried to sound matter-of-fact, but eagerness brightened his voice. When he was my mother's secretary, he had scribed many letters to the old trader.

I sat to take off my boots. The laces resisted, as stiff as twigs. "Oh, we fell on each other's neck with tears of joy."

There was a silence. Through the floor came the thin wail of an infant and a man's curse, then the shrill and snarl of a couple arguing.

"Marcus." Dio put down the lamp and reached for a wax tablet. "I have waited as long as possible to say this, but we are nearly out of money." He opened the tablet and traced a line of figures with his finger. "The rent on this pigeon roost is due soon, and—"

"Tomorrow Spider serves the Norican mare. That will bring us seventy-five denarii." I kicked the unlaced boots into a tangle.

"Seventy-five will not go far to keep five men and two horses." He took a deep breath. "Sell the red one. You do not need them both."

"I am not selling my warhorse."

Dio let out a huff of annoyance. Once a well-fed, well-groomed, well-behaved slave in a patrician house, he had transformed during the difficult escape from Rome. Now soot and grime mottled his tunic, his thinning dark hair hung in sweaty strands, and his tongue was as sharp as a cutpurse's knife. "Those beasts are better kept than we are."

I lurched over to the washbasin and tipped water onto a rag.

He sighed. "With unlimited credit from Gaius Silius to draw on, why must we live like this?"

I scrubbed my face. "I am done with using the money of friends."

"Would not Leonnatus, being your mother's Amber Road agent—"

"Nor will I borrow from him." I lifted the long hair at my nape and ran the wet rag around my neck.

His voice became arid. "What, then? Will we start begging in the streets?"

I slung the rag to the floor. "Curse it, Dio, what do you want me to do? Cross the Danube and comb the wilderness for her?"

"Of course not."

"Perhaps you think I am a coward?"

His face flushed. "Of course not."

But perhaps he did. Not long ago he had seen me stand rooted, numb with shock, when I should have stopped my father from throwing away his life.

I looked past him. A saddlebag on a peg gapped open like a half-wit's grin, showing the end of a scroll case. He had been reading Father's memoirs. "I spoke in haste." He closed the tablet. "We are not so badly off. I can earn money scribing letters for people in the forum. Or curse tablets. There is as much vengefulness here as in Rome."

The cot wheezed bits of straw and stone dust as I slumped onto it again. "Do as you wish. You're free now."

He pressed his lips together. I ought to have told him that our choices had dwindled because a trio of legionaries had recognized me, but I was too dispirited. "Put out the light. Ollius and Cleon have gone down to sleep by the river."

He pinched out the lamp flame and lay back on the floor. Mosquitoes whined in the darkness. The baby below had stopped crying; its parents were noisily occupied in making another one.

"Come with me to the horse farm," I said, attempting conciliation.

"Of course. A Senator's son must not dirty his hands with coin." Tartness soured his voice.

Another day's end. Ten long weeks since Aurima had vanished into the Great Forest with a hired guide, leaving me to retreat alone across the silver Danube, the boatman's oars jostling clots of ice. And thirty-four days, soon to be thirty-five, since the full moon of March when she had promised to return.

Dio, my two guards, even my horse-boy Rufus who worshiped her: they all reckoned she had forsaken us. In the abyss of night, wavering between fear and hope like a sapless fool, I tortured myself by imagining why she had not come back—a marsh fever, a wild beast attack, ambush by some brigand unaware that his coppery-haired victim was a priestess of the Light. Meanwhile I skulked around this cursed frontier backwater, avoiding anyone who had known me as the legion's broad-stripe tribune.

Now, thanks to my outburst in the *taberna*, I was forced to act. To leave Carnuntum, which meant living forever in the shadow of my father's disgrace. Or to attempt a deed of courage and piety to restore our family's honor, which meant crossing the river and looking for Aurima among Germans who had no love for Rome. Ingiomar Ironhand, in particular.

Her father.

In the faint light seeping in from a slice of moon, my gaze caught again on the hanging saddlebag. The cylindrical scroll case was tipped toward me. The small ownership seal stamped into its cap stared like the pupil of a censorious eye.

Oath-breaker's son.

3: ROAD SONGS

The gravel road decayed to dirt outside the town palisade. Our shadows reached ahead, long and thin in the glare of the rising sun. In a few miles this rutted track would join the paved road that ran from the fortress across the broad Pannonian plain, over the Julian Alps, down the spine of Italy to the city from which I was exiled.

Rufus hummed to himself, perched on the bare back of my long-legged blue roan stallion. He had brushed Spider's coat until it shone silver, and the black mane and tail until they streamed like silk.

Dio ambled behind on a hired mule, out of kicking range of my bad-tempered warhorse, Boss. The big sorrel shared my restlessness, tossing his head and jibbing at everything.

Heat, mosquitoes, and misgivings had pricked me all night long. If I went in search of Aurima, I needed my four companions to risk themselves with me. But neither Ollius nor Cleon, whose protection I counted on, had shown up for this early journey to the horse farm. After eight hundred miles of unsettled sea, snow-blasted mountains, and unmapped outlands, this was a fine time for them to have stopped guarding me.

Bees buzzed in tall weeds at the roadside. Dust floated in tawny clouds from our mounts' hooves; overhanging shade alternated with sunlit vistas of wheat and barley. Villas sprawled over placid hills: the estates of newly rich Army contractors, complete with slaves toiling in infant fields and vineyards. Farther away, plumes of smoke rose as more woodland was cleared for farming.

The *Pax Romana*, Pannonian version. Made possible by my old legion, the Fifteenth, defending our provinces from the restless Marcomanni and Quadi tribes north of the Danube River.

I cleared my throat. "Rufus, I want you to come with me." He was still my slave, so I could rely on his obedience—at least until he was old enough to be given the freedom I had promised him.

He cocked his head expectantly.

"I am going to find Aurima."

He gave me a broad grin. This barbaric youth from Thracia, once discarded as worthless, had fed all six of us with his hunting on the wintry journey from Rome.

"Good," he said. The word was indistinct, for he had lost most of his tongue to a villain in the imperial household, but the gleam in his blue eyes was plain enough.

Dio thumped his mule's sides, then hissed in vexation. "Stupid, vile beast! Marcus, will you slow your horse?"

I reined back. "Listen, Dio: Leonnatus will be glad to take you—"

"Did I mishear?" His straw hat had slipped down on his brow. He pushed it back to stare at me. "Did you say you are going to search for Aurima? In Barbaricum?"

"In the Mark, yes. I have decided to join Leo's next trading expedition."

"But . . . Are you . . ." Whatever he wanted to say strangled him.

I was in no mood for his contentiousness. "I do not expect you to come with me." His clerical skills would be useless in the wilds. "I will pose as a horse dealer. A Gaul."

Beneath the hat brim, his face darkened to a muddy red. "I hope . . ." He coughed as if he had swallowed dust. "I mean, there is no need to prove anything."

"To you?" His insinuation of cowardice still rankled.

His mule had fallen back again. He kicked it fiercely to catch up. "Are you serious about this?"

"You should be pleased, after faulting me for irresolution."

Boss folded his ears back, sensing my ill humor. Muscles tensed in his haunches. I tightened the reins.

Dio tried to glare, but his temerity made him blink. "Marcus, you are the head of our house. You swore an oath to gather the *familia* together again, to restore our household altar and the images of our ancestors. How can you let yourself perish in the wilderness?"

Blood heat rose into my face. My honor was my concern, not his. "I need Aurima's help if I am to search for the Eighteenth Legion's lost Eagle," I said, holding back my anger. "So first I must find her. It is simple."

A crow shrieked from atop a sun-bleached shrine to Fornax. Boss hauled at his reins and stamped his formidable hooves.

"You might as well look for a . . . a butterfly in a wasps' nest!" Dio wiped spittle from his lips. "When her father found her mother's murderers, he ripped out their bowels with his bare hands." He dragged in a breath. "What do you suppose he has done to her for sleeping with a Roman? What do you suppose he will do to you?"

Tightness spread across my cheekbones.

"Even if he has only married her off to one of his warriors," he plunged on mercilessly, "how will you feel, prancing up to her doorstep? Eh?"

He was salting the wounds of my most terrible imagining. But Aurima had merely been delayed in marshaling the support of her father and her own people; I was sure of it. Most of the time.

She knew how ardently I longed to reclaim the Eagle captured nearly thirty years earlier, when Rhineland tribes had massacred three of our legions. The defeat, our worst in a century, had since been avenged, but only recovery of the last legion standard would erase the shame.

Dio was still arguing. "There are other places to go. Far enough from Rome to live until Caligula is ... until there is a new Princeps."

My temper exploded. "Hide in some pretentious little Roma Nova? And do what? Live on the pity of the local gentry? What is a man to do whose only ambition has been to bring civilization to the god-cursed barbarians?"

I was shouting so loudly that my warhorse decided to join the attack. He snaked his head sideways, teeth bared. With a cry of alarm Dio yanked on the reins, so it was not his leg but his mount's neck that Boss bit. The mule shrieked like a trumpet and reared, toppling its hapless rider into the dirt.

I had had enough. "Take charge at the farm," I called, though he knew no more of horse breeding than of the mysteries of Dionysus. I kneed Boss into a gallop.

"Faster," I shouted, and the stallion responded, his white forelegs flashing in explosions of dust and grit. We raced past the horse farm, away from the town and the fortress and the Danube. I leaned my cheek into his mane, the cadence of his hooves thrumming through my knees and spine and shoulders. Hair whipped my flooding eyes.

A mile, a mile and a half ... Was I thinking he would carry me all the way to Rome? As if time could roll back on itself, and I would be greeted in the atrium of our house by my parents, my sister, and my older brother—no doubt accompanied by his closest friend, Gaius Caesar, nicknamed Caligula.

Young Caligula had grown up to rule Rome, but Publius would never grow older than twenty-two. I had already passed him by a year.

When at last I brought the panting stallion to a halt, we were on the grassy verge of the stone-laid road to which the dirt track from town connected. Partly visible over a rise, an Army work party labored in a haze of dust and shouts to pave the last segment between Carnuntum and Scarbantia.

I slid to the ground, bracing myself against the horse's heaving side. Patting his powerful neck, I wheezed out a few words of praise. I was hot-breathed too, my thighs quivery, bruised fingers aching from gripping the reins.

Boss dipped his head, tonguing the bit thirstily. The road crew from the fortress would have water, but I did not want to draw their attention. I turned the horse back toward a spring we had passed. Dust-gray, streaked with sweat, he would need Rufus's careful grooming. I wanted him to gleam like a conqueror's steed when I called on Leonnatus this afternoon, for I would need to look confident.

Leo, I would say, *I want to enter the barbarian lands of the Mark clandestinely, so I can recover the last legion standard captured during the Germans' Great Rebellion. Even though previous efforts have failed, I believe King Vannaz will agree to help because I will have the support of his war chieftain, Ingiomar Ironhand, whose daughter Aurima will have persuaded him to support me.*

But first I must find out where she is.

Small birds wheeled across the pale sky, their sickle wings like the knife Aurima had lost in Rome. The new one still waited for her at the silversmith's in Carnuntum.

Wherever she was, she would have sung the sun up this morning.

Austro's priestess has different songs for clear, cloudy, and stormy days; for pleas and praise and thanksgiving, all in an archaic tongue that it was not my business to know. Between ourselves, we talked in braided Latin and Germanic. When Ollius and Cleon heard her correct me, they rolled their eyes. We Romans seldom bother to learn other people's languages; they are required to learn ours.

But not when a man is so besotted that he aches at the sight of his woman bent foraging in the wild woods, or riding beside him on a winter-furred Libyan horse, or standing in a frigid downpour calling on her goddess to keep us safe on our journey.

I thought of her on an icy January morning, singing to Austro while the rest of us huddled in our leaky tent. Melting sleet had dribbled down my cheeks and beard as I held up the tent flap with one hand, trying to keep our fire from drowning.

She dove into the tent, hurling off her drenched hat and cloak. Rufus hooted, and Dio stopped reciting *The Iliad*. From the end of the tent where he was dicing with Cleon, Ollius called, "Will the sun goddess give us better weather?"

A tangle of damp clothing muffled her voice: "So I have prayed."

I had clawed aside the sodden cloak as her cold hands unbuckled my belt. Then, bare and clammy, she wriggled up inside my tunic. Her head popped through the tunic's wide neck. I yelped. "Did I break your poor nose, my love?" she murmured solicitously.

Her hand emerged through the neck hole to tweak the bridge of my nose. "No," she said, "still it is the *nabja* of an eagle."

We both laughed. Aurima's ripe-plum breasts pressed against my chest, her nipples nubbly with chill. A biting freshness breathed from her cold cheeks. I pressed her against me, fumbling beneath damp wool to her muscled legs, parted them, and pushed into the heat that was hidden.

"Ah," she had whispered with a rascal's grin, "so that is not broken, either."

The memory made me ache. Perdition—and I had promised to be chaste while she was gone! At the spring I thrust my head under the cold stream from a pipe while Boss sucked noisily from a trough beneath it.

We plodded on, his head bobbing behind my shoulder. Sunlight glared hot on the paving stones. With the verges shorn of trees and underbrush for the regulation twenty paces on each side, there would be no shade until we turned onto the track leading back to Dio and Rufus. Back to the problem of my two missing bodyguards. Back to preparations for travel into the vast Germanic wilderness, where Dio thought I would die.

Aside from a few scuffles with brigands, the six of us—four men and two boys, one "boy" with short dark-dyed hair that had used to be copper red, her chest bound to complete the disguise—had had no difficulty among the lonely hamlets and strongholds of the Adriatic mountains and eastern Pannonia. Since any trading party of Leonnatus's was sure to be well guarded, I reckoned we would travel with the same impunity in the Mark. Anyway, the king of the Quadi and Marcomanni was well compensated to keep commerce flowing safely through his lands.

On the other hand, Caesar's silver had made no difference to Ingiomar Ironhand, who had tried to annihilate an unthreatening Roman vexillation last year.

What might he have done to her for sleeping with a Roman?

"If he has harmed her, I will kill him," I said aloud.

You? my father would have snorted. *You, who almost let Caligula slaughter you like a sheep?*

What might he do to me?

The bit-rings rattled as the stallion shook his head, biting at flies.

I said, "I am not afraid of him."

The claim rang hollow. Father would have lifted his eyes skyward, despairing of my ever being able to sway a chamberful of Senators.

Boss nipped my shoulder. The track to town forked off ahead, rutty and hoof pitted, shaded by a huge oak tree. "I see it," I growled, and then heard what had alerted him: the rumble of hooves and thin squeal of iron-shod wheels coming up fast behind us.

A courier? No—too many horses, too heavy a vehicle. No one I wanted to be noticed by, in any case.

The occupants of such a high-speed conveyance were probably bound for the fortress, which meant they would stay on the paved road. Still, it was better to be out of sight. I urged Boss onto the dirt track and guided him into the oak tree's deepest shade.

"Turn here," someone called out. The cavalcade slowed, then veered onto the town road in a flurry of gravel. Two armed riders trotted in the lead. Another two flanked a four-wheeled *carpentum* pulled by three mules in line, with a final pair of escorts bringing up the rear. Although dust on the carriage body hid its insignia, I recognized the black-and-white-striped helmet crests of the provincial governor's bodyguards. There was no sign of the governor himself, whose pride in his soldierly vigor would normally have placed him among the men on horseback.

I tugged Boss's head down to keep him quiet. As the *carpentum* jolted past, a woman's pale hand pulled its curtain shut against the billowing dust. A noble lady who, oddly, was headed to the town instead of an official reception at military headquarters.

Spider whinnied a greeting as I caught up with Dio and Rufus. "Who was that in the carriage?" Dio complained. "They nearly ran us down."

I shrugged off the question. "Did it go well at the horse farm?"

He touched his belt purse. "I bargained the Norican up to a hundred, to cover a second visit if the mare does not quicken."

"Fine." I steered Boss away from Spider to keep the two stallions' flattened ears and swishing tails from proceeding to aggression. "Have you seen Cleon or Ollius?"

Rufus pointed a dirty finger. Road dust still swirled around a figure limping from shadow into sunlight. Sweat glistened on a hairless head and a salt-rimed leather cuirass.

Ollius.

I rode ahead to meet him, and got as far as saying, "Where . . ." when I saw that one of his eyes was slitted in a dusky-red bruise. "What mischief is this, man?"

He squinted up at me. "I . . . um." His tongue foraged over dry lips. "Got anything to drink?"

"In a minute." I swung out of the saddle. "What happened?"

"Uh." He backed away as Boss lipped salt from his upper arm. "Those whoreson soldiers."

"You went back to the *taberna*?"

"Said you disgraced the legion. Bragged they'd throw your stinking carcass in the river." Ollius mopped his face gingerly with the shoulder of his tunic. "Don't worry, nobody's dead. Me and Cleon just used our fists."

"Where is he?"

"He, uh, punched a centurion. A patrol took him." He scowled defiantly, knowing I would be displeased. "It was for the family's honor, Marcus."

I bit back a curse. Everyone was obsessed with our honor.

"And"—he sighed—"a trooper brought a message. You're wanted at the fortress."

Ice trailed down the back of my neck. "Did he ask for Marcus Carinna?" Former tribune Carinna, spotted at the *taberna*—or anonymous stranger Marcus Aquilo, patron of two brawling ex-gladiators?

Dio and Rufus reached us then. Amid their exclamations about his colorful injury, Ollius guzzled water from Dio's flask. Finally he blew out his breath explosively. "They want Aquilo." He wiped his chin. "To report to the duty officer. At once." He poured the rest of the water over his shaved head and exhaled again. "I told the patrol me and Cleon was both Roman citizens. That's why they let me go."

"What about Cleon?" Dio wanted to know.

I said, "Ordinarily, they'd beat him into slime for assaulting a centurion. Since he's a citizen, they'll keep him locked up until they decide what to do." Or until I arrived to pay for his release.

The three of them stared mutely at me. Once the ripples spread from the pebble I had kicked into yesterday's pond, dozens—hundreds—of soldiers would be on the lookout for Marcus Carinna, the traitor's son. I hated to delay making my request of Leonnatus, but the sooner Marcus Aquilo showed up at the fortress with his ruffian's beard, sweat-stiff mane, thick Gaulish accent, and wallet of coins, the better.

I would need to take off my ring. The silver ring on my right hand, engraved with the ship that was our family seal, had belonged to Publius. Its twin, my father's, was in the Vestals' keeping. I was the last of the Carinna branch of the Licinii, a noble clan that over the years had given Rome consuls and generals, governors and lawmakers.

It was an irony to make the Furies laugh. Barely a year ago I had won a commendation for forging peace with Ingiomar Ironhand. Now I might be hauled back to Rome for having furtively brought home his daughter, the hostage for that truce.

I thumbed my ring around to hide the signet. "Meet me later at that cookshop by the Temple of Augustus and Rome. Dio, give me all the money we have."

Dio was whacking dust off himself with the battered hat. "But I just . . ." With resignation he dug out of his belt purse the coins he had obtained at the horse farm. "What if you are detained?"

"If I am not back by nightfall . . ."

Then what? Finally I said, "Keep waiting."

4: HEADQUARTERS

When I had left Carnuntum in early fall, the camp was full of pride and celebration after the crushing of Ingiomar's rebellion. Now it sprawled desiccated and forlorn in the uncommon heat, like a forgotten oasis in the desert. Weeds sprouted between roof tiles and drooped from the crevices of barrack walls. Storks had built a nest atop the treadmill that powered the construction crane. Flies swarmed everywhere, sending Boss into a frenzy of tail-lashing and leg-biting.

The disorder was painful to see. Was the distraction of Palatine conspiracies to blame, or the heedlessness of officers who had reverted to sloth? At least the lack of bustle suggested that Ingiomar and his warriors across the river were minding their manners.

Far from being the target of every man's stare, I was hardly noticed. Most soldiers on duty were out of the fortress: felling trees, laboring on the roads, collecting taxes at the customs port, or keeping the peace somewhere else. A few specialists exempt from regular duties trudged between buildings. As I passed through the shadow of the headquarters arch, the guards did not even glance up from their game of knucklebones.

It would be a different story when I returned with the lost Eagle. Cheering troops, tears of joy, sacrifices of thanksgiving, and accolades for the resolute young Roman who had risked his life to search the wastelands of Germania . . . with, I hoped, the aid of his beautiful Marcomanni lover, revered as a priestess by her tribespeople . . .

It was the midday break, so the assembly yard's dusty expanse was deserted, the surrounding colonnades empty. I tied Boss to a post in front of the headquarters building. The camp commandant's brindle bitch came over to let me scratch her ears, wagging her tail in happy recognition.

Not a smart move for a man who wished to be thought a stranger.

My mistake went unnoticed by the sentry at the top of the steps, who barred the way with his javelin. "What do you want?"

"Sent for me," I said in a Gallic grumble. "I am Aquilo."

"Give up your weapons."

I handed over my old legion longknife, sharpened so often that a good third of the blade was gone. Once my father's; briefly my brother's; now mine.

He shouted for a runner. "Some yokel named Aquila says he's wanted. Tell the senior surgeon."

Placidus was officer of the day? *Come back tomorrow*, instinct warned. Someone else would be duty officer. Someone who was not my mentor and friend.

But I was still there when the runner returned. "Come," he said insolently and, after I had followed him through the columned entrance, added, "Wait here."

The duty officer's door was shut. Sunlight glared through the atrium's roof-opening onto a wedge of gray-and-white mosaic floor and a dirty wall. Flies crept on an overflow grille in the empty *impluvium*. Voices muttered from a distant corridor.

The flies whirled up, then settled again as I crossed the hobnail-scored floor to the chapel sheltering the legion's sacred standards. The guards on either side of its open doors braced to attention.

I scratched my chin through my beard. "Just looking," I said amiably.

The silver Eagle sprang out of shadow in the windowless *sacellum*, its wings outspread above the emblem LEGIO XV APOLL: the Fifteenth Legion Apollinaris, dedicated by Augustus Caesar to Apollo, his patron god. More than just a battle standard, it was the symbol of our divinely favored mission to bring order to the world.

Unit and auxiliary emblems and flags flanked the Eagle. Next to the altar a plinth held a bust of Gaius Caesar Augustus Germanicus, for whose good health and good fortune the Fifteenth sacrificed daily. It was one of those bronzes turned out by the score after his accession as Princeps, a bland likeness that did not capture his haunted malice.

I glanced at the back of my left wrist, where a pale "R" glimmered against the sun-brown skin. *Reveniam*, it meant: *I will return*. The vow I had made to my entire household before leaving Rome.

Nailed bootsteps crisped across the floor. A familiar voice grated, "You there! Away from that altar!"

Vatia Glabrio invariably looked unshaven and unclean, even when fresh from the officers' baths. His lank black hair, worn longer than the regulation limit, failed to obscure ears that thrust out almost perpendicular to his head. As the agent in Carnuntum of the Praetorian Guard's intelligence division, the Special Cohort, he was as familiar with Tribune Marcus Carinna as I was with him.

I turned away to hide my face. Fortunately, Glabrio's attention was on the guards by the chapel doors. "Letting civilians gawp at the Eagle! Are you asleep, you ass-headed nitwits?"

"What goes on here?"

Placidus's bellow echoed from the smoke-stained walls. He stood in the duty office doorway, blocking the light from within.

"You sent for me," I said gruffly.

"Are you Aquila?"

"Aquilo."

Glabrio raised his rust-scraper voice: "Placidus, I am responsible for security here. Did you admit this louse-ridden local?"

As if he had not heard, the surgeon waved me into the duty office. Its familiarity gave me a twinge: soot-streaked and fly-wreathed, the grimy walls scaffolded with racks and pigeonholes crammed full of rosters and reports. Even blindfolded, I would have known it by the smells of smoke, wax, sour wine, and old sweat.

"What if he put his dirty hands on the Eagle?" Glabrio persisted from the atrium. "You can't—"

Placidus shut the door, muting the man's rant. He looked at me.

He was just the same. Broad, slightly stooped, with close-cut slate-gray hair. His eyes were calm and disillusioned in a long seamed face. The back of his right wrist bore the rayed-sun tattoo of a Soldier of Mithras.

He held out a big hand. "*Nama Mithra*, brother," he said.

I stared wordlessly, stiff-faced with salt and grime.

His gaze flicked to my own wrists and lingered on the one with the scar. His manner became more distant. "Well, sit down, Carinna—Aquilo— whatever you call yourself." He went around the battered table and lowered himself into a camp chair.

"You have a good eye," I said, abandoning the Gaulish accent.

"That's why the Army pays me like a prince." He dumped bronze styli out of a chipped pot, spat in the pot and wiped it out with his finger, and set it on the table beside a dented metal cup. "I take it you do not care to be recognized."

I pulled a stool under my rump. "Is the Special Cohort looking for me?"

"A dispatch months ago said you were wanted for interrogation."

"About what?"

"Oh, the Special Cohort never explains." Placidus lifted a cloth-draped jug from the floor. "Why did you come back?"

I hesitated over an answer, unsure how much he knew.

"Never mind. Stupid question." He began to fill the two cups. "So it really happened."

"What do you mean?"

He glanced up. "Your father."

"Yes, my father tried to kill Caligula Caesar. Unsuccessfully. When the Special Cohort commander struck him down, he died in my arms."

The surgeon flinched as if I had struck him, and watery red wine slopped over the pot's rim. I cursed myself; I had meant to sound unemotional, not callous.

He mopped the spill, draped the cloth over the jug, and put it away. "I couldn't believe it when I heard. Not Senator Titus Carinna, who helped him survive all those years..." He shook his head. "Some evil spirit must have driven him mad."

"No," I said. "He found something more important than his loyalty to Caligula."

A bee flew through the window and droned around the rafters. I took a swallow of wine and licked my mustache. I knew I ought to arrange Cleon's release, get on my horse, and leave while I could. Instead I said, "Lucius Verginius..."

The melancholy in his face became caution. For me to address him as a peer implied a favor. Or a secret.

I changed my mind about confiding that I had liberated a Germanic hostage. "Things must be quiet in the Mark. The most activity I see here are the fleas on the dogs."

"Why shouldn't it be quiet? Inguiomerus knows his daughter is a hostage for his good behavior." He tapped his puckered lips with a stylus.

I drew a breath. I had been about to call her father by his Germanic name of Ingiomar, which would certainly have aroused Placidus's curiosity. "Yes, of course. I just wondered if Caligula might have had an attack of clemency and let her go home."

It sounded lame, and Placidus's eyes narrowed. "Don't tell me escorting her to Rome sweetened you on that bloody-handed bitch!" He let out a guffaw, then sobered. "Caesar"—with emphasis on the Princeps' proper name—"is unlikely to be so tender-hearted. As for the fleas, you know Poppaeus hates to drive the lads too hard. If they start to sulk, they might spoil his chances of a better posting."

I knew the maxim he referred to: *Don't take risks; keep the troops happy.* To me that meant keeping them busy. To the legion commander, it meant taking it easy on them.

Someone passed under the high window, whistling. Placidus set down the stylus so it pointed at me. His cup was still full.

I could not probe further without revealing that I knew Aurima was no longer a hostage in Rome. I drained the last of my wine and smacked the pot down. "What must I do to have my man Cleon released? That is why I was summoned, isn't it?"

The surgeon drew invisible circles on the table with another stylus. "After your replacement's horse stepped in a foxhole yesterday and fell on him, I spent four hours debriding and setting a compound break of the femur. Four fucking hours." He slapped the second stylus down beside the first. "Then, moments after falling asleep, I am woken to treat First Spear Haterius Velox, who has fractured his clavicle in a *taberna* brawl."

Wonderful. It was not just any centurion Cleon had hit, but the legion's most senior man. And far from inflicting minor damage, he had broken Velox's collarbone.

But I was here to free him, so I said, "I will make...er, Marcus Aquilo will make a gift to his burial fund if he withdraws the complaint." Part of every soldier's pay is automatically withheld for funeral expenses, but Velox was known to be saving for a send-off that befitted his rank.

Placidus grunted. "Let us see what he says." He lumbered to his feet and went to the door.

As he was conveying the message to a runner, I happened to look past them and glimpsed the fringed black cloak of a senior Special Cohort officer. I bolted to my feet and wrenched the door open before Placidus could shut it. The tail of the cloak disappeared up the stairway. "Who was that?"

The surgeon closed the door. "New man filling in as acting Special Cohort prefect. Aelius Lamia. From Hispania." He dropped into his chair again.

The Special Cohort's headquarters for this region—Gaul, Belgica, and the Danube provinces—was far away in the long-pacified Rhone River valley. "What brings him to the wild East?" I sat down.

"Wants to see the frontier for himself, I guess. He's cooking up some kind of expedition with Glabrio." All three styli aimed at me now like a rank of tiny javelins. "Have you broken faith with Mithras, brother?"

It was he who had introduced me to the warrior god Mithras, and had sponsored my initiation into the small group of officers who followed the Lord of Light. After what had happened, how could he think I still believed? I said, "Do not call me brother."

"Unless we fight for Rome, *brother*, chaos and evil will win."

"Rome has become a plaything of Caesars. From now on, I fight only for myself and those who are mine." The few remaining members of my *familia*, the woman I loved, and my blackened honor.

"What about God?"

"If there is a God, I do not believe he cares who wins."

A tap on the door.

Placidus's gaze was baleful now, his goodwill used up. "Then I suppose it makes no difference what you do with yourself."

He rose and opened the door to the messenger he had sent to Velox. It seemed the First Spear was too angry to overlook what Cleon had done to him. For a hundred denarii, however, he would call it an accident.

That was everything Dio had squeezed from the horse breeder, but it did not matter. I spilled all the coins in my belt wallet onto the desk. "Put it in his account. And have my guard freed at once; I must go."

"See to his man," the surgeon directed, and the runner left. "Hold on, Aquilo."

"What is it?" I had a hand on the door latch.

He began to count out the coins. "Are you back in Carnuntum for good?" Perhaps he thought my faith could yet be restored.

"I have already wasted too much time here."

Placidus paused for a moment in his tallying. Although he had just said that it made no difference, he asked, "Where are you going?"

"To fight for what matters to me. As I told you." I swung the door wider.

The surgeon tapped the stacks of coins. "You are short twelve sestertii and five asses."

Dio must have kept it back to pay the rent. "My commission," I said. "For allowing Velox to spar with a man who won fifty bouts in the arena."

Placidus stood up. Our eyes met. Neither of us offered the other a hand.

I will never see him again, I thought. I said, "Tell Poppaeus not to let discipline fall off too much, or I will have to come back."

"Go." He jerked his chin toward the doorway. Almost inaudibly he added, "Mithras guard you."

I stopped at the top of the steps, squinting in the sunlight. So it was not general knowledge that Aurima had left Rome. And, *mirabile dictu*, her father still honored the treaty!

"You there, Hairy One! Forget your nail trimmer?" The sentry snickered as he tossed me my knife.

I took Boss across the assembly yard and let him drink from a fountain. As soon as Cleon was fetched, I meant to look up my former slave Baculus, once the steward of my small household here. He had constantly locked horns with Phormio about household matters, so all three of us were glad when the junior officers' association bought him to manage their baths.

Phormio. How could the past days' worries have driven him from my mind? Here in the heart of the camp where we had lived for three years, every street and structure held memories of my irascible *paedagogus*—tutor, servant, and companion. Phormio would have harangued me to ask Leonnatus for help weeks earlier. He would certainly have railed against my irrational fight in a *taberna*. His silent censure—

I did not notice the squat figure in the gatehouse shadow until he stepped in front of me, stabbing the butt of his twisted staff into the ground by my foot. "So those cocksuckers from the First Cohort had it right," he said. "Welcome back, Tribune."

My light-dazzled eyes could just make out his shape: bowed legs, short muscular forearms, square head on a thick stump of neck. As always, he carried his sturdy vine stick—his "toothpick."

Did that hurt, soldier? That little tap with my toothpick?

"But how you've changed," he drawled, in a mockery of wonderment.

I did not want to wrangle with a centurion whom I had once demoted for extortion. I moved ahead as if he did not block the way, tugging Boss after me.

He stood his ground. Without the added height of his cross-crested helmet, the gray brush of his hair barely reached my eye level. I said evenly, "Let me pass, Festus."

"'Let me pass,'" he mimicked. "High-and-mighty talk for a man who looks like a hairy, milk-guzzling German."

"Running from Caesar? Is that why you're here, traitor's spawn?" Another man materialized out of the sun glare behind him. It was a decurion of the Fifth Gallica auxiliary cavalry, a small man as tough as yew wood. I could not recall his name.

I hardened my voice. "What do you want?"

Festus slapped his vine stick into his palm. "We want to teach you a lesson, you arrogant prick." An evil grin swelled the rubble of pox scars on his cheeks.

The Gallic decurion brought his right hand around. He was carrying a quirt whose two tails were tipped with iron studs, the sort of whip used only on the most unmanageable horses. "How does it feel without a tribune's sash to hide behind?"

As a Senator's son and an officer outranked only by the legion commander, I had never allowed uncertainty or fear to show when facing men like these. Now, despite myself, I looked around for help. A few shapes flickered slowly through the colonnades, avoiding the sun-smashed breadth of the assembly yard. No sign of Cleon. No guards. They had probably been told to keep out of the way.

The decurion snapped his quirt under Boss's nose. The stallion reared back, yanking the reins out of my grip. He whirled and bolted a good twenty feet away, snorting and stamping his hooves.

"Quite a warhorse," the Gaul snickered. As if any other horse would have ignored the threat.

"Back off, or I'll have you court-martialed," I blustered.

Festus kept popping the stick into his palm. "You're lucky it's just us, Tribune." He glanced at the decurion. "Eh, Licnos?" His glee turned suddenly to fury, and he lashed out at my forearm. "All gods curse your family."

The blow might have maimed me if I had not lessened its force by grabbing for the vine stick. Instead of smashing a bone, it struck my wristlet of sturdy boiled leather.

I seized the stick and yanked the centurion closer, yelling, "Boss, to me!"

The stallion charged forward. Festus stumbled over the foot I thrust out. As he went down, I stepped on his shoulder, grabbed one of the saddle horns, and hauled myself onto the horse's back. "Go!"

Boss hardly needed urging. Festus evaded the big hooves by curling up with his arms wrapped around his head. The decurion—Licnos—tried to lash out with his quirt, but Boss shouldered him against the gatehouse wall and hurtled through the archway.

I heard the lockup door slam open behind us. A familiar voice shouted, "I'm here, Marcus."

"With me, Cleon," I said. Abandoning the idea of staying in the camp any longer, I kneed Boss forward. "Time to go."

5: ROME BURNS

The shutters of the big storehouses on the quadrangle were closed against the westering sun. In the long shadow cast across the yard, workers raked rumpled gravel and sluiced down a dusty traveling carriage.

Rufus pointed it out as the *carpentum* that had passed us on the road. I was still too unsettled by what had happened at the Army camp to do more than nod. "They whacked me in the back with a cudgel," Cleon said to Ollius, "then punched me with a *caestus* when I tried to get up. Bastards." He felt his jaw, swollen where the bronze knuckles had hit. "I'll be sucking pap for a week."

"Tragic," muttered Dio, disgruntled that both of my bodyguards favored the search for Aurima. He turned back to the mule's saddle and untied his satchel.

Leonnatus appeared between the double doors of his house, a honey-colored stone villa on one side of the receiving yard. After my boorishness outside the *taberna*, it was reassuring to see him smile.

The old trader was dressed in unusual splendor, a green mantle embroidered with gilt medallions over a blue-striped tunic. Although I had bathed, I was aware of the dinginess of my own tunic and the holes that spitting campfires had scorched into my cloak. My only finery was a gold torc that had been my father's.

As Leonnatus limped down the steps, I said, "Leo, I hope my arrival without notice does not inconvenience you."

"Of course not." He clasped my shoulders in a warm, wine-scented embrace. "It is always good to welcome you here."

"I came to ask for your counsel." For favors, really: not just to join his next trading party, but to stay discreetly within the walls of his compound until it was time to depart.

"Certainly. After you refresh yourself. Come in." Silver gleamed at his wrists as he summoned others to see to Cleon, Ollius, Rufus, and our mounts. I signaled Dio to follow me into the house. A slave took our cloaks.

When another attendant came forward with house sandals, I hesitated before accepting. If Leonnatus refused my request, I might not be staying long.

The trader turned from instructing his steward. "Where is your faithful Phormio?"

He shook his snowy head sadly when I explained about Phormio's bad heart, nodded and smiled when I introduced Dio as my secretary, and drew me forward with an arm around my shoulders. "I have a surprise for you."

The stone-flagged house was cool and dim, fragranced with the rich spices of a recent dinner. Familiar servants bowed to their master, peeking at me from the corners of their eyes. "Perhaps we can talk in your office," I said to Leonnatus.

"Presently." He drew me on past the *tablinum*, empty now, the dark wood of shelves and cupboards almost black in the dimness, and through the door in the far end of the house that led to the arbor and the gardens.

A slender woman in a dark stola rose beneath a tree that shaded the dusty arbor. A necklace of gold and gems circled her throat, and long dark hair in crimped ringlets billowed around her angular face.

I stopped. "Galla?" Half question, half exclamation.

She stared at me.

"My lady Cornelia Galla." Leonnatus was beaming. "Your cousin Carinna's son."

She glided a few paces closer. "Marcus? No."

"Is Sabinus here?" I looked around, as if the governor of Pannonia might be hiding behind an urn full of ivy or a painted statue of Bacchus.

"No, he still . . . Marcus Licinius, is it really you?"

I smiled for the first time in a long while. "It is, Cousin Galla."

"By Juno's girdle! Yes, I can see your father's eyes through all that underbrush." Galla put her hands on my forearms and kissed my cheek. "Are you in disguise, my dear, or just in need of a decent barber?" Her fingers touched the torc, then slipped around my neck and twirled the tail of the hair I had tied back.

I did not mind the familiarity. She was a second cousin of Father's, and much like an aunt to me. I might have asked what brought her here from her husband's headquarters in Poetovio, or teased her about running other traffic off the road in her carriage, but a more urgent longing made me blurt out, "Do you have news of my mother and sister? I have been without word since November."

Leonnatus gave a small start that caught my eye. He put a forefinger to his lips, then touched Dio's shoulder and took him out of the arbor.

Galla returned to her seat under the tree. "Terentia sent me a letter . . . hmm, in February? Yes, she wrote on Parentalia, to . . . to commemorate Titus's death." She trailed off, clearly uneasy with the thought of honoring my father's spirit. "I am sure she said she was in good health."

It was nearly dark in the garden now; a slave lit a cresset beside a small pool, allowing us to see each other more clearly. I had grown so accustomed to Aurima's bare glowing countenance that it was odd to see Galla's face fashionably whitened with lead, her cheeks made rosy with cinnabar.

"She asked me to give you her love, if by chance I saw you."

This sounded fictitious; my mother knew I wanted forgiveness, not love. "And Nina?" I lowered myself into a nearby chair. A servant brought wine.

"Visellius Varro divorced the poor girl, I am sorry to say. She lives with your mother now at Caesar's villa in Antium."

The divorce was no surprise. The governor of Crete and Cyrenaica could not afford to be tainted by his wife's father's treason. But I ached for my sister's humiliation.

Galla's voice faded to a whisper. "Why did he do it, Marcus? You were there. Did Caesar take against him, make some sort of threat? Or was it a fit of lunacy? A stroke?"

Why? It was a question I had been spared as Marcus Aquilo, when no one knew me as the son of a would-be parricide. But I had no better answer for her than I had had for Placidus. It was impossible to explain: too complicated, too agonizing, too shameful. I shook my head and sipped cool wine.

She said, "He never boasted, of course, but he was so proud of his boys."

His boys. My brother and my brother's dearest friend. Not, until the very last, me.

Moths fluttered around the cresset. Beside my chair the pool's surface puckered, spreading rings, as fish rose to gulp gnats.

"But why—" Galla started to ask.

I cut her off: "Are Mother and Nina safe?"

"I believe so."

"And Sabinus? Does he believe so, too?"

"Yes, Marcus, my husband believes so too."

"And how safe am I?"

"As long as you are still related to Caesar, my dear, Sabinus is in no haste to comply with the Special Cohort's squawking about you. Something about a missing Germanic hostage?" Lifting one plucked eyebrow, she sipped again from her cup.

Aurima's tribe bordered his province, so of course the governor would have been informed of her disappearance. I tried to sound uninterested. "Do you know what has become of her?"

"I thought you might know." Galla's eyes were guilelessly expectant.

She would be fishing for news to give her husband. Should I explain that Aurima had promised to keep her father committed to peace on the frontier?

Oh yes, Sabinus would say, *and the Danube River will flow with wine one day.*

I changed the subject: "And Caesar has not demanded my return?"

"He has much else on his mind. Assassination attempts by those he trusted, the desecration of Jupiter's temple on New Year's Day, the Praetorian Prefect's suicide . . ."

I shook my head. Caligula's woes seemed to be occurring in a different world. I would be glad to distance myself further while slogging through the Mark.

Where had Leonnatus gone? I should be speaking with him about the trip.

"The worst," she said, "is that we are losing the advisers who urged him to moderation: first your father and the Senate Leader, then Graecinus, Priscus, Macro . . ."

I pointed out, "There is still Lepidus," our family's patron, who was Caligula's brother by marriage.

"Gods grant he will remain patient."

It was astonishingly bold of her to speak, even indirectly, of Caligula's removal or death. In curiosity I studied her painted face. The firelight betrayed small imperfections: fine creases fanning from the corners of her eyes and nose, a tiny scar that nicked her upper lip. Cornelia Galla was no meek Roman matron. She was a schemer and a beguiler, Father had once said, who could steal a man's navel without his noticing.

She began to tell me about the Princeps' recent marriage. Gradually her voice faded into the chirping of insects and distant clatters from the kitchen. I tipped my head back and watched bats dart in the lingering blue of the sky.

Servers came out with platters of savory food. Leonnatus reappeared and seated himself quietly. A flute began to croon. "—besotted with his sister Agrippina's baby," Galla went on. "He calls him 'little Nero' and talks about adopting him as his heir."

I had once told Agrippina that Rome could not be handed to a child like an ivory rattle. Not that she listened. The Julii had come to believe Rome was theirs.

"Surely talk of succession is premature," Leonnatus interjected. "After all, Caesar is only twenty-five. The gods may yet grant him a healthy son of his own."

"But what will become of the Republic while that son grows up?" Galla retorted.

Tiring of her unwomanly provocation, I broke in rudely, "Leo, how soon does your next trading mission leave for the North?"

"On the Amber Road? Not for some time, actually. Why do you ask?"

"I may want to . . . send a message. Or perhaps a messenger." I did not look at Galla. "How long is 'some time'?"

"This is not the best season to travel. Besides the great numbers of mosquitoes and flies, fur quality will be poor and slaves are not yet available from summer raids." He shook his head. "I am still expecting a few caravans to come in, but none will go out until September or October when the weather cools."

Nearly five more months!

I stood up abruptly, excusing myself, and bade them farewell. Leonnatus pushed himself to his feet. "Carinna—Marcus Licinius—take another cup of wine, my friend. I have had your usual rooms prepared."

"Thank you, no," I said. "I cannot stay." Told that I could not explore the Mark safely until fall, I was suddenly sure that I must do it immediately.

Something was wrong. Aurima had failed to return from the Mark because she could not.

Earthly life is all there is: so said Stoics like my father. But I had already learned that spirits could reach from another world to this one. It might be, then, that intimate souls could touch each other across great distances. And that the woman I desperately loved was shouting for help.

Perhaps I should have confided in Leonnatus and Galla. His many connections and the governor's power would have enabled an extensive search of the Mark. On the other hand, heavy-footed inquiries might put her in even greater danger.

On the point of leaving, I thought of Dio's regrets and recriminations. Impulsively I said, "Leonnatus, I have no need of a secretary. Dio is a free man; I manumitted him several months ago. It would please me if he can be of use to you."

Confusion flickered in the trader's eyes. The sudden request must have embarrassed him; perhaps he had no use for another secretary. "He is intelligent and discreet, and writes a fair hand," I pushed on. "And he . . . And perhaps you know: my father begot him."

"This is not something to decide in haste," Leonnatus protested.

Galla said sharply, "Leo is too civil to ask what you intend to do, but I have bitten my tongue a dozen times. You cannot waste your life here." From her tone, she must have heard of the filth and drunkenness that he had encountered the night before.

Before I could find a reply, she went on, "Come back to Poetovio with me. Sabinus esteemed you when you were a tribune, and I know he will find you a position on his staff—a good one. You are family, after all."

I shook my head.

"A letter came for you a few weeks ago," Leonnatus said. "You may find some guidance in it."

"A letter?" I supposed at once that it was from my mother. "You should have told me sooner."

"I gave it to your secretary so our visit would not be disrupted." He caught my flash of displeasure. "Lady Terentia trusted him completely, and I assumed you did too. I beg your pardon if I was wrong."

I went through the house calling for Dio but hearing no reply, until one of the slaves nodded to a curtained doorway off of Leonnatus's office. It was a scribe's tiny cubicle, lined with latticed shelves. Someone sat at a desk in the darkness, slumped over crossed arms. Smoke from an extinguished lamp hung in the air.

I backed out and asked for another light. When I shouldered past the curtain again, Dio raised his head. His eyes were pink, and tear tracks striped his cheeks.

I pulled him off his stool so I could flatten the scroll and read it for myself. Dated in mid-March, nearly six weeks earlier, it was not from Mother but from our patron.

M. Aemilius Lepidus to M. Licinius Carinna, greetings. I send this letter hoping that Leonnatus with his many connections will know where to reach you.

Mother was well, he wrote; Nina well; Nina divorced. He pledged to find her a new husband who would value Mother's Antonian blood and overlook Father's madness. It was unfortunate that she had twice miscarried, but her beauty might attract a man who already had heirs.

I cursed. My clever, spirited twin, given like an easy-gaited mule to some undistinguished old man!

My most loving and dutiful wife Drusilla is also well and an ever-greater source of comfort to her beleaguered brother. He busies himself with urban improvements, making up for the neglect of past decades.

Yes, I could well believe that Caligula was beleaguered. Lepidus added a few more tidbits of Caesarian family news, but nothing yet to make Dio weep.

I remind you to maintain silence about the bedchamber episode. As we agreed, only a few senior Special Cohort officers have been made aware of it.

Fine. Neither Aurima nor I cared to reveal that she had attacked Caligula in his bed. There had been no agreement, however, to stop the Special Cohort from pursuing and trying to silence her. I was relieved that my precautions, which included sending her companions to the Mark via several different routes, had not been overdone.

I continue to watch for an opportunity to restore your credit with Caesar. You saved his life twice, which has meaning to him. Alas, his forgiveness seems far in the future. At present he will not let your name be spoken, or your father's.

One day he may agree that, ensorcelled by your Germanic priestess, you did not grasp the choice he was giving you. In the meantime, I must advise you not to return to Rome, or indeed to attract his attention in any way. He has remarked more than once that your mother has tenancy of his grandmother's villa only on his sufferance. Further, word has come to him that your sister may have colluded with that lampoonist who fled the city to escape the Special Cohort. The smallest reminder of your betrayal could harm them, not just yourself.

I have written separately to Leonnatus, asking him to make available the sum of five thousand denarii for any purpose you choose. My dear Drusilla prays that through the intercession of Clementia, wisest and kindest of goddesses, we will see you again one day.

Post scriptum. I must also tell you that in order to extend the Palace to the Temple of Castor and Pollux, Caesar is having your family house torn down.

I let out a grunt like a man stabbed in the gut. My hands jerked on the woven papyrus. I stared and kept staring, as the words *your family house torn down* jumped before my eyes.

As a boy I had dragged my *paedagogus* Phormio day after day to a nearby dwelling being demolished to expand a neighbor's garden. I still remembered the boom and crash of the ram, the dusty unveiling of wall frescoes and painted ceilings, pipes and tiled heat ducts, the exposure and destruction of a family's life.

Torn down. I had vowed to reunite our household, but I could not restore them to a place that was no longer there.

Dio was weeping again. He stood in the doorway, swaying like a stalk of wheat. I had not seen him shed tears before, not even when we brought back Father's body from the Palace. But to him, born and raised a slave, our house was where his place was.

"We cannot set foot in Rome," he moaned. "Or your mother will be evicted, a widow with no home; your sister will be exiled, probably to that r-rock, P-Pandateria—"

He was nearly raving. I started to slap him, but at the last moment merely patted his cheek. "Dio," I said. I swallowed and said his name once more.

"We can never go home," he whispered. Still the tears ran down his face.

"Compose yourself." I made my voice rougher. "You are not dead yet, nor am I."

Leonnatus and Galla were still conversing in the arbor, but in hushed tones. They fell quiet when I neared. I said, "Leo, I will accept your offer of a bed after all." The currents around me had become too violent; I needed a rock to anchor myself to.

He nodded gravely. "Your guards will be quartered with mine."

Galla stood on her toes to kiss me on both cheeks. "Good night, cousin." She smiled up at me, her eyes as brown as saddle leather in the white mask of ceruse. "I will come back tomorrow, unless I am made to witness a close-order drill or something equally fascinating. Things will look better in the morning."

6: FORTUNA'S WHEEL

Dio folded to his knees like a camel. "How can I sleep?" he said in a voice still rough with grief, and sank down onto his pallet. He gave a small gasp and in a few moments began to breathe deeply, exhausted.

The room was suffocatingly hot. I got up and opened the shutters, defying the poisons of the night. Some flowering plant fragranced the cooler air. An owl called, low and melancholy like a lost spirit.

Rage seethed in my gut. My mother had solaced and pampered the fatherless Caligula when he was a boy menaced by the old Princeps' distrust. Now, at the "smallest reminder" of me, he threatened to doom her and my sister to beggary!

How simple it was among the Germans, who allowed any man to challenge a king to single combat. If the king died, it was considered the gods' will and the victor was not punished. A pity I could not smash through Caligula's cordon of guards and dare him to meet me sword to sword.

A pity you have less courage than your father, jeered an inner voice.

When I fell asleep at last, I dreamed of coins. My family house would not be demolished if I paid Caligula a hundred denarii. To raise the money I sold my Libyan stallion, Spider. Caligula said that the payment was short twelve sestertii and five asses. If I wished my mother to live in peace, I must pay two hundred more. I sold Boss. When I spilled the coins onto the zebra skins beneath his couch, he smiled and asked if I wished my sister to marry a kind man or a heartless one. I sold Rufus. Was I willing to protect the tomb that held the ashes of my father and his ancestors? I sold Dio, then Ollius and Cleon, who were not even slaves, and the coins mounted up until I begged Caligula to stop; I had nothing more to give him.

"You are wrong," he said. "And unless you want to forfeit your citizenship, you will hand over to me the girl with red hair."

I awoke sweating in the darkness. Every part of the dream was so clear that I knew it must be a message. If I was to restore my name, I must expect to risk everything. And perhaps, at the end, to be alone.

Although it was so early that the tile roofs of the storehouses still dripped dew, Leonnatus's yard swarmed with life. Slaves trudged up from the river landing, bent double under bundles of cowhides. In a corner of the yard, surrounded by opened bales and a plague of flies, one of Leonnatus's sons graded the hides while a clerk and a tax collector kept separate tallies and the peddlers, two big Quadi, scowled over them.

Cleon and Ollius plodded out of the passage to the guards' barracks, yawning. Rufus hummed as he saddled Boss. "Will I tell them about our house?" Dio muttered, touching the strapped leather bag that held Lepidus's letter and our other valuables.

"Not yet. We will talk down by the river." I gestured. "Bring me one of those Germans."

The brute eyed me sullenly, chewing on his mustache. He outtopped me by a head. "The Goddess's greetings," I said in Germanic.

He echoed the phrase, brows raised in surprise. I continued, "The wife of the Roman governor has a message for Aurima, daughter of Ingiomar. Can you take it?"

If he said yes, I meant to find out where he would deliver the imaginary message. But he made a doubtful noise in his throat, then shook his head. "Send it to Ingiomar," he grunted, and tramped back to his hides.

I sighed. The few other times I had found Germans to ask about her, the answer had always been a shrug or a shake of the head.

I was settling into the saddle when Leonnatus limped out to us. "Will you depart without a farewell, Marcus Licinius?"

I apologized; I had told his steward not to wake him. "I must make plans, Leo."

"A post with the governor could offer protection and concealment. For the time being, you may benefit from both."

"No doubt you are right," I said. I had no intention of returning to talk with Galla.

His brows tilted in resignation. "Very well. Lepidus's funds will be here when you want them. What about your secretary?"

Dio sent me an alarmed glance from astride his mule.

"I have thought further, Leo," I said. "We are become a small family, and I ought not to make it smaller."

Amid shouted commands and loud splashing, a dozen young recruits floundered through a shallow channel toward the nearest island. From where we squatted on the banks of a tiny tree-shaded cove, they were partly visible through drooping branches.

I had told the others the stockpile of bad news: staying in Carnuntum had become too risky, there would be no trading ventures to the Mark until fall, and our patron had warned me not to return to Rome. Dio left to retrieve a tattered map from our attic.

An instructor chest-deep in the river hauled a man up by his hair. "Every dog can swim, beef brains, and so can you." He shoved the man underwater. "Kick!"

Cleon swigged from a wine flask, careful of his sore jaw. "Waste of time teaching soldiers to swim."

"Not if they have to cross a river." Ollius cleaned a fingernail with his knife tip.

"I suppose you can swim in chain mail, Arethusa?"

"Hey!" Ollius sat upright, jabbing his knife into the sand. "There's a fine amphitheater in Syracuse. Let's go there. Cleon and I can start a gladiator school."

"In Sicily?" Cleon made it sound next door to Hades. Normally he was the most amiable of men, ruddy-faced and tousle-haired. Once a champion fighter with net and trident in the top arenas, he had no need to prove his toughness. But like me he was a native of Rome, unhappy in exile.

"Bugger you, then," Ollius said. "Let's ask that woman in the alley behind the potter's. She tells fortunes from spitting in a dish of oil."

Beside them, Rufus shook his head violently. "No," he protested. "Au'ima!"

Ollius, profoundly superstitious, touched an amulet at his neck. "Perhaps a god is angry with us. Have you made unfulfilled vows, Marcus?"

I said brusquely, "I have not given up on finding Aurima and tracking down the lost Eagle. If necessary I will go alone. The rest of you are freed from your obligation to our family."

Their protests masked the swish and crackle of brush as Dio trod cautiously down the overgrown path. He pulled a sealed tablet from his satchel and held it out to me.

"What's this?"

"A soldier was waiting with it at our lodging. I said I would give it to you."

The Special Cohort's Janus-headed seal bound the tablet's halves. Glancing at Dio's face, I saw that he too recognized its menace. I snapped the wax with my thumbnail and opened the leaves.

> D. Aelius Lamia, Acting Prefect, to M. Licinius Aquilo, greetings.
> Urgently need to discuss a mission of importance to Rome and potentially of interest to you. Safe conduct assured. Name a meeting place.
> I will bring Vatia Glabrio and my adjutant.

"A trap," Dio declared.

Cleon agreed. "They'll wrap you in chains and send you back to Caligula."

"Or stick a blade in you and say you fought them," Ollius warned.

Mission of importance to Rome, I read again. *Of interest to you. Safe conduct assured.*

I told Dio to give me a stylus. And beneath Lamia's scribed lines I scrawled, "Meet me in the camp amphitheater at the end of the afternoon watch."

7: ARENA

"He's not coming," Dio said decisively. He slung the satchel strap over his shoulder and began to retreat toward Rufus, hidden on the riverbank with the horses.

"Wait." I looked up at Ollius, who stood atop the shrine of Diana Nemesis by the amphitheater's main entrance. Sunlight gleamed on his bare scalp as he squinted toward the fortress, a few minutes' walk away.

The trees were as still as painted images, laying dark shadows on the grass. Birds foraged for crumbs among plank seats set on shelves of turf.

Cleon loosened his sword in its scabbard again. He had moved out of the shade of the arena wall so he could view the whole ellipse of tiered seats. His black curls clung to his sweaty face.

A trumpet in the fortress had sounded the watch change half an hour earlier. Dio must be right: it was a trap. Troops were probably surrounding the amphitheater now, blocking the exits. What kind of idiot would trust a Special Cohort officer's word?

"We are leaving," I announced, but Ollius's shrill whistle overruled me a breath later. I leaned back against the battered arena wall, wiping sweat from my mustache.

The three newcomers walked down into the amphitheater: a man in a fringed black cloak who must have been Lamia, the acting Special Cohort prefect; his local agent, Glabrio, ambling beside him; and then a man in armor, presumably Lamia's adjutant. Ollius jumped down to follow them, sword in hand.

Lamia stopped in the center of the arena. Glabrio halted beside him with a hand on his knife hilt, scuffing his feet in the dirt like a gladiator settling his stance. The adjutant's gaze flicked back and forth under the brim of his helmet.

Glabrio greeted me with a smirk. "Heard you had a little set-to outside headquarters yesterday."

I made myself smile in return. His jutting ears were as red as blood, translucent in the late-day sun. Perhaps an opportunity would arise to flatten them against his skull.

Lamia's eyes roved from my long tied-back hair to my beard to my irreversibly grimed tunic. "Why are you here in Carnuntum, Aquilo?"

He was a slim and graceful man in his forties. Above a tanned, handsome face, his silver hair swept back in waves that many a woman's *tonstrix* would have spent hours achieving. To me he looked less like a spymaster than a society poet, albeit a poet who might write something snide about you behind your back.

Everyone wanted to know my intentions. "Why do you care?"

He lifted his chin. Oil gleamed on the billows of his hair—crocus oil, my nose told me. "I am leading a detachment to the Marcomanni and Quadi king, Vannius. A mixed force of my own Praetorians and auxiliary cavalry."

"Is there trouble in the Mark?" Dread rippled through me. Had Aurima's return broken Ingiomar's leash after all?

"No, this is a goodwill mission. You know of the campaign in two years?"

I did not bother to answer. Nearly everyone north of Numidia knew of Caligula's planned campaign to outdo his famous father, Germanicus.

"I am going to ask Vannius to provide five hundred men for a new cavalry *ala*," he continued. "I will also emphasize that we expect him to keep his people happy and quiet while Caesar is subduing the Rhineland and Britannia."

"His 'people' are of two different tribes, Prefect. Even though Vannaz is their king, the Marcomanni do not forget that he is a Quadian."

If Lamia noticed my misstep in using the king's Germanic name, he did not show it. "Yes, I know there is some animosity between them. Particularly between Vannius and that wild man of the Marcomanni, Inguiomerus."

I knew that. And he was right: hostility between a war chieftain and his king is ill-omened.

He went on, "But everything has its price. So we will offer gifts to remind the king that being a friend of Rome is an advantage—even to primitive barbarians like him." He manufactured a grin full of small white teeth.

I disliked being invited to sneer with him. "You come from Hispania, I believe."

His handsome face tightened. "From Nola, originally. My great-grandfather was a general in the Gallic Wars. My uncle served as suffect consul with Publius Petronius—" Apparently he was easily ruffled by reminders that his family was not of Senatorial rank. Which, as he clearly knew, mine was.

I said, "My point is that Germans are not quite as you describe them."

"Nonsense! Look at them. Generation after generation, illiterate, grunting to each other like pigs, happy to wallow in the mud. Fortune disdains the lazy."

"Yet they are fierce, loyal, stubborn, and generous. Traits we may admire." Aurima's traits.

"You see, Glabrio?" Lamia told his underling. "That is the knowledge we need on this mission." He turned back to me. "You led a vexillation to Vannius's capital last year. You fought off Marcomanni rebels on the Amber Road."

I smiled thinly. "Last year I was a tribune."

"I want you to come with us."

An opportunity to travel into the Mark with an armed escort! What better chance to seek Aurima? "How many men?"

"Twenty cavalry from the Tenth Praetorians," Glabrio said. "A *turma* of the Fifth Gallica. Twenty-five officers and support staff."

Seventy-five troops in all. "No infantry?"

Lamia said, "This will be a mounted escort, not an invading army."

Silence fell. The prefect rolled something in his fingers, a stone or amulet, that clicked against his ring. Glabrio regarded me with his monkey-bright eyes.

Lamia stopped his restless clicking. "You will come, then?"

"It's seventy miles to Bruna," I said. "You will need infantry to build marching camps along the way."

The prefect frowned. "If we insist on a ditched and palisaded camp every night, Vannius will take it as a lack of trust. He prides himself on the safety of his kingdom."

Glabrio turned his shoulder to me. "Inguiomerus's attack last year has cast a long shadow," he suggested to Lamia.

"Ah, yes: 'Once burned, twice shy.'" He paused, kneading his bauble again. "Need I mention that you will be paid?"

My pride flared up. "I am not a mercenary. Or a coward."

"No—you are a penniless outcast who drinks himself stupid in a *taberna* every night. I offer you the possibility of a reward for doing something worthwhile."

I felt myself flush. "If our mission succeeds," Lamia added more persuasively, "I will send a dispatch to Caesar commending you to the Senate and people of Rome."

"That will delight him. Something to wipe himself with after shitting."

Glabrio muttered, "I think this is pointless, sir."

Lamia studied my face. His eyes were that unreliable color called hazel, which can be gray or green or brown, depending on the light. "Can your oath be trusted?"

"Probably more than yours can," I said.

His small teeth glinted in a perfunctory smile. "I think this is worth a chance, Glabrio." He flicked a finger at Cleon, who had stayed within spitting distance of the armed adjutant. "Send your people away. What I have to say is not for others to hear."

Dio coughed behind my back, reminding me that the sensible choice would be to take Lepidus's five thousand denarii and move to the out-of-the-way Roma Nova I had scorned. Yet what better opportunity would there be to locate Aurima? And then to seek the last of the three Eagles stolen when Quinctilius Varus's legions were slaughtered?

Still, I was loath to trust them. These Special Cohort schemers could be among the few who knew about Aurima's disappearance, and might therefore guess that I sought a safe way to enter the Mark. But as long as I did not lead them to her . . .

When Lamia, Glabrio, and I stood alone by the sword-scarred arena wall, I said, "What is this great secret, then?"

Lamia merely ticked his worry stone against his ring, waiting for Glabrio to speak. The agent shuffled closer. Fried onions gusted on his breath. "Swear not to divulge what you are going to hear."

"Why?"

"The lives of other Romans may depend on it. Is that reason enough?"

I shrugged. "I so swear, then."

"By what?"

What could a man swear by if he had no god, no house, and no heir? "By my personal honor," I said.

Glabrio exchanged glances with the prefect. Lamia picked up the discourse. "The Hermunduri have eight Roman captives they are willing to ransom," he said quietly.

I could imagine only one reason for the Special Cohort to be involved in a covert retrieval of prisoners. "Survivors of the Varus disaster?" I guessed. "It must be a hoax."

"I am satisfied by the proof they provided." Lamia shot another glance at Glabrio. "Recovering these survivors is the real purpose of our mission."

Images filled my mind's eye: scarred and emaciated men, close-shorn like all male slaves of the long-haired Germans, with hollow eyes that had witnessed the bloody defeat of an army that should have been undefeatable. Romans. Romans waiting to come home after twenty-nine years of captivity. "Where are they now?"

"Not so fast," Glabrio broke in. "There is a complication."

Click. Lamia's fingers undulated like a milkmaid's. *Click-click.*

"The Hermunduri king does not want it known that they were enslaved by one of his tribal chiefs," Glabrio went on. "It might cost him his status as a friend of Rome."

All I knew about the Hermunduri, who bordered the Marcomanni on the west, was that Aurima's younger brother had been exchanged in childhood with a Hermunduri princeling to bond the two tribes. "And so?"

"Vannius has agreed to deliver the captives on his behalf."

"Why would he do that?"

"He owes his throne to the Hermunduri king, and wants to put the old man in his debt. He is also a great seeker after wealth, which we are going to provide him."

I shook my head. "This is a tangled web."

Lamia took the lead again. "It is a way to save eight Romans who suffered greatly for doing their duty." He dropped his voice even more. "The Hermunduri have already been paid and the survivors brought into Marcomanni lands. When I meet with Vannius, I will reward him for his cooperation. Then we pick up the men and bring them home."

My heart beat harder. "And you ask me to help because of my service to Rome?"

"You used to talk about finding the last stolen Eagle," Glabrio said slyly.

So I had. He would know, too, that I had boasted about my father having been an officer in the army that recovered the first two Eagles.

Lamia said, "If you are with us, you could be among the first to question the captives." I saw in his mud-colored eyes what he did not express: by learning the location of Varus's last Eagle and retrieving it, I could try to make amends for my father's infamy. He could not have nailed my ambition more surely if he had read my soul.

"We leave in five days," he went on. "Assuming all goes well in recovering the captives, we will return no later than mid-May."

Thus, if all went well in fetching—or rescuing—Aurima, by early June she and I could be putting together our own expedition to regain the lost Eagle, having learned from the massacre's survivors where to seek it.

Lamia clenched his fist on his plaything. "Now you know why this mission is both urgent and secret. And why I want a man who has dealt with Germans as a Roman officer. What say you?"

I said, "I have two conditions."

"Conditions?" He stared at me, surprised out of his self-satisfaction. "By Hercules, he who is offered a gift cannot be choosy!"

I waited. I felt Fortuna sitting on my shoulder.

The prefect arrowed a glare at Glabrio, as if the agent had misled him. Glabrio grinned, his teeth showing yellow as amber in his stubble-shadowed jaw.

Lamia huffed out a breath. "All right. I may as well hear them."

"The first condition," I said, "is that you requisition half a cohort of *auxilia* for your vexillation. The First Alpines, for preference."

"Out of the question! Infantry will slow our progress. And if you are still thinking about nightly fortifications, I will not risk insulting our ally Vannius." He shook his head vehemently. "No."

Damned desk-riding slipperlick! He might be too new to the Germanic frontier to be aware of its hazards, but Glabrio should have educated him.

Common sense told me that the mission would be risky without secure camps. But my longing for Aurima and the prospect of finding the Eagle tugged at me. If he was as adamant in refusing my other condition, I would walk away.

"Second, I will command the vexillation," I said. "The authority to pursue the mission's political objectives will be yours, but the troops will be under my orders."

Strangely, it was Glabrio whose reaction was stronger. "What?" he sputtered. Blood rushed into his face. "Absurd!"

Lamia's expression was odd: chiefly appraisal, with a trace of smugness. Before he could voice a reply, I continued, "The king is impressed by rank. Your detachment should be headed by a senior legion officer, and the Fifteenth's new broad-striper is laid up with a broken leg." *I thank you for that news, Placidus.*

"It would be simplest to reappoint me as a broad-stripe tribune *ad rem*. I will have the narrow-striper Valerius Secundus as my adjutant." I knew and valued Secundus, a quick-thinking, reliable soldier's son. "And Senior Surgeon Placidus will accompany the detachment." The captives might need medical care. "None of this is negotiable."

"But—you . . . !" Lamia frowned at my beard, my unkempt hair. I knew he imagined becoming a laughingstock when I slouched up, half barbarian in appearance, as the commander he had chosen for his expedition.

"The men will not obey you," Glabrio charged.

I thought of Festus and Licnos. "I will see that they do."

"This is ludicrous! How can you expect to regain your rank after your family's disgrace?" His ears were red again, this time with fury. "Prefect, he is mocking you!"

"Be quiet, both of you. Let me think." Lamia looked off into the distance. Whatever revolved in his hand clicked irritatingly against his iron equestrian ring.

Ollius, yielding to boredom, tossed his sword from one hand to the other with his good eye closed. Cleon tucked his own weapon under one arm in order to suck from his wine flask. Dio sent me a confused and imploring glance.

Lamia returned to the moment. "Do you need outfitting, Aquilo?"

I did not. Cumbersome though my armor was, I had declined to leave it in Rome to be confiscated.

The clicking stopped. "Present yourself at headquarters at noon tomorrow, in uniform," he said. "If the legion commander approves, your conditions will be accepted."

A canny decision, worthy of a spymaster. If I botched the assignment, Lamia would be able to shift the blame to Poppaeus.

"Very well," I agreed, then added on impulse, "And I will be paid."

"Paid?"

"As you promised earlier." If he thought I could be bought, let him buy me. I would need the money later to finance my own expedition.

The prefect's mouth shaped an omega of contempt. "How much do you want?"

I said the first number that came into my head: "Five thousand denarii. To be deposited to my account with Leonnatus of Narbo before we leave."

He wagged his head, miming helpless exasperation. "Oh, why not?"

Rarely was Fortuna so open-handed with her favors. Perhaps it was some foreboding of how she might obstruct my search for Aurima that made me add, "Last, I want your promise to ransom me or send my ashes to my mother if I do not return."

"You have no reason to worry. As Glabrio tells me, the Mark is at peace."

"The Marcomanni and Quadi are always at peace, until they are not."

"Very well." Lamia began to roll the stone against his ring again. "If necessary I will retrieve you, insofar as I am able. Satisfied?"

I gave him a nod. "Until tomorrow, Prefect."

Glabrio started back across the arena, sour-faced in defeat. Lamia hung back. "One last thing, Aquilo. Our true mission is a secret to everyone, even the legion commander. The troops themselves will not find out until the time is right." He raised his silver brows. "A precaution in case we run into problems. You understand?"

I understood: bungling a widely disclosed mission to rescue prisoners of war would be a political disaster. Even though it went against my judgment to keep the secret from Poppaeus, I was committed now. I nodded.

"Then congratulations, Tribune." He smiled and strode off with his adjutant.

8: THE TRIBUNE

"Back again?" Poppaeus drawled, as if I had just stepped out to set the night's password. He settled deeper into his cushioned chair and knuckled a shiny dribble off his jowl. "It's been restful here without you."

"Glad to hear it," I said, above water splashing into a nearby basin.

The legion commander flipped a plump hand. "Oh, be at ease, Carinna."

I pulled off the heavy helmet and tucked it under my arm. "I use the name Aquilo now, Legate."

"I will try to remember." He sipped from his glass cup. I was not surprised that he accepted the change without comment. The only charm of Carnuntum's great distance from Rome, he had once remarked, was that it spared him from having to lean with the shifting winds off the Palatine Hill.

He lifted his voice slightly. "Well, Prefect, here he is. Any questions?"

Aelius Lamia lounged on a seat in the shady nymphaeum of the commander's house, resting his own wineglass on his knee. For the first time the Special Cohort prefect was seeing me not just with hair cut and face shaved, but in the full regalia of a broad-stripe tribune: horsehair-crested helmet, muscle-patterned armor of silvered bronze, weapons belt, cloak, boots, and the knotted sash of my rank.

"Actually, Legate, it was your assessment I hoped for," he said with a thin smile. "Forewarned is forearmed, you know."

Poppaeus took a honeyed fig from a server's tray. "My assessment?" He bit into the fig and chewed. "Troublemaker. Opinionated. Knows half as much as he thinks he does." He turned his head to the side, and a boy wiped juice from his broad face with a wet cloth. "Related to Caesar, you know, through his great-grandfather Marcus Antonius. Or great-great-grandfather; I always forget." He pointed to a spot on his chin for the boy to wipe. "Also a cousin of Governor Sabinus's wife, whom you will meet at dinner." He squeezed the boy's buttock and sent him away with a casual slap.

"You speak as though he is not accustomed to taking orders." Lamia waved off a bee enticed by his hair oil.

"I have no complaints," Poppaeus said comfortably. He glanced at me. "Any questions from you, Carinna?" It was like him not to bother with my new name.

I had learned from Glabrio that morning that the mission to Bruna would include an ox-drawn wagon to haul the king's gifts north and the rescued captives south. At a top speed of three miles per hour, which was improbable on the rough Amber Road, the oxen would take a week or more to travel seventy miles. This not only made nonsense of Lamia's objection to the slow pace of infantry, but also doubled the number of nights to be spent without defenses—most of the time in Ingiomar's tribal lands.

Glabrio had scoffed at my concerns. His informers told him the Mark was safe. Why take a chance of offending the king? We argued about whether the decision was military or political: mine or Lamia's. I yielded in the end, for I had no information to disprove Glabrio's spies. He conceded that extra weapons would be issued to the cavalry.

I cleared my throat. "I am satisfied," I said.

Lamia's dangling foot jiggled up and down. "Let us be clear. Legate, do you approve of his leading my troops into the Mark?"

Poppaeus arched his brows. "He did well enough last time."

I shifted. A dart of light touched one of the leather straps hanging on my thigh and bounced off the gilded stud.

Lamia raised his glass and made a show of surprise at finding it empty. Appearing not to notice, Poppaeus snapped his fingers and crooned to beckon his pet cat.

The prefect's eyes narrowed. "Our business is concluded, then." He set his cup on the fountain curb and stood up. "Aquilo, you have a great deal to do before we leave."

"Fear not, Prefect; I have already begun," I assured him.

About to pull aside the gauze fly-curtain that opened onto the garden, he pivoted. "Legate, my report will say that you approved his appointment as senior tribune *ad rem*."

Poppaeus shrugged. "With my broad-striper immobilized, I feel compelled to provide an experienced replacement. Since, as you say, your expedition is crucial."

"So be it." Lamia marched out into the sunlight.

As his footsteps faded away, I murmured, "Thank you, sir."

The legion commander scowled. "The only thing I hate worse than a pimply know-it-all from Rome is a pompous liar from the Special Cohort." He reached down to the cat, which arched its back for his caress.

My mind drifted to Aurima. Riding side by side through a snowy gorge, we had mused about living together. "What will you have in our house?" I had asked her.

I thought she might say, *I will have a fountain that runs day and night,* or *Floors that are heated in winter,* or some other refinement of civilization she had seen in Rome. Instead this iridescent opal of a girl, who had known animals only as creatures to eat or be eaten by, told me, "When I was in Nina's garden, a little beast jumped out at her. I swung my arm like this to hit it away. 'No!' she said. She took the beast in her arms and rubbed it, and it closed its eyes and sang to her. That is what I want in our house. A cat like Nina's, that smiles and sings when I hold it."

I had teased her about it—why wish for a pet to cuddle when she had me?—but now I vowed to give her a cat. Not a sleek, aloof Egyptian feline, but a puffball of a kitten whose antics would make her laugh.

Poppaeus heaved himself out of his chair and stumped over to me. "Listen. There is obviously no chance now that your father will persuade Caesar to promote me"—he paused for emphasis—"and every chance that you will destroy what remains of my career if you fuck up this mission. If you do, I will abandon you. I expect the governor too will withdraw his protection."

"I think the outcome will satisfy you." After being sworn to secrecy, I could come no closer to hinting at rescue of the massacre survivors.

He grunted. "Lamia wants to be confirmed as regional prefect. Make him look good, and you will be fine." The cat, which had curled up on his cushion, gave a yowl of protest as he dropped it unceremoniously on the floor. "But watch out for Glabrio. The man's a snake." He sank into his chair. "If you want to thank me, keep those two from setting Barbaricum on fire. Things are peaceful now, the way I like them."

Instead of the wariness he obviously meant to spark in me, what I felt was satisfaction. At last I was on my way to find Aurima, with the hope of eventually restoring public respect for my family. "Understood, Legate."

"Forewarned is forearmed," Poppaeus cautioned. He winked. "As the man said."

9: THE AMBER ROAD

Even the newest recruit knows the story. It is usually said to have happened to the messmate of a friend in another cohort, although no one ever knows exactly whose friend it was or the name of the messmate. One also wonders at the details, since the victim would have been unable to tell the tale, but the account is accepted for its chilling import.

The cohort in question is supposedly on maneuvers across the river, or escorting an official who met with the Marcomanni king, or on the way back from extinguishing a wildfire that threatened Amber Road trade. Whatever its mission, the nameless soldier has always eaten something he should not have, and he is caught short as the cohort is forming up to march. Without a word he ducks away from his comrades and dashes into the trees to relieve himself. First he runs into a patch of nettles, then briars, then an ants' nest, forcing him to plunge deeper and deeper into the forest. Finally he comes upon a tiny clearing where he can squat in comfort.

But then he cannot find the way back. The trees all look the same. Their thick canopy denies him guidance from the sun. He shouts. No one hears him. The cohort has marched off without him, his friends covering for his absence. He rushes in one direction, then another, running into branches, stumbling on deadfalls, tripping over roots. Shouting, shouting, until his voice cracks. The forest grows darker.

Before long he begins to scream.

And he is never seen again.

Pavor saltūs, we call it: terror of the forest. Dark, dense, virtually trackless, teeming with dangerous beasts, treacherous bogs, and—so rumor said—giant trees that engulf sleeping men at night, the Great Forest is pierced by a single thoroughfare: the Amber Road, a rutted and potholed dirt track that meanders hundreds of miles from Carnuntum to the northern sea where amber is found. Fortunately there was no need for us to stray from the course of this road to reach the king of the Marcomanni and Quadi, for it runs past his stronghold of Bruna, where we were to retrieve the eight captives.

I had made the journey to Bruna a year earlier, as had Valerius Secundus, the narrow-stripe tribune who was now my adjutant *ad rem*. Less than halfway there, we had been attacked and nearly overrun by Ingiomar and his fanatics. But if the Marcomanni war chieftain was as peaceable now as the Special Cohort insisted, there was nothing to worry about.

That did not prevent Ollius from praying to every god he could think of. When he arrived in the last ferryload of men, animals, and supplies across the Danube, my stocky guard wore so many amulets that he rattled like an Egyptian priestess. Cleon, whose own trip preparations had involved making brothel owners richer, hooted at the sight.

Even though I had given up on all gods but Fortuna, I did not laugh. Self-assurance that was once natural, bred into me as a Senator's son, now had to be purposely summoned and sometimes arose with too much force. Discovering at an early meeting with my junior officers that the *turma* of Gallic cavalry was headed by Licnos, the decurion who had joined Festus in attacking me, I had flattened him with my fist. Now I prowled the staging area with Secundus, bawling at drunken troopers, idle muleteers, and swaggering Praetorians. No one on this expedition would dare think me fainthearted.

The first night's campsite was on the north bank of the Danube. I ordered the carts drawn protectively around tents and picket lines, while Lamia's Praetorians and the Fifth Gallica patrolled the inner and outer perimeters. Any attacker striking so near the frontier would have to be suicidal, but this was good practice for less settled areas.

After reviewing orders for the morning with my junior officers, I walked the camp. Off-duty troopers sat by their fires, gambling or polishing gear. Mounts and draft beasts, fed and watered, dozed at their tethers. I spoke quietly to Rufus and patted my horses, who snuffled drowsily into my clothing.

The flap of Placidus's tent was closed against visitors. The surgeon had been surly after being drafted into the vexillation, but I reckoned his mood would improve when he learned of the captives to be delivered.

Glabrio crouched beside the fire outside Lamia's tent, scratching in the dust with a stick. Two shaggy Germans leaned over him, scouts of his who would rove the countryside as we progressed.

The Special Cohort agent's boot scraped across one side of his drawing as he straightened up, but I recognized the telltale Y. The Amber Road runs north along the Marus River for what would be the first third of our journey. At that point the Thaya joins the Marus from the northwest. The road continues between the two rivers to Bruna, some forty-five miles north of this confluence.

Before Glabrio's foot swiped them away, I thought I saw other lines: one below the Thaya and another above it. Aurima had told me that was Quadi territory, except for lands her Marcomanni father had gained when her Quadian mother died. There, in Ingiomar's stronghold of Hoheneih, was where I expected to find her.

"What are you mapping?" I said.

"Where they live." Glabrio glanced from one German to the other. "Central to our route, you see, so they will have no trouble getting local information."

I nodded a greeting, an acknowledgment, a good night.

A light burned inside Lamia's tent. When I went in past the Praetorian sentry, the acting prefect was dictating to his secretary, an elderly man who wheezed over his wax tablet: "—river crossing completed . . ."

Lamia broke off and looked up. I wanted to ask when he would inform the troops of our clandestine mission, but did not know if the secretary was privy to the secret. "Just making sure all is well, Prefect."

Lamia let his eyelids droop halfway. "For a well-bred patrician, your language was remarkably salty today."

I let that pass. There was no hope of commanding obedience unless fear of my authority surpassed the men's contempt.

His eyes opened fully. "Just remember what matters, Aquilo. Deeds, not words."

Full dark settled at last on the encampment. It was still unseasonably warm, and most off-duty troopers slept in the open under cloaks or saddle blankets. The night buzzed and crackled with snores, horses' whickers, subdued voices, an occasional clatter of a mess tin or piece of equipment, and, farther away, the eerie howls and shrieks of wild things. The smell of the Danube, sour and rich with decay, filtered through the trees.

I paused to look up outside my own tent. Stars bespattered the sky. Sometimes I wanted to believe, as others did, that they were the souls of the dead.

If it was true, which spark of brightness was the soul of my father?

Guide me, Father, I prayed. *Help me return eight lost men to the civilized world, so I may in some way atone for what I forced upon you.*

The white river of souls flowed unheedingly over my head. Desolation swelled within me.

Then it was gone when Cleon groaned, "Bed at last! I'm asleep on my feet."

"Where have you been?" I snapped. "I didn't see you."

"You said not to be obvious." My chief bodyguard's sun-flushed face glowed in the flame of a nearby torch. "So don't bite my head off." He followed me into the tent.

A lamp guttered in the far end where my armor and weapons hung on a stand. The cover over my breastplate had been pulled up so that light reflected in its silvered slopes, magnifying the brightness. Ollius was curled on a carpet in the forepart of the tent, his cloak over his head. Dio rose from a seat, blinking and rubbing his eyes.

I unbuckled my knife belt. "Did you take Father's memoirs to Leonnatus?"

"I already told—"

"And my will?"

"Yes, he locked your will and the master's memoirs in his strongbox."

In my fatigue it struck me as unfortunate that a slave must speak of the man who sired him as "master." Now that I had freed Dio, perhaps I should give him permission to call himself my father's son.

What was I thinking? That would demean me, as well as my brother's memory.

I bent over a basin to splash my face. After months of whiskers, the water felt foreign on bare skin.

Dio went on, "But I did not think it right to let him keep this."

I wiped my face on the partitioning curtain. Looking up from the coarse folds pressed to my jaw, I glimpsed in his hands my father's gold torc.

"Dio, I told you I would not risk losing that to some light-fingered *calo!*"

"You will not lose it," he said, "if you wear it."

I stared at him. A memory came to me of Father wearing the neck ring of twisted cables, given to him as a token of friendship by Caligula's father, Germanicus, and I realized that what I had considered an expensive ornament was in truth an emblem of tested valor. An emblem I had not earned.

I took it in a damp palm. The metal was warm; Dio must have kept it inside his tunic. I spread the ends, slipped the ring around my neck, and tightened it. It would not show beneath my neck scarf when I was in uniform, but I would feel it there. And perhaps trying to live up to what it meant would be justification enough for wearing it.

Cleon yawned. "Lucky they have you running things, eh? Maybe the Silver Sheep will put you up for a medal."

"You should have more respect for a Praetorian officer," scolded Dio, who had grown up with an urban slave's awe of the imperial guards.

"Don't nanny me, you pen-pusher," Cleon shot back.

"Besides," I said mildly, "it is golden fleece, isn't it, that crowns the most prized sheep from Hispania?" The interior of the tent dimmed as I pulled the cover down over the breastplate.

Dio blinked, mollified. Cleon grinned and booted the cloaked lump that was Ollius. "Up, darling. Your turn on watch."

Ollius's yawn was contagious. I could not think of anything I had failed to do. Anyway, Secundus was in command until the start of the last night watch. "Get some sleep," I said, and swung my booted feet up onto my camp bed.

Aurima, I am coming for you.

In the morning, I offered ritual prayers to Jupiter and Apollo and sacrificed a cock—perhaps last night's loser—while the troops stood in a dutiful hush. Assured of the gods' favor, the vexillation formed up. With a jingle of buckles and spurs, troopers hoisted themselves onto their horses, socketed javelins into saddle-slings, and adjusted sword hilts close to hand. They faced me two abreast with Lamia's Praetorians in the lead, black helmet-plumes nodding and javelins bristling. The oval shields slung on their backs bore the scorpion of the Praetorian Guard, gold on red. I gave the order and we set out for the Amber Road, cheered on by the locals who could now resume plucking travelers at the river's edge.

A traveler leaving the Roman frontier does not at once plunge into the Great Forest. First he must evade a horde of seedy inns and shacks offering drink, gambling, fornication, and other farewell enticements. Our grinning troopers pranced past women of every age and shape, and boys too, who called out and waved.

We made good time, for the Danube floodplain is as flat as a coin. As we rode on, the web of wheel marks across the Marus delta merged into a single rough thoroughfare through fields and fens. This was the famed Amber Road: two carts wide, sometimes three; scarred with wheel ruts, studded with deep-rooted rocks, crisscrossed with the trace of dried rivulets, and littered with leaves, fallen branches, and dung. Scraggly undergrowth overhung the lip of the sunken roadbed; trees reared above it, the tallest of them farther away, so that we seemed to be cradled in the pocket of a slingshot.

Here and there, where a clearing had been hewn, round huts sprouted like mushrooms. Rudely clad folk stopped what they were doing to gape. "Why are you here, Romans?" a bold youngster shouted in Germanic. "Go back where you came from!"

I ignored the taunts, surveying hovels heavily laden with thatch, each with its fenced garden, woodpile, brew shed, cow, and barking dog. Apart from the disturbance our passage aroused, it was the sort of rustic idyll we Romans like to think we sprang from.

"Hmph." The plumes of Lamia's helmet swayed as he looked around. "This is the Mark you were so worried about, Aquilo?"

"No," I said. "This is not the part I was worried about."

We ambled on. I asked, "When will you tell our men about the captives?"

"Not today. At the halfway mark, perhaps. There is still too much risk of word being carried back to the fortress." The prefect darted a glance at me from under his helmet brim. "Have you said anything to your own people?"

"I gave you my word." His obsession with secrecy was irritating. I reckoned he would not admit that the sun crossed the sky unless one of Apollo's horses shat on his head.

At any rate, by the time we were halfway to Bruna I should have learned a great deal more. Pulling my neckcloth over my nose against the dust, I trotted back along the column in search of the two Quadi scouts. I wanted to learn what they knew about Aurima and Ingiomar without Glabrio flapping his big ears in the background.

We were passing an inn and stableyard that sprawled for a hundred paces along the road. In a pen walled against predators, sheep bleated greetings to our parade of horses, men, mules, oxen, and rumbling carts. I shouted to Glabrio about the scouts.

"I sent them out at dawn, Tribune. They may not be back until tomorrow."

"Why did you not inform me?"

"I did tell the prefect." He paused a moment as a reminder that he reported to Lamia, not to me. "By the way, I asked them to see what they can find out about Inguiomerus. And his family." He turned his swarthy face toward me. "Reckoned you might be interested." The glint in his eyes could have been merriment.

Confirmation, if I had needed any, that he and Lamia knew Aurima's escape from Rome might have nullified the truce. But it was in their interest to keep this news from the provincial populace, who might take fright, and from the troops, who might take revenge on me.

"Let me know as soon as they return," I said, and pulled up my neckerchief again.

As expected, the heavy wagon carrying the gifts—the eight captives' ransom—soon became an encumbrance. It lurched over rocks and ruts, dragged by two spotted oxen who plodded along like tortoises. After it came the surgeon's cart and the remounts, then orderlies and slaves leading pack animals bearing officers' baggage. Farther back in the dust-choked column, mules pulled the carts carrying tents and supplies. I began to think my estimate of ten miles a day had been too optimistic.

Other traffic on the road was sparse. A southbound herd of long-horned cattle milled across a farmer's flattened wheatfield after the drovers ceded us the road. A trio of sun-beaten scruffs, occupation unknown, overtook us with their guards and pack horses.

Gradually the huts and commercial establishments thinned, and the trees closed in. In stretches the sky shrank to a tattered blue ribbon between alders as tall as ten men.

The troopers' high spirits began to fade. Their mounts spooked at cries and crackles in the forest, false alarms that became tiresome. After taunting each other about relieving themselves in the woods, they reverted to everyday grumbles about withheld pay, overpriced wine, and the odds of missing Germanicus's birthday games next month.

Licnos's evil glare followed me. By now his two black eyes were fading to purple and yellow, and he could breathe through his nose again. He and his Gallic troop obeyed orders without demur, evidently having absorbed my message.

Sweat ran under my helmet's cheek plates and glued my tunic to my skin, but I was in a good humor amid the familiar road smells of trampled earth and manure, sweaty men and horses, hot leather, and the sour tang of polished steel. I studied the road ahead, hoping to see Glabrio's two scouts or other natives who might know about Aurima. Here in her own land, I was sure to find out soon where she was.

The engineer and his assistants had pegged out the campsite when we arrived. To judge by the worn grass and hewn saplings, it had been much occupied by other travelers since I had used it the year before. Lamia rode up as I watched tents being pitched and horses led to the riverbank. "No sign of trouble so far," he observed.

I said, "No sign of Glabrio's Quadi, either." But they might turn up before dark.

"Aquilo." The prefect's tone made me look at him. "My secretary suffers from weak lungs, and this dust has utterly disabled him. I will need to send him back with the next convoy that passes. Will you lend me yours?"

I said, "He is a free man." Did he think I could give Dio away like a spare cloak?

"I think he will make a good impression on the king. He's good-looking and speaks Palatine Latin—although I don't suppose a barbarian can tell the difference."

Balding Dio, good-looking? "Fine," I agreed. It was a simple enough request.

Again I wanted to urge him to inform the troops about the massacre survivors, but I was reluctant to be brushed aside once more. Some distance away a cavalry horse broke free and had to be restrained from trampling a half-unpacked tent. With my eyes on the animal I asked, "What condition are they in, the survivors?"

"Not bad, for men who have been used as slaves since Augustus's day."

"Can they walk? Ride?"

"One of them, a centurion, was blinded when he was captured," Lamia said. "I believe a couple of others are lame. The rest should be able to walk."

"They will not walk home while I am in command." Once the wagon was unloaded, I would have seats put in it for them.

Before he moved away, I said, "Show me the gifts we are taking to Vannius." The wagon had arrived on the ferry with its cover lashed down, and in all the hubbub I had not yet seen what made suitable ransom for eight Romans.

Six bundles of swords, not legion *gladii* but the longer cavalry *spathae* the Germans preferred. Ten saddles, two to a bale. Another six sacks bulged with the short sharp angles of iron ax heads. A long crate showed glimpses of the wrapped statue of a headless man, with the head separately swaddled. A protruding marble toe and the strap of a general's boot hinted that the body was that of a generic military hero, destined to wear Caligula Caesar's head.

"Vannius will be pleased with that," I said. "I hear he fancies himself *imperator* of the East, Caesar's spiritual brother."

The prefect snorted at this assessment. "At least he will have more good swords than most barbarians who call themselves kings."

Surely he knew that Vannius needed weapons to hold off the Iazyges in the east and the Lugii in the north. Many who are new to the frontier are surprised to learn that there are barbarians behind the barbarians. Without our support, the Quadi and Marcomanni would be shoved across the frontier into Pannonia by eastern tribes hungry for their land. Naturally enough, Aurima refused to see any benefit of Roman intervention in her homeland.

If the Quadi scouts reported she was dead, what would I do?

"Are you well?" Lamia asked, for I had closed my eyes to shut out an image of her long limp body, of an ashen face half hidden in hair whose dark dye had faded.

"I am fine," I said, watching Rufus wash my unsaddled horses. When Lamia kept looking at me, I added, "It was a short night."

He clapped me on the shoulder, a liberty I had not invited. "Relax, Aquilo. We have capable officers; you need not fret about everything."

In view of his lower social rank, the comment and contact were patronizing. But a friendly overture ought not to be rejected.

Relax, man. Fortuna grant that Glabrio's scouts would return soon to report that she was alive and well.

10: PAYBACK

"His secretary?" echoed Dio, on the verge of tipping hot water into a basin. "Do you think I have too little to do for you?"

"Of course not." I set my helmet on its stand. The tall red crest swayed a little in the lamplight. My orderly poured a cup of wine. "More water," I told him. There was no need to sweat out more than necessary of the precious Baeterran Leonnatus had provided. When he had thinned the drink to my satisfaction, I dismissed him.

"You can be my Trojan horse," I said softly in Greek, apt to be incomprehensible to big-eared soldiers.

"Eh? Oh." Dio unbuckled my belts and body armor as I sipped the wine. In the same language he asked, "Is something wrong? You look troubled."

"Just tired." Perhaps I was becoming as secretive as Lamia, not wishing to admit my worry about Aurima. I peeled off my damp tunic and bent to wash.

Dio reverted to Latin. "This is a strange land."

"You and I have ridden through wilder country," I said through my hands.

"Yes, but"—he handed me a towel—"here it seems that men live on the sufferance of the trees. Do you feel it? If the cutting and burning and grazing stopped, the forest would close in like a wound healing over. This dirt road would vanish."

I wiped my face. "Dio, that is as fanciful as saying eels are born out of mud."

"No, I think not. Aurima knows it too. To her, trees have spirits. As do rivers. You know how she talks to them. In the city or a town, we see more than she does. But in the countryside or wild land, she sees things we do not."

I had always honored her prayers to the sun and moon, to the earth and storms, but to me it was no different from the peasants on our Volsinii farm sacrificing to the nymph in the hill spring or to Ops at sowing time. Most of Italy had long ago been tamed; there were no more great forests, and the powers most to be feared were men.

I resolved to be more tender of her beliefs when I was with her again. I would even beg forgiveness of a tree before felling it for firewood.

Sluggish with fatigue, I thought to ask, "Have you eaten?"

"Your orderly brought us beans and barley." I heard Dio snapping creases out of my tunic. "Rufus didn't mind, but the Titans wouldn't touch it. Said it was slaves' food."

After dining on the prefect's roast lamb myself, I could not fault Cleon and Ollius—or Dio himself—for scorning soldiers' food as poor rations. My thoughtlessness shamed me; it is a poor *paterfamilias* who neglects those he is duty-bound to protect. "I will see to better fare for you tomorrow."

I slumped onto my cot. The last thing I remembered was Dio saying grouchily, "If I am the prefect's secretary, I will be able to see to it myself."

An unholy screech knifed through the soundness of sleep.

I scrambled to my feet. Now there were men's yells, horses neighing in alarm—*merda*, was Ingiomar attacking? I yanked my sword from its scabbard and ran through the tent, nearly colliding with Cleon and Dio.

Horses whinnied and pulled at the picket lines. Mules brayed and stamped. Awakened troopers rolled out of their cloaks and stumbled from tents. But I could see no clashes with the night patrol. No rushing shadows darted past the perimeter torches.

A bear? Wolves? Predators might associate woodsmoke with food, cooked or on the hoof.

The torch I grabbed on the run lit the remains of a brawl: men splayed on the ground near the horse lines, picking themselves up, trying to slink into the dark. Not Germans—men in the blue tunics of the Fifth Gallica. Licnos himself, curse him, was hauling one of his men to his feet.

"Stand to attention!" I roared.

Rufus sprawled over a saddle with the back of his tunic yanked up to his waist. He struggled to his feet, eyes wild in a face smeared with dirt and grass. Beside me, Ollius swore aloud.

I understood at once. "Rufus, point them out."

The boy pulled down his tunic. He glared around at the four Gallic troopers frozen in the torchlight, then threw himself at Licnos.

A knife glinted suddenly in Ollius's hand. He and Cleon started forward. "No," I said, barring their way with the flat of my sword. Someone hauled Rufus away from the decurion.

By now most of the camp was goggling at the fracas. The horses and mules still snorted and fidgeted.

Dio thrust my own tunic at me. I handed the torch to Cleon and a moment later, more decently covered, pointed my sword at the saddle. "Explain this, Licnos."

The decurion stood rigid, eyes aimed straight ahead. "No idea, Tribune. Boy must have had a bad dream."

Rufus tried to wrench free. Agony flared across his face, and he sagged.

I was so furious it dizzied me. "Take these men's names," I told Secundus. "All four of you, be in my tent at the start of the first watch. Everyone else, as you were."

To Dio I muttered, "Talk to the boy." Marching back to my tent, I caught a glimpse of Lamia and Glabrio among the crowd. It was hard to be sure in the flickering light, but I thought the Special Cohort agent had a smirk on his ill-shaven face.

There was nothing in the tent to smash, or it would have been broken by the time Dio edged in past the entrance flap. I swung around. "Is Rufus all right?"

"The attempt failed; I think they expected him to be mute. His shoulder was dislocated. The *medicus* has just put it back."

"I thought they were disciplined enough to keep their minds on the mission. To forget about my father." I slammed the edge of my fist against the tent pole. The canopy shuddered. "Not this god-cursed outrage, to shame me before the entire vexillation!"

Secundus arrived, helmet tucked under his arm. He had ordered the four malefactors to stand facing their standard for the rest of the night.

"I want you to discipline them in the morning," I said. "In my presence. They must understand that they did not just offend me; they broke a law of military conduct."

"What sentence shall I pronounce?"

"Think of something appropriate. I am too angry."

About to take his leave, he paused. "I believe the boy would be better off in the medical tent tonight, but he wants to stay with his horses." He raised a questioning brow.

I smiled sourly, thinking of Boss's temper. Anyone who molested Rufus within range of my sorrel stallion would regret it. "Then let it be so."

Pink clouds streamed across the sky, deepening to fiery rose. As the sun vanished, the trees seemed to grow taller, looming over the road like immense fortifications.

I turned my horse back toward the camp. Another day's march had ended, and Glabrio's scouts had still not returned.

That was the cap to a day of disharmony. Sentenced to three days of walking or riding mules, Licnos spat whenever I passed him and his fellows tramping behind their mounted comrades. Their bilious tempers spread until most of the troopers were sneering and growling at one another. Salutes and salutations were omitted and sullenly corrected, orders sloppily executed.

The two Praetorians on patrol were talking about how infernally tedious this expedition had been when one of them held up a hand and said, "Listen."

Horses coming. Not Glabrio's two scouts; so many riders that their hoofbeats merged into a heavy rumbling. The two Praetorians spread out ahead of me, javelins lowered.

Straining my eyes northward through the graying light, I recognized the man in the lead. Probably he had come from Vannaz, king of the Marcomanni and Quadi, but it seemed equally likely to me that Fortuna had sent him. Vangio, the king's nephew, would surely be able to tell me what I needed to know.

11: PRINCE OF THE MARK

"I am Vangio, son of Erminlinda," he announced, identifying himself with his mother's name as his tribespeople do. He was a dozen years older and half a head taller than me, with a beard the color of burnt honey and a very high forehead, so that his features seemed to have sagged into the lower half of his face. Arriving in company with an escort of five warriors and our own advance patrol, he was as amiable as his limited Latin allowed. "Vannaz— you Romans say 'Vannius,' *ja*?—who is the brother of my mother, he sends me greetings to give." Like most Germans, he had trouble with our multiple verb tenses.

Red-faced and sweating, as we all were, Lamia did not rise from a folding stool over which a couple of slaves were erecting a canopy. Everyone in the camp who did not have a duty, and others who did, found a reason to wander by and stare at the newcomers.

The prefect was dubious, I saw, about the Germanic princeling's ride-tangled hair, sweaty tunic, and dust-grimed short trousers. But Vangio wore a torc at his neck, three armlets, and a cuff on each wrist, enough gold as if he were a king himself.

I said, "You must be thirsty. Come and have something to drink."

Vangio's mustaches parted over a grin. His men were already sucking on their own aleskins. With a nod to Lamia, he followed me to my baggage cart.

I had introduced myself earlier as Aquilo, and received a glance of puzzlement. Now, lifting off my helmet, I asked quietly, "Do you remember me?"

"*Ja.* Last year, with Ingiomar you make the peace. I remember." Was he still smiling? His deep-browed face resembled a dolphin's, but his beard hid where the dolphin's smile would have been.

When my orderly had drawn a cup of wine for me, I held it out to the king's nephew. "This was a gift to me from an old friend. I offer it to one who may be a new friend, Vangio of the Quadi."

His blue eyes showed appreciation, and he gulped deeply from the cup. That is the way Germans drink their ale, but the Gallic wine was far sweeter and heavier.

"One to four," I said to the orderly while Vangio, crimson-cheeked, struggled not to cough. When the refilled cup came back to me, it was thinned with four-fifths water.

"It takes a brave man to drink it straight," I said. "I myself must mix it first." I sipped, then passed him the cup again.

He drank, more cautiously this time. We smiled at each other.

I took the leap that I had avoided with my fellow Romans: "Do you know where to find Inguiomerus's daughter?"

Only because I watched intently did I see a cloud shadow his eyes, and then he was staring at me with equal force. "Why do you think I know?"

"Because she was to marry your brother."

The heat in my voice disquieted him. He put down the cup. His fingers touched the hilt of his sword.

I tried to calm myself. "She was a hostage for peace. I have a right to ask."

Vangio's hand slipped off the sword grip. "*Ja*, she was wife to Sido."

His brother's wife! Impossible. She had been a maiden when I met her.

"No, I speak wrong. I mean, wife she was to be. Now, not."

"What are you saying?" I was too stunned to think of urging him to speak Germanic, which I might have understood better than his Latin.

"Some *erlmann*, a high man, he takes her." Incoherent emotion mottled his cheeks. "She runs from Rome, comes to father, but no more *mavî*, no good for wife to my brother."

I picked incredulously through the tangled stammer. "She was attacked? Taken?" Had I returned her to the Mark only to be ravished by some tribal chieftain?

Vangio licked spittle from his lips. "Not attacked. Maelo say that she —" He made a gesture of pulling someone closer: *she invited it.* "Inguiomerus has much anger."

This was no time to reveal that I was the high man whom Maelo had accused. "Where is she now?" I demanded. But before he could reply, the question I should have asked struck me: Was Ingiomar angry enough for revenge?

Revenge on seventy-five Romans who were unprepared to build a fortified camp, were still nearly a week's march from captives whose lives depended on them, and were burdened by a wagonload of ransom from making a hasty retreat to Carnuntum.

I felt suddenly as though I were floundering through a turbulent sea, a monstrous creature following beneath me with jaws open wide.

Vangio had spoken to me. I croaked out, "What did you say?"

"I said, since a long time nothing on her do I hear. On the *dulthi*, the holy day, of Austro I ask, 'Where is Aurima? Why is Austro's priestess not here?'" He spread his hands. "People know nothing."

Austro's festival was at the spring equinox, a good month ago. Aurima would not have missed the celebration, unless . . .

I forced saliva into my mouth. "Do you think she is dead?"

Vangio looked into the distance for several heartbeats before turning back to me. "Gladly I want to think not so. Vannaz—Vannius—he does not want peace to end." He patted his chest. "Me, also." His forefinger touched my breastplate. "You, also?"

Others had drifted closer, perhaps drawn by Vangio's reaching for his sword. His five warriors, my two bodyguards. Secundus passed through them. "Is everything all right, Tribune?" His eyes dwelled on Vangio.

I made a gesture of dismissal. But then I was seized by talons of fear —for Aurima, for the soldiers whose lives were my responsibility. As I swallowed past the torc that seemed to choke me, the thought came of my father watching from the other world.

I took a deep breath. "Is Inguiomerus planning to attack us?" The steadiness of my voice surprised me.

Vangio's mustache drooped. "Vannius is thinking not. But that is why he send me, so Inguiomerus knows protecting by the king you have."

If Ingiomar Ironhand decided to punish Romans for debauching his daughter, our protection by the king of the Marcomanni and Quadi might matter little to him—and the presence of Vannaz's nephew and five companions would not help us much. I said, "I need to be sure."

"I am not sure, Aquilo."

"Will you go and find out?"

"Go? To Hoheneih, you mean?" Vangio cocked his head uncertainly. "This is not— Vannius does not send me here for this."

"I need to know whether he means to attack us. And where Aurima is."

"Why . . ." He stopped himself. I read the rest in his eyes: why her whereabouts mattered to me; what my role might have been in provoking Ingiomar's anger.

"You?" He was astonished. No doubt he had imagined her despoiler as a small, ugly brute with rotten teeth and hobnailed boots.

Well, I did have the boots.

"You can help us make a decision," I said. "Come with me. But I urge you to say nothing about Aurima."

Lamia's face was still sun-flushed when I arrived with Vangio and ordered a council meeting. As we stood in a circle in the prefect's large tent, I told the others, "There is a possibility we are in danger. Inguiomerus may have ended the truce we struck with him."

"Why?" Secundus asked. His eyebrows went up when no one else asked the question. Placidus was still grumpy, and Lamia and Glabrio already knew the answer.

My adjutant's face hardened. He was not a fool.

I waited in trepidation for Vangio or one of the Special Cohort men to reveal that the truce was no longer secured by a hostage, but they did not speak. Finally I said, "We are not sure of anything yet," and watched Dio write down my words. Lamia's coughing secretary had gone home that day with a passing troop of beast-catchers.

Vangio said he had not heard of Ingiomar assembling his warriors. Secundus countered, "Aquilo and I know he has ambushed troops before on the Amber Road."

"We will know more when my scouts return tomorrow." Glabrio tipped his chin to the north, as if his bat ears might pick up the sounds of their arrival sooner than ours.

Lamia shifted in his chair. "If Inguiomerus is indeed planning an attack, we can retreat and gather a force to crush him." His worry stone clicked against his ring.

"Ordinarily I would agree, Prefect," Glabrio said. "But it would be a pity to delay our mission to Bruna." I assumed he meant that men held captive for twenty-nine years should not have to wait weeks or months more for rescue.

Placidus spoke for the first time: "Why? Is the king going somewhere?"

Lamia said, "The Special Cohort has its orders," which meant "Not your affair."

I thought it ridiculous that they hid the existence of Varian survivors from the senior surgeon, but that was a side issue compared with the threat of assault. At any rate, I was in accord with Glabrio on this matter. I said, "Unless the scouts tell us we are in danger, I suggest continuing to Bruna as quickly as possible."

"I have a better idea." Lamia's fingers stilled on his stone. "Let us invite Inguiomerus to meet with us."

Damn the man's naïve political ambitions! He probably thought he could bribe the war chieftain of the eastern Marcomanni with smooth talk and a few ax heads.

Lamia gestured toward Vangio, fingers fanned coaxingly. "I am sure you can persuade him, Lord Vangio. He is an important man. He will not turn down a chance to confer with the regional prefect of the Praetorian Special Cohort, will he?"

I glanced at Vangio, who had already expressed reluctance to confront Aurima's father. His brows wrinkled in uncertainty.

"Is Ironhand likely to agree, Senior Tribune?" A cryptic question about the safety of an arranged meeting from Placidus, who had heard my tales of Ingiomar's deceit.

I said, "I expect he will honor the authority of his king's nephew." Probably. "But it may take days to find him—three days, four—while we sit here like geese in a pond."

Before anyone else could speak, Vangio protested in stumbling Latin, "Vannaz— Vannius must say yes before. He does not want Inguiomerus angry to make."

Lamia pounced on this. "That settles it, Aquilo. It would be risky to wait here without knowing Ironhand's aims. The wise course is to retreat to

Carnuntum." He lifted his fist to his mouth, like a gambler kissing his dice.

A commander is expected to listen to his officers' opinions, but he need not defer to them. "We will continue to Bruna," I said, a blunt reminder that the decision was mine.

Glances were exchanged.

"Patrols will be doubled for as long as necessary," I added. It was for Aurima's sake, not to save my men or eight Roman captives, that I refused to retreat. Such was the prejudice I had declared to Placidus, yet I did not care for its taste in my mouth.

In the morning the troops were informed that we were entering the domain of an unfriendly German chieftain and needed to heighten our vigilance.

The Fifth Gallica's *duplicarius*, who had not taken part in the assault on Rufus, asked if punishment would be lifted for Licnos and the others. I said back-alley bullies did not have the same rights as loyal soldiers. That won snarls from the footsore malefactors, still loath to ride mules, and endeared me even less to the rest of the *turma*.

Vangio was saddling his mare when I cornered him to voice a fear that had poisoned my sleep: "If Aurima's father thinks she is dishonored, will he kill her?"

"He cannot do that." He sounded shocked. "The Council of Women must decide."

"The Council of Women? Who are they?"

He swung into the saddle. "Women from all around." Gold glinted as he swept his arm in an arc.

"They decide on women's matters?"

"On all things important to our people." He flicked the end of his reins at a fly on the mare's neck. "For some tribes—Batavi or Chauci, maybe—it is a council of warriors, *ja*? But with us, women. They are more *frôda*, I think? I do not know the Latin."

Wise, I translated mentally. Would a council of women condemn Aurima for having had a Roman lover, no matter how much it infuriated her father? Were they wiser than he was?

I almost told Vangio the story that came to me then, but forbore. He might be too prudish to appreciate it.

It had started with my guards throwing dice as we waited out a snowstorm in a mountain hut. Cleon had tossed Ollius one of the brass coins they won and lost by turns—a new *sestertius* showing Caligula's sisters as Vestals. "Not that again," Ollius complained. "If those three are Vestal Virgins, I'm the fucking Pontifex Maximus!"

Aurima had asked to know why it was bad for a priestess to have a man or bear a child. I said a virgin was thought to be pleasing to the gods because of her purity.

"If a woman makes a good man happy, if she bears a child and cares for it, why is she not more pleasing to the gods than a girl who bleeds because she is empty?" she had said, or something like it.

I recognized the mistake I had made in getting involved. But snow had climbed high in the doorway of the hut, and there was no escape.

Aurima landed a final blow: "So Roman men think a woman is more excellent if they have not put their cock in her."

Rufus choked on a laugh. None of the rest of us had dared to respond.

"This Romulus and Remus," she had said scathingly. "It is too bad Rome did not begin with two sisters."

Vangio must have noticed my smile of recollection. "She is important to you, *ja*?"

"We are promised to each other," I said. "I gave her a horse as a bride gift." I patted Spider's silver-gray neck. "This horse."

A while later he said, "Aquilo." He had an air of decisiveness. "I go to Bruna, talk with Vannaz. If he says yes, I come back and we are going together to Hoheneih."

I said, "Fine." But on this wreck of a road, it would take him at least three days to reach the king's stronghold. Another day to talk with Vannaz; that made four altogether. By then we ourselves would be within a day of Bruna, and Ingiomar's plans—if any—would have already been made clear.

The prince and I were then riding at the head of the column. It was still early; mist swathed the forest. Crows in the treetops rattled out warnings. *Cavē, cavē*: beware. Vangio said, "We leave now. I try to come soon."

I held out my palm to him. He took it awkwardly, for handclasps are not a custom among Germans. Without letting go he said, "You are *erlmann*, Aquilo?" With his other hand he touched his gold neck-ring.

I had forgotten I wore my father's torc. "I am," I said.

Vangio nodded to his warriors. When their hoofbeats drubbed away into the distance, I hoped I had his friendship, and that it would aid me in finding Aurima.

12: NO STARS TONIGHT

Late that afternoon, I rode out to meet Glabrio's scouts. The two men were wild-haired and hot-faced, their mounts foam-flecked and blowing. "Are you pursued?" I demanded.

They shook their heads. "Wanting to be here by dark," puffed one. "*Die geiste.*"

The ghosts.

I handed over my wine flask as their horses plodded toward the camp. "What did you learn about Inguiomerus?"

"We went to Grozhauga," said the younger of the two. "Not to Hoheneih."

"Why? Where is Grozhauga?"

"A long day of riding." The other pointed vaguely to the northwest. "Berinhard is *fraujaz*." He took a swig of wine.

I knew the word *fraujaz*, similar to our term *dominus*. "Who is Berinhard?"

"A chief of the Quadi," said the younger.

"A friend to Rome," volunteered the older.

I wanted to shake them until I had the right answer. Slowly and clearly I said, "I need to know if Inguiomerus intends to attack us."

The older scout grunted in surprise. The younger one shook his head. "Berinhard says, 'Tell the *Fledarmûs* all is peace in the Mark.'"

Flying mouse? Wasn't that Germanic for "bat"? I realized whose nickname it must be. "So the vexillation is not in danger?"

"By Tiwaz, Tribune, we hear of no danger to vexillation," he said, and my heart unclenched for the first time since I had spoken with Vangio.

We were coming into camp. Others surrounded us, preventing me from asking about Aurima. Glabrio took the scouts away while a *calo* led off their weary horses.

When I told Secundus the news, he said, "That should improve everyone's mood." He ran a hand over his head, making his mouse-brown bristles stand up like a close-shorn carpet. "By Bellona, it's improved mine!" He grinned.

And mine. If Ingiomar did not intend to attack, Aurima must have soothed his initial anger. That made my own scheme to seek her in Hoheneih less perilous.

Lamia called a council meeting to discuss the scouts' report. We drank his good wine and agreed to offer an extra morning sacrifice to Fortuna Romana.

"Mithras be thanked," Placidus said. "Now Aquilo will stop badgering me about wearing that cook-pot on my head"—a quip that made Dio smile faintly at his note tablet.

The quartermaster Aprilis added, "We should also ask Apollo for continued fair weather. I see no stars tonight." Slogging through rain and mire would add days to the journey.

As the meeting ended, I said, "Glabrio, I must talk to the Quadi. Where are they?"

"Probably dead to the world, Tribune. They nearly fell asleep in their food."

Lamia interjected, "Surely you can question the poor fellows in the morning, Aquilo." I expected a favorite aphorism, and he did not disappoint: "Make haste slowly."

I could not wait for morning. I caught up with Glabrio on the short walk from the prefect's tent to his own. "Did your scouts have any word of Inguiomerus's daughter?"

He stopped. "In fact, they did. Well, one of them did: Tudrus."

My heart thudded faster. "Tell me."

Glabrio's back was to the nearby torch, so I could see only the shape of his head and his jutting ears. "Tudrus overheard her name when Berinhard, the lord of Grozhauga, was talking with his brother. Aurora, is it not?"

"Aurima. What did they say?"

Glabrio shook his head. "There was too much noise to hear clearly. He had already asked a number of questions, so he thought it would be dangerous to probe."

I was disappointed. "Is that all?"

"Sorry, I know it is no more than a hint."

I had to talk with this Berinhard. The scouts had said Grozhauga was only a day's ride from here. Could I leave the vexillation long enough to find him?

As Glabrio was turning away, I said, "If we cannot find Inguiomerus to ask his intentions, why not ask her?"

"Well, yes, but who knows if she is there?"

"I think it is worth finding out."

Glabrio heaved a sigh. "Very well, I will send one of the scouts tomorrow."

I nodded. "I will go with him."

His swarthy face slackened in surprise. "Aquilo, you squeezed the prefect to have command of this vexillation. It makes no sense to go off on your own."

He was right, but I could not pass up this precious clue. "Secundus is capable of taking over for a couple of days."

He rasped a fingernail over his beard stubble. "I don't know," he said at last. "I think the prefect must agree to this. I will speak with him."

I stood up. "We will speak with him together."

Lamia's body servant was massaging him with scented oil when I entered with Glabrio. Dio sat cross-legged on the ground, scribing something on a writing desk in his lap.

I broke into the prefect's dictation without preamble. "We may have an opportunity to find out from Inguiomerus's daughter what her father is planning."

Lamia propped his head on his arm to listen. I explained what Glabrio's scout had overheard, while the agent himself slouched on a seat with his arms draped on his knees.

When I was finished, Glabrio pointed out, "I doubt whether this will pay off, Prefect. But I feel I should accompany him. With a Praetorian escort, if you permit."

Damn him! It was as I had feared: they would unleash me to track down Aurima, then take her captive and haul her back to Rome. "I do not need you or your Praetorians," I said. "You should stay with the vexillation."

"I agree that questioning this girl may be important"—Lamia sneezed at the perfumed oil—"but under the circumstances, we should not divide our limited forces." The flesh on his shoulders jostled to and fro under the servant's hands.

"I am willing to go to Grozhauga by myself, with my two guards and a slave," I said. "I will leave tomorrow morning and return the next afternoon."

"Two days," Lamia mused. "We could withdraw to the Danube in that time."

Such caution seemed more reasonable now, if I—his senior liaison with the Marcomanni—was to be absent. I wanted to advise him sensibly, but as Cicero says, desire blindfolds the eyes of the mind. When I forced my thoughts away from Aurima, I was able only to imagine the massacre survivors, now men in their fifties, sixties, or older, waiting to be ransomed in Bruna.

In a voice I tried to keep noncommittal, I said, "Withdrawal could be awkward, Prefect, if it turns out there is no need."

The servant's hands batted Lamia's back lightly, *patter-patter-patter*. The prefect jerked himself up on his elbows. "Stop! How can I think with you pounding me?" He went on as the slave backed away, "Your men found no signs of rebel activity, Glabrio?"

"Nothing out of the ordinary, sir."

With a sigh, Lamia made his decision. "We will continue on to Bruna, then. Aquilo, see what you can learn from the girl, and rejoin us in two days." He glanced at Dio. "Of course, your excellently trained freedman must stay here; I cannot spare him."

Though I did not like dividing my *familia*, I had no excuse for needing a scribe. "Very well," I agreed, ignoring Dio's glare of accusation at being left behind.

Emerging from the tent ahead of Glabrio, I found Secundus waiting outside. He had overheard most of the discussion. As we walked to my quarters, he said, "I will be honored to have temporary command." His raised brows showed he thought it a questionable gift.

"Do you remember that ruined tavern south of the Thaya?" I asked.

He nodded. "Near where Inguiomerus ambushed us last fall."

"I will rejoin you there. If I am late arriving, carve 'Fifteen' into the doorpost so I will know you have already passed." I clapped him on the shoulder. "In the meantime, make Lamia happy and you may finally get your transfer to the Praetorian Guard."

It should have shamed me to neglect my duty, but I was too elated at being on Aurima's trail. I longed for Dio's presence, so he might see I still knew how to laugh.

"Don't worry, Marcus," Cleon said. "If she's there, me and Ollius will rescue her."

The two bodyguards and Rufus sat in my tent, eating smoked fish and dates and drinking my fine wine. It was very late now, and I knew I needed sleep before riding to Grozhauga. "Ollius is coming with me. Cleon, you will stay and look after Dio."

"Look after him? What do you expect to happen in two days?"

"Nothing, I hope. Yes, Rufus, you are coming too."

Cleon scowled. "That's daft, Marcus! Let Ollius stay and wet-nurse Dio."

"Dio cannot defend himself," I said. "He needs you, Cunctator." That had been his arena name, "Delayer," because he prolonged bouts to bring audiences to a frenzy.

"I should be the one going with you. I'm your chief guard, ain't I?"

Ollius snapped, "He needs a guard who can use a sword. Not a fork and a fishnet."

"When the master bought out your contract, you bugger, you only had —"

"I know: thirty-seven wins," I interrupted. "But I am the head of our house, Cleon, and you will do as I say."

"So you let him have all the fun," Cleon snarled. He flung his fish at Ollius and stalked out, stiff with sore pride. Ollius caught it, popped it in his mouth, and smirked.

13: CUPID'S ARROW

I would have missed the turnoff to Grozhauga had the scout guiding us not pointed it out. At first it seemed to be just another deer trail.

Entering it, we passed from partial sun into the shadow of titanic oak, alder, and beech trees. Their foliage closed over the track, shutting off all but rare snatches of daylight. The night's light rain, which had only laid the dust on the Amber Road, here set free an overwhelming flood of scents: of leaves, fronds, evergreen needles, bark and moss and fungus, of lavish growth and slow decay.

The west-trending path twisted around massive tree trunks and ledge outcrops, concealing itself from one moment to the next. Tudrus, the older of Glabrio's two scouts, rode ahead out of sight. Ollius's mare ambled near Boss's haunch, so the stallion's tail could swat flies from her face. Rufus brought up the rear on Spider, behind a pack mule.

Uneasiness coiled in my stomach. The Amber Road was a lifeline back to civilization. Leaving it behind made me less certain of being able to return.

Nonsense, of course. Yet I could not forget having seen Dio perched beside the wagon driver when the rest of the vexillation marched off toward Bruna, in his dark eyes the reproach of a dog being deserted by its master. When I lifted a hand in farewell, Cleon had spat to show his displeasure.

I had explained everything to Ollius and Rufus, so there was no more to be said now. Tudrus, a scar-faced Quadian with greasy gray hair, seemed to be out of humor at having to retrace his path to Grozhauga. He offered only sullen grunts in Latin: "Here," when we came to the turn; "Pig," to explain a noise in the brush. When I asked why Berinhard might have mentioned Aurima, he muttered, "Dunno." I did not reckon my luck would be any better if I tried my modest Germanic.

So we were all quiet as we started along this green tunnel, so narrow that outreaching bushes and boughs licked at us as if tasting every traveler. I endured my share of wet smacks, leaves, and insects. Ollius fingered his lucky charms, sliding his eyes back and forth like pieces on a game board. I understood his apprehension; we Romans prefer the countryside to have a horizon.

This told me, too, that I was not the only one longing to be out of here before dark. *Pavor saltūs* arises from more than just the denseness of the forest. Many trees of the Mark are immensely tall and thicker than several men can span with outstretched arms, so that one might reckon them to be older than mankind. It takes only a short leap to imagine them as the daylight shape of spirits that at night escape their woody bounds, consuming prey to feed their abnormal growth. That is a common night fear of Aurima and her people, but more enlightened men are also afflicted.

Moreover, it was an excellent setting for an ambush. Riding from a patch of sunlight into deep shade was like being struck blind. An elephant would have gone unnoticed in the trees, let alone a band of spear-launching barbarians. I hoped fervently that the scouts were right about Ingiomar's inactivity.

Ollius was unsettled enough to break the silence. "Think Caligula will get a son on his new wife?" he asked, apropos of nothing.

"He is due for some good luck," I said.

We rode for a while longer, the rustle, thud, and jingle of our small troop overlaying sounds from the forest. Rufus hummed. Mosquitoes fed on us like vultures.

"Strange, ain't it?" Ollius said. "I mean, he's hopped into more beds than a flea."

I lifted my feet as Boss splashed through a brook that ran across the track. "Strange, you mean, that he has no living children?"

"I know the gods don't gift every man with sons," he said piously.

"If there were gods, I would thank them for not allowing him to reproduce," I said, which shut him up.

Instead I passed the time thinking about what we might find at Grozhauga—"Big Hill," it means in Germanic. Would Aurima be there? I imagined her greeting me, arms wide, her long coppery hair flying as she rushed into my embrace.

No, her hair would not have grown long yet. Still, it would be thick when I forked my fingers through it, as we met in a lengthy passionate kiss. . . .

Should she not be there, I would demand to know where to find her. If she was safe, I would send her word to expect me on our return from Bruna. If my premonition had been correct and she was in danger . . . well, I would cross that bridge if necessary.

We stopped for a meal in a clearing with a streamlet running through it. After the horses were unsaddled, the mule disburdened, and all the animals watered, we crouched in a slant of shade, gnawing on yesterday's bread and passing around a jug of vinegary *posca*.

Tudrus approached me as I was rerigging the mule's pack. "We are near," he said, wiping sweat out of his eyes with his beard's end. "I go to tell Berinhard."

"No," I told him. "We go together." The Quadian lord would not be given time to organize a hostile greeting.

While the others readied themselves and their mounts, I walked to the edge of the clearing. Gnats danced in the shadows; the trees shimmered with the chittering of birds. I passed yellow flower tufts that burned like beacons in the shafts of light. A tree on the right brushed my shoulder with heart-shaped leaves, like a host's touch of welcome. On the left, saplings formed ranks around a barren oak. The ferns at my feet glimmered with splotches of sunlight like a scattering of *aurei*.

I walked farther into the trees, enjoying the coolness, until something stopped me. Bird chatter, the tiny crackles of twigs and leaves. Far off, a chime like a silver *cymbala*.

Deeper into the wildwood, the light dimmed. Birdsong grew fainter. The chime became a thread of sound, and then a single strong, sure note.

In the romances my sister Nina used to read aloud, a dart from Cupid makes a lover's heart jump into his throat. In the dimming forest, my heart leaped at that sweet sound as if it would strangle me. In such a way had Aurima summoned me in Diana's wood, before we came to love each other.

There was a great crackling of branches and brush behind me. "Marcus," Ollius's voice called. "Where are you?"

I turned. He glimpsed me through the trees and plunged toward me, panting. "What are you doing? Mars' cock, I thought—"

I grasped his shoulder. "Listen. Do you hear?"

"What?"

"Listen!"

He was breathing too noisily. There was no music, no silvery chime.

"Aurima," I said. "Ollius, I know she lives. And she is thinking of me."

"What? How?"

I said I did not know.

"Come on," he muttered. "Let's get going."

For most of the next hour we followed Tudrus with nerve-racking care, probing for movement among the trees, straining for unusual sounds. When two does and their fawns leaped out across the track, we all jerked as if hit by lightning. Their flight into the woods produced a burst of nervous laughter.

Light grew around us as the forest thinned. The path began to widen, and a final turn around a dead tree brought us out on a rise that sloped down to a twisting stream. Except at a ford where the trail crossed, the banks, undercut by winter freshets, rose high above a flow that looked barely knee-deep.

Four ponies cropped grass on the far side of the stream. A bare-chested rider slouched atop one of them with a trousered knee bent casually across its withers. A second man stood beside his own mount, braiding wildflowers into its mane. The rider greeted Tudrus, and two more heads popped up from the grass. Not quite the warlike confrontation I had been worried about.

Tudrus introduced me in Germanic: an officer of the Roman Army here to see Berinhard. By then all four of the Quadi were mounted. One of them held an ax across his thighs; the others wore swords.

I rode to the stream's edge. "Do you speak Latin?"

Three of the men looked at the fourth, whose cheek scar made a white streak in his fair beard. He said, "*Modicum.*"

A little was better than none when it came to spouting one's credentials. "I am Tribune Marcus Licinius Aquilo, on special duty with the Praetorian Guard of Gaius Caesar Augustus," I said. "I am here to talk with Berinhard."

"I am Chlothar, brother of Berinhard." It was a bellow, as if the white-streaked warrior wanted Caligula himself to hear it. "Your spears and swords, give them to us."

"There is no need," I said. "Rome is at peace with the Marcomanni and Quadi. We have no anger toward you and your people."

Chlothar muttered to the others. They turned their ponies, making room for us to cross the stream. He said, "We take you to Berinhard. Come."

14: FEAST OF WELCOME

Berinhard's stronghold sat on a saddle-shaped hill enclosed by a palisade. Smoke rose from cook fires outside thatched huts that squatted under the walls. Chlothar blew on a cow horn, and women stooped out of the huts to stare at us. Curious ponies crowded against the brush fence of a corral. In the farther distance grazed an oblivious herd of splay-horned cattle.

The palisade of Grozhauga had no gate. Instead, the walls ended in an overlap to slow down attackers. I gazed at it, longing for a woman with red hair to come flying through the opening, hands outstretched to me.

Tudrus was conferring with Chlothar. I rode over to join them. To avoid mispronouncing the man's name, I merely said, "Where is your brother now?"

Chlothar stroked his white-streaked beard. Tudrus explained, "Berinhard gives a feast of welcome." He gestured toward the stronghold. "He makes ready for you."

"You like!" Chlothar boomed in Latin. "Much food!" His blue eyes twinkled.

Was German hospitality so spontaneous? I asked warily, "Did he expect us?"

The scout grinned through his draggly mustache. "He knows us from far away. He is Quadian!" He pointed to a nearby meadow dominated by a broad chestnut tree. "A good place to camp there, Tribune. I come soon, take you to feast."

It was too hot to deploy the small tent we had brought, so we spread our bedrolls, saddles, cooking gear, and other impedimenta under the tree. I fetched myself a basin of water, stripped, and sponged off while Ollius perched gingerly on a folding stool. Rufus took the animals, one at a time, to wash them in the stream. Tudrus had disappeared.

Ollius was peevish. "I could have come on foot, Marcus. My arse ain't been so sore since I swapped my father's trick dice for a pigeon pie." He wiped the back of his neck with his grimy scarf, wincing at the movement. "You really think Aurima is here?"

I told myself to stop glancing up every few seconds to see if she had materialized. "I think we will soon know more about her," I said, scrubbing under my arms. "Cheer up; you are about to be feasted by a Germanic lord."

Ollius lifted his own arm and sniffed. "Too bad I forgot my silk dinner tunic."

I rinsed the sponge in the basin. "Take care not to drink overmuch. If Berinhard decides to help himself to our horses and weapons tonight, we cannot be snoring like pigs."

He shook his wine flask. It gave a faint slosh. "Reckon he might be in league with Ironhand?" He uncapped it and drank.

"It's unlikely." I washed between my legs. "They are Quadi. Even though Inguiomerus married a Quadian, he's a Marcomannian. The two tribes don't care much for each other." In fact, it was impressive that Vannaz could ride both horses at the same time.

I had planned to wear my armor to meet with Berinhard. The point was to impress him, after all. But Glabrio had argued that the Quadian *frau-jaz* was an ally, and that I could dress informally without forfeiting authority. So even though I had brought my full uniform, I decided that wearing it would be too confrontational. Not to mention too hot.

As summer twilight rose from the meadow and the surrounding trees, I buckled my new knife belt over my best tunic, settling the old long-knife's hilt and sheath into the valley of my spine. My fingertips paused on one of the decorations of engraved silver leaves inlaid with niello. Aurima had urged me to buy the belt from a market stall in Scarbantia. I had resisted; the old one had been Father's before it became mine, but the leather around the prong-hole had worn thin.

A pang of memory stabbed me. I blinked it away.

Rufus had brushed and saddled Boss, who now looked finer than I did. Spider, Ollius's mare, and the mule grazed contentedly on hobbles. "Rufus, I need you to stay here on guard," I told him. "We will bring you something from the feast."

The boy smiled and mimed gobbling food with a spoon. I roughed his hair companionably, complimented his work with the beasts, and reached for my cloak.

The amulets around Ollius's neck ticked against each other as he fastened the cloak pin for me. Not trusting our barbarian hosts, he had laced up his stiff leather cuirass and was wearing his sword. His scalp had sprouted a silver fuzz. I was about to jibe, *Going gray, old man?*, when he said, "We're early. No sign of that goat-faced scout yet."

"I want to take a look around without a guide." My heart was jittering like spit on a hot griddle. I settled my torc more comfortably beneath the cloak. "Come along," I said. "Let's see if they have dancing girls."

"So! You are Aquilo. From Rome, so Tudrus tells me."

Berinhard's long braided hair and thick beard were as silver as rain.

About my own height, which made him short for a German, he had the brawny arms and shoulders of a woodcutter. "It is long since we have in our *halla* a Roman."

One glimpse of his eyes undid all the friendliness promised by his joviality. They were like pebbles in an icy stream.

The feast hall, the *halla*, was a reed-roofed longhouse set near the top of the hill on which this walled settlement crouched. Dirt paths meandered around trees, roundhouses of wattle and thatch, barns, workshops, a spring-fed pond. Ollius and I had caught the inhabitants by surprise. Dogs barked. Women, children, a few old men, and crop-haired slaves stared as we entered through the overlapping gate: two grown men in short skirts, a sorrel horse four hands taller than the local ponies.

I looked around, trying not to be obvious about it. No redheads. No Aurima.

It was easy to see where the warriors had gone. Several of them lounged with drinking horns outside the big *halla*, which gave off an invigorating scent of roast meat. Chlothar strode to meet us, raising his own horn high in greeting. It was huge and hollow, not from a cow but an aurochs, with capacity enough to stupefy any drinker I knew.

"Come!" He beckoned us vigorously to enter.

We passed between doorposts carved with grotesque faces to bar evil spirits. Inside, the savory aroma of roast pig and wild onions swirled over a reek of sweat and ale. I had a glimpse of high smoke-hazed rafters and shield-hung walls of upended tree trunks before we were met by ten or twelve other Quadi warriors. Arrayed in gold rings and tattoos, sweat-glossed in leather or fur vests and woolen trousers, they jostled each other to approach. Some wore their hair in twisted tufts that looked like horns.

Our scout Tudrus was among them, grinning through his stringy mustache. In quick glances I tried to make out whether any of the others were familiar from last year's truce negotiations, but the late-day light was too uncertain, the throng too restive.

I saw no women. Why had the brothers not brought their wives to welcome us?

The silver-bearded *fraujaz* had pushed through the crowd of his companions toward me. After his exuberant greeting I said, "It is an honor to meet you, Berinhard of the Quadi." He was speaking Latin, so I did too. "I bring greetings from my cousin Gaius Caesar Augustus."

"You are a cousin to Caesar?" The glittery pebble-eyes studied me more closely.

Chlothar, his cheek-scarred brother, jerked a thumb at Ollius. "You with head of egg! No sword in *halla*. Give to me."

I hesitated. We had, in fact, passed a rack of swords and spears outside. As for the women, it was possible they did not attend feasts with visiting outlanders.

I nodded to my bodyguard, who grudgingly unbuckled his sword belt and handed it to Chlothar. We still wore our knives, of course. A man must have a blade to eat with.

"Come, come," Berinhard urged, sweeping his arm toward the interior of the feast hall and its meaty, mouth-watering fragrance.

I took a step, fighting an urge to demand, *Where is Aurima?* But after such an effusive welcome, no doubt he would willingly answer this question as we dined.

The crowd parted, opening a path toward a long table strewn with slabs of bread, chewed bones, tipped-over cups, and spills of ale. Evidently the feast to which I was invited had already been in progress for a while.

"Seize him," Berinhard called out in Germanic.

I was not a guest. I was the next course.

I pulled my longknife. "Ollius, your sword!" I drove my elbow into Chlothar's belly, but did not see whether Ollius snatched back his scabbard because Berinhard gave a roar and flung himself at me.

"Tudrus!" I shouted. "Where—"

The *fraujaz* wrenched me around, clamping his arm across my neck. I stabbed backward, piercing clothing and flesh. Berinhard's breath blasted out in a hot and carnivorous howl. His grip loosened. I spun and swiped the longknife toward his throat.

Everything moved as slowly as in a dream: my hand slicing the air, a scrim of blood streaming off the blade's edge, the chieftain's blue eyes widening above his silver mustache, his own hand rising in a doomed attempt to ward off the blow.

Someone bear-hugged me from behind. Heaving furiously against the restraint, I jabbed at an arm within reach. Voices bellowed. Hands clutched and pulled.

I could not see Ollius. Had he regained his sword?

A warrior with a forked beard seized my knife wrist. I threw myself against the man behind me and kicked out to stop Forked Beard from breaking my arm. My boot caught him in the crotch. As he began to fold, I fell on top of the bear-hugger.

Before I could scramble free, I was flung on my face. A foot stamped on my arm, and my knife was wrenched away. Someone knelt on my back.

I thrashed like a crushed beetle, unable to breathe. My eyesight darkened. *Do not let me die like this*, I begged whoever might be listening. Whoever might care.

Dimly I felt kicks and punches. A bellow in Germanic. The unbearable weight came off. As I gasped for air, a hand clenched in my hair and pulled my head back.

They were going to cut my throat. Faster than smothering, at least. Would Lamia retrieve my ashes?

Yet the slash did not come. I glimpsed Ollius fighting his way toward me, armed with his knife and a shield he must have yanked from the wall. No sword. Blood trickled down his face. He was dueling with three Germans at once, moving like a cat, like the Occisor—Killer—he had been in the arena.

I tried to get up, but my legs were pinned. I could not break the grip that arched my neck backward.

"Marcus," he shouted, thrusting his shield against the knife of a lunging warrior. "Marcus, hold fast, I am coming."

An armlet glinted. Berinhard was reaching toward his brother's shoulder, where Ollius's sword belt hung. "No," I croaked as the blade slid from its scabbard, but my cry was almost voiceless.

Ollius turned, following my horrified gaze, as Berinhard roared and chopped down with all his weight. The Spanish steel split the wooden shield in half and took off Ollius's forearm in a spray of blood.

Any man but a trained gladiator would have collapsed. Ollius reversed his own weapon like a dagger and pressed inside the chieftain's reach. "Mars and Diana!" he screamed, plunging his knife through gouts of his own blood into Berinhard's breast.

Chlothar seized the sword blade and pulled it from his dying brother's fist. Clutching the hilt two-handed, he stabbed Ollius through the cuirass.

Ollius fell back. His foot slipped in blood, and he sprawled on the earthen floor. Amid the thunder of voices, I seemed to hear the chatter of charms and amulets when he fell. His face was turned in my direction, but his eyes saw nothing.

O Mithras, receive his soul.

"Wodunaz curse you," Chlothar bellowed. He lurched toward me, brandishing the sword still slimed with Ollius's blood.

Staring at his anguished face, I steeled myself to die like a Roman. But the blow that hit me came from behind, so I never saw it.

15: THE BOAR EMERGES

It was soft and warm where I lay. So there really was an afterlife! But in this warm, soggy cloud, or bed, or hell, my head hurt so much that I could barely crack my eyes open. When I did, there was only darkness. I wanted to cradle my skull in my hands, but my wrists were stuck together.

Unlikely to be paradise, then. Especially since it stank. Or perhaps that was me. My bowels would have opened when I died.

I slipped into the black again.

At some time I remembered Ollius. The rest of the prayer for a sword brother came into my mind: *Receive his soul, O Mithras; I bear witness that he has lived and fought with courage and honor.*

Was Tudrus dead? Had Rufus escaped? I needed to get off the cloud and find out, but rolling over made my head burst and my stomach erupt.

When I woke again in bright daylight, it was to a loud buzzing and a feeling of tiny feathers touching me all over. "Pull him out of there," someone said. The buzzing rose in pitch as I was dragged by the ankles onto hard ground. Squinting through a cloud of flies, I made out the shapes of two trousered men, black against the sun.

"He cannot see," said one. "Let him see us."

Chickens clucked and scuttered away as the two men walked around me. When sunlight shone on them, they stopped.

No, definitely not paradise.

The first man was tall and lean, with a thick roan beard and long loose hair that was still mostly red. "Maelo," I said. Thirst made my voice no more than a wheeze.

His eyes remained expressionless, his mouth grim beneath the shaggy mustache.

"Tiwaz be thanked," said the other man, "his wits are not porridge after all." His smile bared broken white teeth like fangs.

He was no shorter but much broader, a boar to Maelo's wolf. His hair, as pale as a cold winter sun, was tied back with a thong; his long beard lay plaited on his massive chest. Although he was still smiling, his eyes beneath dark brows were cold.

I had seen him only once, an occasion I would never forget. "Ingiomar," I said. The breath caught in my dry throat, so it must have seemed that I was afraid. I knew I was probably looking my death in the face.

When he was forced into a truce by the capture of his daughter, I had promised she would marry a king or prince of Caesar's choosing. By now he would know from Maelo, who had been her guardian in Rome, that she had chosen me.

Shame and anger overcame my fear. I was wearing only my tunic, stained with vomit and smeared with dung. Chlothar and his comrades had taken my father's torc and my family ring, tied my wrists, and thrown me on a midden like a dead dog.

I struggled to get up. The flies crawling on me rose and hovered, then lit again. I croaked, "Maelo, cut me free." My knife belt and knife were gone too.

Aurima's uncle eyed me, stroking his roan mustache between thumb and forefinger. "The turd is impatient," he said in Germanic.

"He does not know yet that he is shit," Aurima's father said.

I writhed and twisted onto my knees, then struggled to my feet. The world spun, my head yammered, and my eyes went dark. "Where is she?" I rasped into the blackness. "What have you done with her?"

"By the god of thunder, she even taught him our language!"

Ingiomar's slap caught me unprepared. Unable to break my fall, I sprawled back onto the midden.

"Before you die, you are going to be sorry you touched her," he said, and spat into my face.

His breath came harshly as he moved away. He said something about horses.

"Is she dead?" It burst out of me, raw and agonized.

Ingiomar turned. "I did not kill her," he said. "But she is going to wish I had."

I managed to lurch to my feet again. Wherever she was, I would find her. "Enough, old man. Free me, or feel Rome's anger in fire and blood."

"You still do not understand, turd." He grinned again. "Rome gave you to me."

"What?"

It was only a taunt. Had to be.

The dung heap lay beside a decrepit shed near the palisade. I squinted toward the longhouse where Ollius had died. A handful of men milled there, some on horseback and others waiting by their mounts. I rasped, "Where is . . ." No, better not mention Rufus; if he had escaped, perhaps they did not know about him. "Where is my scout? Tudrus?"

Ingiomar raised his voice: "Friduric, bring our horses."

A young man leading a black pony ambled over from the group by the longhouse. "Hah! He believed it, *Fader*."

Believed it?

I blundered away from the midden and reeled a few steps, but the overlapping gateway hid any view of the tree in the meadow.

The young man grasped my wrists. In a daze I wrenched myself free. "What is going on?"

"Be still or I cut off your thumb," he said, brandishing his own thumb to be sure I understood.

Backing away, I stepped on something that rolled under my bare foot. His hand shot out and caught the binding between my wrists so I did not fall.

It was Ollius's severed forearm, stiff as a log, that had tripped me. Beneath its wriggling crust of flies his naked body was bluish white, drained of blood that had streaked and smeared and dried on his limbs where the tunic had not covered him. Dark spatters freckled his shaven head, still turned to one side. One of his eyes was missing.

The chickens dared to waddle back. I tried to throw something at them, but it was impossible with my hands tied. They scattered as I kicked frenziedly, hopping and spinning on one leg like a madman. "Fucking carrion-eaters! Filthy scavengers! Bloodsuckers! Harpy monst—!" My breath caught in my dry throat. I began to cough.

The young man pulled me away. I tried to stop coughing. My eyes leaked tears.

"Idiot," he growled. "It is not the birds. They come to eat the flies."

The group from the longhouse was gathering around Ollius's corpse. Maelo said, "I knew the dead man in Rome, *fraujaz*. Let us burn him."

"He killed Berinhard," Ingiomar snapped. "And if we take more time, Chlothar is going to find out this turd is still alive." He gestured impatiently. "Tie him, Friduric."

The young man knotted a length of rope to my wrist binding. I said in hoarse Germanic, "Where is your sister?"

His gaze sharpened. He was yellow-haired like his father, but his gray-green eyes were Aurima's: large and deep-set, the long lashes tipped with gold.

"Tell ... I am going ... to find her." I coughed again. I would not beg for water.

The other Germans were mounting. "Why not ride the big one, *fraujaz*?" someone called out.

"This is no time to try a new horse," Ingiomar said.

Maelo said, "The Roman calls him Boss." He said the name in Latin, *Umbo*. I blinked the blur from my eyes. There they were: both my horses, brawny Boss and fleet Spider, heads high among the smaller ponies. Maelo's son, Odo, grasped Spider's reins. And Rufus, unhurt and unbound, held my sorrel warhorse.

Odo, a lanky, beard-fuzzed youth, laughed at my expression. "He is free now, not a slave with a slave's name. Show your Roman master what you think of him, Rudra."

Rufus hesitated, then took a few steps forward. He moved differently: head up, shoulders squared. Perhaps it was the way he had walked as a boy, before a stone slung at a Roman tax collector had cost him and his family their freedom.

My skull was throbbing as though it would crack and spill my brains onto my shoulders. My salvaged young Thracian, whom I had admitted into my *familia*, had joined in this treachery. Would he spit on me now? Lift his fist to strike me?

"On your horses," Ingiomar barked. "We are leaving." Rufus drew back and scrambled onto Boss.

I twitched my head to shake off flies. All my senses came untethered, and I nearly fell. What had happened? What had I wrongly believed? Why could I not figure anything out?

Friduric took the rope knotted to my wrist bonds and tied it to his pony's doubled-up tail. He yanked on it to test the knots, then vaulted show-ily into the saddle.

I set my bare feet. The black pony took a few paces after Ingiomar, Maelo, and the others until the rope came taut. I leaned against the pull.

Friduric looked around. "So we are playing, hey?"

He chirruped to the pony, and it backed up. That was what I had waited for. I rushed him, diving over the pony's rump with my bound hands outstretched to haul him out of the saddle. He gave a startled shout.

I might have succeeded in unhorsing him and flinging myself onto the pony's back, had the exertion not broken whatever thread of awareness tied me to the world. The last I knew was a distant shrieking, wild and angry. The Furies, I thought.

There is an old story about Theseus who, on his way to Athens to claim his kingship, encountered the cruel Procrustes. Procrustes would offer weary travelers a bed for the night, provided it fit them. To taller travelers he gave a short bed, then lopped off their legs until the body no longer overhung the bed frame. Other journeyers were given an unusually long bed, and racked until they stretched from one end to the other. Theseus killed the blood-thirsty robber by making him fit in one of his own beds—the shorter one, I think.

Procrustes would have admired the effect of Friduric dragging me on my back behind his ambling pony. I demanded that he slow down to let me stand. At some point I may have pleaded, although I hope I did not.

Stones, tree roots, clods of hoof-torn turf, and broken branches pum-meled and gouged as I jounced and twisted over them, the pain hardly felt in the greater agony of my arms straining to part from the shoulder joints. My loincloth tore off, my tunic shredded; but with eyes screwed shut in the effort of holding up my head, I did not see my own nakedness. Over and over I told myself not to let them hear me scream, until I no longer remembered why my teeth were gritted and my body turned to flame.

"Mar's." A whisper. "Mar's."

Something nudged my cheek, but I hurt too much to open my eyes. I drifted back into the not-knowing of the otherworld.

A drop of wetness splashed on my nose. Thinking I was being pissed on, I forced a soundless curse through cracked lips.

Sandaled feet beside me. Long reedy legs. It was Rufus's tongueless slurring of my name that I had heard.

Another splash. Cool. Not piss.

Water?

Holding the goatskin bag close to his side, Rufus tipped the bone nozzle downward. I moved my head. The trickle rained on my cheek, then into my mouth.

Ale.

I swallowed greedily. More, more, more.

With his other hand the boy began to urinate onto a stump, making an excuse for the sound of plashing liquid. Beyond him Boss cropped grass placidly, screening us from the Marcomanni.

Rufus finished. He pinched off the mouth of the goatskin and moved away, although my thirst was far from slaked. "Rudra," shouted Odo, "are you going to drink it all yourself? Bring over that ale."

I scuffed my cheek against my arm so the track of spilled drink would not betray the boy. Perhaps it made no difference; my face was swollen with insect bites and crusted with snot and tears.

"How fares the Roman turd, Friduric?" Ingiomar's voice. "Is he wolf bait yet?"

Feet swished through the grass. I wanted to spit something defiant, but could not summon a gnat's weight of strength. Like one of Procrustes' broken victims, I lay in searing pain with my arms above my head. The very thought of moving was unbearable.

"Still alive," Friduric said. He sounded disappointed.

"Roll him over."

Wedging a foot under my side, Friduric pried me up onto shoulder and hip. I gasped through my teeth. My eyes, bone dry and tearless, squeezed shut against the hurt.

Neither of the others spoke for a few moments. The torn flesh of my back and buttocks shrieked with exposure to the air.

"I want to see the meat tear off his bones, *Fader*. I want to hear him scream when his arms rip off his body."

"You must be careful, then. If his head hits a root or a rock and he breaks his neck"—Ingiomar swigged noisily from an aleskin—"then he is just food for dogs."

More footsteps. "The boys can take the body into the woods," Maelo said. "Let the foxes get rid of it."

Friduric said in disgust, "The pig-stubborn Roman is not dead yet."

"No?" Maelo said. "Hmm," the noise he made while stroking his beard.

"Then I think we must tie him onto a horse for the rest of the journey."

Ingiomar's voice was sharp-edged: "Why do you say that, my brother?"

"The gods are not ready to take him. Forcing his death may anger Nerthuz."

"I have never found Nerthuz unwilling to drink a man's blood."

Maelo made some response, but the guttural Germanic had faded to a sound as peaceful as the whisper of wheat in a summer breeze. And I was gone.

16: HOHENEIH

"He looks strong enough to kill three hens," the cook's assistant said.

"You have to clean them, Meino," the old woman said without looking up from shelling beans. "He must not have a knife."

"Then you can do it, Roza." He whacked me in the shin with a fire-blackened stick. "Get going, turd. Fat ones, mind. And pluck them bare, or I give you this stick up your backside."

I understood that I was supposed to do something, even though some of the words were ones Aurima had never taught me. Pain splintered my back and buttocks as I straightened up from the wall of the meat-smoking shed.

It must be July now, or even August, six weeks or more since I had been dropped in a heap on Rosmunda's doorstep. She had cared for me with minimal diligence and without pity until I was able to shuffle around. Since then I had been at everyone's command, a filthy, smelly, scratching creature with a scruff of beard.

The cook's assistant said, "I heard this Roman was highborn, of the clan of Caesar." He frowned at me. "Are his wits gone?"

"The *fraujaz* told me to keep him alive. He did not say to make him clever."

Meino grunted. He held up three fingers to me. "*Driô.*" Tucking his fists in his armpits, he flapped his arms and bobbed his head. "*Haninnan.*" He pointed across the barnyard with his stick. "Clear enough? Go!"

Limping off to find the chickens, I heard Rosmunda say, "For Helle, I suppose? With me it was cheese. When my time was near, I could not . . ." Her voice faded.

In place of my father's treasured torc, a slave collar chafed my sweaty neck. Made of thick, ill-cured leather, it was fastened with laces tied at my nape in a glue-welded knot. Anyone with a sharp blade could have sawed through the ties, but no one here in Ingiomar Ironhand's stronghold was inclined to help his daughter's despoiler.

Crawling back from the gates of Hades, sweating with fever, the first words I had managed after "Where am I?" had been to ask for Aurima. "Not here," Rosmunda had said shortly, waving flies from my lacerated back, and then, "Gone," when I asked again, and finally, "We do not talk about her."

I had sought Aurima everywhere inside the palisade, but could find no sign of her. None of the men and women who had accompanied her to

Rome, and had returned via the Julian Alps while I brought her home across the Adriatic Sea, would speak about her.

The hens squawked indignantly when I cornered them. I had only ever killed birds with a sacrificial knife, and had never plucked or cleaned one. All my life, slaves had done such things for me.

I was able to strangle the unfortunate birds by imagining Ingiomar's head on their scrawny necks. Rosmunda criticized my attempt at plucking and stripped off the last feathers herself. After she gutted the carcasses, tossing the offal to drooling hounds, I gestured toward Ingiomar's *halla*. "I take to Meino?"

She looked around for someone to accompany me, for I was not supposed to go anywhere alone, then sighed and set aside the basket of shelled beans. Before she could heave herself to her feet, I said, "I know where to go. You rest."

She peered around again, saw no one who could object, and sank back on her bench. Before picking up the basket again she leveled a bony finger at me. "You come straight back. Understand?"

"I understand," I said docilely, intending to steal into Ingiomar's *halla* if I could. There, if anywhere, I might hear news of his daughter.

Although set on a flatter hilltop, Ingiomar's walled stronghold was otherwise much like Grozhauga. Tree-shaded paths wound past storage barns and byres to five or six longhouses, all heavily thatched almost to the ground, their front doors facing east to honor the goddess of light, Austro, whom Aurima's mother had taught her to serve.

The feast hall was the largest building, set a stone's throw from a giant oak tree dedicated to the warrior god Thunraz—the tree for which Hoheneih, "High Oak," was named. I hobbled toward the cookhouse, an open shed near the hall. In truth I could walk almost normally once my joints loosened, but like the dull-eyed stare and rudimentary Germanic, the limp might lead people to underestimate me.

Behind the vacant gaze I watched carefully for Ingiomar, whom I wished to avoid, and Rufus, who was avoiding me. I saw him strutting around with Odo now and then, the two of them bare-chested and trousered, with hunting dogs at their heels. He was free now, and triumphantly so. If I asked him for help, he would certainly refuse me.

A trio of young children came flying around a corner. "Roman, Roman," they shrieked, darting at me like horseflies. "What's under your shirt, she-man?"

I was barelegged, with a ragged tunic hanging loose to my knees. By contrast every male German higher than a pony's hock wore breeches, ridiculous as it was in the summer heat.

When one of the little pests made a grab for the plucked hens I had strung on a stick, I swatted his fingers away. The children laughed and made grasping motions with their hands. "Give us silver, Roman."

They were handsome brats, flaxen-haired and tawny-skinned, cavorting like colts. Yet as young as they were, they knew Rome gave presents to win their tribal leaders' favor. When we could offer barbarians the rewards of the *Pax Romana*, what in Hades prompted them to fling themselves onto legion swords in the name of freedom?

"You little ones, be off." Friduric was leading his black pony up the path from the main gate, long javelins bobbing in a sling. "Alberich, does your mother know you are not weeding the beans? Hadewic, are you not supposed to gather feathers?"

The three scattered with gleeful shrieks. Friduric's mouth twitched in a half smile that vanished when he realized I was looking at him. Wisps of hair stuck to his brow, and sweat stained his faded tunic a darker red down his chest and under his arms.

"Good hunting?" I asked, conscious of the ludicrous bird carcasses I still carried.

He scratched his beard, eyeing me. "No," he said, and kept walking.

"Friduric." I fell in beside him. "Vannaz the king did not have eight men from Varus's army, did he?"

Ingiomar's son took a moment to decide whether he would answer. "No."

He pulled harder on the reins as his stride lengthened. His pony stretched its neck, reluctant to move faster.

I had not needed his confirmation. I already knew that Lamia and Glabrio had betrayed me.

They had planned the expedition to Bruna to request recruits for Caligula's coming campaign. When I appeared unexpectedly, the two of them had hatched a scheme to make me vanish forever in the wilderness. Success would impress Saxa, the Special Cohort commander in Rome, and no blame would be attached to Caligula Caesar, who must not appear to have taken revenge on me for my father's betrayal.

Glabrio knew of my interest in the lost Eagle. I was sure he had persuaded Lamia to entice me with the story of rescuing survivors of the Varian disaster—survivors whose existence, strangely, could not be revealed to anyone else. Recalling Lamia blithely inventing details of these nonexistent prisoners, I ground my teeth. *One of them, a centurion, was blinded when he was captured. I believe a couple of others are lame.*

To further ensnare me, he had given me all I wanted: command, colleagues, money, while Glabrio sent his scouts to arrange an ambush with Berinhard. By now the spymaster and his underling would have returned to Carnuntum, bearing the sad news that I had been slain in a foolhardy search for Ingiomar's daughter—or, if they could conceal the bloodshed at Grozhauga, that I had vanished in the forest while seeking her.

Why had I not been more cautious? Distracted by worry for her, I had leaped at the chance of finding out where she was. And had fallen right into the trap laid for me.

I was breathing hard to keep up with Friduric. Infuriated by my weakness, I huffed, "What is your father going to do with me?"

Friduric slowed, then stopped. "He is going to kill you."

I marveled again at seeing Aurima's eyes in her brother's face. He leaned closer. "Does that not frighten you? Or are you too stupid, after that blow on the head?"

I had to tilt my chin to meet his gaze. The slave collar rubbed against my throat. "Where is Aurima, Friduric? What has he done to her?"

His face changed; the mocking grin uncurled into a grim line. "Do not remind me why I should tear out your guts." He strode off, hauling his tired pony by the reins.

There was no hope of being rescued or ransomed. If Leonnatus asked what had become of me, he would be told the lie of my death or disappearance. Dio and Cleon, believing the falsehood, might already be on their way back to Rome.

For a black moment I felt overpowered by my enemies' spite. I would have died on a dung heap if Ingiomar had not gone there to gloat over my corpse. Was it so much better to be alive in the indifferent wilderness, with a slave collar around my neck and my hand stripped of a ring that might have identified my bones?

Meino appeared suddenly beside me. "Give me my hens, you useless *goukh!*" He snatched the stick of chickens out of my hand.

I cast a sidelong glance at the *halla*. Too late: Rosmunda was scurrying toward me. "I told you to come straight back." She poked me in the arm with the rusty blade she used to dig weeds. "Get going." Another poke.

She herded me back across the settlement like a stray calf. Hunters grinned, trudging home with their hounds, and women and girls tittered and whispered as they straggled in from fields and flocks. Even the handful of other slaves, short-shorn captives from distant tribes, smirked as they carried water or chopped wood or churned milk.

"In with you." With a final prod, Rosmunda drove me into the cave that was my prison. "See if a night without food teaches you to pay attention."

A protest rose in my throat. I was famished, having eaten only a cup of barley porridge at daybreak.

The door clapped shut and the heavy bar fell into its brackets. She scuffed away.

My stomach grumbled. I sank painfully to the ground, bracing myself on the rough earthen wall. Dug into a knoll overlooking the western end of the palisade, the shoulder-high cave stank of spoiled milk and meat. At present, I was the only perishable kept in its cool darkness.

Through cracks in the door I could hear people calling cheerily as they went their separate ways, as in one of old Vergilius's *Bucolics* celebrating the tranquil routine of farm life. Unfortunately I belonged in a completely different story, and was about to be erased from this one.

He is going to kill you.

Fool! Why had I not asked Friduric when that would be? Not soon, I hoped, for escaping would take more strength than I had regained. The gate guards knew I was forbidden to leave the palisaded settlement, and I had not mended enough to fight my way past them. Horses were out of reach, grazed outside the walls by day and kept under guard at night.

And I still had no idea where to find Aurima.

Perhaps I should have prayed to Fortuna. Told the goddess why I was worthy of her favor and vowed a silver tripod to her temple on the Quirinal Hill if she granted me what I needed. But after what had happened, I no longer believed even in luck.

By the last of the daylight, I wrote six names in the earth with the stub of a stick: *GLABRIO. LAMIA. CHLOTHAR. INGIOMAR. MAELO. FRIDURIC.* Six men who would pay for what they had done to me.

As I did every night, I labored to keep my sinews from tightening with scar tissue. Stretches, squats, running in place. This night, a small victory: I could touch the spot above my ear where I had been struck in Berinhard's *halla.* It was the first time I had been able to flex my shoulders so freely since being dragged behind Friduric's horse.

Voices and laughter floated from Ingiomar's hall. The *fraujaz* and his warriors were drinking, as usual, with much hooting and shouting. Maybe Rufus was among them.

As I did every night, I also said to Aurima in my heart, *Wherever you are, I swear I will find you.* Sucking a pebble to slake my thirst, I lowered myself painfully to sleep.

The bar rattled in its brackets. "You want to wake everyone?" a man said in a noisy whisper.

"Watch out with that sword! You could cut off my leg."

The bar came free and *thunked* on the ground, and the ill-fitting door rasped open. Faint light framed two trousered figures.

"You forgot the torch, *dumba.*"

"Whiskers of Wodunaz! I mem—remembered the sword, didn't I?" A snigger.

I got to my feet. Even without a torch, they could not miss me in this cubbyhole.

"There he is. You, Roman, the *fraujaz* wants you."

I recognized Friduric's voice. The other man, who held the sword, sounded younger. "Call him 'the turd,'" he said, "as your mother's brother named him." A snort of amusement. "Come out, turd."

I took a wavering step forward, groaned, and lurched sideways. "Hammer of Thunraz!" Friduric said. "I am not going to carry him, Egino."

"I can . . . walk," I protested. I shuffled out of the cave, gasped, and reeled against Egino. He fended me off, cursing. For further distraction I trod on his foot. Then, twisting the sword from his hand, I spun clear of them both.

It felt splendid to be armed, to see them gape like newly landed fish. I wagged the sword point at the cave entrance. "In there, both of you." Locking them inside would give me time to look for a horse I could steal.

Neither one moved. Glancing at Egino, Friduric said, "When I count to three . . ."

"Are you stupid? He knows how to use that sword."

"There are two of us, *ja*?"

"Get in there," I snapped. "Or one of you loses a hand."

Egino whirled and pelted toward the *halla*, bellowing for help. There was no point in pursuing him; Friduric could run me down without difficulty.

"So," Friduric said. He spat, evidently a comment on Egino's bravery. "Hand me the sword, Roman. The gates are closed, the *heribanan*"—he nodded toward Egino's shouts—"is given. You cannot get away."

I swept the sword blade between us. "I can take you with me."

"Do you still want to know where my sister is?"

I flicked a glance at the hall. Egino had gone in; I had only a few moments to do whatever I could. "Where is she?"

"Give me the sword." He put out his hand.

"Tell me first."

Men were pouring out of the hall. Someone pointed, and they veered in our direction. "Tell me!" I shouted.

Friduric tilted his head toward the south. "Look in the water house of the witch." He grinned sardonically.

"Witch?" Aurima had used that word, *fêla*, to describe her mother's mother. She meant the woman was a magic worker, but I did not believe in magic.

He held out his hand. "Quick, or you die now."

I tossed the sword on the ground at his feet.

Then the horde was upon us, yelling and waving whatever weapons they had found. They stumbled to a halt at the sight of Friduric holding me by my slave collar with his sword point between my legs. Silence fell, except for their panting breaths and the thud of footsteps as others raced to see what the commotion was about.

"F-Friduric. You have captured him!" Egino managed to grin.

Ingiomar strolled around the throng, carrying his drinking horn. He eyed Friduric impassively, then raised the horn and dashed his drink into Egino's face.

He turned back to Friduric. "Bring him to the hall."

17: DARK OF THE MOON

Willing hands grabbed my arms and hustled me roughly over the dark paths, dragging me when I tripped over my feet.

A torch staked outside the *halla* lit its open doors. Inside, flames from a central firepit gleamed on a shiny earthen floor sunk a step below ground level. Thick smoke reeking of ale and grease loomed over a long trestle table littered with scraps of meat and discarded drinking horns, a fetid reminder of the feast of treachery at Grozhauga.

My captors hauled me past overturned benches, through withered rushes and cracked bones, dried dog turds and ale spills, and threw me down beside a carved chair at the end of the table.

Coughing, I picked myself up as the rest of the warriors streamed in and resumed their seats with much joking and crashing of benches. All the activity stirred the smoke into gray swirls, which rose to become chimeras and many-headed hydras in the rafters.

Panic began an icy cascade through my veins. Perhaps Fortuna had given me the luck I was too proud to ask for, and turned her face away when I failed to make use of it.

Ingiomar sauntered up to me with a braided leather rope looped over his shoulder. "On your knees."

"Fuck you," I said.

Shaking his head, he turned to Friduric, who had arrived on my other side. Then without a pause he swung around and punched me between the shoulders.

I had begun to take a step forward, alerted by instinct, but the sledgehammer blow drove me sprawling to the ground. My elbows would not support me, and I collapsed on my face.

Hands fumbled at the back of my collar. When I dragged myself up, cursing in rage and frustration, I was on a leash knotted to the arm of Ingiomar's carved chair. He grinned down at me. "Do you like my hall, Roman? Look around us, on the walls." The knife in his fist gestured to left and right.

Through the smoky blur I saw a row of battered shields: the curved rectangles of Fifteenth Legion infantry, the flat oblongs of the First Alpines, the ovals of the First Hispanic Aravacians cavalry: all units I had commanded the year before, when he ambushed us. There were not many, but the insult did not need more emphasis to sting.

Farther away hung round shields of an auxiliary cohort I did not know, with a flagged standard whose staff was snapped in two. Ingiomar followed my gaze. "Our *vexillum*," he said. "The First Marcomannians. Broken on the day my wife was found."

"I did not murder . . . your wife." My voice caught in my dry throat.

He signaled to a long-braided woman, big with child, who was replenishing the drinking horns. As she leaned over him, I saw that the ewer she held was of heavy silver, skillfully embossed. A gift from Rome, no doubt, in the days when his loyalty was valued.

"Give me to drink," I said in Germanic.

Ingiomar ignored me to lean toward Maelo, who had shoved himself onto the nearest bench. The woman turned away with her pitcher. I swallowed dryly. It was a sign that the *fraujaz* did not care about keeping me alive.

"Ingiomar," Maelo began, and dropped his voice so low that what he said next was inaudible. But he tipped his head at me, so I could guess it.

"I am still going to kill him," Ingiomar said, and shouted down the table, "Ha, Fulco, your beard is drinking more than you are."

A burst of laughter. Maelo spoke louder to be heard over it: "But she lives."

Ingiomar slitted his eyes. "So you think he must live, too?"

"I told you, he is a cousin of Caesar—"

"You also told me that his father tried to kill Caesar. I think Caesar is not going to weep at his death." He leaned back and gulped ale from his horn.

"Brother, you don't understand." Maelo's voice rose. "When Caesar comes north with his fifty legions, we do not want him angry with our people."

"And how does he know to be angry, *brother*?" Ingiomar snapped.

"Because, you fool, he has informers!" Maelo used the Latin word, *delatores*. "We are lucky that Vannaz has not already found out—"

"Hammer of Thunraz!" Ingiomar jumped up and struck the pommel of his knife on the table. Dishes bounced and clattered. "Vannaz bends over for Rome's prick and thinks it is a gift!" He swept his arm around. "Do you see the empty seats at this table, Maelo? Do you remember when it was full of young warriors eager for riches and fame? Now we do not raid, because Vannaz gives us iron and salt and cattle. We do not take good land across the great river for our children, because Rome forbids it."

The other men at the table bellowed support, hoisting their drinking horns. Maelo tried to speak, but Ingiomar shouted over him, "Romans killed my wife. And when I trusted you, my wife's brother, to keep my daughter safe, you let a Roman dishonor her."

Although I had had to guess at some of the words in his rant, I grasped this. "No," I croaked. "I love her."

Ingiomar swung his head around. His eyes glinted in the firelight like polished steel. "And you think I do not?"

"Kill him," Friduric demanded.

The other warriors, too, began calling out, "Kill the Roman! Kill him!"

My bowels cramped. So many times I myself had shouted, "Kill him," when a gladiator had fought poorly. And when he was dispatched with a thrust, I had cheered.

Amid the commotion, an unmoving gleam of red gold far down the table caught my eye. Rufus sat stiffly beside Odo, who was yelling and shaking his fist. Odo jabbed him in the ribs. Rufus glanced at him, startled. Then his face, too, contorted into a grimace. His fist shot into the air, and he bayed with the others, "Kill!"

Ingiomar raised his hands. The men gradually quieted.

I had backed away to the full extent of the rope without realizing it. He glared at me, head lowered, beard bushing out on his chest. "In two nights, when the Moon God hides his face, we take you to the *mora* of Nerthuz." He looked up. "What do you say, my shield brothers?"

Shouts of approval. Someone called, "*Fraujaz*, we need strong arms for the harvest. Let us give him to Nerthuz after."

"The Earth Mother has waited long enough for this Roman, Radulf. I, the father of Aurima, have waited long enough."

He pointed his knife at my face. "First I cut out your eyes, for what you saw." He showed his teeth, as sharp as fangs. "Then I cut off your balls, for what you did."

He tucked the blade into his belt and held out both hands, fingers clawed. "And before we give you to Nerthuz, I pull out your *edri* with these hands." More shouts, howls, laughter.

I felt my face grow cold. When the bodies of his wife's murderers were found in the forum at Siscia, their gaping belly wounds had been gouged by fingers, not by a knife. Thus had he earned the byname Ironhand.

"Friduric." Ingiomar sat down again, raking sweaty hair off his brow. "Take him back to the store place." He scooped up his ale horn and held it out for a refill. "Be sure he has not made holes in the walls. Or under the door."

Friduric came toward me. "Wait," I said, clot-tongued with thirst. "Give me my father's ring, old man."

Ingiomar looked up, scowling. Standing as straight as I could, I held out my hand.

"Will you take it from me?" He peered around with exaggerated dread. "Or is a legion coming to help you?"

The warriors hooted. I tried to keep my voice steady. "It belonged to my father. And to his father and grandfather before him."

His lips twisted in the thick blond beard as he studied me. "Chlothar took everything," he said, and turned away.

The night had become dense and heavy, shrinking the stars to dim glimmers in the sky. As Friduric pushed me forward with a hand on my slave collar, I said, "What is *mora*?"

At first I thought he did not intend to answer. He steered too close to a tree, and low-hanging leaves slapped us both in the face.

"A place where the earth cannot be walked on," he said at last. "We make offerings to Nerthuz there that are not to be seen by the sky gods."

A bog. Where my body would disappear and never be found.

"Friduric, help me," I rasped. "For love of your sister. Just leave the—"

He twisted the collar tighter. I clawed at the throttling strap, but could only stumble onward as he shoved me along. At the cave entrance he thrust me inside. I fell onto hands and knees, wheezing as light from the *halla* vanished and the bar slammed into its brackets.

I pounded the earth in rage. I swore revenge on him and his vicious father. I cursed Maelo and Odo and Rufus, and the others who had shouted for my death. I called down vengeance on Chlothar and Lamia and Glabrio.

Finally I had to stop. So great was my thirst that I had no voice. I licked the earthen wall, but tongued up only grit.

Two nights. So I must escape tomorrow or tomorrow night, or die maimed, smothered in oblivion.

While I lay sleepless, so dry I could not think, there came a faint tap at the door. It was the merest ghost of sound, hardly more than the click of a fingernail.

Rufus! I thought, my heart lifting. The boy had come to deliver me after all.

"Are you there?" someone whispered in Germanic. A female voice.

I scrambled up. "Aurima?" Her name seared my throat, but it was a joyful pain.

"No," she said, and my hope died. She added, "I bring you drink."

I said nothing. It must be a trick.

The whisper came again: "Kneel down away from the door. Do you understand?"

I said, "Yes," more a gust of air than a word. I backed away and lowered myself torturously to my knees.

"I have a knife, so do not move."

Bold and defiant. Like Aurima. I rasped, "Who are you?"

She might not have heard, for the bar was scraping as she lifted it. A moment later she cracked open the door.

My opportunity. Wrench it open, knock her down, grab the knife and silence her, and be off over the palisade.

I did not move. Part of me thought I was dreaming, and did not want to wake.

She placed an object inside and hastily shut the door. The bar fell into place with a *clunk*, and I heard her hiss with vexation at the noise.

I groped my way to the door. She had left me an aleskin, plump and yielding. I yanked the nozzle free and took a gulp without pausing for a cautious sip. Awful, sour barley ale. It tasted better than the finest aged Falernian I had ever drunk.

When it was empty, I sank to the floor and savored my restored well-being. It was several long minutes before I thought to whisper, "Are you still there?"

"Yes."

"Who are you?"

A brief hesitation. "I am Helewidis."

"Helle? You are Helle, the wife of Friduric?"

"Who has told you?"

"Aurima told me. 'You are going to like Helle,' she said. 'She is a sister to me.'"

In the silence we both heard shouts from the direction of the hall. She said hurriedly, "Hide the aleskin. I come for it later."

"Wait. Tell me, is she well?"

"I . . . think so."

I could not have said to her face the question I most wanted answered, but the barrier of the door between us made it possible. "Is she . . . done with me?"

"I must go."

I heard the rustle of her skirts. "Helle, wait! Tell me where to find her."

She must have stooped and spoken next to the door, for the murmur was soft and clear: "I came because you said you love her. But I cannot go against the *fraujaz* and my husband." From farther away she whispered, "May your gods receive you."

And she was gone.

I would find Aurima somewhere to the south, near a river or a lake, in the house of a sorceress. Her mother's mother, Hroswitha?

She had told me her grandmother could cast *zoubar* with a wave of her amber-headed staff, could turn herself into an owl after dark and fly away. Instead of joking about my inability to pronounce "Hroswitha," why had I not asked her where this witch-woman lived? How far from Hoheneih? Hours? Days? Once I fled the stronghold, would I stumble upon her "water house" if I took a trail that led southward?

The next night would be all but moonless, favorable for escape, yet I could not hurry a stolen horse along a forest track in the darkness. Fast-paced pursuers the next morning would not find it hard to overtake me.

Ingiomar's threats echoed in my head. *I cut out your eyes . . .* I saw Ollius's face, spattered with blood, and the swarming socket where his eye had been.

Then I cut off your balls . . .

Perdition! By morning I would be a gibbering imbecile unless I could bring myself under control. I would have given anything to doze off quickly and sleep without dreams, but Morpheus appeared no more inclined to heed me than Fortuna had.

Then I seemed to be in a different cavern beneath the Palatine Hill, a dungeon stinking of ordure. Caligula Caesar emerged from the swirling smoke, elegant in a gold-striped mantle, with a laurel wreath crowning his fair hair.

I gripped the bars between us. "Release me, cousin! For the sake of our fathers' friendship, will you not forgive me?"

"Why, Marcus, I forgave you long since," he said with that charming Julian smile. "Don't you know you are free?"

"But I will be caught. I cannot go fast enough or far enough by night."

"Then flee by day, young fool."

"When I am constantly watched?"

He sighed. "In the midst of Rome, can you find nowhere to hide?"

I knew it was not Rome we were talking about. "And struggle on foot through the forest? Catch food with my bare hands?"

Caligula frowned. "I said you would be free." He covered his nose with an edge of his mantle, then drew it down for a moment. "Not that you would escape death."

I had no interest in dying. I needed to rescue the woman I loved and pay back the men whose names were scrawled in the dirt.

Irritated by my stubbornness, he drifted away.

"Wait," I called. "Wait!" And woke myself up.

There were footfalls outside. "—what the *fraujaz* did to the Romans who killed Ammisia," a man said in slurred Germanic. "By Tiwaz the Just, I did not know I would see it myself."

The footsteps came up to the door. The bar rattled in its brackets. "Sleep well, turd," someone shouted. They brayed drunken laughter as they left.

I had twenty-four hours to escape. How was I to manage it?

In the darkness, a voice that might have been Caligula's said to me, "Do what they do not expect."

91

18: ITHACA

Loud gabbling outside my cave the next morning faded as Rosmunda opened the door and I limped into the daylight. A score of people—farmworkers, cowherds, washwomen, little children—stood gawping at me as if I had just flown down on a cloud.

I met the stares with a sour grimace. I was starving, and my scanty sleep after dreaming of the dungeon had been broken by nightmares of Ingiomar throwing me into a sucking swamp. Added to that, my bladder ached after guzzling Helle's ale. I pushed through the bystanders.

"Imagine," someone said. "Him, with beautiful Aurima!"

"He must have forced her," someone else muttered. "Filthy beast."

Feet shuffled after me. A hand pulled down the wide neck of my tunic, exposing my scarred back. "Mother Nerthuz! Look at that."

I wrenched free and pulled the garment up across my shoulders. I was used to the warriors' casual blows and kicks, but women had kept their distance. Evidently the sentence of death pronounced last night gave them, too, the license to harass me. Were they going to follow me all the way to the waste pit?

A man's gruff voice said, "You women go back to your work, now."

"I want to see if his pizzle is different."

"Yes, we want to see."

Curse them, they wanted to see if Romans were made like other men! I had half a mind to show them, but I would not shame Aurima by letting them gape at my privates.

I rounded on them. "See all you want tomorrow night, you crows! Go away."

They startled back, but none showed any embarrassment. I did not see the heavily pregnant blonde who had served Ingiomar's drink, and who I thought was Helle. Perhaps she had more affection for Aurima than to come and gloat.

"What is all this?" A familiar voice: Maelo's. "Does no one have work today?"

Reluctantly the observers drifted off. I went to the far side of an empty cart, where there was privacy. When I turned, Odo scowled at me, leaning on a hunting spear. Maelo was stooped in conversation with Rosmunda.

"Roman," Maelo said in Latin. Above the briar-bush beard his eyes were chilly, as if he had not pleaded for my life the evening before. "I am telling Roza that Odo goes with you everywhere today. If you attack him or run away, he does not kill you. He cuts you." He gestured to the back of his own leg. "Understand?"

"You think too highly of your son," I said. "I am not afraid of a bare-faced boy."

Odo turned as red as a stormy sunrise. The beard he had been trying to cultivate for a year was still just a few patchy bristles.

"Caesar has not forgotten that I am his cousin," I went on. "Remind Ingiomar that only a fool risks angering the Princeps of Rome."

"You are paying a blood price for the death of his wife, Ammisia. My sister."

"Is it going to please her spirit when my friends take revenge on you?"

Maelo stared at me, eyes flickering with calculation. I pressed my advantage: "Set me free. All I want is to make sure Aurima is well."

"She is well," he said. His lips parted as if he would say something more, but he merely cast a hard look at his son and stalked off.

"Odo, where does Hroswitha live?" I said the name as well as I could.

"Quiet! Do not talk to me."

"Is she not your grandmother, too, your father's mother?"

Aurima had liked to talk about Hroswitha, her *amma*. Somewhere in the Illyrian hills with snow spitting down from a bruise-dark sky, she had told me, "My *amma* says it is good luck to be kissed by the North Wind." She tipped her face back with snow melting bright on her eyelashes. "Does he have a name in Latin, the North Wind?"

I told her his name: Aquilo. Burrowed into the covers with arms around each other, we had talked about ...

"*Mola*," I said suddenly.

"What?" Odo looked up from digging a stone out of the path with his spear butt.

It was a game we had played, asking the name of random things in each other's language. She had mimed a turning mill wheel and asked me the Latin word. Could the "water house" be a mill? Did her grandmother run it? Live near it?

"Does your father's mother ..." I began, and stopped. I could not recall how to say "mill" in Germanic.

"Shut up," Odo snapped. "Eat."

One of the dogs was lapping porridge out of my bowl, which Rosmunda had left on the ground. I limped toward it and the hound backed away, waving its tail appeasingly. They were used to my scent now, or perhaps I had come to smell German.

I wiped the bowl clean and sucked my fingers. As Lamia had been fond of saying, *He who is given a gift cannot be choosy.*

Odo's stare was contemptuous. He probably thought he could never be humbled enough to eat a dog's leavings.

My belly rumbled. "More, Roza?" I begged.

She tilted her head without looking up from whatever she was pounding in a mortar. The crusted pot of porridge stood on a flat stone behind her, still steaming ripples into the morning air.

Her pestle thudded: *whump, whump, whump*. Chickens burbled, pecking at anything that might be a grain of barley.

As I crouched by the pot, I said, "It cannot please Nerthuz to make a sacrifice that is *turpis*." Foul. I showed Odo the inside of my arm, black with ingrained grime, and went on scooping up porridge with my fingers. "In Rome we wash sacrifices in living water." That was not strictly true, but if they took me down to the stream that ran outside the stronghold, I could study the landscape and the trails.

Odo sounded angry that he had to speak with me after all. "Father says you are going to be crazy today, like a fox in a trap. Thinking of escaping. Thinking you are going to be saved." He gave me a steady, serious look. "Tomorrow you are going to be afraid. You are going to shake and cry and beg for your life."

"No," I said with all the conviction I could muster. "Tomorrow the Fifteenth Legion is coming for me."

Rosmunda cawed in derision. "You laugh?" I exclaimed. "Then perhaps they are coming today." I summoned strength into my shoulders and arms, leaped, and swung onto the lowest limb of the great oak. Perdition, the pain!

"That tree is holy!" Odo grabbed for my foot, but I had already clambered higher.

"I must see if they are coming," I said. I scrambled further up, scraping myself on bark and branches, clinging to every handhold.

Below me Roza said, "Calm yourself, boy. Let Thunraz take him."

"But he is for Nerthuz," Odo said wildly. "Come down, or I come after you!"

"If you do, you die first," I shouted back. Twigs and acorns showered past as I climbed, and the sky beyond the waving leaves grew brighter.

At last my nerve gave out. I was so high that the tree had begun to move with me, the branches swaying and rustling when my weight shifted. Stopping with one bare foot jammed in the crotch of a limb and my hands on the next branch, I peered through a gap in the foliage.

The palisade lay far below, the thatched longhouses penned in it like a herd of hairy aurochs. Beyond it spread a valley surrounded by forest. A stream wound across the valley floor past a scatter of huts, green and yellow fields of grain, and brush-fenced pastures where cattle grazed.

It was a placid summer morning. Birds soared and dipped across the sky. Between the huts I made out a smith pounding on a blade, an old man scraping a hide, a couple of girls tending geese, women spinning in the shade of a tree.

A broad track crossed the stream and disappeared among trees to the east. I crawled out on a springy limb, opening a larger sight hole, and saw wheel marks crossing the valley from the south. Beyond Hoheneih in all directions were endless trees. No gaps to show nearby steadings, no smoke to mark human hearths. No water mill.

My breathing had calmed. I closed my eyes, then opened them again. Xerxes' million-man army could be a mile away and no one would know it in this wilderness.

"I see them," I bellowed in Latin. "One . . . two . . . six cohorts of the legion! The governor leads them. He has brought a wing of cavalry . . . The standard is just coming into sight . . . the First Tungrians. And two auxiliary cohorts: the First Mountaineers and the Second Armored Hispanians. Fetch your father, Odo! Quickly, quickly."

Odo had stifled his shouts for me to climb down, no doubt realizing that the fewer who knew of my antics, the less disgrace there would be to him. "Shut up," he cried, sounding very far away. "You are lying."

Of course I was lying. But the warning from the sacred oak of Thunraz that a Roman army was on the way achieved its result. A man who knew Latin shouted a warning. Dogs barked. A horn blew. Women screamed for their children. The gates swung shut. Half a dozen men leaped on horses, shouting for the gates to open, and galloped off to the east. Confirmed in my surmise that that was the direction in which the Amber Road lay, I laughed, pleased with the chaos.

But now I had to climb down. It crossed my mind to simply release the branch and let myself fall. Before my heart could beat twice I would be dead, avoiding the torture Ingiomar planned. Aurima was safe; her uncle had as much as said she had no need of me. If I tried and failed to escape tonight, I might become the trembling, weeping, pleading wretch that Odo had predicted.

No, I would not. First I would dig a sharp rock out of the cave wall and cut my throat with it.

I descended the tree slowly, looking around when the leafage permitted. At the well-maintained palisade, where sturdy new poles gleamed yellow beside the gray of older stakes. At the twin gates, the only way out, that were always manned and at night were barred. At the rotting gray roof thatch of Ingiomar's hall, splotched with moss and soot-streaked around the smokehole, and at the flower-speckled roof of a hay barn between the *halla* and the horse pen.

About twenty feet above Odo's head I bestrode a stout bough and grinned at him, letting my feet dangle.

"Get down," he muttered nervously. Folk were still running and shouting at each other. No one had noticed yet that he had lost a captive.

"Why?" I taunted, knowing he was anxious lest his father or Ingiomar appear.

He paced sideways, looking for a clean spear-cast through the leaves and branches. "Come down now! Or, by Wodunaz, you are never walking again."

"Want to see me fly?" I made to stand up. Twenty feet was still enough of a drop to break my neck.

"No!" His voice quavered. "Come down. I swear not to hurt you."

"No, I am going to wait here for the Army." I swung my feet.

"What?" He glanced around as two young men ran toward the gates, carrying shields and spears.

I might have compelled him to tell me where his grandmother lived, but it was too late: Maelo had arrived. He saw me, cursed, and knocked his son flat with a single blow. I laughed when he cursed me too, but when he took aim at me with Odo's spear, I dropped the last few feet to the ground.

"Calf-wit," he muttered, punching the spear butt into the pit of my stomach. My breathing stopped, and it seemed I might cheat Ingiomar after all.

I dreamed of snow. Snow sifted down from the top of Thunraz's oak, hiding me amid foliage that was covered in white. I stood on a branch in perfect ease, neither cold nor fearful, seeing all the way to the fortress of Carnuntum on its bluff above the Danube. All was as usual there: no rescue mission preparing to depart, no troop-laden ferries crossing the river to the Mark. Nothing moved but an eagle high over the snow-dusted trees, sailing the air with its great wings outspread.

"Come to me," I called. With a few strokes of its wings the eagle glided down, so close that I could see the fierce eye and the scything beak.

"Ithaca," it said to me.

I leaped into the snowy air to join it. And flew away.

A dream of death, or of life? After coming to my senses in the cave, I had slipped into an exhausted doze. Was the eagle my father's spirit counseling me to die with dignity? An omen that troops were coming, after all? Or did "Ithaca" mean that I, like oppressed Odysseus, would at last be reunited with the one I loved?

I sat up all of a sudden, panicky that my last precious night was rushing away. The abrupt lunge made me gasp. My belly ached from Maelo's blow, and my shoulders from the monkey tricks in the tree.

But it was not so late; sunlight still lanced around the ill-fitting cave door. I levered myself to my feet and peered through a crack. Distant voices mumbled, then passed. I heard the slow clop of an unseen horse being led up the path from the gates.

Do what they do not expect.

Damn my foolery! I had meant to steal some kind of digging tool before I was shut in here—a shard of crockery, perhaps, something I could have hidden in my mouth or armpit. Now I had nothing. The rotten stick with which I had written names in the dirt had crumbled.

Wait—Helle had not retrieved her aleskin yet. I picked up the limp leather bag.

She might have made it herself. A wrapping of colored thread bound the lips of the bag to the hollow bone mouthpiece. A thong dyed the same color would have closed off the contents, had I not drunk them all.

I wrenched at the mouthpiece and tore at the thread with my teeth until the small piece of bone came free. A tool.

This rabbit burrow had not been excavated with desperate prisoners in mind. It was dug deep enough to keep butter and milk cool, and fitted with a door strong enough to defeat most hungry animals. Every inside surface was damp earth smoothed like plaster, including the two-foot-thick wall into which the door was set.

I started beside the doorpost, where an earlier effort I had made with bare hands showed as a pitiful dent. The hollow bone had quarried only four or five small trenches in the earth when a deep, distant rumble froze me. But it was nothing; just the late-day thunder that never brought rain.

With the next scoop, raw dirt chafed my knuckles. The bone had snapped.

So I dug with my hands. The left one first. A little later, the right.

I worked steadily as the light faded from gold to rose to gray. The earth was hard-packed, stony, and seamed with roots, but I did not care. I dug like a man bailing a sinking boat. As I dredged, I imagined freedom: finding Aurima, reaching Carnuntum, swearing charges against Lamia and Glabrio, returning with troops to capture Ingiomar and Maelo and Chlothar. Sparing Friduric, perhaps, because his wife had been kind.

Gradually I deepened a slot in the earth beside the doorpost. As soon as I broke through, I would reach out and dislodge the end of the bar, then push the door open. In a population without lamps, everyone but the feasting warriors would be asleep. And they would be making too much noise in the *halla* to heed the fall of a crossbar.

Male voices broke into the sounds of my labor. I stopped at once and squirmed back, away from the hole I had made.

The bar scraped out of its brackets and fell on the ground. The door opened, letting in distant torchlight that darkened as Friduric edged into the hut, sword drawn.

I glared up at him. *Like a fox in a trap*, Odo had said. Precisely how I felt.

The heap of excavated dirt told its own story. "He has been busy, *Fader*," Friduric said over his shoulder.

"I reckoned he would," said Ingiomar Ironhand. He filled the doorway, a dark mass of a man with some weapon of his own in his hand. "Bind his wrists."

Friduric beckoned with the sword. I pulled my feet beneath me to stand up. "No," he said. "Sit. Hands behind you."

He stepped behind me, sheathed his sword, and hauled my arms together. His hand slipped. "Ah, *Fader*"—he clicked his tongue—"he has drawn first blood himself."

Helpless anger shook me as he wrapped a thong around my wrists several times and knotted it. "You are dead men," I rasped in Germanic.

Friduric snorted, amused.

"Here is something to think about," Ingiomar said, "if you expect you are going to escape and gallop away." He tossed what he was holding at me. Wetness sprayed across my neck, and the thing fell heavily into my lap.

He backed out with Friduric after him. Not until the doorway was empty was there enough light to see what he had flung across my thighs.

I gasped and jerked myself up, trying to get away, but retched and fell. And then, in grief and anger, roared aloud.

Ingiomar laughed and slammed the door. But even with daylight turned to murk I could see it, knowing it by the white sock that extended up from the big pale hoof. Boss's left foreleg, chopped off at the knee.

19: THE ANGER OF THUNRAZ

Noise hissed inside my head, red and black with hatred. At the same time everything I had to do was very clear, as if I had the eagle vision of my dream. From the distant hall came the shouts and howling laughter of Ingiomar and his warriors.

My wrists were slick with blood from torn fingers. I wrenched and pulled at the binding until one hand slid free. Then both hands. I rolled my shoulders, heard myself moan, stopped, wiped my eyes with my tunic, and crawled back to resume digging.

Now I had a better tool.

The bar scraped slowly in its brackets. I went still, curling my fingers around the leg bone. I had not heard any footsteps scuffing on the path.

Very quietly someone set the bar on the ground. An inch of paler night appeared at the door's edge.

I rose to my feet.

The gap widened. A voice murmured, "Mar's?"

I almost spoke aloud, but recalled myself in time to whisper. "Rufus?"

He thrust his head inside. I gripped the bone tighter. "Why are you here?" If he had brought me a knife, perhaps I ought to thank him for his kindness. Even though I did not intend to kill myself.

He backed away and beckoned. I edged out the door.

Rufus saw what Ingiomar had thrown to me. His mouth opened in shock.

It was very dark; any last fragment of moon had not yet risen. The only lights were a torch outside the feast hall and two at the gates. No one else seemed to be abroad. I closed the door. Rufus helped me set the bar into its brackets, gently and without sound.

So quickly had Fortuna's wheel spun that I could hardly believe I stood in the open air, separated from liberty only by a palisade. I squeezed Rufus's shoulder to thank him and urge him toward a quiet spot where I could tell him my plan.

He took my hand off his shoulder, leaving a bloody palm print. I said, "You are not coming?"

He shook his head.

"Ingiomar will guess who helped me."

"Go," he whispered. "Au'ima needs."

He seemed to have become leaner and leggier just since I was captured. His red hair had grown long enough to be tied at his nape. I could no longer call him "the Thracian boy"; he was becoming a young warrior.

"Leave me, then. You cannot be seen with me." I thought of something. "Rufus."

He turned back. I was stripping off my bedraggled tunic.

"When the sky lights up," I said softly, "let the horses loose."

He nodded, touched my upper arm in farewell, and glided into the darkness.

I stood for a moment, watching the hole he had left in the night. If he was not careful, his life would be as much at risk as mine.

Aurima needs.

I pissed into a patch of dirt beneath a tree, stirred it with my toes, and daubed mud over my pale face, chest, limbs, and loincloth. All was still quiet. I crept toward the torch outside the doors of the *halla*, hardly noticing pebbles and tree roots under my calloused feet.

The night was warm and still, as if smothered by the surrounding forest. Snores buzzed inside the nearest house. Woodsmoke floated from the hall, carrying the usual scents of ale and roast meat. Someone inside was chanting a sonorous battle saga. They are great boasters of their own heroism, the Germans. A few others joined in but stumbled over the words. Something fell with a crash, and there was laughter.

I reached the shelter of the great oak and pressed myself against its trunk. Some bird or animal rustled high in the branches, dislodging acorns that plopped beside me.

The drunken singing resumed as I crouched there. Feeling around my feet, I gathered up a few dead branches as long as my forearm.

The next minutes would be the most dangerous, for I would come into the gate guards' view as I crossed to the front of the hall. And anyone leaving the feast might see me in the light of the torch planted outside the open doors.

A whicker came from the horse pen. One of the sleepy animals greeting Rufus, I guessed. Not Boss. Never again would I ride my sorrel warhorse, nevermore share an exhilarating gallop with him—

To stop these thoughts I darted rashly from the tree into the open.

A man's shape loomed into the lit doorway of the *halla*. I shrank down behind a holly bush. Luckily, it was a sot who stumbled back to the feast after relieving himself.

I had barely recovered from that alarm when something wet and cold nosed between my thighs. I gasped and turned so quickly I nearly fell. One of the hunting dogs waved his tail, happy to find company at this hour.

Boneheaded cur! All I needed was for someone to glance over and wonder why a dog was wagging his tail at a clump of holly.

A startlingly clear voice said, "The nights are long when the Moon God is away."

A second voice growled at him to stop complaining. Had they not agreed to take gate-guard duty tonight so they could watch the *fraujaz* sacrifice the Roman tomorrow?

I raised myself over the holly until I could see the two of them at the foot of the slope. They squatted inside the closed gates, passing an aleskin back and forth. Three more hounds stretched out around them, heads resting on forepaws.

Merda! The hounds were bound to hear or smell me and start barking.

There was an alternative: to retreat around the oak tree and approach the hall from the rear. But that would take time. Time in which Rufus or I might be discovered.

The dog next to me raised his head, nostrils twitching. I noticed then a delicate tickle on my arm hairs. A breeze was drifting across the valley.

Perhaps there was a Fortuna and she loved me after all, for this rising zephyr wafted from the gates toward the *halla*. I was downwind of the three hounds.

Moments later the oak leaves were whispering to themselves. Acorns pattered to the ground. The tips of the torch flames fluttered. And I ran, followed by the dog.

I had just reached the corner of the hall when one of the hounds at the gate let out a sharp bark and stood up. I flung myself against the thatched side wall, out of the light.

"What is it now?" one of the gate guards exclaimed.

My four-legged companion trotted down to join its fellows. "It's that dog of Wido's," said the other guard. "What are you doing so late, Blackie? Settle down now."

I risked a glance. One guard slouched on a low post fixed to stop the gate's swing. His comrade tussled with the four dogs, all clustered around him with waving tails.

I slithered toward the torch in front of the hall. With wounded hands as stiff as boxers' mitts, I thrust my two longest sticks into the flame until they flared alight. Shielding the glow, I slipped back against the side wall, pried up the top layer of thatch, and touched the burning sticks to dry straw beneath.

The thatch smoldered. I huffed on it. A spark of brightness came first, then a flicker of flame. Propping the upper layer with a twig to let in air, I moved stealthily down the side wall and kindled the underthatch in two more places.

The breeze was still alive, hiding my small noises from the gate guards. I stole across to the nearby barn. The doors stood open, for there was nothing inside but a hay wagon. I slipped in and set my remaining twigs and branches afire. Some I stuck into the walls; others I tossed into the hay drifts.

None of the fires had shown themselves by the time I ghosted back to the hall. How long would it take? Surely some of them would spread ...

As at Grozhauga, the drinkers had left their weapons in a basket outside, a sensible practice since ale and armaments do not mix. An Army shortsword in the basket was a lucky discovery. Probably taken from a legionary, unless some idiot politician had sent it straight from the smithy to Ingiomar.

A yellow light caught my eye, flaring inside the hay barn.

I swung one of the hall's heavy doors shut, and then the other. The symbols carved into them glared black in the torchlight: tridents and diamonds, upward-pointing arrows and spirals. Three stout boar spears stood in the basket. I thrust them one after the other into the pull rings on either side, barring the doors. Last I yanked the grease-spitting torch from its holder and pushed it into the thatch beside the doors.

By now the dogs were barking. The guards had turned, but would have seen only swaying shadows as I swept the torch sideways.

"*Fuir*," I shouted. "Fire!" I snatched the shortsword from the basket and ran down toward them, hoping the mud that darkened my skin would disguise the slave collar until I was close. "Save the *fraujaz*!"

At first they only gaped. Then the night lit up. Our shadows jumped on the inside of the gates in a fiery glow from the hay barn. "Go," I screamed to the nearer guard, a big-bellied man with dull shock on his face. He began to lumber up the slope, a sword scabbard bobbing on his hip, and I chopped at his neck. Blood gushed, dyeing his fair beard scarlet, and he toppled.

Because of the gyrating shadows the other man was slow to recognize what had happened, but when I came toward him, he thrust at me with his spear. I lopped it in half with my sword, then lunged forward and drove the blade between ribs into his heart, as Ollius had taught me.

The dogs barked and danced excitedly. I was about to start clearing them away with my sword when an uproar of banging and shouting burst from the hall. Flames at this end had climbed the thatch to the gable, and gouts of smoke billowed along the roof where I had seeded fire. The spears jolted in the pull rings as men inside flung themselves against the doors. The dogs raced up to add their clamor to the din.

Then, above the barking and shouting and hammering and the snarl of the fire, I heard the frantic whinny of horses. The sound ripped me from my stupor, and I threw myself on the crossbar that secured the gates. It was counterweighted, so a downward thrust tipped the other end up and out of its bracket.

I dragged one gate open. The guard I had stabbed lay in the path of the other. I hauled him to one side, remembering to wrench off his soft leather shoes and shove my feet into them.

The horses were screaming. By now they could see the barn blazing across the way and feel its heat. Embers soared into the sky like stars climbing homeward. People spilled groggily from their homes, shrieked, and ran back inside for valuables. Ash and scraps of thatch swirled through the air like snow.

I could not keep back a smile of malicious gratification. If Rome's *vigiles* thought it was difficult to put out a tenement fire, let them try to save a straw-roofed hamlet.

The ground began to vibrate under the soles of my feet. Time to go. Clumsy in my borrowed shoes, I ran out through the gates. Peasants goggled from their huts, faces lit by the conflagration inside the stronghold. Hidden in the fire-shadow of the palisade, I scuttled into the ditch beneath it.

The pounding of many hooves rumbled louder. I stopped and half turned. The whole fear-maddened herd of horses thundered through the open gates and hurtled down the path, scattering apart in a storm of fire-gilded dust, then drawing together. They splashed across the river and streamed up the trail that led eastward through the forest to the Amber Road. Spider must have been among them, but I could not spot him in the erratically flickering firelight. Silently I wished him luck.

I kept slogging around the outside of the palisade in my too-big shoes. The fire inside roared, a huge beast devouring prey that shouted and shrieked. Wisps of burning straw, sparks, and ash rose in the smoke, whirled lazily, and sailed downwind.

I had made chaos again, this time even more successfully than before. And now I was free. Free until morning, at least, when Ingiomar would start combing the countryside for his escaped Roman on an escaped horse.

Even if my nose had not told me, the stain on the palings would have signaled the place I sought. I paused, at the last minute debating my choice. But lacking any better solution, I took a deep breath and pinched my nostrils shut between lacerated thumb and forefinger. With a dead man's shoes on my feet and a sword in my other hand, I leaped into the one place no one would look for a fugitive: a heap of horse dung.

It was not as bad as it might have been. Hot days without rain had withered most of the droppings into crumbly packets of half-digested hay. And I had long since grown used to the odor of horse manure.

I wriggled into the heap, shoving the sword down beside me, until all but my face was submerged. The dry grass prickled, itched, and stung everywhere my skin was torn.

Smoke shone a garish orange overhead, shot with sparks. To a chorus of yells, a building inside the palisade collapsed in a crash of timbers. It must have been the barn, not the hall with Ingiomar in it, for a while later he was shouting hoarsely for dirt to be thrown on roofs.

I writhed deeper, clearing a crooked channel for air. Cocks were crowing, confused by the unnatural light. I tucked my damaged hands into my armpits to obscure the smell of blood.

I had slain two men. Yet I felt neither satisfaction nor regret, and did not even wonder at my ruthlessness. The soul within me was numb, indifferent. Nothing mattered except finding a concealed young priestess, and then vengeance.

"How many horses are still missing?"

Ingiomar's voice was so close that it roused me immediately from sleep to defiance, thinking I was discovered. My involuntary twitch startled a nimbus of flies, which hovered uncertainly before settling again.

"Three of ours," said a younger voice. "And the Roman's silver stallion."

My face was buried, eyes squeezed shut against the crumbling dung, but the direction of the men's voices placed them atop the earthen rampart inside the palisade. If they looked down, they would see the midden, and perhaps me. I hoped my skin was still filthy enough to hide any bits that might show.

"Find him," Ingiomar said. "He is on the horse, I know it."

My groping hand tightened on the sword hilt.

"There are many tracks, *fraujaz*." The younger man sounded frustrated and weary.

"Tell Friduric not to come back until he has the turd, dead or alive."

The man spat in discontent. Exhausted, no doubt, from fighting fires.

I thought they had both gone, but a few moments later I heard another voice: Maelo's. "What if he is not found?"

Ingiomar snapped, "He burned my hall, Wodunaz curse him! He killed Fulco and Adalwulf. By all the gods, I am going to find him or his chewed bones!"

"It is strange that the dogs cannot track him beyond the gate."

"He stole a horse! Or do you think he grew wings and flew off?"

"I think the gods have not favored us since you sent Aurima away. Look at the anger in the sky."

"Was it my doing that the oak tree caught fire? I have always honored Thunraz!"

"You have displeased him somehow, brother. Unless he wills it, you are never going to catch the Roman. And then the legions are coming after us."

Ingiomar snorted. "Thunraz did not free him. It was that slave Rudra your son hunted with. The boy you said we could trust."

I stiffened, suddenly recalling my bloody handprint on Rufus's shoulder. Or had he been seen releasing the horses?

"Maybe it was not the slave," Maelo said.

After a pause Ingiomar asked, "What is this?"

"I found it inside the store place. That is your son's mark sewn on it, is it not?"

The aleskin Helle had brought me.

"Friduric did not help him escape!"

"Are you sure? Perhaps that is why he says he cannot find the Roman."

"By the Hammer of Thunraz! Odo, bring me my horse."

A few minutes later, hoofbeats echoed from the gateposts and dwindled away. No question about it: sowing chaos appealed to me. Maybe Friduric and his father would kill each other and the search would be abandoned.

What had Maelo meant by "Look at the anger in the sky"? I widened my air hole, slowly and cautiously, until a patch of blue showed overhead. A patch soon blotted out by a cloud like dirty wool.

The weather had changed. That was the reason for the breeze last night: after weeks of hot sun, rain was coming. Perdition! A downpour would ruin my hiding place. Would it hold off until dark?

I had no choice but to stay cramped and inert amid the increasingly smelly manure. My body reminded me that it was thirsty and hungry, that it itched and hurt.

If I had actually stolen Spider, I might be on the Amber Road by now. That was where I hoped Ingiomar would look for me, because when it was dark I meant to go another way. Toward the south.

The day was endless. Heat baked me like a chicken in a casserole. My scalp crawled so intolerably with sweat that I had to bite my knuckles to fight down the urge to scratch. Feeling, or imagining, the wriggle of maggots on my face, I breathed into a hand cupped over my nostrils.

Dogs barked and whined. One shoved his nose into the dung heap, but was clouted away by a searcher: "Leave that stinking mess!" I heard the huts being ransacked, the cattle scattered with wild whoops to make sure I was not hidden among them.

Groups of newcomers straggled in, laughing and shouting greetings to each other, eager to view the promised human sacrifice. Many rode out more grimly to hunt for me. I overheard a woman I thought was Helle, fretting about where to shelter so many guests with the *halla* burned down.

Clouds thickened. The air grew damp. Search parties trotted back, glum-voiced. I listened for Ingiomar or Friduric, but did not hear them. In my uneasy imaginings they tortured Rufus, demanding a confession before he took my place in Nerthuz's bog.

Meat roasted somewhere. Spitted pork, a side of beef, a haunch of venison? But Germans ate horsemeat, too. My dry mouth filled with bile.

Wagons groaned and squealed up the road and through the gates of the stronghold. Nearer I heard grunting and panting, scraping and crackling. "Lend a hand," men shouted. "Bring it over here. Hurry now." They sounded so close that I dared not poke a hole to see what they were doing.

Someone whistled sharply. A few minutes later came the rumble of horses' hooves. Boys yipped to drive them on, voices bright with excitement.

Another growl. I cursed my traitor belly. Was the noise loud enough to carry?

But it did not come from my guts. It was thunder.

A racket of barking and snarling broke out. Men's shouts silenced the dogs. Arriving horses nickered back and forth.

"You have him?" It was Maelo's bellow.

"Only his horse," Ingiomar called back sourly.

I smiled. He would have to explain to all his followers and friends that the victim for his sacrifice had escaped after burning down his house. How embarrassing for him.

"By the Hammer of Thunraz!" he snarled. "Why are the horses penned out here?"

Maelo must have moved farther away, for only a few words of his reply were audible: "...Too many people...wagons..."

A louder rumble shivered the air, with a deep booming echo like a cauldron falling from a great height. The anger of Thunraz was upon us.

There were cries of alarm. "Inside," Ingiomar roared. "Friduric, see to the gates!"

The day darkened. Cooler air rushed through the crannies of dried dung. A far-off rustle grew louder like a river gone rampant. Thunder boomed again, to distant shrieks.

And the rain came. Gently at first, then heavier. I dared to clear a sight hole.

An enclosure had been made with fences of woven brush dragged from who knew where. The horses inside it ranged uneasily. There was no one in sight to calm them; Ingiomar and his men had vanished. Even the doors of the peasants' huts were shut tight. No one wanted to tempt the wrath of the god of thunder.

The downpour was drenching me in a stinking soup. Even though someone might be looking out over the palisade, I had to move.

I thrust my head out of the mess. Just then two young riders came hurtling out through the gates, each leading a second horse. One was Ingiomar's white-faced chestnut, another Friduric's black pony. Beside the pen the two boys threw themselves off, dragged sections of fence apart, and chivvied the horses inside.

As they struggled to unsaddle the four animals, lightning flared across the sky. In the flash, I caught sight of Spider's elegant head above the twitching ears and bristly manes of the other mounts. Excellent. I much preferred my own horse to stealing one of the German ponies.

The boys yelped, scrambling to gather up saddles and saddle blankets. I had frozen where I was, visible from crown to ears in the manure pile, but neither of them glanced in my direction. Heads bent under the teeming rain, they staggered back toward the stronghold with their arms full of saddles. The gates crashed shut as soon as they had passed through.

I rolled out into a mire of disintegrating droppings. Found my feet, tottered, and steadied myself by leaning on the sword. Gloriously cool, cleansing rain poured over me. The dead warrior's shoes were lost somewhere in the ordure, having succeeded in hiding my scent from the dogs.

Stumbling and lurching across the wet grass, I headed for the horses. My eyes were fixed on where I had last seen Spider, a pale shape in the darkness.

I tripped over a saddle blanket that one of the boys had dropped. With a pause to fling it around my shoulders, I pulled apart the fences that the boys had hastily shoved together and let myself into the pen.

The ponies shied away. Fumbling through the downpour, I spoke meaningless calming words, patting a hairy flank here and a neck there and hoping not to be stepped on. I could hardly see. Desperately I called the roan's name once and then twice, fearing to raise my voice too much despite the noise of the storm.

And suddenly he was there, mouthing my shoulder, his dark eyes wide and white-rimmed. "Spider," I said, and felt my own eyes fill with tears as I laid my cheek against his neck. I threw the sodden blanket over his back, caught his mane with my free hand, and flung myself up on him. We would have made an orderly escape had lightning not flashed and thunder boomed right on top of us.

The ponies went mad, squealing and thrashing. Spider reared, and the blanket slipped beneath me. In another instant I would have been on the ground amid the hooves of stampeding horses.

I threw myself forward, clamped my arm around Spider's neck, and whacked his haunch with the flat of the sword. He lunged forward with his forelegs still in the air, crashing into a pony that went down.

Then I somehow had both arms around his neck with the sword still in one hand. It was amazing that I did not accidentally cut his throat. "Go," I cried. He bolted ahead, on all four feet at last, plowing through the ponies like a trireme through fishing smacks. It was dark again, and I did not know if he saw the fence. I leaned forward anyway to help him jump, waiting for the smash of his chest into the barrier stuffed with branches, but he lifted off and flew over without touching it.

Somehow I stayed on when he landed, and despite the almost constant flashes of light and thunderous booming, I was able to turn him toward the southern end of the valley. The other horses fled out behind us, some following, others scattering.

The rain on my cheeks, as it ran into my mouth, was warm and salty. I was free.

20: HROSWITHA

The water mill had clearly been built by Romans.

It sat on the far bank of the river, two stories of wood topped with red tiles. Straw had been stuffed into gaps where the tiles were missing, so that the roof looked like a badly barbered face. The wooden wheel stood still, dragging a slow trail of froth into a pond trapped by a dike of stone and earth. Chickens in the yard scavenged grain.

I lay on my belly in the shade of alders on the riverbank. It was the second afternoon since I had fled from Ingiomar's stronghold, and I had been watching the mill since midday. Birds twittered in the trees, no longer alarmed by my presence. Bees droned in and out of sunlit patches. My stallion munched grass in the shade behind me, his hooves rustling now and then as he moved.

I had been sure that once I found the mill, Aurima would be there. That certainty had sustained me through hellish hours on and off the forest path, haunted by fear of pursuit. Once a handful of Germans had ridden past toward Hoheneih, grumbling about their failure to find me, while Spider knelt behind a huge deadfall and I held his muzzle to keep him quiet.

But the mill seemed deserted, with no one to ask about Aurima's grandmother. Perhaps it had been abandoned. Perhaps I had taken the wrong trail. Perhaps I was lost in the Mark, with every man's hand against me.

I was so tired that this possibility held no more power to terrify. After a little rest, I would go in search of food. With no way to make fire and no time to set snares, I had eaten nothing but berries for nearly three days.

So I dozed off, and as in every snatched bit of sleep during my flight, Ingiomar Ironhand found me. I would regret trying to escape, he growled. Now I would be cast into Nerthuz's bog, tied to Rudra. Did I know that my accomplice's name meant not only "red" but "blood"? I shouted and struggled as he tied me to his horse's tail . . .

"Wake," a voice growled. Something poked me in the ribs.

I lashed out. My hand brushed long skirts and seized a bare ankle.

A stick whacked my elbow. I let go and staggered up, my heart galloping.

Blue twilight filled the glade. The trees pressed all around like armed men. Before me stood a shadowy thing as angular as an obelisk.

I swayed dizzily, clutching my numbed forearm with swollen fingers.

I had sawed off the slave collar with my sword, but this creature could probably see the discoloration of my neck, or the scabs where I had nicked myself.

Sunset-lit clouds outlined long dark robes. White hair flourished in a wild dandelion fluff around the head, so fine that I could see the shape of the knobby skull. The beardless face was a dusky blank.

The birds had gone quiet, as if spellbound.

I trembled. Could not stop. Hunger and exhaustion, no doubt. I would not believe that this was Nerthuz, come to claim the sacrifice she had been cheated of.

I looked away, down at the moss and ferns where my sword had lain. It was gone.

The dark creature stepped closer, raising a long rod. To my horror, I had no strength to run. I opened my mouth to shout to Spider when a ray of sun shot from beneath low clouds and struck flame at the head of the rod.

An amber-headed staff.

"I am looking for Aurima," I croaked.

Silence then, except for a buzz inside my head. Or perhaps a mosquito's whine.

"Great is the Goddess," her grandmother said. "You live."

"Worthless," a man was saying in Germanic. "Let me tell Ingiomar he is here."

An older, crackly voice: "You want to help Ingiomar, after what has happened?"

"What use to us is a half-dead slave who stinks of horse shit? Ingiomar is offering twenty head of cattle for him."

"The Goddess did not save him for you."

I kept still. Rain rushed and rustled, yet I lay in dry comfort. Images drifted behind my closed eyes: a low doorway through which I had stumbled in the lightless night, a fire flaring crazily on fanged walls, a dark figure who had fed me.

But Aurima was not there, and my hoarse questions about her had brought no reply. So I listened now, hoping to discover what I had not been told.

The younger man retorted, "How can he help her, *Amma*? He fell off his horse!"

"Hush. Take him more of the pottage."

I rolled over, since there was no longer any point in pretending to be asleep. Hay rustled and prickled beneath me. A knob prodded me in the side: the pommel of my sword, which I had lain upon. My filthy loincloth was gone.

A child holding a wooden bowl glared at me. No, not a child. Though no taller than a boy of seven or eight, he had a beard that was powdered white. At the end of his short arms were hands as muscular as mine.

I scrambled to my feet, trying to wrap my crippled hands around the sword hilt.

Hroswitha's cracked voice said, "Put down your weapon. There is no danger."

I had seen dwarves juggling or telling jokes at fashionable dinner parties, but had never met one. I eyed him, from dust-smutched tunic to boy-sized breeches and bare feet, and then up again at his scowling face. He smelled strongly of barley flour.

"Do you know who I am?" I rasped.

"A Roman slave," he retorted, the way one would say *A wormy nut.*

Hroswitha began slicing a loaf of bread. "Ingiomar sent men here for you."

I kept my eyes on the glowering dwarf. "Why not take the twenty cows, then?"

Jerking his chin at Hroswitha, he spat out, "Because my *amma* thinks you can save Aurima."

"Save her from what? Where is she?"

"By Wodunaz's beard!" The dwarf thrust the bowl at me. "Eat this, or starve."

"Where is she?" I needed to be running, riding, fighting—doing something. I glared from one to the other, angry and fearful. My sore fingers cramped on the sword hilt, and the point quivered.

Hroswitha said, "First you eat. Then we talk."

"Tell me now!"

I took a step closer to her, warning the dwarf with a slash of the sword to get out of the way. My legs, as weak as weed stalks, barely held me up.

He threw the bowl. It hit me on the forehead, drenching my face and bare chest in hot, viscous stew. I reeled back and fell down. The sword flew from my hands.

The old woman yelled. He shouted back at her. I slumped on the ground in a half swoon, clawing barley, greens, and bits of meat off my cheeks and into my mouth.

"Out!" Hroswitha shouted. "Both of you, out!" She seized her amber-topped staff.

"*Amma,*" the dwarf protested. Flour puffed up as her staff whacked him across the shoulders. He pulled me to my feet, surprising me with his strength, and yanked me forward. I collided with a door that gave way, and the two of us burst out into the rain.

It was a cold torrent, washing color out of the world. Blinded, I slipped on wet grass. As I fell again, I managed to hook the dwarf's legs out from under him. We sprawled together in a thrashing tangle.

"Where is she?" I panted. Seizing the hair above his ears in both hands, I slammed his head against the ground. When it smote the turf, rainwater splatted out on either side.

His eyes swirled in their sockets. His hands clutched my wrists, trying to break my grip, but in my madness I was stronger than he was. "Tell me!"

With a desperate lurch he rolled me over. The earth fell away. Flailing helplessly, I tumbled into the river.

It was warmer than the rain. After a moment of floundering in panic, I found my footing and stood up. The water was no higher than my waist.

The dwarf crouched on the bank with his hands on his knees, breathing hard. "You cannot save her," he cried into the rain. It was a wail as much as a shout.

I lunged out of the water at him. Then, finally noticing my surroundings, I paused.

The dwelling I had woken in was a small longhouse hooded with thatch. A thin streamer of smoke rose from mid-roof into the rain. Great trees the height of a basilica surrounded it on all but the river side. A path along the bank led downriver to the mill, barely visible through sodden foliage.

The water house.

Alarm struck me: What had Aurima's witch-woman grandmother done with Spider while I slept? Had she butchered him to make her spells, with heart and eyes and liver? *Had I eaten him?*

"Where is my horse?" I cried out. The dwarf nodded sullenly toward the end of the longhouse.

I found Spider dozing in a low-roofed byre, along with a broken-horned cow, its calf, and some chickens. In the gray afternoon light I checked the horse's feet and legs, looking for injury from our flight through the forest, but he seemed sound. Rubbing his head, I murmured into his cocked ear, "Courage; we are not yet finished."

Avoiding the cow's horns, I slipped around a wicker screen that partitioned off the byre. From the smoky rafters of the main room hung bunches of withered leaves and flowers, looped cords and lines, and baskets of many shapes. A pot steamed over a hazy firepit. Benches nudged a crude wooden table. Atop a small chest lay a spindle with a partly spun skein of wool. Much like the byre, the room smelled of musty hay and herbs, woodsmoke, and animals.

I plucked a cloth off a ladder to dry myself. Three days after frenzied digging in the cave, my fingers were still so battered and swollen that I had to rub with my palms.

The dwarf was hunched on a seat, head in hands. Wet flour streaked his straw-colored hair. Between him and me, licking up spilled stew from the floor, stood a wolf.

I froze.

It was colored like the forest floor, yellow-brown-gray, with a ruff-collared head that looked too large for its lean body. When it had finished its appetizer, it would surely go for the dwarf's throat. Had it already killed the old woman?

My sword was out of reach. Carefully I put one foot behind the other to step back.

The wolf looked up, yellow-eyed. So did the dwarf, but his eyes were red. "Tig," he said tiredly.

The wolf licked its jowls and sat down by his knee.

I dared not relax. "Is it going to eat me?"

"She. Her name is Tig." He eyed me blearily. "Come closer so we can find out."

The she-wolf nosed me, her hot moist breath on my thighs and her fangs a hair's breadth from my balls. I wished I had not been so quick to wash the smelly horse muck off my skin. But horses were probably on her menu, too.

Apparently I smelled German enough to satisfy her curiosity. She went back to lapping at the wet patch on the floor. Keeping an eye on her, I tied the cloth around my naked hips and retrieved my sword. "Now," I said, sitting on another bench with the blade across my thighs, "tell me where Aurima is. No, wait. First tell me who you are."

"I run the mill," the dwarf said. With a deep breath he added, "I am her brother."

I did not think I could have heard right. I even twitched my head to shake water out of my ears. "She has two brothers," I said. "Friduric, and Ingo who"—I did not know the word for "fostered"—"lives with the Hermunduri."

"No. She has three brothers: me and Friduric and Ingo."

"She never told me . . ." I let it go to ask a more urgent question: "Where is she?"

"You do not know?"

"How could I know? I have been a prisoner at Hoheneih."

"It was your people who came for her."

"My people? Romans?" How had Dio and Cleon managed to track her down? I let myself relax. "She is safe, then."

"Safe?" The dwarf's cheeks flushed red. "Safe with horse soldiers who seized her and killed her slavewoman?"

My heart slowed and beat more heavily in my chest. I lifted the sword off my lap and spiked it into the dirt floor. Leaning toward him with both hands on the hilt, I said quietly, "Tell me about these horse soldiers."

"There were ten of them, with a cart." His voice calmed to match mine. "Their helmets had black feathers. The leader was a man like this." He put his hands against his temples, palms forward, like bat ears.

Vatia Glabrio and a troop of Praetorians had taken her. What was he doing in the Mark, after all these weeks when I had been a prisoner? "When was this?"

"Two nights ago."

Only two? Then there was hope of catching them. "Where did they go?"

"Toward Hoheneih," he said, and my heart jolted.

"No, impossible. They did not pass me."

"Then they have turned onto the trail to the Amber Road. It is a longer journey from here, but easier."

Toward the Amber Road. The road to Carnuntum, then to Rome.

I made a sound in my throat. The she-wolf sat up and growled softly. The dwarf scratched her neck, and she lay down again with her slanted yellow eyes fixed on me.

So the Special Cohort had succeeded, after all, in finding the woman who nearly murdered Caligula in his bed. Glabrio meant to send her back to Rome for punishment.

"And you let them take her away?"

"Ramis tried to stop them," he said. "The Roman killed her with his sword."

"And that beast"—I stabbed a finger at the wolf—"that beast did not attack him?"

"I had to tie her up. The Roman said—"

"He spoke Germanic?" I knew neither grandmother nor grandson had Latin.

The dwarf clicked his tongue in exasperation. "A man of our tribe was with him, a two-face named Tudrus. He said, 'Get rid of Tig, or the Roman kills your *amma*.'"

Tudrus. The Quadian scout who had set up my betrayal at Grozhauga.

I had been too free in accusing this little man. Even with the aid of a tame wolf, how could he, an old woman, and a maidservant have overcome a troop of cavalry?

A horde of angry Germanic warriors would be another matter. I said, "You sent word to Ingiomar, *ja*? Perhaps he has gone already to save her." The news that Romans had stolen his daughter would surely have made the *fraujaz* abandon his hunt for me.

"Ingiomar?" Hroswitha hissed the name. "It was Ingiomar who sent them." She bent over the pot and slopped more stew into a bowl, her movements brusque and wrathy.

"He sent the Romans here?"

I did not kill her, he had told me. *But she is going to wish I had.*

What sort of man would betray his daughter to his enemies? Did he loathe me so much that he would let her die on my account?

I lifted the bowl and began to shovel stew into my mouth. "I need a sharpening stone," I said between mouthfuls. My sword had spawned flecks of rust.

Hroswitha said, "There is something more you must know, Roman."

"What?" I paused, fingers in the bowl. "What more is there?"

"They did not take only Aurima," Hroswitha said. She gestured toward what I had thought was a small chest, and now saw was a cradle. "They took her child, too."

21: MAGIC

"Child?" I said stupidly.

Aurima's grandmother looked at me unblinkingly, like an owl.

"She has a child?"

"I see you did not know."

"No, I..." I could not grasp it. "My child?"

When I had last seen her in February, she had said nothing, not a word. I tried to count backward. If this was July, nine months ago would have been November, when we left Rome. Yes, my child.

Hroswitha said, "Ten nights ago, when the face of the Moon God was half turned away, the Goddess gave her a healthy boy."

A boy. A son. Our son.

"And the horse soldiers took him too?"

"The Roman with big ears said she must bring him," the dwarf answered.

I saw Glabrio's swarthy face, his lascivious smirk. Imagined him tugging on Aurima's freckled shoulder, hoisting her, who had given birth just a week earlier, into a cart. Through a fog of rage I blurted, "Why?"

"He said Caesar waited for her."

For a moment no one spoke. Sensing the strain in our talk, the she-wolf had begun to pant with excitement. I frowned mindlessly at the noise, and then saw that she had lifted her black lips away from her sharp teeth in a joyous feral smile.

"So," I said. I set down the bowl and got to my feet, steadying myself on the sword. "I am leaving in the morning. Can you give me food to take with me, and show me the way they went?"

The dwarf stared at me. Coldly I said, "You are not really her brother, are you?"

He lifted his chin, squaring off like a belligerent ram. "My mother is her mother. My father was Ansigar of the Quadi."

Aurima's half brother, then. "I do not know your name."

"Thancmar. And I am going with you."

"My name is Aquilo. And you are not." This little man and whatever undersized pony he rode would only hamper me. "It is faster if I go alone."

He snorted. "Oh, do you know the way to the Amber Road?"

Being a Roman used to engineered roadways, I reckoned that all I needed was for the dwarf or the grandmother to aim me in the right direction. "I cannot stop you. But I am not waiting for you."

"If you fall off your horse again, Roman, I am not waiting for you either." He clicked his tongue to the wolf, who leaped to her feet and followed him out into the rain.

Hroswitha stood at the table grinding herbs. As I approached, she put a blue stone the size of my palm on the tabletop. I set about sharpening the sword blade.

"*Amma*," I said after a while, "what did she call the child?"

She did not seem to mind being addressed as *grandmother*. "It is for you to give him his name."

I would name him Titus, for my father.

For several moments we each tended to our work while rain dripping through the smokehole hissed in the fire. What did she think of me, this old woman whose daughter Ammisia had been wantonly murdered by Romans? Did she imagine I had betrayed her granddaughter?

I ran the edge of the sword back and forth over the sharpening stone with even, measured strokes. "I did not know about the horse soldiers," I said without looking up.

"Ingiomar did not tell you?"

I moved the sword down to hone its point. "He said only that I was going to wish I had never touched her."

Hroswitha did not respond. I glanced up into her faded gray eyes.

She held my gaze for several moments, then reached out to still the sword blade. My fingers were bleeding across the sharpening stone.

"Sharp enough," she said.

The names I had scrawled into the cave's earthen floor crowded my mind's eye: *INGIOMAR. GLABRIO. MAELO. FRIDURIC. CHLOTHAR. LAMIA.*

Glabrio would be first.

Hroswitha said, "Thancmar is going to take you by a shorter way. If you are fast, you can reach the Amber Road before them." Then I—or we, if my stumpy companion kept up—could ambush them on their way to Carnuntum.

More questions about Aurima, Glabrio, and Ingiomar jostled on my tongue, but I was too bewildered and weary to voice them. For now, I knew as much as I needed.

I stood up. "Find me clothes." I wanted to see to Spider.

"Thancmar is going to feed your horse," Hroswitha said, as if I had spoken my intent aloud. "Sit." She went behind the screen into the byre.

Her demeanor unsettled me, smothering any thought of disobedience. I sat, hoping to be brought a shirt or cloak.

After a moment I put my hands on the table. They were like paws, the fingers dark and bloated, bloody where blisters had broken and scabs had torn off. The right hand was worse than the left, with swollen knuckles and two nails gone. Acknowledging the agonized throbbing brought cold sweat to my brow. How would I be able to ride, much less wield a sword against Aurima's captors?

I hid my hands again as Hroswitha carried in a small bowl of yellow milk. Muttering softly, she stirred in the pounded herbs and a dollop of honey. I was beginning to salivate when she turned and plucked the lump of amber from the head of her staff. Holding it over the fire so that the heart of the flames danced within it, she started to chant in the same antique Germanic her granddaughter employed to pray to Austro.

I did not believe that a witch's potion could turn me into a frog or a beetle. This was probably a sleeping draught to calm me and restore my strength. Or could it be something more lethal, perhaps to turn a hated Roman into a corpse?

Without interrupting her prayer, Hroswitha gestured for me to lift my hands. Carefully she touched the glowing amber to each ruined finger, ignoring my winces. Then the blood-warm amber touched my forehead, tracing what felt like the jagged lightning bolt that was the Germanic symbol of Sunu, the sun.

I sat stiffly, hands curled in my lap, as she plunged the amber into the potion she had made and set the dish by the fire's edge. Her prayer to Austro came to an end.

I was about to rise when she sat opposite me and extended her hands, palms up. After a moment I laid my hands on hers.

With her thumb she touched the "R" carved into my wrist. "Is this a god-sign?"

"It marks a vow to my family."

She closed her eyes, her thumbs stroking the sides of my hands.

At first I felt only cool, smooth old skin against mine. Then a thrumming like a cat's purr. Warmth rose into my palms. I jerked in surprise, but her thumbs held me.

The warmth became heat. With her eyes still shut, she said, "I pray to the goddess of life to heal you, Roman called Aquilo. I ask her to give you the strength and courage to free Aurima, daughter of Ammisia, and her child. And if you hurt or abandon Aurima or her child, I pray that the goddess makes you burn in fire."

The curse startled me into yanking my hands away. She regarded me pitilessly, white eyelashes flickering. She had spoken in common Germanic so I would understand.

"That is not needed," I said.

"Then do not fear; it is not going to happen."

What I had assumed to be a drink had thickened at the fire's edge into a cream. She daubed it stickily on my fingers and bound my hands in strips of cloth. Last, uttering another incantation, she laid her staff's amber head in each bandaged palm.

I felt foolish. Was this the magic for which she was renowned? There could be no meaningful difference in my wounds by morning, when I would have to remove the wrappings. I must never tell Aurima that her priestess grandmother had cast no better a spell than I could have bought for two *asses* from a charm peddler in the Subura.

Sleep would not come. My gullet burned, choked with fury at Ingiomar and Glabrio. I raged at the fear and misery Aurima must have suffered at their hands. Hauled off in a cart like a sack of flour from the mill—a week after giving birth! She must think I had broken my pledge to her, that I had fled Carnuntum and left her to the mercies of the Special Cohort.

I twitched and sighed. No matter how I lay, my hands throbbed in agony. I needed to rest, but longed for daybreak when I could begin to give chase.

On the other side of the firepit, Thancmar heaved himself to his feet. "*Amma*, I am going to the mill," he called up to the sleeping loft above the byre. The wolf's breath huffed as she followed him through the doorway.

There was no reply from the loft. I imagined Aurima's bed there beside her grandmother's, sweet-scented with dried flowers and herbs. Saw her climbing up and down the peeled-birch ladder, until the child within made her too ungainly.

Could the infant be saved, a tiny just-born creature? Or had Glabrio's roughness already doomed it?

Although the fire had died to embers, the room seemed suddenly hot. Lifting a bandaged hand, I felt heat in my cheeks. I hissed between my teeth. Now, of all times, I must not fall sick.

From the loft came a squeal of wood on wood, and a moment later damp night air flowed down on me. Hroswitha must have opened a shutter. I listened for the creak of floorboards as she returned to bed, but a gust of coolness brushed my face instead. A windflaw had probably blown through the open window. Or else ...

No, fool, you have been too long among the spirit-ridden Germans.

But in a strange way it pleased me to think of a feathered creature gliding above the forests, silent wings spread wide, until its night-adapted eyes found my brave beloved. And perhaps it would send her a dream that I was on my way to save her.

A thick mist hung over the river when I stumbled outside, still half asleep. When the hem of my damp shirt trailed across my hand, the bandage slid off.

I blinked, unbelieving, then unbound my other hand. On both of them the blistered skin had healed, the gashes had closed, the missing nails had grown again. The swelling had gone, and there was no pain. I could fold both hands into fists.

When I looked up, Hroswitha's eyes met mine. Mist spangled her puff-ball of hair, so that it seemed a starry cosmos above the planet of her skull.

"What has happened?" I asked gruffly.

Her smile was as thin as a knife's edge. "The Goddess heals." Her dark robes began to fade into the mist, and the last of her disembodied words floated to me: "I merely helped her to enter you."

She buried rags spotted with my blood and Thancmar's to propitiate Nerthuz. Otherwise the Earth Goddess might waylay us, greedy to taste the life spirit of unknown travelers. Hearing the old priestess's adjurations as I knotted braids of hemp into a bridle, I looked again and again at my hands. No matter how often I reminded myself that no well-educated Roman believed in magic, the evidence of my eyes did not change: the skin was unmarked, smooth but for the calluses of my slave work at Hoheneih.

The old linen breeches and shirt I wore had once been someone else's, and ancient sweat of man and horse still permeated them. Spider nosed me all over, inhaling my strangeness. I tied on a makeshift rein, stood back, and looked at my staunch little stallion. He flicked his ears toward me, snorted, and nodded up and down.

"Time to go," I told him softly, and led him out of the byre.

Thancmar looked up from tying a fat aleskin on a small dun pony. He had lashed another bulging sack behind his saddle, presumably full of food. Striving for a resolute start to this ill-founded partnership, I greeted him with "I see we are not going to starve."

The dwarf glowered, red-eyed. His hair rioted like a fistful of broom-straw, and he wavered on his feet. "Is that a horse or a deer?" he sneered as Spider high-stepped fastidiously through the wet grass. Libyans are desert horses, after all.

So much for comradery. I hoisted myself onto my stallion's bare back and adjusted the sword slung across my shoulders, rolled in a blanket that would serve as cloak and bedding.

The she-wolf sloped through the underbrush, sat, and placidly scratched her ear. Thancmar's pony snorted and sidestepped. Spider's nostrils went wide, his eyes bulged, and he bolted, nearly dislodging me. Shivering and sweating, dark eyes sickled in white, he finally allowed me to halt him behind the longhouse.

Thancmar shuffled around the corner with the curious wolf padding beside him. Spider squealed and backed away.

"Get your beast out of here," I said furiously. Although Tig was wagging her tail, Spider kept crabbing backward. Even foals still wet from birthing have a terror of wolves; it is innate in the species.

"We need Tig. She warns us of danger. Eh, Tig?" Bending to ruffle his pet's fur, the dwarf almost toppled over. I realized that with the day just sprung and a desperate journey ahead of us, he was so drunk he could barely stand up.

Hroswitha appeared in the thinning mist. "Thancmar, shut Tig in the mill."

"But, *Amma*, his horse must learn—"

Spider laid his ears back and snapped his tail back and forth. Even though he was not a warhorse like my murdered Boss, my anger had infected him. He stamped his forefeet, a warning that he was about to charge. The she-wolf prudently slunk behind her master's stubby legs.

I was on the point of leaving the dwarf and his pet and setting off by myself. But before I could knee Spider, the old woman lifted her staff and ordered, "*Rôva.*" Be still.

While moisture pattered from the trees onto ferns and shrubs and Tig howled and scratched from behind the mill door, the dwarf clambered aboard his pony. His trousered legs thrust out comically on either side of the beast's barrel. He glared fiercely, daring me to ridicule him. Once I would have laughed at such a sight, but as Ingiomar's slave I myself had too often been the butt of mockery.

By the time Hroswitha had finished what I hoped was a final prayer for Austro's protection, the sun was burning through the fog. When she came to me, droplets of mist still sparkled in the thistledown of her hair and glittered on her pale lashes.

In a voice fissured like crazed glass, she said, "I did not think you were the man for my daughter's daughter." She tapped my leg with a bony finger. "Prove that you are."

I followed Thancmar on the familiar track to Hoheneih for a short distance; then he veered onto a trail to the east that I had bypassed. The clearing we came to had once been a grove of young trees, to judge by the chopped stubs that remained. Moss had been ripped by boots and hooves, leaving dark scars. Oblong patches of barren earth, spaded flat, showed where tents had been pitched. Black scabs of firepits pocked the clearing.

"They waited here half a moon for the baby to be born," Thancmar said bitterly.

"How did they know she was with child, when I did not?" I asked, but he just shook his head. No doubt her condition had eventually become obvious to all the local folk who brought their grain to be milled.

Over the sour reek of wet char hung the stink of a latrine trench, invisible in the ground mist. Evidently it had been left uncovered, contrary to Army routine. Glabrio must have reckoned that after all, no one lived nearby except barbarians.

I was unexpectedly aware not only of the mess my own people had left, but of the insult offered to the spirits of the place. Perhaps Hroswitha's spells had made me more Germanic. Or perhaps it was coldly Roman to welcome another reason for revenge.

The dwarf gestured to the trail, which continued under sodden and drooping foliage. "This is the way they have taken Aurima and the baby," he said, though the hoof-shaped rain puddles and horse dung already told the story.

Gazing at the damp imprint of a wheel, I imagined her in that cart, Glabrio's helpless prisoner—now with a head start of three days on us. "Let's go," I said, heeling Spider forward.

"Stop, Roman! This way, it is farther to the Amber Road."

"Then why did they take it?"

"Wait and see," he said, and turned his pony around.

The shorter way led into a drowned forest.

After crossing the mill dam to the Thaya's southern bank, I pushed the pace, splashing through rivulets that spilled across the trail. To any pursuer, our traces in the rain-sodden turf would be as obvious as a sign painted on a forum wall.

Around midmorning the arching trees thinned, then parted, and we came upon a ghostly lowland. Hundreds of bone-gray trunks thrust up from a white shroud of mist, their stiff limbs contorted as if struggling to breathe.

I stopped behind Thancmar. The trail descended into a muddy slough, then disappeared into a green-scummed pool and was lost in the mist. I strained to see where it reemerged. "Must we go through this?"

"It is the fastest way." The dwarf reached for his aleskin and took a couple of mighty swigs.

I gave Spider a nudge. He stepped ahead and then back, uncomfortable with the sponginess beneath his feet. "Have you been here before?"

"Stop talking!" he hissed. "You will disturb them." He groped in a saddlebag, pulled out strips of cloth, and held one out to me. "Tie this around your face."

I sniffed it dubiously. It was oiled and smelled strongly of mint. "Disturb whom?"

"Do you want to catch your Romans, or not?" He tied the cloth over his nose and mouth, like a river-raker about to haul a dead body from the Tiber. I did the same.

His pony inched forward, its hooves denting the soggy turf. He stopped it at the water's edge and reached back a hand. "Let me have your neck-ring," he said, muffled by the mask.

"What?" I was distracted by low shapes in the mist.

"We are giving it as an offering to Nerthuz. To keep us safe." He glowered at me impatiently, his hand still outstretched.

As apprehensive as I was about entering this doomful swamp, I would not sacrifice my gold torc in the hope of easing his fears. Was it not enough that Hroswitha had already given Nerthuz our blood? "No," I said, and kneed Spider past him to splash into the stagnant pool.

"Roman!" he called after me, panicked.

I held up a healed hand as a reminder that his grandmother had asked Austro to protect me.

Water swirled fetlock-deep around Spider's legs as he took a few more cautious steps. His ears swiveled, alert for danger. I urged him farther into the mist.

The sky vanished. Through the haze appeared channels of green water that snaked around mudbanks and islets of grass. Lifeless trees, attenuated and grim, loomed like frozen sentinels. Some had fallen, their bare branches fanning from the water like the ribs of ancient monsters.

I hesitated. From behind us came a flurry of splashes, and Thancmar pushed his dun pony into the lead. "Follow me."

We crept between the dead trees on a path he alone could discern. The horses scrambled up onto grassy hummocks, then stepped down into water that might be knee-high or belly-high or barely above their hooves.

I tried to restore my bravery by fixing my thoughts on Aurima, but she seemed far away, part of another life. In the blinding mist I could not see how far this swamp extended, could smell nothing but mint, and could hear little through the cloth tied over my ears.

Friduric might be following us, wading soft-footed through the mud. Or something less corporeal that dwelled in this spectral boneyard ... perhaps the "they" that Thancmar dreaded ... ?

Get a grip on yourself, man. This was only a backwater where the flooding river had long ago killed a stand of trees. Any competent engineer and work crew could drain the area in a pair of weeks. I distracted myself by planning how it might be done: where the canals would be, the berms ...

Ahead of us, a flock of small white things lifted in unison and ghosted into the mist.

Spider snorted and jibbed. My heart jolted.

Birds. Only birds.

Then I felt him lurch. He trod on a submerged branch whose other end whipped from the water like a striking snake.

I could not risk losing him to an injury. I slid off his bare back into the water. Feeling the way with each step of a bare foot, I led him by the bridle behind Thancmar's pony.

And on. And on. It began to seem that we had entered an underworld, an Erebus swarming with unseen wraiths who waited only for a spill of blood to show themselves. I was Odysseus, with Thancmar as a drunken, diminutive Teiresias guiding me deeper and deeper ...

Then they struck—"they" from whom we were hiding our faces. The black clouds of minute, bloodthirsty insects were too real, their bites too painful, to sustain supernatural fantasies. We struggled forward, slapping and scratching, and were at last rewarded when the trail climbed to higher ground, among trees that lived and breathed.

By then Thancmar and I were as wet as the horses. As restorative as it was to enter the rampant green forest and unmask, too little sunlight penetrated to dry our clothes. Before long my inner thighs were stinging. Neither Spider nor I was accustomed to bareback riding under such conditions, and my wet breeches abraded hot patches in my skin and on his back.

It was a temptation to fling the cursed trousers into the underbrush, but they might be useful if I needed to pose as a native. I wrapped them around my waist, dried myself and the horse as well as I could, and remounted.

Other narrow trails and animal paths crossed or joined our track. Several times I stopped to listen, fearing an ambush. Thancmar's euphoria at our safe passage through the swamp had revived his disdain for me. "Did I not say that Tig could warn us of danger?" he needled.

We came to a wide bend in the track. "Wait here," the dwarf called out. He hopped off, hung his reins on a branch, and disappeared into the trees.

I waited irritably, scratching my itches, with half a mind to ride on alone. He would have to catch up after he had eased himself. But then I heard his voice, raised in the same singsong chant in which his sister and grandmother spoke to divinities.

"This place is sacred to Thunraz," he explained upon returning. "We cannot pass without his blessing." He undid the lashing of the aleskin and took several gulps.

A similar ceremony was repeated near an old beech tree. Offerings had been thrown into its boughs: a bronze armlet, a glittery string of beads, a knife, small game with fur or feathers. The dwarf thanked the tree spirit for allowing us to pass, tossed a silver ring into its foliage, and again slaked his thirst from the aleskin.

I had held my peace all this while, but now impatience got the better of me. "If you stop at every tree and bush, we are not going to find your sister in time."

"Spirits are everywhere, Roman." He waved his arm around. "I know we must hurry. So I stop to honor only those who are most old and powerful." He took another swallow of ale and wiped his mustache with the edge of his hand.

I nudged Spider forward. "I am not waiting for you, little man."

Thancmar remounted from a fallen tree, muttering to himself. Although he continued to stop now and then, his prayers grew appreciably shorter.

My thoughts returned to Aurima. Over and over I imagined her bewildered and frightened, believing me dead. Ten Special Cohort cavalrymen made stiff odds, even if Thancmar was any sort of fighter. I needed a plan.

Spider balked as a chipmunk ran across the twisting trail. After the morning's ordeal, he was as edgy as I was. I soothed him: "It is nothing."

Then, behind us, a horse screamed.

22: METAMORPHOSIS

At first I thought the dwarf and his pony were being attacked, but he too had turned to look behind us. A man's cry of fear undercut the frenzied shriek. With a wild thrashing of foliage a grayish blur streaked around the curve of the trail toward us, and it became obvious what had agitated him.

"Tig!" Thancmar jumped off his pony and embraced the panting wolf, heedless of the green scum streaking her wet fur. Wagging her tail triumphantly, she licked his bearded face.

Spider panicked, bunching his haunches to flee. I kicked him up the bank into the forest. That was near enough to the horse's own inclination that he smashed a good hundred feet through the trees before I could stop him.

I slid off and freed my sword from its bindings. Keeping far back in the foliage, I crept toward the sound of men arguing in Germanic.

There were two of them, both afoot. One was still wrestling with his pony, a white mare, which twitched and bucked in fright. The other had been unhorsed. His mount watched as he picked himself up, as if surprised by what it had done.

I knew both men. The one who had lost his seat was Wido, a narrow-faced brute with a blotchy scar on his head where a slab of hair and flesh had once been sliced away. He had used to enjoy knocking me down when I could not lift my arms to defend myself. The other was lanky Egino, who had fled when I held a sword on his friend Friduric. Both of their ponies were wet to the flank. Somehow they had followed us through the swamp.

Wido was saying, "Hit the bitch, stupid! Make her pay attention. You, Harefoot!" He snapped his fingers at his own mount. "Come here."

Their spears lay scattered across the track. Not hunting javelins, but heavy *frameae*: man-killers. "Must have been . . . chasing a deer," puffed Egino, trying to quiet his pony. "Thank Nerthuz it did not stop. Since all you did was scream like a woman."

"Shut up! All you did was dance in the road with your horse."

"Maybe it was a wolf spirit seeking the Roman. That is why we are not hurt."

"Hah! Tell that to the *fraujaz*. He wants the Roman's head, not tales of spirits." Managing at last to catch his pony, Wido slapped its nose for its temerity.

Hiding behind a tree, I rose quietly to my feet with a stone the size of an apple. One moment ... two ... three ... Finally both of them were looking elsewhere. I hurled the stone into the foliage on the other side of the trail.

Both of the Marcomanni whirled toward the swish and crackle. Egino clutched the reins of his jittery horse even tighter. Wido ducked to pick up a spear.

By then I was leaping down onto the trail. I flung the wet breeches over Egino's head and without pausing lunged at Wido. He had enough warning to half turn, and my sword caught him under the arm. I shoved it hard through cloth and flesh. He coughed and fell with the sword caught in him, so I let it go and grabbed his spear instead.

Egino had just yanked the clinging breeches off his face. For an instant he gaped at me. Then, with extraordinary slowness, he reached for a battle knife sheathed beside his saddle. I threw myself at him, driving him back against his mount, and rammed the spearhead between his teeth. His legs buckled. He slid to his knees, trailing blood down the saddle and his pony's side, until it stepped away and he fell into the grass of the trail.

I wrested the spear free and glanced around wildly to see if I had missed a threat. Nothing stirred but the two ponies, backing away from the explosion of blood. I dropped the spear to grab their reins. If they fled home to Hoheneih, the search would quickly turn in our direction.

"Thancmar!" The shout broke apart in my throat, and I had to call his name again. Once more I turned around to make sure the two warriors had been alone.

The dwarf peered through a stand of ferns. "Mother Nerthuz save us!" He jumped down the bank with the wolf at his heels.

The ponies' fright nearly lifted me off my feet. "Keep her back," I shouted.

He caught Tig by her ruff. "You k-killed them both?" He waddled over to the two bodies. "These are Ingiomar's men, Wido and Egino."

"Make the fucking wolf go away, so I can give you these fucking ponies to hold!"

Something in me had changed. I never would have thought I could look a man in the eyes and kill him. The two gate guards at Hoheneih had been mere shapes in the dark.

"We could have just taken their horses. Made them w-walk back."

"Listen, little man," I said, savage with nerves. "I am not going to be captured by Ingiomar again. Send that beast away and hold these ponies."

My sword thrust had just missed a belt on which Wido carried a sheathed hunting knife. I gouged a new prong-hole and buckled the belt on myself. His body did not want to give up my sword; I had to stand on it to free the blade. Hot bile rushed up my throat.

Thancmar was as white as Luna marble. "The *fraujaz* is going to think I did this."

"Then let us make sure he knows it was me."

A few minutes later, I stood back to assess the effect. Heads awry,

Ingiomar's two men sat facing down the bloodstained trail, propped on sticks, ready to greet him when he came for them. Animals might ravage them first, but the macabre gesture satisfied me.

I thought of one more thing. The soles of my feet were tough, but there was no point in courting injury. I took Wido's soft leather shoes and put them on.

As I turned to reclaim the ponies' reins from the dwarf, I saw the horror in his eyes. "Do you wish to return to your mill?" I said. "Sorry, it is too late now."

I expected my savagery to have dissolved Hroswitha's magic. But except for grime and other men's blood, my fingers were still whole and unmarked. It seemed the goddess of light did not scorn vengeance.

Thancmar stood guzzling from the aleskin as if he had been crawling through the Gedrosian Desert for weeks. "Easy," I cautioned him. "The day is not yet done."

I climbed onto Egino's pony. With the sword snugged on my back, Wido's hunting knife at my waist, and two spears in a sling hanging from the saddle, I felt better equipped for whatever else we would encounter. The spare mounts might be needed for Aurima's rescue, and in the meantime a respite would allow Spider's back to heal.

Thancmar knotted the aleskin, sighed, and sagged against his pony's side with his arms flung over its back. "I thought . . . we were just going to bring her home," he said in a muffled voice. "So everything can be the same again."

"It is only beginning," I said harshly. "The soldiers who took her are not going to say they made a mistake and hand her over."

"But you were a . . . a *tribunus* . . . Are they not going to obey you?"

I laughed. My laugh was starting to sound like Caligula's humorless bark. "No, half brother. Unless we catch them, they are going to kill your sister. Get on your horse."

He straightened up. One hand flopped atop the aleskin, but he moved it away. After he mounted, I gave him the reins of Wido's pony. As we continued along the trail, each towing an extra horse, the she-wolf went the other way, released from whatever command he had given her, to investigate the bloody disorder we were leaving behind.

The shred of twilight sky that I could see turned deeper and deeper blue as the trees drew it slowly into their dark grasp. I could barely see my companion now. He had scribed a ring in the mossy turf around us with the point of his sword and had pronounced a lengthy incantation on it. From Aurima I knew this was a conjure circle, a ring of magic to keep us safe from wild animals and prowling spirits.

He wanted to light a fire for further protection, but I would not risk anyone being drawn to our camp. It was disquieting to know that Ingiomar had already sent two sets of pursuers to the mill, expecting me to look for Aurima there. After warning Hroswitha and Thancmar of my escape, the first group had unknowingly passed me on their way back to Hoheneih. Later the *fraujaz* had sent Wido and Egino to make sure I had not turned up. Discovering that the little miller was gone, they must have guessed he was helping me to flee and had chased us until Tig overtook them.

"Used to her, that's why," the dwarf was saying. "Knew Tig when she was a pup." He rambled on with slurred praise of his pony's speed and cleverness.

To avoid thinking about Ingiomar's tenacity I said, "Tell me about your father."

"My father?" Thancmar broke off a piece of the barley bread that he had boasted of baking himself. "My father was Ansigar of the Quadi. He won Ammisia, sister's daughter of the great king Marbodo, against many, many others who wished to marry her." He chewed. "The king favored him, and Ansigar came to have a war band of his own." I heard a crunch. He grunted and spat out what might have been grit from the millstone. "All he lacked was a son, a tall and handsome son that other men might envy."

The aleskin glugged. "Instead," he said, "the gods gave him me. So he left the beautiful Ammisia. He went to fight Romans with the Cherusci, and was killed."

I did not comment. In Rome, a dwarf born to a noble family would be exposed at birth. Poorer parents might raise him to beg outside temples or turn cartwheels at parties.

"Afterward, only Ingiomar dared to marry a woman who birthed creatures like me." He belched. "He did not like me, of course, so I went to live with *Amma*."

"At the mill."

Thancmar scratched insect bites on his arm. "I could not be a warrior like Friduric, so he had the Romans build the mill for me. Back when they still loved him."

I had no reply. In a way I knew what the malformed boy had undergone, for I too had lived in my brother's shadow. Then I was ashamed of the comparison, for I had been free to overcome my failings.

When I got up quietly to check on the horses, his voice drifted to me across the small clearing: "We need a fire, Roman. There are bears, and worse."

"Go to sleep; Tig protects us," I said, although I had no idea if the she-wolf was near. She seemed prone to wandering off when it suited her.

Despite his fears he was snoring, wrapped in his saddle blanket, when I returned. I tried to make myself comfortable with Egino's saddle under my shoulders, gazing up at the ragged patch of stars that the trees revealed. One of my hands rested on my sword hilt, the other atop a pair of the dead men's spears.

I was undecided whether or not to leave Thancmar behind. There did not seem much advantage in dragging along a drunken dwarf to help free Aurima. On the other hand, he was her brother—or half brother, anyway—and he had volunteered to come. Who could tell whether a little man with a tame wolf might not be useful?

While he slept, I tried to guess which constellation hung fragmented overhead. Checked on the horses again. Examined the dressings plastered on Spider's sores, hoping I had applied the same herb Aurima used for healing.

During the journey from Rome she had healed me, too, never doubting that I was the man I imagined myself to be. Dementedly in love, I had been able to forget that she and my father had acted because I would not—believing myself bound by my oath to Caligula, by my faith in a God of Truth who rewarded honor and duty. A faith now scoured away as ruthlessly as moss on a campground.

Why had I not saved in my memory every moment of our traveling together? That would not be all I had of her, would it?

Half asleep, Spider grunted in contentment as I stroked his neck. I murmured into his ear, "I am a father." He sighed and put his head on my shoulder.

Without my knowing, she had nourished within her a child we made. The grandson my father had hoped for, so that our family would not end.

I heard his voice from a year past, telling me of his first fatherhood as we traveled home from celebrating some client's son's naming day. Holding back the litter's curtain as I walked beside him, he had said to me, "I went to sacrifice to Juno Primigenia, hoping your mother's labor would be ended when I returned. Yet it was still a day before the babe was born."

I kept my eyes on the bobbing head of my horse. Beyond it, the pavement's irregularities sprang out in the shifting light of the footman's torch.

"He ailed from the beginning," Father said. "One hopes, of course. But it does not do to become attached to young children."

He had never before spoken to me of his firstborn, Titus, who lived less than a year. Perhaps I needed reminding of the importance of indifference to one's offspring.

We were passing the end of the Circus Maximus. A great bonfire near the Temple of Janus honored the god of beginnings.

"When Publius was born, I was on campaign and did not see him for two years. I still remember coming home from the North"—a smile crept into his voice—"and finding him there in the atrium, a strange little boy with dark curls."

I had plodded on silently.

"'Welcome, Papa,' he said. And my heart leaped with joy."

He fell quiet. After a moment he gave a sigh, almost inaudible over the bearers' shuffling steps, and let the litter curtain fall between us.

Grief at his sacrifice of Publius and himself filled my eyes. He would have been horrified, of course, to find himself the grandsire of a half-German boy. Perhaps he would never have gotten over it. But the family, in whatever unorthodox, unpatrician form, would go on.

Did this unseen creature, this new little Titus, look like me? Were his eyes blue like mine, or silver-green like his mother's? Was his hair fair or the color of copper?

Something large rustled in the underbrush a knife-cast away. The horses stamped in unease. Not thinking of bear or boar, much less of the *lemures* of two unburied men, I shouted, "Get away," in a voice strident with willingness to kill whatever obstructed me.

Thancmar convulsed in his blankets and sat up.

"Your turn to stand guard," I told him, as whatever had rustled faded into the night.

23: VENGEANCE

"I was not afraid," he grumbled. "Not for an eye-blink." He twitched the reins to quicken his pony.

He had been in a sulky mood since first light. Supposing him to be vexed by the spirits of murdered men and disrespected trees, I tried to tease him out of his temper. "Yes, you were. You yelled loud enough when you sat up to wake the king in Bruna. Did you think I was going to cut 'S P Q R' into your hide and send you to Hades?"

"Cut what?"

I had forgotten that Germans are illiterate. "Letters that mean 'the Roman Senate and people.'" I pulled my pony's head away from a clump of grass. The trees on one side of the trail had retreated, opening up a meadow gay with wildflowers. As we trotted along, the sunlit view did much to lighten my own mood.

"Aurima tried to teach me letters," he said. "A waste of time. Why look at marks on tree bark when you can hear a singer tell a tale?"

"Writing is useful if you want to send a message to someone far away."

"Huh. Is your tree bark going to send itself?"

"No."

"Then the messenger can tell your message. Better, probably." His caustic tone added the unheard words "you simpleton."

On impulse I asked, "Did Aurima leave me a message?"

"Eh?" He slitted his eyes.

"Before the soldiers took her. Did she write on tree bark and say to give it to me?"

"No." He flicked something off his trousered thigh. "Of course not."

I had judged too many untruthful soldiers to believe him. "Did she, Thancmar?"

"Stupid girl," he burst out. "Always talking about Rome, about men with black faces and gardens inside houses and stone shapes of women with no clothes. Trying to make writing for our people. I hated that she was different. That you made her different."

He dropped the rein of the pony behind him, kicked his own steed, and charged forward as if three-headed Cerberus were after him. The wolf raced happily alongside.

"Wait," I shouted. The trail climbed a slope. I urged my own mount after him, hoping to catch up before he pitched over the top into a ravine or a patch of briars.

The dwarf hurtled over the crest. I slowed my pace, and was glad of it when the *woo-ooo* of a horn sounded on the far side of the hill.

I tugged my mount and Spider off the trail and into the trees. The pony Thancmar had been towing remained in plain sight, but I dared not retrieve it.

Leaving my two horses tethered, I took a spear from the sling and climbed the hill under cover of the woods. Easing over leaf litter and moss, I darted from tree trunk to windfall to cluster of ferns, keeping the spear low to avoid branches and foliage.

The light through the trees grew brighter. I crouched low, thrust a few twigs into my hair to obscure the shape of my head, and crept closer to peer over the hill crest.

The landscape below looked oddly familiar. A pasture dotted with cows spread across a valley bottom. Thancmar was talking with the cowherd while Tig crouched nearby. Beyond them, a sprinkling of huts and a corral with a few ponies bordered a trail leading up to a hill fort. The palisade had no gates, just an overlap to snare assailants.

A trickle of cold ran down my spine.

There on the right, which had been the left when I arrived with Ollius, Rufus, and the scout Tudrus, were the pasture and the chestnut tree where we had camped. This was Grozhauga, Berinhard's stronghold. Or perhaps Chlothar's, since Berinhard was dead. Where Chlothar had killed Ollius, and thrown me on the dung heap with his mutilated corpse.

Men were streaming out of the gateway in response to the horn blast. Thancmar turned and raised a hand to greet them. Casually, he cast a glance uphill.

Sorry, half brother; you are on your own.

Presumably he was known in this part of the Mark. After all, there could not be many dwarves. But how would he explain what he was doing here? Was he going to betray me, the Roman who had made his sister hatefully different, who had begotten a child of enemy blood on her? He might reckon that Chlothar could raise enough warriors to rescue her without me. And by sending word of my whereabouts to Ingiomar, he could collect twenty cattle for himself.

A tall fair-haired man strode ahead of the others, sword in hand. When he reached Thancmar, he sheathed the sword and held out both arms in welcome. I did not need to see the white streak in his beard to recognize Chlothar.

The cold spread through me.

INGIOMAR. GLABRIO. MAELO. FRIDURIC. CHLOTHAR. LAMIA.

This trail to the Amber Road ran right by his stronghold. Why had the dwarf not told me we would pass Grozhauga?

I watched him enter the palisade with Chlothar. The others gave the wolf ample room as she trotted behind her master. Slithering backward from the hilltop, I heard the frantic whinnies of horses inside the walls who caught her scent.

What to do now? If he betrayed me to Chlothar, a search might sweep up the hill at any moment.

The pony Thancmar had abandoned wandered over to join mine. So I had three horses now, two of which might be recognized as belonging to dead men.

While they cropped grass in tattered patches of sunlight, I hunkered down against a tree trunk to think out the best course. Caution urged me to backtrack and find a secure place to hide for the rest of the day. Then, leaving the ponies, I could try to sneak across the valley with Spider. If the night sky stayed clear, there would be a sliver of waxing moon to help me find the track on the other side. And after daybreak it would be less than a full day's ride to the Amber Road.

On the other hand, there was danger in waiting for nightfall. Even if the dwarf did not expose me, Wido's and Egino's bodies were sure to be discovered before long.

I could try now, in daylight, to circumvent Grozhauga by forcing my way through the forest, but nothing unnerved me more than the possibility of losing myself among the trees. It was infuriating to know that even I, a civilized man in Rome's eighth century, was not immune to *pavor saltūs*.

Damn Thancmar! Why had I let him complicate my mission?

Hoofbeats drummed on the trail. I grabbed the spear and scuttled to a place where I could see.

Thancmar rode over the top of the hill on his pony, his short legs outthrust on either side. He reined in where he had left me, peering into the trees. "Roman," he hissed. "Are you here?"

I held still, expecting Chlothar and his men to pour over the crest behind him.

He rode a few more lengths down the trail. "Where are you? Chlothar expects me to return. I need to speak to you!"

As far as I could tell, he was alone. I rose quietly and stepped out behind him. "Here I am," I said, aiming the spear.

"What are you doing?" He turned his mount so quickly that he slid in the saddle.

No sign that he had been followed. I lowered the spear. "I said nothing about you," he insisted, nudging his mount closer. "I said Tig went off when I was hunting, and I found her nearby." His gaze flew to the hilltop, then back.

"You are not a good liar, half brother. Your hunting spears are still tied to your saddle."

"I said I did not see anything to chase." Thancmar grimaced. "Now they think I am a bad hunter." This disturbed him. "Chlothar wants me to stay at Grozhauga tonight."

"So what are you doing here?"

"I said I dropped my luck charm when I rode up the hill."

"That is a better lie, Thancmar."

"I..." He looked down, running the reins back and forth between his hands.

I said, "Are you still with me? Or is this as far as you go?"

A stubborn and suspicious look came over his face. "I am hungry and thirsty. And I do not want to ride all night."

I could not trust him with my plan. "Do you still want to free your sister?"

"Of course!"

"Then do this one thing: before moonset, leave Grozhauga and hide in the woods on the track to the Amber Road. What do you say?"

He nodded guardedly.

"Wait for me there."

"What are you going to do?"

"Do not ask." I scuffed the grass with my toe. "I hope you find your luck charm."

I took a few swallows from the flabby aleskin and ate stale bread and some cheese before he rode back to rejoin Chlothar. Too late I realized I should have warned him not to drink too much, but perhaps he would figure that out for himself.

What I intended was neither sensible nor prudent. But Chlothar had taken the life of my loyal bodyguard. My family ring. And my father's gold torc, given to him by Germanicus Caesar himself.

I returned to the horses and untied the roll of clothes bundled behind my saddle. The still-damp breeches unfolded into my hand, along with Egino's torn tunic, which I had used to wipe his blood off his mount's side.

Aurima, take heart. I will be with you soon, beloved.

While waiting for the sun to sink, I began my preparations.

The boy at the door of the *halla*, a youngster whose balls could hardly have dropped, held up his hand to block a limping stranger who leaned on a spear shaft. His eyes widened at the bloody bandage, the empty knife sheath on a belt girding a filthy tunic, the sagging breeches. He tried unsuccessfully to deepen his voice: "Who are you?"

Squint-eyed and sour-faced, I whacked his shin with the spear. "Out of my way."

"Hey! Leave that outside, whoever you are."

"So says the stripling with two good legs." I pushed past him into the entrance of the *halla*, where silver-maned Berinhard and his companions had greeted me so perfidiously, and where Ollius had died. In the smoky feasting hall beyond, a score of men crowded noisily around a table cluttered with food and drinking horns.

I did not have time to see whether Thancmar was there, for the boy was intent on his duty as door guard. "Listen, you! No weapons in the hall, by order of the *fraujaz*."

"That is Chlothar, *ja*?" I spat on the ground, then wiped my beard reflexively. My tangled hair was much shorter than most warriors', but I hoped the bloodstained binding on my head distracted from it. "I do not want to go in, you stupid pup."

"Then what do you want?"

One of the diners had noticed our standoff. "Need help, Ivo?"

I pushed my dirty face close to the boy's and snarled, "I want to see your *fraujaz*. I brought him something."

"What?"

"Just fetch him, pup."

At last he said, "Stay here," and went into the feast hall.

Fear fluttered in my stomach then. I had stepped of my own will into an arena full of lions. If Chlothar recognized me, or if I tried and failed in what I meant to do, I would die—quickly or slowly, however the dice fell. Aurima would be lost, the infant as well, all because I was set on avenging the honor of my *familia*.

Freezing my features in the scowl I had adopted, I glared after the boy Ivo. Thancmar was not at the table. Good; he must have heeded my warning. Best of all, I saw none of Ingiomar's men among the Quadi warriors.

Chlothar rose from the end of the table, looking toward me. Barechested in the heat, he was more muscular than I had remembered. My heart raced as he lumbered through the smoke toward me, responding good-naturedly to the sallies of others.

When he came into the aura of torchlight by the open doors, a handful of rings woven into his beard glittered at me. Among the plain circlets of hand-hammered gold and copper was one of silver that bore a signet. And on the bulge of his upper arm, crimped so it would fit, was my father's gold torc.

My apprehension hardened into resolve. He asked who I was. "Meino of the Marcomanni, son of Rosmunda," I lied.

His eyes narrowed. "I do not know you, Meino."

I had counted on the *fraujaz* of Grozhauga being unacquainted with a cook's assistant from Hoheneih. "I bring a gift from Ingiomar Ironhand, if you want it."

"From Ingiomar?" Chlothar looked me over more carefully. "Where is it?"

"Outside."

His gaze lingered on my bandage, stained with Egino's blood. "What befell you?"

I let him see the quirk of a grimace. "Ingiomar's gift threw me."

The lines around his eyes relaxed. "Hah." His mustaches spread in a grin, and he turned toward the doors.

Suddenly the boy was there. "Let me go with you, *Fader*. I want to see what Ingiomar gave you."

Merda! How could I discourage the man's son from accompanying him?

"Yes, let us go and see this gift of Ironhand's." A man with elaborate wrist tattoos disentangled himself from his bench at the table.

I grunted disapprovingly and shook my head.

"What?" Chlothar said.

I lowered my voice. "I rode him hard after he threw me off, and he is tired." I flicked my eyes meaningfully toward Chlothar's companions. "In the morning he is going to be twice the horse."

"*Ja?*" He raised his palm to the tattooed warrior and the others. "Tomorrow, my brothers. For now, I give two little flowers of bronze to whoever drinks the most and can still stand up!" The diners cheered raucously and shouted to the serving women.

Little flowers of bronze. Probably a pair of the bronze rosettes weighting the leather strips at the shoulders and waist of what had once been my padded undertunic. I should have known that my armor had become part of Chlothar's plunder.

"Come, lad." Chlothar circled a big arm around the youngster's shoulders and pulled him forward. I followed them, so beset by misgivings that I almost forgot to limp. No one followed.

Spider gleamed like a pearl in the light of the crescent moon. "He belonged to that Roman," I explained, hobbling faster to catch the two eager Germans. "Ingiomar sends him to thank you for your help."

"The one who raped his daughter, *ja?* It was a pleasure to help." Chlothar slowed and turned to me. "Did he catch the turd yet?"

"Since I left, perhaps." I hardly knew what I was saying, so intently was I studying his vulnerable spots. The bushy beard hid his throat; his massive biceps protected his armpits; knife-tangling breeches covered his lower belly. This was going to be difficult. And the boy—would I have to kill him first?

We were nearly to the brush corral. My pulse hammered in my throat.

"Ah," Chlothar sighed. He had caught sight of Spider, whose chiseled profile rose above the smaller ponies in the pen. Scenting me, the stallion pushed the ponies out of his way and came over to the fence. His nostrils flared inquisitively.

I hung back so he would not betray me with a friendly nuzzle. "Does the gift please you?" Up under the ribs and into the heart; that was what Ollius would advise.

"I am very pleased." Chlothar beamed. He began to swing toward me, arm wide, opening his chest as a target. My right hand on the spear loosened

—

And he tugged his son against him. "Look, Ivo. Now that is a horse, *ja?*" They both turned toward Spider.

I reached under my sleeve and grabbed the knife I had bound to my upper arm. The spear fell with a thump. Chlothar spun around, letting go of his son.

I yanked the boy against me and pressed the knife to his throat. He wriggled furiously. "Tell him to be still," I hissed, "or he dies here."

Chlothar edged along the fence, closer to me. "What are you doing?"

"Do not move, either of you." I backed away, dragging the boy. In my desperation I bore down too hard on the knife blade. Ivo squeaked, and blood oozed onto my thumb.

Chlothar froze. "Let him go. He is just a boy. Ivo, be still!"

My captive stopped struggling. I inhaled deeply to calm myself. "Is he your only son? Good. So am I, an only son."

"You must be moon-witted." Chlothar glanced up at his palisaded stronghold. "One shout and my men will be on you."

"Not before your boy dies. Give me what I want, and maybe he lives."

"What do you want?" His eyes danced all around, seeking a way to disarm me, to get the upper hand without sacrificing his son.

"First, the silver ring in your beard."

"Silver . . . ? What? Which one?" His fingers hovered over the brambly mass.

"That one. Hurry."

He plucked at the ring, winced, and jerked it free.

"Ivo, put out your hand. Take it. Good." Without easing the pressure on the knife I grabbed the ring from the boy's fingers and thrust it in my mouth, next to my cheek.

"Thief," the boy choked. "I am going to kill you!"

"Now the gold ring on your arm. Quickly! My hand is tired."

Chlothar wrested the torc off, leaving a dark circle in his flesh. "Take it, Ivo," I ordered. I meant to drop it inside my tunic, where it would be caught by the cinched belt.

The boy grasped the torc. But instead of letting me take it from him, he struck me on the kneecap with it. "Kill him, *Fader!*"

My knee buckled at the blow, and I nearly cut his throat without meaning to. He squirmed around, flailing with his fists. I cracked the hilt of the knife down on his head.

Seeing his son crumple to the ground, Chlothar must have thought I had slain him. He roared and launched himself at me, his face contorted with rage. I had barely time to turn my wrist before he knocked me to the ground beneath him.

And then he lay still, a heavy weight upon my chest and hips, with wetness flooding between us. His ale-soused breath gusted once, and then . . . did not.

I struggled to push him off. The knife had driven deeply between his stomach and heart, and every last *ligula* of blood in him must have pumped out on me. Only clamping my teeth on the treasured ring kept me from vomiting.

The boy Ivo still lay senseless on the ground. I hoped I had not killed him. Perhaps I should have hoped I had, since I had slain his father.

Spider tossed his head and shied away at the stench of blood. I ripped off my tunic, which had soaked up the worst of it. So far, all was quiet within the palisade. I pulled Egino's hunting knife from Chlothar's body, wiped it on a dry part of the tunic, and slid it back into its sheath.

What else? The torc, which had caused it all. I snatched it up, fitted it on my neck, and squeezed the ends together.

The stallion tried to sidle away, but I seized his rein and leaped onto his back, then caught the tethers of the two ponies I had penned with him. Leaving behind the bodies that lay motionless in the last light of a setting moon, I urged all three horses toward the notch in the distant trees that would lead to the Amber Road.

24: GHOST

Only stars lit the sky when Spider saw the wolf. He stopped, jolting me out of a drowse. The two ponies crowded against him. Predator and prey stared at each other, motionless.

"Tig," I said hoarsely.

"Roman?" Thancmar stepped out of the woods in front of me. "Where —?" He staggered backward. "Keep away from me, *geist!*"

Indeed, I felt as boneless as a ghost. "I am thirsty," I croaked. "Fetch me ale."

After more convincing, he brought me the refilled aleskin. I stretched out a hand—a hand that still bore no traces of clawing and digging in the cave at Hoheneih.

"What happened?" He caught sight of the ring on my finger, and then must have noticed the torc around my neck. "Where did you get those?"

I just shook my head. I was mortally tired. "Can you see to lead the way?"

"Now? In the dark?" He swigged from the aleskin himself. "What happened?"

"Later," I said. "Lead on. If anyone comes, hide."

I swayed in the saddle, half dozing, drifting in and out of time. My knife haft chopped down on the boy's skull, and he slumped silently. Chlothar sprang, arms outstretched, and collapsed upon me. And there was blood: blood all over my arms and legs, my cheeks and chest and cock, blood marking me as a killer of men.

Thancmar's pony picked its way carefully along the trail, broadened now to a cart track, with the three other horses following in single file. Overhead, partly hidden by foliage, stretched the white avenue of the Milk Road, the *via lactea*, which Aurima called Wodunaz's Way. The stars cast our shadows beneath us.

At daybreak we stopped in the same clearing where my little troop had paused on the way to Berinhard's. I should have made an effort to wash myself in the brook, but cleanliness, that most Roman of virtues, no longer seemed to matter. The streaks and spatters were part of me, like a soldier's tattoo or a slave's brand.

"Chlothar is dead," I told Thancmar. When he said nothing, I added, "His son too, perhaps, but that was not meant."

After leading us through a night that to him was infested with spirits, he was white-faced and shaky. "Dead?" he echoed, about to lift down our provisions bag from his pony's back. For a moment his hand lingered over the hilt of Egino's battle knife. "Are you going to s-say why?"

"He swore to kill me. And when I did not die, he let Ingiomar take me."

"His men are going to come after you. After us b-both."

"I told them Ingiomar sent me. They are going to look in the other direction for me, near Hoheneih."

His lips twisted beneath his yellow mustache. "My people are very, very good at tracking, Roman." He drew out of his saddlebag a roasted chicken, twisted it, and tossed half into my lap. "Here: your last meal. From Grozhauga."

I stared down at it without appetite. But there was still Aurima to be saved, and I needed strength.

The she-wolf sat down beside me. I glanced at her. Her yellow eyes blinked, and she licked her lips.

"Tig, here," Thancmar ordered.

The wolf moved over to gaze raptly at her master's food. I tore into the chicken with my teeth. Chew, swallow. Chew, spit out gristle, swallow.

"She was happy with the child," Thancmar said abruptly. "She was going to take him to you in Carnuntum." He tossed a shred of chicken. Tig snapped it out of the air.

I stopped eating. The meat lumped in my mouth.

He went on, "She said you had lost so much, but here was something found."

I tried to resume chewing, but could not. My sight fogged.

Distantly I heard him tossing away the bones and repacking the provisions bag. He came back. "She did not write on tree bark," he said, and held something out to me.

It was a shard of unglazed pottery, perhaps part of a broken dish. On one side she had scratched two words in sprawling, misshapen letters:

TE AMO.

When I got up, Thancmar was waiting by his mount's head. He looked somewhere else as I wiped the heels of my hands across my eyes.

Behind me Tig crunched the remains of the chicken. I walked past Spider, taking a moment to rub his neck, and hoisted myself into the saddle of Wido's pony. "Lead on, brother," I said. "You are doing a good job of it."

The wolf vanished again, no doubt to lie up in the growing heat. Her absence calmed Spider, our two captured ponies, and me.

Late in the morning we encountered a trader's mule cart traveling west. It was laden with boxes packed in straw, probably pottery or glassware. The creaking of wheels and driver's curses warned us in time to conceal ourselves in the trees before it rumbled past, escorted by four tough-looking armed guards. No doubt their valor would be tested when they came upon the havoc I had caused at Grozhauga.

Not an hour later we reached the Amber Road, so much broader that it seemed a great thoroughfare. It was the third day since we had left Hros-witha and the mill.

The road was somnolent in the summer sun. Trees overhung the verges, their leaves unmoving. Flies buzzed. There was no traffic in either direction.

Thancmar's pony whisked his tail, spread his hind legs, and pissed voluminously. Thancmar woke from a doze. "Now what?"

"Now we watch."

"What if they have already passed?"

I dismounted stiffly and walked into the road. Glabrio's troop would have left a swarm of hoofprints heading south, as well as the wheel marks of their cart. But the only recent traces were those of the pottery merchant, who had been northbound before turning onto the track to Grozhauga.

Thancmar looked up the road toward Bruna. "Something comes."

We moved into the trees again. The scuffing he had heard resolved itself into five men on horseback, twelve or thirteen more on foot. No helmets, no armor. Not Romans.

"Slaves," Thancmar muttered. "Lugii, I expect."

I said, "Wait here." Half hidden in dappled shade at the road's edge, I led my pony toward the approaching men. If Thancmar was right, they were on their way to the slave market in Carnuntum.

The captives shuffled in single file, each linked to the next by a rope noosed around his neck. Or hers, for there were women among them. Their wrists had been bound, and the men's legs were hobbled. All were clad in filthy rags.

I bent down and lifted my pony's forefoot as if inspecting its hoof. By now the guards could see me, although mottled shadows obscured the blood and dirt on my chest and breeches. In case they were unscrupulous enough to think of adding me to their haul, I casually touched Wido's battle knife as I straightened.

The guard in the lead ambled closer. "The Goddess's greetings," I said.

He halted, squinting in the sun. Sweat had soaked the headband holding back his long hair and stained a dark V down the front of his tunic. "Do I know you?"

They are keen on knowing who is who, the Germans. "I am Meino of Hoheneih, searching for an escaped slave," I said, pretending to study the captives shambling by.

"You, too? We just passed your *fraujaz*'s son." He thrust a thumb over his shoulder. "You are all looking for the Roman to be given to Nerthuz, *ja*?"

I had not guessed that Friduric was so near. I managed to nod.

The guard winked. "The gods have not been good to Ingiomar lately." He turned back to his coffle of slaves.

"Wait," I said. "Have you heard of any Romans on the road? Soldiers?"

He reined his horse around and examined me more closely. "It is said there are horse soldiers at the Little Man's Mill. And by the bridge this morning"—he nodded over his shoulder—"I saw a Quadian whose horse had a Roman mark."

The Thaya bridge was only about five miles to the north. And the lone rider was likely to have been Glabrio's scout Tudrus on a cavalry-branded mount. "Good," I said. Depending how far ahead he had been ranging, the Praetorians and Aurima would pass us on the Amber Road this afternoon or in the morning.

"Good, is it? Well, remember, Meino: when you see Romans, let them have the road." Kneeing his mount, he loped back to the column.

When guards, slaves, and the cart that accompanied them had disappeared around a bend, Thancmar thrashed through the underbrush with the three other horses in tow. "I heard him," he said. "Friduric must have come straight from Hoheneih looking for you."

Like a good gambler, Ingiomar had hedged his bets. On the chance that I had fled east rather than south, he had sent his son to watch for me on the Amber Road.

"Maybe that is good news," I said. "Can you persuade him to help free your sister?" Friduric was surely accompanied by at least four or five men. With them on our side, we would have a far better chance of overpowering Glabrio's ten troopers.

The dwarf made a disgusted face. "He is not going to help. He does what Ingiomar says."

I did not believe it. Friduric might have gone along with banishing Aurima until her baby was born, but he would not be callous enough to surrender her to a Roman execution squad. "Everything depends on him. Tell him you came to save Aurima."

"Me? Roman, he is not going to listen to me."

I was tired of being called *Roman*. "If he asks, you know nothing about me. Or about anything happening at Grozhauga. You did not stay there, because . . . because Chlothar made sport of you." I paused. "Can you say that to him?"

"Never mind Friduric! Chlothar's men are going to catch us very soon." He was frightened now, not just angry. "Because of you, Roman, there is no hope for my sister."

"My name is Aquilo," I told him irritably. "Go find your brother. Say you are alone. Tell him he must help you take Aurima away from ten Romans."

"It is not ten men. Also there is the leader with big ears, there is Tudrus, some slaves, and the man with the cart. At least five and ten."

"Who is this man with the cart? You said nothing about him."

"He is big, strong, with hair like ice. They quarrel, him and Big Ears. After the baby is born, Big Ears wants to take Aurima the next day. The ice-hair man says no. He shows eight fingers." Eight more days.

A suspicion rose in me. "This man, did he have writing on his arm?" I sketched the Mithraic sun sign on my own wrist.

"*Ja*, just so. When he spoke to Aurima, I saw the mark."

Placidus had come with Glabrio. My old friend had taken part in abducting Aurima and her newborn child. So be it; let him not hinder me, or I would kill him too.

I said, "Very well, let us say fifteen men. Tell Friduric he is going to be a great warrior for helping to save your sister."

Thancmar's resistance gave way. He sighed. "You think they are coming soon?"

I had been trying to work this out since the slaver reported his sighting. There were not many suitable places to bivouac on this stretch of the Amber Road. The nearest, less than a mile north of us, was likely to be where Friduric's men were camped. That might also be the site Glabrio was making for. But if Tudrus told him a band of Marcomanni occupied it, the Special Cohort agent could not risk them accosting him with demands to release their priestess. He would wait until morning, hoping they would have moved on.

I could be wrong. The rider might have been someone else, the troop neaer than I thought, or Glabrio too pigheaded to stop before reaching the campsite he wanted. *Maybe, maybe, maybe.* My head buzzed with weariness; I was too short of sleep to think clearly.

"I don't know," I told Thancmar. "Go now, so Friduric can make ready. The man said he is nearby."

In the meantime, I needed a place to hide the horses and myself. Why not the ruined tavern, where I had told Secundus I would rejoin the vexillation? Not far from Friduric's camp, it would enable me to watch the road and swoop down to rescue Aurima when he and his Marcomanni attacked Glabrio's troops.

"Follow me," I said. "We need to get off the road."

The tavern sprawled at the roadside. Nearly smothered in vines, brush, and saplings, it had caved in beneath a massive oak that crushed its rooftree. Because the oak had been felled by lightning, the ruins were thought to be cursed by Thunraz. So I had been told last fall by a native guide, who crossed to the far side of the road in passing it.

"We cannot stay here," Thancmar gasped. "This place is *fluokhôn!*"

I was out of patience with his superstitions. "Go, then," I snapped, pointing up the road, "if you think you can sleep better in your brother's camp." He kicked his pony and clattered off, his spears rattling together in their sling.

The thunder god was unlikely to care if the tavern housed three horses and a weary man. I waded through tall grass into a gateless courtyard, pushed past a side door that hung by a rotting leather hinge, and stepped gingerly into a dark space reeking like a fox's den and as thick with foliage as if it had no walls. My entry startled small inhabitants who scurried out through the doorway or up through the caved-in roof.

When I had cleared enough room and made sure none of the greenery was toxic, I brought in the horses, who huffed and stamped uneasily before settling. I unsaddled the two ponies and trudged outside through the overgrowth.

Faithful to his promise, Secundus had incised "XV" in one of the doorposts. He had believed then that I was alive. I wondered how Glabrio had explained my death.

Watch out for Glabrio, Poppaeus had told me. *The man's a snake.* When I was finished with him, Special Cohort Agent Vatia Glabrio would destroy no one else with his venomous bite.

Shadows blanketed the Amber Road as I jogged between the wheel ruts, scuffing up flurries of dust in Wido's shoes. The clearing where I expected to find Friduric was not far north of the old tavern, just past a rocky hillock bristling with scrub brush. When muttering voices sounded above my footfalls, I edged off the road.

Knowing I was useless in my fatigue, I had let myself sleep for a few hours in the tavern, counting on the horses to wake me if anyone approached. I woke revived, found that Thancmar had not returned from talking with Friduric, and decided to investigate.

The voices continued as I lizarded up the rocky knoll, wriggling through dry grass and bushes on hands and knees. Near the summit, I slithered on my belly until there was a view through prickly brush.

Thancmar's pony grazed beside three others near a litter of blankets, saddles, and open packs. Only three! I had hoped for many more. Friduric sat on a stump, skinning a hare. I recognized his two companions from Hoheneih: a man known as Mangy Face for his thin and patchy beard, who was breaking up dead wood beside a firepit, and a scarred grayhair with a ruined eye who squatted over a sack, rooting through its contents.

"Do you hear me?" Thancmar stood confronting Friduric like an undersized messenger of the gods. "Aurima needs help." He coughed on smoke from the kindling fire. "Give me some ale; I am as dry as a stone."

"There is no more." Mangy Face thrust another stick of wood into the flames.

"Do you want me to curse you, you liar?"

"He is not lying," Friduric said. "There is none for you to get drunk on, dwarf." He spitted the hare and set it over the fire on a pair of forked branches.

Had Thancmar only just arrived? Well, I could not fault him if he had stopped to nap, since I had done the same.

"We could fetch ale from Grozhauga," One Eye argued.

"Beg from those gutless Quadi?" Friduric retorted. "Better to drink piss."

I was lying on a sharp edge of Aurima's pottery shard, which was tucked inside my shirt. Slowly I rolled aside and set it beside me. *Te idem amo, Aurima.*

Thancmar had stumped over to his saddle and was rummaging in his baggage. One Eye grumbled, "My balls are going to burst if we stay here much longer."

"Missing your wife, old man?" jeered Mangy Face.

"Go, then," Friduric said indifferently, beheading a second hare with his hunting knife. "The *fraujaz* knows you cannot obey if those tiny berries of yours ache."

Thancmar had found his own aleskin and was draining it with his back turned to the others. *Stay clearheaded, little man; you know too many secrets.*

Mangy Face sat back on his heels. "How could a soft Roman live in the forest for so many nights? The turd must be bear food by now."

"Or a tree goblin got him," One Eye said. All three muttered an incantation.

If they had come directly to the Amber Road from Hoheneih, they would not know that I had killed Egino and Wido, or that the Quadian Chlothar had been murdered by a man claiming to be a Marcomannian. What a shame I would not be able to watch when vengeful Quadi arrived to accuse Ingiomar!

As Thancmar tossed down the empty aleskin, Friduric demanded, "So why are you here? Do you know where the Roman turd is?"

"I am here because our sister is in danger. Why are you not listening to me?"

"Why do you think I care about her? Whatever happens, she earned it by lying with that cursed Roman."

"Her child is born. A boy. Goddess be thanked, they are both well."

"I do not care if they both die." Friduric threw the second skinned hare to Mangy Face. "Spit this for me. Is the other one burning?" He crouched over the fire.

Darkness was gathering in the trees. Although I needed to leave while there was enough light to see by, I lingered to hear whether Friduric would agree to help us.

Thancmar tramped closer to him. "I told you, Fridi, the Romans are taking her!"

With an oath, Friduric thrust scorched fingers into his mouth. "Taking her where?" From his tone, he did not know his father had delivered Aurima to Glabrio.

"To the Romeland, because she tried to kill Caesar." He gestured northward. "There are five and ten of them, coming this way. Help me free her."

Friduric unfolded to his full height. "Help you?" Regarding Thancmar, who stood no higher than his nipple, he laughed. "What are you going to do, little man? Trip them as they go by?"

"Friduric, she is our mother's daughter!"

"Aurima tried to kill the Caesar?" interrupted One Eye. "By the ax of Wodunaz, I call such a woman a hero!"

Thancmar nodded vigorously. "And she is Austro's priestess. If we let the Romans come into the Mark and take her from us, we deserve the Goddess's anger."

"Does the *fraujaz* know she is in those devils' hands?" Mangy Face growled.

Germanic leaders can lead only if their followers are willing, so I waited for Friduric to agree to rescue his sister. But Thancmar, who until then had been doing well, went too far: "It was the *fraujaz* who told the Romans where to find her."

"Is that so?" Friduric loomed over the others, hands on his belt. "Then if she loves them so much, let her live with them. That is my father's decision."

"They want to kill her," Thancmar protested.

"Hah!" He spat into the fire. "She is going to warm an officer's bed in Carnuntum, you wait and see."

I did not know what was said next, for I was crawling backward down the knoll. Now that Friduric knew his father's will, he would not oppose it. Nor would the others, no matter how much Thancmar tried to rouse their resentment of Rome.

It was ironic that twitchy little Thancmar had forgiven his rebellious sister, while Friduric, the tall, strong warrior, held fast to his grudge. That made it easier for me to hold to mine, which I had made while writing his name on the floor of a cave.

I did not remember trees growing so thickly at the foot of the knoll. Away from the last of the daylight, the forest was blacker than cuttlefish ink. Within moments unseen branches speared at my face and deadfalls clutched my ankles. I stumbled in what could not possibly have been a straight line.

Something large lifted from a high bough and spread its wings overhead. A single soundless beat fanned air against my cheek. I fell into a terrified crouch, imagining myself seized by the steely talons of a tree goblin. Whatever that was.

The owl glided away with a shrill cry. I paused on all fours, trying to calm myself by thinking of Hroswitha. Why not believe in magic when it served me?

I staggered a few more paces and fell over a rotten tree trunk, gashing my knee. When I got up, I was panting. My torc pressed against the blood-beat in my neck. Carefully, to avoid falling again, I turned in a circle.

A glimmer of light through the trees caught my eye: Friduric's fire. Reoriented, I lurched to the edge of the empty road, colored gray by a quarter moon and a scattering of stars. Many tired steps later I plodded through the tavern's weedy yard and found the three horses where I had left them. They crowded around, grunting and blowing through their nostrils. It would have been hard to say which of us was more relieved.

I threw down the saddles and blankets to make a bed and fell upon it. Curse it, I had hoped to hear whether Rufus was suspected of aiding my escape.

With a deeper pang of dismay, I realized I had left my talisman, Aurima's *TE AMO* shard, on the knoll. But that was of little importance. I had thought of another plan, one that enmeshed Friduric despite his reluctance, and in a few hours she might be able to tell me herself that she loved me.

25: NEMESIS WAITS

"Maelo thinks Friduric let you escape, but Friduric says it is not so," Thancmar said. "He blames a red-haired boy who freed the horses. Others say the boy was right to save them from the fire." He held up his palms, balancing the opinions.

I eased out a sigh of relief. If Rufus or Helle had been harmed, I would not have forgiven myself. Nor would I have been forgiven by Aurima, who loved them both.

We sat nearly nose to nose beneath the tree that had collapsed the tavern roof. Our horses champed weeds and grass in the early light. Birdsong quickened around us.

The dwarf licked his lips. "But some think..."

"Some think what?"

He squirmed closer. "That Dunkara took you," he whispered.

"Who is Dunkara?"

His voice sank even lower. "The sister of Austro. Goddess of darkness. Of death."

I laughed.

"Quiet!" Thancmar rolled his eyes toward the lightning-struck oak taking shape against a pale lavender sky. "How can you not heed gods or ghosts?"

"There are no gods or ghosts." *Not in the daylight.*

"*Jawâra,* there are, and Friduric better fear them." He drew out a few inches of knife blade, then thrust it back into the sheath that lay in his lap. "His own sister is going to be put to death, and he says she has earned it!" He scowled. "Gods hear me, I need a horn of ale. Or two. I could drink two without stopping to breathe."

Given the size of aurochs' horns, I thought so much ale would render him useless. Perhaps that was what he wished for. "Is there anything to eat?"

Thancmar rummaged in his pack. "Friduric said that Ingiomar is so angry, he is going to burn the house of any man who shelters you." He handed me a stale barley cake.

"Is he likely to burn the mill? Or your grandmother's house?"

"He is afraid of my grandmother." He gnawed on a strip of dried meat.

"So if he burns it, he is fucked."

He stopped chewing. A wondering smile lifted his blond mustache. "He *what*?"

A lesson in the pitfalls of translating Latin verbatim. But it made us both grin.

While we were watering the horses at a spring-fed pool that might once have been the tavern's fishpond, Thancmar said, "We must make an offering for Tiwaz's favor."

"I am planning on it."

"Let us give him your gold neck-ring."

"Tiwaz is the god of war, *ja*?" I said. "So let us give him blood."

He stared glumly into the weed-choked pool. Battle nerves, I guessed.

I felt no fear, only elation, eagerness, and determination. "Don't worry about Glabrio's troops, Thancmar. I am going to take care of them. When they scatter, you take Aurima and the baby."

"Suppose Friduric catches us?"

"You are always saying how fast your horse is. Now you can prove it." Spider thrust his head against me, drooling water. I held his chin to my chest, taking heart from his trust. "Afterward, we meet north of the bridge."

"Aquilo." Thancmar pulled his dun pony back from a bank of nettles. "Tell me about my sister and Caligula Caesar." He took a deep breath. "I know she tried to kill him but he was saved by his gods. Did she use a knife? How did she escape?"

"If she told you no more, perhaps you are not meant to know it."

"I am going to fight for her. It does not seem much to ask."

I bent for a handful of dry grass and began to groom my horse. "Well, then. Yes, she used a knife. She was in Caesar's house." There was no need to say that she had inveigled herself into his bed without my knowing. "A boy helped her escape."

"It was a brave thing," he said wonderingly.

"She is the bravest woman I have ever known."

"Yes," said Thancmar, suddenly smiling.

All at once I was happy too. Soon it would be resolved, one way or another.

26: AMBUSH

We had barely stuck our heads out of the tavern when Thancmar hissed, "Get back!"

A train of mules was plodding north in a low haze of dust, loaded with plump bundles—perhaps cotton or linen cloth for the market in Bruna.

We had done our best to hide our presence at the smashed tavern, but it hardly seemed to matter: the muleteers averted their eyes from the thunder god's devastation. The string of pack beasts slogged past and disappeared up the road.

Thancmar gathered his reins. "If I follow close behind them, I can see the Romans before they see me."

He would have to pass Friduric's encampment first, but that was not a problem. Even if his half brother spotted him lurking behind a caravan headed north, he would assume that Thancmar was foolishly set on saving Aurima by himself.

As he was about to mount his dun pony, I held him back. Livelier hoofbeats were coming from the north. Peering cautiously through the skewed opening that was once a window, I saw Friduric, Mangy Face, and One Eye riding toward the tavern, bent over with their eyes fixed on the road. I reached for my sword.

"Tracking me," Thancmar whispered. "Or you."

Friduric held up his hand, and all three stopped. The mules' passage must have obliterated the traces they were following.

Mangy Face eyed the tavern. "The grass is beaten down."

Friduric scanned the road surface. "One horse." He gestured from the seamed road to the ruined building. I felt Thancmar stiffen beside me.

One Eye edged his pony away from the tavern. "They had good ale here, remember? There was a spring in the back."

"Go have a drink, then," snapped Mangy Face. "If you want to be struck dead by Thunraz."

"Shut up," Friduric said. "I cannot think if I must listen to the whining of little girls." He raised his voice. "Thancmar!"

"*Skita*," Thancmar mumbled. "What now?"

I asked quietly, "Are they going to come in?"

He ran a finger across his mustache. "I think no." Before I could relax, he added, "But Friduric is pigheaded enough to throw fire on us."

"Thancmar, I know you're in there! Come out!"

I did not like the options. I had intended to surprise Friduric at his encampment, reckoning we could outrun him until he chased us into Glabrio's troops. The chase would be much longer if it had to start from here, and we might be overtaken.

The three Marcomanni were still muttering to one another on the far side of the road. Trying to get up their nerve, I reckoned.

"Well, I prefer not to be roasted," I said. "Are you willing to ride?"

He drew in a breath. "Goddess grant that Friduric does not stop us."

"Shout your war cry and ride him down, man."

The dwarf looked at me oddly, and I regretted the casual brutality of my remark. What he was about to do took courage, more than ought to be demanded of a miller.

Diffidently I held out my palm. "Are you willing to take the hand of a Roman?"

"I am willing to take yours," he said.

Instead of besieging Thancmar with further demands, Friduric and his two companions trotted farther down the road. They stopped by the track to Grozhauga. Their words were inaudible, but it seemed that something had alerted them.

Thancmar's pony shifted restlessly in the high grass, eager for a signal to go. He patted its neck. "Someone is coming," he said. "I hope it is not—"

Trousered riders burst out onto the Amber Road. Three, five, nine— all Quadi. One of them was the tattooed man who had wanted to accompany Chlothar and his young son to the horse pen. "Murderers," he roared at Friduric.

"Haimo!" Friduric said. "Are you moonstruck?" He wrenched his pony's head away an instant before the other man's ax would have cleaved its skull.

"He called it a gift from your father." Haimo wheeled his mount around for another blow. "So here is my gift to Ingiomar!"

Friduric kicked his pony out of range and nearly collided with Mangy Face. "What are you saying? My father made no gift—"

"Marcomanni liar!" Two more of the Quadi closed on him. Friduric pulled his sword from its scabbard.

An attacker lunged at One Eye, who ducked the blade and stabbed the man's pony in the neck. It screamed and staggered, unseating its rider. Another Quadi warrior was slashing at Mangy Face. Blood slatted through the air. Accusation and protest fused in a clamor of shouting and neighing.

I stared transfixed through the viny overgrowth, as if at a staged combat in the arena. When another rider raced toward the fight, I was shocked to see it was Thancmar.

"No," I bellowed, but he was not listening. Instead he hurtled toward Friduric, who had been unhorsed and was trying to block Haimo's ax with his sword. Haimo lopped the blade in half with a swing of his heavy ax head.

Friduric dropped the useless hilt. As Haimo circled for a killing blow, Thancmar shouted, "Here, brother! Jump up behind me." He held out his hand.

Friduric pulled him out of the saddle and hoisted himself onto the pony. He bolted northward, leaving his half brother splayed in the road. One Eye and Mangy Face galloped after their leader. Those of the Quadi who were still mounted pulled their unhorsed comrades up behind them and tore off after the Marcomanni. Within moments the road was empty except for Thancmar's body, sprawled amid scuffled dirt and grass.

When I reached him, he was on hands and knees, sucking in gulps of air. I yanked him to his feet. My plan had been turned on its head, and time was precious.

He wheezed and stumbled as I hauled him back to the tavern. Unnerved by the turmoil, the penned horses jostled and stamped. I grabbed the reins of Egino's white mare. "Go," I said urgently, boosting him into the mare's saddle. "Find your sister."

After he barreled off, I seized the reins of the last pony, threw myself onto Spider's back, and put my heels to him. He surged after everyone else.

I came upon the mule train first. It was in disarray, unsettled by the brawling barbarians who had streamed past. The muleteers broke off their tugging and prodding to yell curses as I overtook them. The pony I was towing sideswiped a mule that shrieked its displeasure.

Spider thundered on like an avalanche. Trees and bushes shot past, blurred by my wind-tears. Disaster lurked underfoot, the road's ruts and humps and holes hidden by drifts of dust, but like any stallion he wanted to lead the horses running ahead of him. The rocky knoll loomed to one side, then fled back behind us.

I tightened my sweat-slick fist on the reins of the towed pony. "Find her, find her," I muttered. Spider flicked back his ears, his black mane streaming.

Friduric's former encampment swept past. The road in front of us still lay bare. Where were they?

I wiped my eyes on my forearm. A damned herd of deer was flitting across the road ahead. Spider checked his stride. I kicked him hard. The last doe stopped short, frozen, as I galloped by with the spare pony.

Beyond a curve in the road, a sudden storm of birds rose into the pale sky. Rounding the turn, I saw the pandemonium I had wrought.

Scattered across the road and its verges, a dozen Praetorian troopers had been caught unawares: helmets still hanging at saddle bows, long *spathae* scabbarded, shields slung on their backs. Their once-orderly ranks had been demolished by Germans who were battling each other. Behind the brawl I caught sight of a cart with an awning over it.

Then something odd happened: the pony I had been tugging along crowded up against my knee, white-eyed with fright. Over my shoulder I glimpsed a streak of gray bolting through the yellow dust. Tig.

The decurion who commanded the troopers yelled for them to withdraw. I yelled in Latin for them to engage. In a turbulence of horses, Praetorian began to fight German.

A few lengths from the front line, I pulled Wido's hunting knife from its sheath. The drumming of hooves exploded into the *whump* of collision, whinnies, shrieks, yells, a crash as a cavalryman fell. Spider found a gap and surged through it. I swung at another trooper about to cross my path. When he yanked his horse aside, it tripped over its feet. I did not see if he jumped free, for I was past, forcing my way toward the cart.

It was Placidus's medical cart. Thancmar had halted by one of the wheels. Still mounted on the white mare, he held the reins of his dun pony that Friduric had appropriated.

At first I could discern only a shape beneath the sunshade. When she stood up and pushed back the canopy, her hair glowed like a new copper *as*. "Aurima," I cried, raising my knife in a triumphant salute. She stared blankly. She did not recognize me.

In the next moment, Placidus cut between us on his bay mare. "Back, you savage," he bellowed in Latin. He was unarmored, as always, and had not drawn the longknife I had always told him to carry. "This woman is protected by Caesar's order!"

"Let Caesar stop me," I shouted back, whacking his mare's flank with the flat of the hunting knife. She jibbed aside, and I rode on.

Thancmar had taken a bundle into his arms. Aurima balanced for an instant atop the wheel, then leaped onto the dun pony. "Hurry," I shouted, although in the tumult she could not have heard me.

A rider on a yellow horse charged her with sword drawn. Beneath the brim of the black-crested helmet I spied the swarthy face and glaring eyes of Vatia Glabrio.

"You, woman!" he blared. "Get back in! Get back!"

The cart driver jumped down and fled. I jammed the knife into the waist of my breeches, hauled on the baldric until the hilt of my sword came into my hand, and pulled it free of its bindings. "Glabrio," I roared. "Here, you whoreson."

The man who had delivered me to die at Berinhard's hands, and who had torn Aurima from her grandmother's home mere days after she gave birth, whirled his horse. "By Serapis!" he blurted, eyes agape. Then some instinct for survival awoke him, and he flung up his blade just before I would have spitted him from belly to backbone.

Our swords met with a *crack*. The impact jolted up my arm, but I hardly noticed. I heeled Spider past his horse, and turned to engage him again.

"Praetorians, to me!" he yelled wildly. He wore no armor. It was a hot day, and with the Mark at peace he had not expected trouble.

Bad assumption, whoreson.

Glabrio hauled his mount's head around and booted it in the ribs. I swerved in front of him, trapping him against the now-empty medical cart.

He tried to push past me. My horse slammed him into the side of the cart. The vehicle rocked on its wheels.

He slashed at me. I blocked the blow. We pushed against each other, sword against sword, our horses so close that Glabrio's knee pressed against mine.

I felt the strain in my sinews as he tried to force my sword down. Fear gave him strength. "You should be dead," he gasped.

"You first," I growled. With my other hand I yanked the knife from my belt and jammed it into his liver.

When I tugged the knife free, he came with it, folding over his saddle-bow and toppling to the ground. I wiped the blade on my breeches and slid it back into its sheath. How easy it had been, after all, to kill my first Roman. My own countryman.

A swale in the road hid Aurima and Thancmar. Perhaps my senses were so blunted from stabbing Glabrio that I stared northward for too long, for a trooper caught me unawares. Jostling aside one of the riderless ponies, he rode up on my left.

I ducked and tried to knock his sword aside with mine. The parry was a weak one. His blade caught me on the upper arm, but he was not able to take another whack before Spider veered out of range.

By now the road was a melee of Quadi and Marcomanni grappling furiously with Praetorian troopers and with each other, loose horses plunging here and there with reins flying, braying mules tugging at their couplings, and noncombatants dashing for shelter. Placidus leaned over a casualty, giving instructions to his assistant. He glanced up at me, then at Glabrio's body, and bent to his work again. The scout Tudrus watched from horseback, well away from danger.

For a moment my path was clear to follow Aurima, or so I thought. I had just set heels to my horse's sides when a sudden movement caught the corner of my eye. Someone panted in Germanic, "Not so fast, turd."

I wheeled the stallion around. A lean bearded figure with rampant yellow hair confronted me on a sweat-rimed pony. Dirt and gore streaked his tattooed chest and his breeches, and his sword dripped bright crimson.

"So. You and Thancmar, making trouble, *ja?*" Friduric smiled, showing his white teeth. "Let us . . . finish this." He swung his leg over his pony's back. Pain tightened his face as he set both feet on the ground. His breeches were slashed down his right thigh, and blood oozed down his leg.

"You are wounded," I told him. "I am not going to fight you."

"Too frightened, turd?" He spat on the ground between us.

My battle fury had ebbed, and I could not bring myself to attack. The reasons I hated him—for dragging me behind his horse, for throwing me in the cave to await torture and death—now seemed owed more to his father's account than his. "No," I said. "For your sister's sake."

Friduric lurched forward, sweeping his sword toward Spider's foreleg. I jerked the horse to a stop.

His blade quivered close to Spider's knee. "Do you want me to cut this one too?"

I had not guessed Boss was his doing. Blood began to throb in my head.

Without a word I dismounted. Friduric's teeth glinted again beneath the muddy-blond mustache. He stepped back from my horse and waved the tip of his sword at me. It was not a short stabbing sword like my *gladius*, but a cavalry *spatha* three feet long.

I swatted Spider away and pulled the hunting knife from its sheath. Sword in one hand, knife in the other, I crouched to face Ingiomar's son as Cleon and Ollius had drilled into me. To get inside the reach of his *spatha*, I needed him to attack first. And the fight would have to end quickly, before any Praetorians could intervene.

Shifting his lamed leg, Friduric waited for me to move.

"I like your wife," I said. "Helle. Pretty name."

He twitched as if a hornet had stung him.

"Pretty woman." I watched his eyes.

Veins stood out on his forehead. His face darkened.

I smirked at him. "She came to me, you know."

Friduric roared and charged, slicing the *spatha* in an arc meant to behead me.

I twisted under his guard, stabbing my sword at his navel. His other hand shot out and gripped my wrist, stopping the thrust. I punched the knife upward toward his throat, but it tangled in his unkempt beard.

His grip was like a vise, squeezing my wrist hard enough to snap bones. Numb-fingered, I realized with shock that I would be forced to drop my sword.

No. I could not die just when I had found Aurima again.

Friduric pulled me toward him. I saw his arm sweep down, glimpsed the *spatha*'s descending pommel. The next I knew, I was sprawled on my back with my skull vibrating. I tried to sit up, but was stopped by the point of a blade.

Friduric looked down at me with the tip of his sword hovering over my throat. As my sight cleared, I saw my own *gladius* under his foot, inches from my right hand. I still held the knife in my left, but it could not reach him now.

Satisfaction smoothed his face, and a crooked smile lifted a corner of his sweat-stringy mustache. "I am going to give Helle your heart," he gasped.

"Give your father my cock and tell him to suck it."

"You can give it to him yourself." He stepped back. "I am taking you to him."

"No." I reversed the knife hilt, pressing the point below my breastbone.

"Stop," Friduric shouted, lifting the sharp-edged *spatha*. Whether he meant to kill me after all or just slice off my fingers I do not know, because while he was still in his backswing, I rolled over and stabbed the knife into the calf of his wounded leg.

He stumbled back and crashed down like a felled tree. I struggled to my feet, reaching for my sword.

"Tig, kill!" a voice bellowed.

The wolf flew through the air and fastened onto Friduric's forearm. He roared without words. The *spatha* fell as he clawed at her head.

Man and beast blurred into a thrashing tumble. Legs flailed in woad-blue wool, splattering blood and foam. Worse were the noises: Friduric shrieking; Tig growling, deep and wet, through a jawful of living meat.

He was screaming, "*Broodher.*" Brother. I was almost sure of it.

"Aquilo!" Thancmar grabbed my arm. I could not take my eyes from the carnage.

"Come away!" The dwarf jerked me toward him. "Make haste!" He pushed Spider's reins into my hand.

I managed to mount on the third attempt. Troopers near us had backed away, trying to calm their terrified horses. Others crowded to see. No one took their eyes from the wolf's attack. No one moved to save Friduric. He was a barbarian, not one of them.

But I was not one of them either, was I?

Thancmar was already astride his pony. We rode north, past the men who had been in Glabrio's detachment. Past Quadi and Marcomanni who had thrown down their weapons. Through a scattering of crumpled bodies, most of them German.

The Praetorian decurion, now the ranking officer, should have ordered us stopped. But no one shouted or blocked the way.

When we were clear, Thancmar put two fingers in his mouth and whistled. "She always comes," he said. He whistled again.

Tig lolloped after us. Her fur was darkly matted, and her tongue drooled pink.

My gorge rose. I said thickly, "Your brother . . ."

Friduric's *spatha* hovered before my eyes. The faded blue of his trouser leg patched at the knee, his foot planted atop my fallen sword.

Collect yourself, man. It counted for nothing to lead in thirteen laps of a race and fail in the last. Once the decurion formed up his men, they would be after us.

"What?" said Thancmar.

I turned my face away. And, to my shame, spewed over my horse's side.

He and the wolf were far ahead when I regained control of myself. At least Aurima had not seen me retch like a boy witnessing his first bout.

The horses were kicking up huge amounts of dust. Or was it mist rising from the river? The trees and stump-studded riverbanks, the dips and hillocks and twists of the road had become hazy, as if a gauzy fly-curtain had drawn around me.

Soft-bellied lordling, Ollius said in my ear. *Now you know what it's like.*

I had almost caught up with Thancmar when the Thaya bridge came into sight. It was a crude thing of split tree trunks with the bark still on, just wide enough for a wagon.

Tig raced ahead as our horses thumped across the deck of halved logs. She was a beast from a nightmare, her bloody fur coated with road dust. All at once she stopped and crouched, growling.

Something stirred in the trees on the far side of the bridge. I lifted the sword lying across my thighs.

Aurima rode out of the forest astride the dun pony. Coppery hair blown free of its thong floated around her head. One hand nestled inside a bulging sling that hung around her neck and under one arm.

Her face lit when she saw us. She heeled the pony forward.

There were many things I had planned to say, but I could recall none of them. My head seemed filled with bees.

Aurima threw her free arm around Thancmar's neck and kissed his bearded cheek. "Thank you, brother. As many times as there are stars, I thank you!"

"Thank the Goddess, not me," he grumbled. He nodded at me. "He is wounded."

"Marcus," she cried. An exclamation or a question, I could not tell which.

They both looked at my arm, so I did, too. Blood seeped from the sword-slash below my left shoulder. The side of my breeches was black with it, and my shin and foot were striped crimson.

Then the infant in its sling squalled, so piercingly that anything I might have tried to say would have made no difference. I cleared my scalded throat and spat. When the baby finally drew breath, I rasped, "We must hide."

27: ODYSSEUS RETURNS

This was a far better afterlife. Sunlight glowed through my eyelids. Sweet-scented grass pricked and tickled. The bees that had crowded my head droned farther away.

I hated to open my eyes. Last time, I had found Ingiomar and Maelo glaring down at me. But I was as dry as day-old bread.

One might be infernally thirsty in the next world, perhaps. However, I would not expect to have an arm on fire, too.

Two faces looked down at me. One was long and black, with thick-lashed dark eyes and nostrils as big as goose eggs. The other had a shorter nose that had been broken at least once, bright blue eyes, and a beard that was darker blond than his head hair.

Spider stepped back as I propped myself on my good arm. "Thanc-mar," I said. "Where are we?" He had led us off the Amber Road onto a narrow track, then along a winding game trail through the woods. I did not recall reaching this meadow, or dismounting, or dropping into the grass.

"Safe." He unbent himself, his belt creaking. "Rest while I see to the horses."

Safe. At least for now. The Praetorians would not risk losing them-selves on an unknown forest byway. Anyhow, they would have their hands full deciding how to handle a dead officer, not to mention native combat-ants they had engaged by accident.

I watched Thancmar's ungainly waddle as he towed my horse toward the two others: the big, almost leonine head on a body that was some god's idea of a joke, stubby-armed and squat-trunked, stumpy legs as bowed as a saddle tree.

As many times as there are stars, I thank you!

Why had she not embraced me, her true heart, who had been through so much to rescue her? Me, the father of her noisy infant?

"Where is Aurima?" I called after him.

He said she was seeking something. A word I did not recognize.

My sword lay by my hip. By spiking it into the ground, I managed to pull myself one-handed to my feet. My guess about the bees had been wrong; a hive of them had moved into my wounded arm, and they were all enraged.

The meadow was clasped in a lazy loop of river—a stream, really, no wider than a spear-cast. The westering sun slanted down along it, and swifts dived on insects glittering like flecks of gold above the pea-green surface.

My bare feet slewed in a strip of sand at its edge. The warm water rose up my legs to my hips, with no more current than a *tepidarium* pool. I wrestled off the stained and stinking breeches with one hand and sank to my knees on the grassy bottom, my tunic floating around me. My skin awoke to the stream's silky caress, then to the sting and sear of my wounds.

It seemed impious, now, to make use of the river without paying tribute. I sank forward, submerging my head and shoulders, and said in a cloud of bubbles, "Thank you, spirit of the stream."

I surfaced and took a great breath, flinging back my wet hair. A streak of blue caught my eye: Aurima looking at me from the meadow, the sling around her neck, greenery in her hand. I did not think she was smiling.

Turning away, I groped for the breeches and began to scrub myself with the fisted cloth. My palms and fingers ached from the unaccustomed strain of wielding weapons.

Now what? Or rather, now where to go with Aurima and our child?

I must retrieve my people: Dio and Cleon and, if he wished, Rufus. And bury Ollius's bones. After that, where would we go? No place within Rome's borders was safe from the Special Cohort. Nor could we take refuge in Ingiomar's or Berinhard's lands.

Thancmar brought the horses down to drink. Over the noise of their splashing I said, "Have you told Aurima about Friduric?"

"No."

"Let me tell her, then. I once vowed to kill him."

"So did I." Thancmar pulled on his pony's halter. The beast was trying to chew on the wad of breeches in my hand. "I must be the one who tells her."

The harshness of his voice silenced me. I resumed swabbing the trail of dried blood from my elbow.

"I need ale," the dwarf growled. He lost his grip on Spider's rein, or perhaps let it go, and the roan stallion plunged into the river with a splash that drenched us both.

"*Skita!*" He threw the other two horses' leads into the air and marched up the beach. "I am going hunting."

I rose, streaming water, and flung the sodden breeches over my shoulder. Thancmar's pony plodded after him. Spider stamped his forefeet one at a time in the shallows, enjoying the splatter. The white mare still sucked water, her belly as round as a filled aleskin.

I took her reins and pulled her out of the river. By now my arm was hurting badly. I grimaced at the cut, whose purple lips still oozed blood.

When I looked up, Thancmar was gone. I listened for a rustle of foliage or crackle of twigs beneath soft-booted feet, for hooves or voices or jingling harness on the track far away. But the only sounds were birdsong and the rasp of the dun pony cropping grass.

How could I fear the wilderness, after all I had undergone? The "R" on my wrist was a pledge that I would not die here. There was still vengeance to be taken, justice to be done. *LAMIA. INGIOMAR. MAELO.*

I tied the pony and whistled to Spider. He surged from the river, snorting, and pranced onto the beach. Water showered around him like jewels as he shook his black mane. Teeth bared, he neighed a trumpet call of self-satisfaction.

"As if you did it all yourself," I said.

There was dead wood aplenty inside the forest fringes. On my third trip to drop dry branches on the beach, Thancmar reappeared with a hare and a pheasant. His gaze shifted to my breeches spread on a bush to dry, and he frowned at my bare legs. Wordlessly I took the pheasant from him, and wordlessly he bent to build a fire.

The sun disappeared into the trees. I glanced at Aurima's brother to see if her absence worried him, but he was grimly intent on striking a spark.

The first twigs were smoking when she trudged through the meadow from upriver, carrying the baby cradled in its sling. She stopped a few paces away, and we looked at each other.

I could still see in her the maiden who had arrived in Rome less than a year before, edgy with hostility that hid her terror of the monstrous city and its million beetling inhabitants. It was her courage, her refusal to give in to her ordained fate, that had drawn me to her.

In our months apart, the red-haired girl who once was slim enough to impersonate a boy had become a woman. The sleekness of one bare arm and the curve of her cheek hinted at new fullness of breast and belly and thigh. More alarmingly, her green-gray eyes, which had used to be restless and intense, now looked at me with cool reserve. Yes, that was it. She held back something of herself. As if . . .

As if she no longer loved me.

Was it any wonder she had rushed to Thancmar first? With matted hair and beard, plucking feathers off our next meal like a kitchen slave, I bore no resemblance to the Roman she had left in Carnuntum. Certainly no one would confuse me with Perseus, savior of Andromeda.

I said hoarsely, "Beloved."

Aurima knelt and reached out to skim her fingertips along an arc of my golden torc. The scent of sweet hay and some broken plant came from her. And milk.

"I came for you." I forced a smile. "Is that not worth at least one of the stars?"

She stared, puzzled.

"No matter," I said gruffly. It would be petty to let my hurt pride diminish her joy in her half brother's valor. "Thancmar was intent on saving you. He has a hero's heart."

He looked up from the fire. Aurima's eyes gentled. "So I have always known."

My magnanimity failed to ease the knot in my chest. I swallowed thickly. "Let me see my son." I tried to hold out both hands, but could lift only one arm.

"In a moment. Open your mouth."

She fished a handful of leaves out of her sling and pushed them between my teeth. I tongued the bitter stuff.

She pressed her forefinger to my lips before I could spit it out. "No. Chew."

I mashed the weeds distastefully with lips drawn back. She took the child from her sling, but I had only a glimpse of a pink wriggling thing, much smaller than I had expected, before she laid it down beside her. With a grunt of protest I strained for a better look. Feathers from the half-plucked pheasant floated around us.

"Thancmar, for the Goddess's sake take that bird," she snapped.

"I am starting the fire, Riemy!" He thrust a branch into smoldering twigs.

I swept the carcass off my lap. The infant waved chubby arms, as if approving.

Aurima spread my wound open with finger and thumb. I spat the stringy leaves into her beckoning palm. She kneaded the poultice, then pressed it into the cut.

Golden lashes hid her eyes as she worked, and her wide mouth hooked down. She was muttering—an incantation, perhaps, to her goddess. Through a blur of pain-tears I fixed my gaze on the freckles I once had counted in kisses, a terra-cotta spatter across her nose and cheeks. Was this strange, brusque woman the glad and tender lover who had done much to heal my grief on the journey from Rome?

She would have been at least three months pregnant when she left me. And she had said nothing about it.

Shifting from knee to knee, Aurima pulled up her skirts and tore a strip from the hem of her undertunic. I looked away, questions crowding on my tongue, while she bound the cut. At last I could silence myself no longer. "Why did you not tell me?"

She knotted the bandage silently, eyes down.

"She was afraid," Thancmar said, as if it should have been obvious.

"Afraid!" I tried to find answers in her face. "Of what?"

A tear tipped over the edge of her eyelid and slid down the side of her nose. She bit her lip, but tears continued to spill from her reddened eyes. She scooped the infant into her arms and began to rise.

I forgot everything else in a rush of fury. "Afraid of your father? Did he hurt you? Did Maelo let him hurt you?"

She stared blindly down at me, then stooped and held out the child. Reflexively I clasped him to my chest, but the shift in weight toppled me backward into the grass. When I lifted my head, his hazy blue-gray eyes stared back at me.

From overhearing my sister and mother with their friends, I had supposed that all babies were beautiful and that one could immediately see their parents' traits in their faces. This infant was wrinkled and hairy. His face was round and flat, his nose a nub, and his mouth barely budded. Oddest of all, his skin was yellow.

What had she eaten that resulted in such an unnatural child? Had the cold and privations of our journey poisoned it? Or had it been stricken in the womb by Aurima's sight of some ugly little man of the Silk Kingdom?

Aurima glimpsed the horror in my face. "You have never seen a new baby?"

When would I have had the chance? I said, "I thought . . ." but was too confused to finish. The infant grabbed my torc, blowing foam through pursed lips. I tried to wrest the tiny fist free, but the baby had a grip like a mussel on a rock.

"Austro blessed the seed from which he grew. That is why he is the color of the sun. He has so much hair because Beranaz, the Great Bear, came to me in a dream." She smiled fondly at him. "But these god-signs will fade away, now that he is in the world."

"And his skin is so loose because . . . ?"

"Ramis said . . ." Her eyes filled again. "My poor Ramis s-said it is because he is going to be much bigger. A big man."

The future big man let go the torc, seized the end of my nose, and tried to pull it toward his sucking lips. Aurima snorted a spray of giggles through her tears.

My anger flared. "Take him." My touchy pride was chafed anew by what seemed to be discrediting of my virility, my trust, and the trials I had suffered to find her.

My clumsiness as I struggled to my feet infuriated me further. I thrust the infant at her and strode up through the darkening meadow toward Spider, snatching my breeches off the bush as I went.

The roan stallion's whiskery muzzle tickled my chest as he sniffed the baby's unfamiliar scent on me. I leaned against him with my good arm along his back, and after a moment he went back to grazing, reassured that I had no mind to disturb him.

The first stars glinted above, barely brighter than the pale blue in which they were set. Down by the river, firelight gleamed on skinned carcasses on a spit, on Thancmar's belt buckle, and on the globe of a woman's breast, soon obscured by a hand cradling a small round head.

Ithaca, said a voice inside me.

The returning king.

His wife's treacherous suitors.

The bow that only he could string.

I studied the stars, composing myself. Once the Great and Little Bears had emerged in the dark sky, I braced against a tree and wrestled my way painfully into the wet breeches. A half-naked man is always at a disadvantage with a fully clothed woman.

Aurima and Thancmar looked up as I rejoined them by the fire. "We have things to talk about," I said.

28: BEAR CUB

As she spoke, Aurima looked down at a pleat she was kneading into her sleeveless overtunic. "He said, 'I am going to send him to you in pieces if you make trouble, whore.'" She used the coarse term, *lupa*, that her father would have learned in his Army days. "Everyone knew. The farmers who came to mill their barley. They said that Friduric dragged you behind his horse. That Father tied you like a dog."

The creased cloth became a wadded knot in her fist. "No one wanted to help you. They were all afraid." Her cheeks reddened with anger, bright in the fire's glow. "I begged *Amma* to use her skill, but she said she must save it for me."

Thancmar said, "It is good that she did."

I looked over the flames at the dwarf, who was digging bits of meat out of crannies in the pheasant's carcass. His eyes flicked up to me for a moment, then dropped again to his task. "Riemy needed it on the night the Goddess brought forth the baby."

Aurima's ragged voice was almost lost in the hiss and pop of the fire: "I thought Dunkara was taking me into the darkness." She smoothed the sleeping infant's hair.

My mind recoiled from imagining what she had undergone. I shook my head in stunned denial.

"But *Amma* did not allow me to die." She swayed her head, mirroring my gesture. "Then my father sent word that he was going to sacrifice you to Nerthuz on the night the Moon God went to light the dark world."

I did not know how to console her for such anguish. My powerlessness flared into rage. "And he was willing for Glabrio to take you to Rome." It was a dreadful vengeance for the dishonor he reckoned she had brought to her murdered mother's name.

Now that she was safe, the deaths I had already caused might have satisfied my lust for revenge. Maelo and Lamia would pay in some severe fashion. But I would not relent with Ingiomar Ironhand. Of the six of them, he owed the most.

I shifted on the log where I sat, trying to ease the pain in my arm. "We must leave at first light tomorrow."

"To where?" Thancmar asked belligerently. "*Amma* needs me at the mill."

"Can she protect you from Ingiomar?" The *fraujaz* was bound to learn that he had set his wolf on Friduric.

"Let him try to punish me for saving my sister's life," he retorted.

Amazing, I thought: the pigeon had become a fighting cock.

He turned to his sister. "But, Riemy, the mill is not safe for you and the little one. You must go to the Hermunduri. Ingo can protect you."

"No," I said. They frowned at me.

I had not forgotten that Germanic women, and especially priestesses, have more liberty to make decisions for themselves than Roman women do. But the responsibility for her and the hairy infant was mine.

"Do you think she is safe with you?" Thancmar said. "Where? In the Romeland?"

"We are going to Bruna," I said.

Going north to the king's stronghold must have been the last thing the dwarf expected. His eyebrows jerked up in surprise, then down in a scowl.

"To Bruna?" Aurima repeated uncertainly. Her hand curled protectively around the fuzzy crown of the child's head.

I said, "We have friends there." Or so I hoped. With Vangio's help, Aurima and I could appeal for his royal uncle's support. Then, with the five thousand denarii from my patron and the five more I had squeezed out of Lamia, I could order supplies through Leonnatus's agent in Bruna to launch my delayed search for the lost Eagle. If Cleon and Dio were still in Carnuntum, Leo could arrange for them to rejoin me. Us.

Although I had begun to feel very tired, I was illogically confident in this plan. Somehow Vannaz would be persuaded to smile on a man who had killed at least five of his tribesmen. And somehow I would redeem my honor, even though Glabrio's death made me a cold-blooded murderer in the eyes of Rome.

Thancmar interrupted my thoughts: "Riemy, listen. It is dangerous to be with Aquilo."

A shiver ran down my arms. Aurima was dauntless, but she was still a woman. Surely she would be dismayed and disgusted to learn of all the blood I had spilled. Let Thancmar tell her of my savagery, of the deaths of the two gate guards, of Wido and Egino, of Chlothar and perhaps his son, of Glabrio and Friduric. I need not sit by to see how it offended her.

Toiling to my feet, I dislodged a brand at the edge of the fire. Aurima flinched, startling the infant into a thin wail. Even to my inexperienced ears, it sounded like the prelude to a full battle cry. "Give me the child while you talk together," I said.

The baby was so surprised when I scooped him from his mother's arms that he fell silent. I stepped carefully around the fire, cradling him against my chest. He was small enough, head to rump, to cup in my right hand.

My fire-shadow sprawled ahead on the little beach as I moved away. "What an unsightly creature you are," I told him. "If I did not know how beautiful your mother is, I would think you were found in a bear's den."

He did not like my comment, or perhaps the fact that I had spoken in

Latin. His toothless mouth opened and the battle cry shrilled out, preventing me from hearing Thancmar tell Aurima of the slaughter I had carried out between here and Hoheneih.

She came upon me some time later as I stood up to my knees in the dark river, sozzling the baby's lower half. "What are you doing?"

The grab she made for him bumped my sore arm, and I lost my grip. The child slipped beneath the surface without a sound.

We both lunged after him, colliding with each other. Each of us seized a different limb—I an arm, Aurima the opposite leg. Together we hauled him from the water. I let go of the tiny arm and leaned closer to be sure he still breathed.

Big pale eyes blinked up at us. "Ha!" he crowed.

Aurima clutched him against her. "What were you doing?"

Her anger erased my smile of relief. "He needed washing," I protested. I had thought it considerate to take care of the matter myself, instead of returning him befouled to his mother's lap.

"You could have drowned him!"

Beneath the shrill of rage I heard a more tremulous vehemence. On impulse I asked, "What were you afraid of, beloved? That I was not going to want him?"

The hostility bled out of her, and she seemed to shrink upon herself. She murmured something I could not hear.

I put my good arm around her shoulders and ducked my head to listen, but her capitulation was all too brief. She pulled away, clutching the infant. "Why did you not come sooner to find me? After Father sent me to *Amma*'s, I waited for you. I waited and waited." She wept amid her fury, gulping as tears ran down her cheeks.

I opened my mouth to object, only to close it without a word. Mired in fear and hope, I had delayed too long in Carnuntum.

"When he said he was going to sacrifice you, there was nothing I could do. Nothing!"

I had no excuse for my tardiness in rescuing her, or for blundering into my enemies' trap. Talking became impossible, anyway, when the baby added his howls to her sobs.

She waded out of the water, joggling him. I trudged behind, following the swath her dragging skirts left in the sand, and sank onto the log before the dying fire, stupefied with pain and weariness.

Aurima settled back on her heels. The babe was still shrieking. She pulled open the wide neck of her undertunic, baring a breast that was as round and heavy as I had imagined. I longed to cup it in my hand, and resented Thancmar for seeing her nudity.

The infant quieted at once, fastening on her nipple like a limpet. Maybe it was a sea creature he resembled.

"No," I said aloud. "A bear."

Aurima glanced up. "*Beran*," I explained, gesturing at the baby.

Her eyes widened. "What is happening to you?"

My elbow was bloody. I looked down at my hands. My fingers were as battered and blood-crusted as on the night Hroswitha had salved them. My ring, which had slid so easily back on my hand, was now sunk in swollen flesh.

"Thancmar!" Her voice rose, panicky. "Thancmar, look!"

The hurt was suddenly much worse, so fierce it made my eyes water. "*Zoubar*," I said. Helpfully I added in Latin, "Magic." But the words made no sound.

Evidently I had lost enough blood to scatter my wits, for I did not remember much of the journey to Bruna. Thancmar led us on deer paths and fox trails to avoid any pursuers on the Amber Road. Aurima doctored me every day with potions and poultices, but I was still in pain when we entered Vannaz's mountain-cradled stronghold. We found a place to stay that seemed safe, and I fell gratefully into sleep.

When a noise finally woke me, I was surrounded by bars of color, some thick and some thin—red, yellow, ivory, green, blue, and more—mounting high into darkness. Mysterious yet pleasing, except for a reek of stale urine so strong that I thought I must have pissed myself many times over.

I groped for my sword, but my hand had become a wolf's paw. A child with long wheat-colored hair jumped up and ran away crying, "Mama."

Odd, I thought hazily. Was that my son grown older, the bear cub?

The next time I awoke, I heard the sweet sound of liquid plashing into a cup. Aurima leaned over me. "Drink this." She tried to lift my head.

"Let me do it," said a deeper voice. I glimpsed a brawny crouching thigh, a studded belt, a broad expanse of tunic. An arm like an iron bar slid under my shoulders and tipped me up to drink.

I swilled ale as if I were hollow. Finally, turning my face aside, I gasped, "Cleon." This must be a dream. Cleon should have returned to Carnuntum.

"Marcus." He was grinning, his broken teeth bright in the half-light. "I feared they'd be hauling you out of here by your heels."

I reached up, and he gripped my hand so hard I winced. "Dio?" I croaked, trying to see past his bulk.

"Here, Marcus." Dio edged forward, pitcher in hand. Though he too smiled at me, deep lines scored his high brow. As he grasped my hand, a heavy silver bracelet slid down his wrist. "Where is the boy?"

"Boy? Rufus?" I tried to recall. "Oath-sworn to Inguiomerus."

"What?" Cleon's face curdled with anger. "The little dung-rat!"

"Ollius is . . ." I began, but my throat closed.

Dio made a small noise.

Cleon sighed. After a moment he said thickly, "Knew he wouldn't desert you."

"Where's...Lamia?"

"He left for Carnuntum a few days after you disappeared," Dio said. "We decided to stay here in Bruna. Thought we'd have a better chance to find out what hap—" he gulped—"what happened to you."

My bleary eyes wandered over the multicolored walls. I managed to say Aurima's name. Her hand took hold of mine, tenderer than the men's. "Beran?" I whispered.

"He is well," she said, and I let myself sink into sleep again.

"I do not believe in magic," I said stubbornly.

Aurima looked up from a patch she was sewing on my tunic. "Things you do not understand are sometimes magic."

The bandages that had turned my hands into paws were gone. My pink and swollen fingers were scabbed with healing wounds, the torn nails regrowing. I could not forget the shock of seeing them by firelight, torn and bloody, when moments earlier they had been unscathed enough to stroke the tenderness of a baby's skin.

"Tell me again what Vannaz said."

"He wants you to come to him when you are well."

"Is he going to make your father pay for what he did?" Ingiomar's pursuit of us seemed to have ended—so far, at least.

"It is not for a king to punish his chiefs." The thread broke. She hissed, annoyed.

"What about the Council of Women? Do they not give justice?"

"Later, *min hersa*. Rest. Let the Goddess heal you."

The baby mewed. As she turned to look at him in his basket, the stacked colors behind her blurred. This was the storeroom of a cloth merchant, as I should have guessed from the smell of ammonia used to set the dyes.

With a sigh of frustration I closed my eyes. The sword-slash in my upper arm was taking more time to mend than I could bear.

She said, "I pray the Goddess has kept Thancmar safe on his return to the mill."

I grunted. The dwarf had guided us back to the world of time. In Bruna, folk who traded with Rome knew that Portunalia had just gone by, or maybe Dio had said Vinalia. At any rate, it was mid-August—over three months since I had led my vexillation across the Danube, cocksure of regaining the respect I had lost.

I must have sighed again, or groaned, for Aurima tried to distract me: "Spider misses you; the farmer says he goes around and around in his pen." She paused. "You have not told me of Boss. Is he still in Carnuntum, your warhorse?"

"He is dead," I said. Reminded of the man who had bragged of killing him, I added with unthinking vindictiveness, "As dead as Friduric."

"Friduric is not dead." Surprised, I opened my eyes. She placed her bone needle carefully in its reed casing. "But I do not think he asks the gods for long life."

Someone out in the front room asked, "How much for three ells?"

I felt compelled to say, "He wanted to please your father." In a Roman, such dutifulness would have been praiseworthy.

Aurima caught her breath in a sad chuckle. "My father is never going to give up avenging my mother." She turned the tunic right side out and held it up, but the glistening in her eyes would have made it hard to inspect the work.

I hesitated. She had not told me what she thought about my bloody path from Hoheneih. "Aurima," I said at last, "I have sworn to kill him." A fine boast for a man with one good arm and no more strength than his own newborn son.

The doorway of the storeroom dimmed. The merchant's wife, a thin, fig-faced woman from Pannonia, entered with the stocky simpleton who was their man of all work. "There," she told him, pointing. "The nettle green."

As he lifted down a folded length of cloth, she turned to Aurima. "My lady," she said respectfully, "how does your man today?" Her eyes lingered on my wounded hands.

"I am better," I said in Germanic.

"Praise to the Goddess." The woman turned back to her helper. "There, the elderberry also. He wants to see them both. Careful, *dumba!*"

The man added a roll of dark reddish fabric to his armload and trailed his mistress out of the room. Had she heard me say, "I have sworn to kill him"?

I muttered, "We must leave here."

Aurima picked up the baby, who was beginning to fuss. "They think you were wounded by Romans. They will not give you away." The cloth merchant had been told that I was German. However, repeated visits by Dio and Cleon were bound to raise his doubts.

I needed to get onto my feet. Movement would stir up the good humors and heal my arm. I sat up and reached for Aurima's shoulder to help myself stand.

She ignored me to investigate the infant's wrappings. He let out a wail.

A little girl with wheaten hair peeked into the room. "Does he need a dry cloth, Lady? May I do it?"

Unwilling to be seen struggling, I lay back so they could put him next to me on the pallet. I should have been thinking about the future, about lost Eagles and vengeance and being court-martialed for killing Glabrio, but the girl's earnest chirps and Aurima's softer voice were lulling.

Light from the doorway polished my beloved's cheek, the straight bridge of her nose, a curving strand of red hair that she pushed back behind her ear. The tender glide of her neck hid in shadow as she looked down. She would bare it to me, her head flung back, as I teased her nipples with teeth and tongue, as her thighs clasped me tight . . .

O gods! Would she never again long for me?

Who would have thought that a man with a suppurating arm wound could also ache with lust? I turned my back on Aurima and her apprentice and pretended to sleep. After what seemed a long time the pretense dissolved, and became darkness.

29: KING AND CAESAR

Like most Germans the merchant and his family retired with the sun, so the knock on their door after dark alarmed the household.

The merchant himself came to the curtained doorway of the storeroom. The candle he held glittered on rings and pierced coins in his beard that marked him as a man of means. "My lady," he said, turning his eyes away from Aurima, who in the summer heat slept only in her shift, "a man at the door is saying your name. I think he is a Roman."

By then I was on my feet, sword in hand. Without speaking Aurima rose and laid the baby beside me, then pulled on her sleeveless tunic and followed the merchant.

I strained my ears over the baby's whimpers. He paid no heed to my murmured command to hush, so I crouched and gave him the distraction of my smallest finger. He clamped onto it with enthusiasm.

The front door scraped open. I clenched one fist on the hilt of the sword and the other on my son's tiny hand.

Footsteps approached. The curtain swung open. I saw Dio's dark shape, outlined by the light Aurima carried behind him.

"Marcus? Are you awake? I have news."

The curtain fell shut as Aurima set down the candle in its saucer. She reached for the infant, who uttered a yelp at being taken from my grasp.

I sat down, easing my fingers off the sword grip. "What is it?"

"I have been doing some work, scribing and bookkeeping and inventory, for Aldric." He noticed my frown. "I thought you knew him; he is Leonnatus's agent here. He has just received a message from Leonnatus with news from Rome."

I made an impatient gesture.

Dio took a deep breath. Lowering his voice to a whisper, he said, "Caesar has lost his wits."

This seemed blackly humorous to me. "How can they tell?" I said. After betrayals and assassination attempts by those he trusted, compounded by desecration of Rome's holiest temple, Caligula must have been living in a fog of fear and desperation.

Dio batted away the sarcasm with a flap of his hand. "People who saw him said he was like a wild man. He tore his hair and clothes and ran through the streets to the Temple of Capitoline Jupiter, screaming to the gods."

Dread startled me out of mockery. "Why? Has something happened?" A great military disaster? Some tremendous natural cataclysm?

"Julia Drusilla has died. May her shade rest in peace."

"His sister?" Aurima breathed.

His best-loved sister. With a sigh I laid aside my sword. "What did she die of?"

"She was ill; that was all Leonnatus said. Maybe summer fever."

Maybe poison.

I looked away. *Oh, Drusilla.* How could anyone who knew her have harmed her?

I had been half in love with her as a boy, when my brother and I were sent to visit Mother's great-aunt, who was also the grandmother of Caligula and his three sisters. The Drusilla I had known was kind and innocent, as unlike her ambitious older sister and vindictive younger one as if she had been born in a different family.

Could someone have murdered her to weaken her husband Lepidus's chances of succeeding to the principate? Or—viler yet—to deprive her brother of the only person who truly cared for him?

Hunched before my eyes in a horse stall, Caligula had shrieked, *Gods, no more! O Furies, let me be!*

Dio said, "Aldric is supposed to keep it quiet until Caesar is himself again." Any rumor of weakness might encourage Rome's enemies—and even its allies—to sharpen their swords.

"Something else." He glanced at Aurima. Cradled in her embrace, little Beran played with my silver ring, which hung at her neck along with her amber pendant. "Lamia knows you are here. The king sent him word."

I tried to focus my scorched eyes on him. "How long ago?"

"Well . . . long enough that he is on his way from Carnuntum."

I cursed to myself. By what foul luck was the Special Cohort regional prefect still on the Pannonian frontier, when he had a quarter of the world to make trouble in?

Dio's gaze fell to my hot and swollen arm. "What are we going to do, Marcus?"

Here in Vannaz's stronghold, Lamia would have to think twice before kidnaping a priestess of noble blood. My own situation was more grave. It is military policy for the murder of an officer to be prosecuted. If the prefect brought a detachment of soldiers with him, how was I to avoid capture?

Aurima stopped humming as she rocked the baby. I blinked, unable to meet her gaze. "I think we must make a bargain with the king," I said slowly.

Hoheneih and Grozhauga had been rustic settlements; Bruna pretended to be a town. Flanked by two lean rivers that merged to the south in a marshy slough, it perched atop a low hill in a pocket of higher hills. Longhouses buried in gray-speckled thatch jostled timber-and-mud buildings roofed with Roman tiles. Round huts hunched under slabs of turf. No two buildings stood in a line; no wall, or roof gable, or door frame was completely straight.

As we twined through the haphazard scatter of houses, barns, and workshops, Cleon squinted in the sun. "It's not smart to make your woman so angry," he said.

My wounded arm throbbed fiercely beneath the bandage. Trying not to cling to the stave I carried, I said, "A wife should obey her husband."

"'Wife,' is it?" He grinned. "You're getting more like us common folk all the time. None of that nonsense with priests and contracts and golden veils, eh?"

Aurima had insisted that she was well-known to Vannaz and could make our case to him better than I could. Perhaps she was right, but I had had enough of being helpless. I would not have a king reckon me willing to hide behind a woman's skirts.

Think you're helpless now? an inner voice whispered cruelly. *Imagine yourself with only one arm.*

A stone twisted under my foot, and I stumbled into the path of a cow pulling a cart full of wood. Cleon grabbed my sleeve and hauled me against him as the cow plodded by. The cartwheel spat dirt and dung onto my leg, and the woman driving clicked her tongue at my waywardness.

Moments later, he seized my stave to beat away a pig rummaging in the lane ahead of us. I steadied myself on a roof post, glad of the pause. "So Lamia told you . . . Berinhard and . . . Chlothar killed Ollius and me?"

"Crocodile tears by the bucket," Cleon said. "Too bad you couldn't hear his eulogy of you. 'Bravely volunteered to explore a possible threat to the vexillation. Foully slain by treacherous Germans.' And Bat-Ears trying not to smirk, the little pus-bag."

Since Dio's warning the night before, I had become more confident of defying Lamia. If he threatened to drag me back to Carnuntum, I would counter with a threat to inform the legion commander and the governor of his lie about Varian survivors. Anyway, he would soon have something more serious than Glabrio's slaying to worry about, unless Caligula regained his senses.

My strength waned on the last of the climb to the market square, and I had to stop again to rest. The broad greensward, which last September had swarmed with traders, travelers, and their caravans blocked by Ingiomar's rebellion, was almost empty now. At the far end, picketed horses and mules near a scatter of Roman tents must be the remnants of Glabrio's detachment. The only wheeled vehicle I saw was Placidus's cart.

Something new caught my attention: a small temple next to Vannaz's *halla.* Much like the Temple of Vesta in the Forum, it was circular with a portico of painted columns and a tiled roof. Could it be a shrine to Austro, who was usually worshiped in the open air?

I was curious enough to investigate. After climbing the steps, I leaned on the stave to catch my breath.

There were no interior walls where a *cella* would normally be. Instead, I was confronted by Caligula Caesar. In a pose characteristic of his great-grandfather Augustus, the armor-clad Princeps gazed over my head, pointing skyward, with a commander's cloak draped over his other arm. The sculpted torso was stockier than Caligula's own, and his head looked peculiar atop it. Well, perhaps only to me.

As if he were a sacred tree, reverent Germans had flung tributes onto him. A gold necklace hung from his raised arm, and a thong bearing a silver ring had caught on one of his ears. A dead rabbit lay at his sandaled feet.

I would tell Aurima about this sign of Vannaz's homage to Rome, I thought. No, I had forgotten: she must have seen it earlier when she went to announce our arrival to the king.

"Greetings, cousin," I murmured to the painted marble face. It was the statue I had seen wrapped on its way to Bruna.

Caligula smiled at me.

I blinked my blurry eyes. Heat seeped from them and from my nostrils. I had become a fire-breathing chimera.

A faint clamor surged louder and nearer: excited barking, cheerful shouts, neighing, the thump of hooves, the screech of wheels.

From the step below me Cleon muttered, "What a monster."

He was looking at the dead boar that had just appeared, along with the king of the Marcomanni and Quadi and the rest of his hunting party. Standing under the temple's architrave, we watched Vannaz stroke his horse's neck and joke with Vangio while the others crowded around the pig's carcass on a handcart. Bristly hounds threaded through the mob, and servants brandished bloody boar-spears like military standards.

Cleon trotted down the steps and shouldered his way into the crowd. When he spoke to the king and his nephew and gestured toward the temple, their eyes flashed to me. Vannaz nodded.

My heart beat hard. If the king gave Aurima and me his protection, we would be safe from both Lamia and Ingiomar. When I recovered, I could order supplies through Aldric to launch a search for the lost Eagle.

Inhaling deeply to clear my head, I descended the temple steps carefully. Although I had met the king at last year's truce negotiations, I did not look the same now with shaggy hair and an uncut beard. Only the gold torc and my family ring, jammed back onto my smallest finger, lent any distinction.

Vannaz was tall and thick-chested, as might be expected of a man strong enough to rule not just one but two warrior nations. He had a boxer's face, with a crooked nose and broken cheekbones. One brow was scar-smashed; the other arched above shrewd pale eyes. Scratches and stabs from underbrush scored his cheeks and arms, and twigs had snagged in his loose ginger-brown hair and beard. A musk of blood and sweat emanated from him.

"The Goddess's greetings," I said hoarsely in Germanic.

Surprise lifted his mismatched brows; then a keener interest narrowed his dark-gray eyes. "The Goddess's greetings," he replied.

I turned to his nephew. Had he been involved in betraying me to Berinhard?

Vangio gave his dolphin smile. "Aquilo, *mîn friund.*" He held out his palm to me. I extended my own hand, watching his eyes to see if he showed any pleasure in its disfigurement. As he clasped it, his brows drew together in a frown. I was gratified that I had not let myself wince.

As the rest of the hunting party flooded into the thatch-covered feasting hall, Vannaz led us to a half-built Roman-style house on its other side. We passed between brick pillars awaiting their marble cladding, into an atrium where a tiler was setting tesserae inside an outlined drawing, and down a hall. I strove to match the king's pace, the butt of my stave striking harder on the wooden floor. The walls seemed to ripple as I swayed between them.

Vannaz pushed aside a door hanging. The floor of the room we entered was pounded dirt, well saturated with spilled ale. Several crude stools draped with animal skins ringed a firepit filled with dead ash, and smoke-dulled murals of a deer hunt chased around the walls. A window let in light from a garden.

The king lifted his pinned cloak over his head, pitched it onto an empty seat, and threw himself onto another stool. The long hunting blade sheathed at his waist reminded me of my treasured Army knife, stolen when I was left for dead at Grozhauga.

I straightened, tightening my grip on the stave to keep myself steady. In careful Germanic I said, "Vannaz, I am Marcus Licinius Aquilo. I was senior tribune of the legion in Carnuntum. Now I am the husband of Aurima, daughter of Ammisia." There was satisfaction in saying the word *frijo*—husband—as if I had earned the crown in a contest at some great festival.

Vannaz found a leaf in his hair. "Aurima is not here with you?" He combed his fingers through his beard. Small twigs and bits of tree moss fluttered from his hand.

"No." I sensed that he expected an excuse, but I did not want to give one.

"Then sit, Aquilo. First we drink."

I propped my stave against a folded-back window shutter. Cleon leaned against the wall beside it.

As I lowered myself to a seat beside Vannaz, Vangio dropped down on his other side. "I thought that black beast was going to spill Folcher's guts," he said in Germanic.

Vannaz's grin showed teeth as damaged as the rest of his face. "So did Folcher."

While we waited for ale, they traded reminiscences of the hunt that meant nothing to me or Cleon. Drinking is part of important decision-making among the Germans. Of course, *Truth in wine* is one of our sayings, too.

Voices from the *halla* pulsed through the open window in time with the beat of my blood. My bad arm throbbed. Buzzing flies lit on my bandage, swooped on my hands.

So quiet was the entry of a stout, bent-backed woman with steel-gray braids that I noticed her only when Vangio exclaimed, "*Amma!*" She too leaned on a stick, but hers was slender with a ring of green serpentine at its head. When the king and his nephew rose and bent to welcome her, she held Vannaz's shoulders and kissed his cheek, then Vangio's. Gripping her staff, she gathered the grimy skirts of her white robe and sank onto a seat near the window.

Vannaz said, "My mother, Gisila." Austro's chief priestess in the Mark.

Why was she here? With painstaking correctness I greeted her in the Goddess's name.

Gisila turned toward me. Her deep-set eyes were milky with cataract, her toothless mouth sunken. On her bosom lay an amber disk like Hros-witha's.

Servants carried in a sloshing cask and an armload of auroch horns. Vangio exclaimed in satisfaction.

Cleon refused the offer of ale. He was taking his bodyguard duty seriously. When Vangio and I had been served, Vannaz lifted his foaming vessel. "Long life and glory for Gaius Caesar Augustus Germanicus," he said in guttural Latin.

He and Vangio gulped ale. I did not.

The king lowered his horn. "You do not drink to the Princeps?"

"I am not going to drink to you either, Vannius." I forced saliva into my dry mouth. "Since I entered your lands, Quadi and Marcomanni have joined with Romans to rob me of my life and honor."

Vannaz was not provoked by an offense to his dignity. He waited.

My hot dry eyes met his. "Should a true king not protect me, my wife, and my child from those who betrayed us, captured and tortured us, and sought our deaths?"

Belatedly I thought I should have spoken in simpler Latin, but Vannaz had understood. He fisted his free hand on his knee. "Name me these men."

"Inguiomerus of the Marcomanni. Maelo, his wife's brother. Friduric, his son. Berinhard of the Quadi, who is now dead. Chlothar his brother, who is dead. Vatia Glabrio, who is dead." I paused for breath. "And Aelius Lamia."

"Do I hear my name?" said a smooth voice. Pushing aside the curtain, the black-cloaked Praetorian prefect stepped into the room.

30: THE MAN WITH TWO TONGUES

I staggered up, dropping my drinking horn to grab for the knife I did not have. "What trick is this, Vannius?"

"Aquilo," Lamia said. "Back from the dead! My congratulations."

The king's craggy face showed no surprise. He stood up too, so that all five of us were eye to eye.

I seized my stave and veered toward the doorway. Vangio blocked my path. "Aquilo, the king must both of you hear. That is why my *amma* has come—to hear."

"This man ordered my death and my wife's abduction," I sputtered. "I will not stay if he is present."

Lamia shot back, "So says a traitor who has just killed one of my senior officers."

No doubt he had hurried to reach Bruna; his face was pink and the disheveled waves of his silver hair made him look dissolute. But the air of debauchery was contradicted by predatory calculation in his hazel eyes. He had not given up hope of delivering news of my death to Rome.

Vannaz held up both hands, one wrapped around his great curling ale-horn. "I did not plan this, Aquilo. But I ask you to stay. For both of you I have questions."

Despite my anger, I knew his goodwill was crucial. I slumped into my seat, eyes on Lamia.

"Vangio, fetch another horn. And a seat for the prefect."

His nephew went out. Lamia swept the hem of his cloak beneath him and took Vangio's stool. His gaze moved. "Cleon. Gave your trainees a day off, did you?" He must have informers here in Bruna, if he knew my bodyguard had been earning his bread by teaching close combat to young warriors.

Cleon's broken teeth glittered in his dark beard. "I'd like to set 'em on you, Prefect 'Eight Survivors.'"

Lamia narrowed his eyes, feigning perplexity. "What do you mean by that?"

Of course he would deny having invented the eight captives. With Glabrio dead, the existence of the hoax was my word against his. So faithfully had I kept my promise of secrecy that no one else could confirm the deception.

We will see whom the governor believes, you two-tongued rat.

The old priestess sat unmoving with her hands clasped in her voluminous lap. Vangio returned, thumped down another stool, and refilled the huge horns. As little as I cared to drink in Lamia's company, I was too thirsty to refuse.

We all quaffed ale. My head swam when I stopped for breath.

Vannaz lowered his horn and swiped a hand across his wet mustache. "So how is it, Prefect, that a Roman tribune dies at Grozhauga, and while I am asking how this happened"—his gaze shifted to me—"the Roman lives again and runs from Hoheneih?"

Lamia's answer was immediate: "As you must recall, great king, my scout Tudrus reported that some of Berinhard's guests at Grozhauga had attacked Aquilo. Berinhard was killed while trying to protect him, as was Aquilo's bodyguard, and we were told that Aquilo died of his wounds. Incorrectly, it seems."

"No," I said thickly. "Berinhard and Chlothar attacked us. They killed Ollius. Inguiomerus took me prisoner."

Vangio spoke up. "Prefect, from here you went Aquilo's body to get. When no body was there, you did not look more?"

Lamia's ring finger ticked against the drinking horn. "Chlothar handed over ashes he said were Aquilo's."

"Did you send them to my mother?" I blurted out.

The prefect contrived an apologetic grimace. "I did."

Appalled, I almost missed the king's next words. "And now Chlothar is killed. By a man from Hoheneih, it is said." He mimicked Lamia: "Incorrectly, it seems."

I was still fixed on the prefect's sham ignorance of my survival. "Your informers . . . must have told you Inguiomerus meant to put me to death." I dragged in a breath. "And you did nothing to rescue me."

Tick, tick went Lamia's ring on the hollow horn. "Vannius, has he told you why he helped that woman, a sacred hostage, to defy our gods and laws by fleeing Rome?"

Vannaz lowered his own horn from his lips. His gaze flicked from Lamia to me. "Madness of love, *ja?*"

"She tried to kill Caesar. Stabbed him with a dagger."

The king's face stiffened. He looked at Vangio, who shook his head. Even in my heat-haze I understood that Ingiomar and Maelo must have kept that secret close.

"Aquilo's father made an attempt on Caesar's life, too," Lamia went on. "You see what a brutal pair they are, he and the woman. Like speaks to like." A curl at the corner of his mouth hinted at his pleasure in the adage, and in the weight of his accusations. "I have come, as Caesar's representative, to bring them back to Roman justice."

Vannaz took a long swallow of ale. He jabbed the tip of his horn into the earthen floor and wiped his ginger mustache with the back of his hand, not looking at either of us. "What do you think of this?" he asked his nephew in Germanic.

Vangio tilted his brows. "Love madness, *ja*. Murdering Caesar?" He shrugged.

"She did it for me." I slipped into their language. "He caused great pain for my family." My thoughts were beginning to disconnect, slipping from my grasp like fish in a pool. I had to grope through the muddle in my mind to recall my intentions. Obtaining the king's protection: that was most critical. Then, when my arm was healed, I could . . . Aurima and I could . . . With his help, we could go into the wilderness for . . .

Unable to follow our exchange, Lamia burst out in Latin, "Great king, during the recent skirmish between the men from Grozhauga and Hoheneih and my Praetorians, this monster Aquilo also killed one of my officers."

Anger focused my wits. I dashed my horn to the ground and struggled up. "That whoreson took my wife captive a few days after she gave birth. He deserved to die." Tottery without my stave, I reeled forward.

Lamia mistook my unsteadiness for an aggressive lunge. His ale splashed across my feet as he jumped up, whipping back his cloak, and reached for a knife to defend himself. Its sheath, I saw, rode on a belt decorated with engraved silver leaves inlaid with niello—the very belt I had worn to Berinhard's feast.

With an inarticulate roar I seized his cloak and wrenched him toward me. He thrust both arms up to break my grip. "What in Hades—"

"You paid Berinhard to kill me." I yanked his knife from its sheath, meaning to drive it between his ribs.

An iron grip stayed my hand. I resisted, but Vannaz's fingers crushed mine.

"He has my belt." I struggled, enraged. "And my knife."

"You're raving." Lamia picked up the blade that Vannaz had forced me to drop. "This knife was forged for me in Hispania five years ago."

It ought to have been the Army *pugio* stolen when I was attacked at Berinhard's—its guard incised with *ROMA* and *AMOR*, its blade worn from sharpening—but as the fury cleared from my eyes, I saw that it was indeed much newer. "Where is mine?" The longknife that my father had carried in Germania and I had worn in Pannonia, that had taken his life and my brother's, was not just a weapon; it stood for my family's sacrifices for Rome.

I swept my confused and embittered glare to Gisila. The old woman's milky eyes, deep-set under tufty brows, seemed to be fixed on the view from the window. She was not watching us, but listening.

I needed no more proof that Lamia had conspired with Glabrio to have me killed. He would pay.

LAMIA. INGIOMAR. MAELO.

I turned to the king, who had resumed his seat. My tongue felt like boiled wool. "Again I ask you to protect me, my wife, and our son, Vannaz *kuninga."*

With a sigh Vannaz got up again. He crossed the firepit in one long stride and crouched beside his mother's seat. They conferred quietly.

I realized I was at the window. How had I come to have the stave in my hand?

Bees circled a straggly rosebush in the garden. "How goes it, Cicero?" Cleon said beside me, his voice hardly audible over the buzzing.

Gisila beckoned me with her green circlet-topped staff. She was only a couple of steps away, but the distance seemed great. I flinched when she raised a hand, but she wished only to feel my face: forehead, nose, cheeks, beard. She mumbled something.

Vangio's eyes widened. Vannaz objected, "But, *Muoter*, he is Roman."

"What is it?" Cleon demanded. "What's she saying?"

"My grandmother says . . . inside him they fight." Vangio's big forehead wrinkled in apprehension. "Austro and . . . and the Dark One. That is why he burns."

Cleon felt my arm. "Diana's tits, you're as hot as a furnace. Let's get out of here."

I did not budge. "What is your decision, Vannius?"

"Great king, you are a valued friend of Rome," Lamia interjected. "But if our laws are treated less seriously than they deserve, Caesar will be very disappointed." He cocked his head, eyes glinting at the king. Draped in black, he looked like a crow waiting for some injured creature to die.

"Take your threats and . . . god-cursed lies back to Carnuntum," I slurred. There were two Lamias now, the pair of them crouching to fall upon my strengthless body.

"Listen to me," the king's voice grated.

I clutched my stave, swaying. What a poor job I had made of this! Had I not kept Aurima from coming, she would have easily persuaded Vannaz and routed Lamia.

"My mother says that you both speak truth. But she cannot read your heart, Aquilo, because of the fire in you." He looked from one of us to the other. "I am going to ask Tiwaz the Just for the deciding. Before then, Prefect, you must not put a hand on this man or his family. And you, Aquilo, must not hurt any man who offends you."

"How soon may I expect your judgment, great king?" Lamia asked.

"That is for Tiwaz." Impatient now, Vannaz strode toward the doorway.

I said, "I need . . . a safe place for my family."

The king had gone by the time I forced the plea off my withered tongue. Vangio, behind him, paused long enough to say, "Do not worry about that, Aquilo. First, the war inside you must end."

31: PATERFAMILIAS

Wound fever was something that happened only to others. Unfortunate casualties of Ingiomar's ambush the year before. Soldiers who sliced open their feet chopping wood or digging a ditch. Public-works slaves with fingers crushed by paving stones. And now me.

Some men bear such debility with fortitude. Not I. I was furious. Why must it enfeeble me, when I needed to be tough and alert to protect myself and my family? I thrust away Aurima's hand when she tried to wipe my perspiring face, and shut my teeth obstinately against the concoctions she brewed. When Beran's wails pierced my restless doze, I groaned and grumbled at her. I blamed her for not knowing as much magic as her grandmother.

Once I woke, facedown, to find her smearing ointment on the rough weals and pits of my back. I told her to stop, but she ignored me.

I heard the slap of sandals. Then Dio's horrified exclamation: *"Roma Dea!"*

It was the first time he had seen what a ruin Friduric had made of my back. "Begone," I muttered. "Go back to your abacus and tablets."

As if I had not spoken, Aurima said to him, "Hold this, please."

Should I be surprised that no one listened to me, respected me, obeyed me? I pressed my cheek into a pillowing cloak and screwed my eyes shut. Ollius rose out of the depths into my mind: *Marcus, hold fast, I am coming.*

"Is his arm better at all?" Dio murmured.

Her reply was muffled: "I fear that somehow I have displeased the Goddess."

A drop of wetness kissed my shoulder.

"He has a strong spirit, Aurima. Think of all he did to find you."

I wanted to escape into sleep. But I was too aware of their breathing, the rustle of Aurima's stola, the maddening drone of flies. The touch of her fingers on my ravaged skin was like cool water in the throat of a thirsty man.

Silent tears gathered on my eyelashes. I blinked them back, all the angrier for pitying myself.

"Marcus, I have good news. I think." Dio's voice, starting robustly, softened into uncertainty.

I wanted to grumble, "What?" like a sullen child, but made myself turn to him.

"Aldric has had another message from Leonnatus. Leo asks him to find a first-quality piece of amber suitable for a pendant. It must be the color of clover honey, and no more than a *scrupulum* in weight."

My gaze lit on Aurima's own amber pendant. Hers was darker—almond honey, perhaps. *Merda!* Who cared about honey or amber or tradesmen's orders?

"The order came from your mother," Dio went on. "She wants the pendant as a wedding gift for your sister."

So Lepidus had found some widowed old crock for Nina, as I feared.

"It is to be sent to Narbonnese Gaul. I imagine . . ."

Pertinax.

Lucius Pertinax, Nina's longtime admirer. My poor sister, reduced to abandoning the bustling, gossipy Rome she loved in order to marry a provincial farmer. Evidently no one of better birth had wanted her, since she could not bear children.

Stung with shame at the memory of what had happened to the last child she carried, I turned my head away.

"I was not going to . . ." A pause. "Very well. According to Leo, your mother said Nina asked for amber because it comes from the region where you disappeared. And it is to be"—I heard Dio swallow—"the color of your hair."

I wanted to laugh and weep at the same time. "Go," I mumbled into the cloak. "Go away. Leave me alone."

He sighed. Aurima said quietly, "Dio, he is not himself."

"I know. It is not you he is angry with. Or me."

"No?"

"When a *paterfamilias* dies, the oldest son becomes head of the household."

She murmured wordlessly. Her cool hand anointed the dip of my spine.

"It eats at him that he cannot keep the *familia* safe."

Father. Father. Father. I could almost slip into the overlapping darkness of the word's tender petals.

"That is why I give him my heart, Dio. He is a *haistra*. Do you know what that is? It is a young . . . a young *eih* . . . oh, I do not know that word in Latin either. A tree . . ."

An oak tree. Hoheneih, the tall oak, the oak of Thunraz. She did not desire me for my courage, my rebellious spirit, or even the passion of my lovemaking . . . but because I was a sapling, a young oak.

While I was puzzling over that, I lost the light.

Lamia had brought with him the same cavalry units as before, this time unencumbered by oxen. Tents, carts, horses, and mules clogged the broad pasture in front of the king's hall, with the familiar standards of the Fifth Gallica and Tenth Praetorians planted beside the headquarters tent. Perhaps they had been chosen in the hope that Glabrio's murder had intensified their hatred of me.

They could not see inside the litter Vangio had brought. I had demanded a horse, but was patronizingly rebuffed. Apparently the king had made a place for us to stay until our fate was decided, so we left the cloth merchant's house with our meager possessions. The small fair girl, the man's daughter, sobbed as Beran was taken from her.

Aurima had embraced Vangio when he arrived. The curtain in the storeroom doorway was drawn back to ease the heat, and I saw his thick arms wrap around her. When she stepped back, his big paws remained on her forearms. She laughed self-consciously, perhaps knowing I could see the two of them, and pushed his hands away.

Now, as Cleon strode beside the litter, I watched while the king's nephew tickled my infant son's chin, twitched Aurima's long skirts away from a clump of dung, and told her things that made her smile.

She had been betrothed to his brother, who had wed someone else while she was gone. I saw how fond she was of this porpoise-faced princeling, and my blood seethed.

The place that had been set aside for us was a room in the king's new house, next to the great hall. Vangio made much of its amenities, pushing open the shutters to display the garden like a landlord showing an apartment for rent. My injured arm shrieked from having been bumped and the baby was squawking fretfully, so finally I snapped, "Go, man; you have done enough."

Aurima said a few soft words to him. He smiled wryly, reclosed the shutters against the bright sunlight, and left. With a mumbled excuse Cleon followed.

Sighing, Aurima sank onto a couch opposite mine and uncovered a breast for the fractious child. "Fat-witted oaf," I grumbled. I spoke in Latin, or thought I did.

She looked up sharply. "It is his doing that we have shelter under Vannaz's roof. Is it not more pleasant here?"

"I would feel better if he kept his hands off you."

She watched the baby suckle, stroking his feathery hair.

Some jealous impulse made me say petulantly, "I am thirsty."

"You can shout until someone comes, or wait until I have fed your son," she retorted with sudden venom.

I stared at her. Even in my dull-witted state I realized what I had done. But my pride had already been battered too much; I could not apologize for being a needy wretch instead of the stalwart warrior she expected.

In a few minutes she said, "Vangio was like a brother to me when I was small."

It was an offer of truce, but I was not sensible enough to accept it. Instead I said crudely, "He does not seem worried that you may end up being strangled for treason."

She sat quite still for a moment, then plucked her nipple from the baby's mouth with an audible pop, jumped to her feet, and bolted toward the doorway, clutching him.

"Wait! I just— My arm—"

But she swept from the room, and I could only curse myself.

The afternoon passed. I drowsed in the heat, or tried to, my cursed wound pulsing with pain. On the edge of sleep, I would think I heard Beran's distant wail and imagine it meant Aurima was returning.

After twilight fell with no sign of her, I sat up and shouted for attention. Eventually a harried-looking woman in a stained overtunic came in, her face shiny with sweat. I said, "Where is my wife? Aurima?"

She said she did not know and turned to leave. "Wait," I said. "Bring me something to drink. And a light."

After she left, I stumbled to the window and opened a shutter. On the far side of the garden the great hall teemed with noise: shouts, laughter, the crashing of benches, snatches of song—the same racket I had grown used to hearing from Ingiomar's *halla*. I savored for a moment the memory of that building on fire, its thatch roaring flames into the night.

Where had Aurima gone? If she meant to teach me a lesson, I had learned it. I would be as stoic as a Spartan. I would give her the gratitude she deserved. I would do everything she suggested without complaint.

Darkness sifted into the room. I drowsed, feverish and thirsty and alone.

This was unbearable. I had not realized how desolate her absence would make me. I fumbled for the stave Cleon had left by my couch, shuffled to the dimly outlined doorway, and went out into a windowless corridor. A faint light lured me in one direction. Eyes fixed on it, I collided with an unseen stool and crashed to the floor.

A woman and a girl rushed up. "Where is Aurima?" I demanded, wrenching away from a grasping hand that smelled of grease and sweat. "Aurima, the priestess of Austro, where is she?"

"Are you all right? Are you hurt?" they gabbled. Perhaps they had been supposed to see that I did not wander.

I spoke louder. If she was nearby, maybe she would hear. "Where is my wife?"

"No, no." They tried to push me toward my room.

"Aurima!" I called out anxiously. "Where are you?"

Someone else loomed up behind the women: a broad German who

blotted out the distant glow. "Be calm, Roman," he rumbled.

I swung my stave at him, but he caught the end of it and wrested it away. "Look," I panted, "I just want . . . to know where . . . Aurima is."

"Not now," he said. He pulled me against him. For a moment my face was smothered in a beard that stank of everything he had ever eaten or drunk. Then he manhandled me down the corridor with an arm clamped around my shoulders.

The pressure against my wounded arm took away what little breath I had left. I could not even swear at him as he pushed me down on the couch. "Stay here, eh?" He swung the shutters together and latched them.

"My wife . . ." I gasped. "Aurima."

"Not now," he said again. His footsteps moved away.

Too tired to struggle further, I fired hoarse demands at the faces that peeped palely from the doorway. "Bring me my wife," I rasped. "Where is Cleon, my guard? I want to see Vannaz the king."

Instead of Vannaz, I was visited by his mother. Gisila floated in like a large cloud, preceded by a slave with a candle and followed by another with a cup and a dish.

I looked up eagerly at their approach, but my spirits turned sullen when I realized the old woman had not brought Aurima. I glowered at her.

Despite the night's heat, she wore a dark shawl over her once-white robe. Her cataract-blinded eyes were opalescent, and her nose jutted over the caved-in mouth. "You are making a lot of trouble in my house, young man."

It took me a moment to decipher the imprecise words. I said, "I cannot find my wife and child in your house, mother of Vannaz. Where are they?"

"Is Aurima your wife? Her family did not give her to you."

"I chose her. And she chose me."

She sank down on the other couch. Golden beads on her soft leather shoes winked in the candlelight. "Is it Aurima who taught you our language?"

Cudgels at Ingiomar's stronghold had taught me, too. "Gisila, the Praetorian Lamia wants to take her back to Rome." My voice cracked with desperation. "She is in danger."

"Oh, not here. Not in Bruna. No Roman defies my son's command." She nodded emphatically. "In the Goddess's name, I promise you she is safe."

I longed to believe her, but I had already made the mistake of trusting too much. "Where? Where is she?"

"She has many friends here. Maybe she visits them."

Like Vangio?

My anger flared. I had had enough of German women doing as they pleased. "I want her with me. Now."

She laughed softly, her jowls jiggling. "You are hungry, and your arm hurts, yes? So you make trouble. Here, I have brought you something to eat. Fill your belly and calm yourself." She beckoned the second servant forward.

The woman uncovered the dish she carried, but I had no appetite. I stared in fury and distress at the dish of stew, then at the brimming cup.

"There, now." Gisila rose from the couch, lightly despite her bulk. "No more trouble, eh? Aurima is safe, and the baby."

I said nothing, for I was already tipping the cup to my lips. The ale was bitterer than I liked, but every brewer's draft is different. I swilled it down in gulps, looking up only as the king's mother twinkled out of the room with the two servants and the candle. Leaving me, again, in the dark.

In my dream Aurima leaned down and gently kissed my cheek. I tried to speak to her, to embrace her, but was too weary. She must be smuggling me out of Bruna, I told myself. There was a wet little sneeze, the sort Beran made, and I sank in relief and contentment beneath the straw that concealed me.

32: IN THE HANDS
OF THE GODS

The cart rattled and bumped over ruts, its wheels squalling on the axles. I squeezed my eyelids tighter against glaring daylight. My head felt as if it had been cleaved in two. More urgently, my bladder was bursting. The last time I had been so drunk was after celebrating Caligula's first birthday as Princeps with my Mithraic brethren.

We must have left Bruna by now. I would sit up and draw Aurima's attention...

But I could not move. She had wrapped me like a sausage from shoulders to toes. "Stop," I croaked.

Someone said, "At last." In Latin.

Light stabbed me in the eyes. I could see nothing. Fighting against whatever pinioned my limbs, I shouted, "Aurima, free me."

"I am afraid your woman is not here to help you," someone else drawled.

Panic seized me. I struggled harder, flopping like a landed fish. Shapes emerged from the blare of light: a wagon driver, turned on his seat to stare; the bobbing head of a horse and then that of its rider, whose black helmet-plumes nodded with the horse's stride. Ahead and behind and all around rode cavalry troopers with javelins slung. Behind them, trees.

"Stop," I rasped again, in Latin this time.

Lamia raised his hand. Junior officers relayed the command.

"Free me."

I hardly knew what I was saying. Agony racked me. Where was I? Where was Aurima?

The driver clambered down into the cart. "Turn over, you stupid cunny."

I had been tightly rolled in a cloak whose edges were trapped beneath my weight. Released, I hauled myself up by the cart's high side and threw a leg over it.

The column was on the Amber Road, headed south. Toward Carnuntum.

Bile surged into my throat. I half fell to the ground, staggered a few steps, and collapsed onto hands and knees. My belly and bladder emptied together, and my eyes streamed tears.

The troops would be laughing at me. *Stand up,* I raged at myself. But something evil had me in its grip, as helpless as a rat in a mastiff's teeth.

"You were drugged," someone said beside me. Cleon.

Pain hewed my skull like an ax blade. My stomach heaved again, but there was nothing more to bring up.

"Take this," Cleon said as I slumped back on my heels. It was his neck-cloth, stiff with old sweat.

I wiped my face with a trembling hand. My jaw was bare. Badly shaven, the skin smarting. My rough fingers slid down to clasp my father's torc. Still there.

"It was supposed to put you to sleep. Poppy-tears, likely. The *medicus* reckons you were given too much." Cleon's eyes did not meet mine. "Here." He tucked his hand under my arm and hauled me to my feet.

Vannaz's mother. The bitter ale.

"Aurima?" I said. "Aurima—is she here?"

"She's all right. The prefect will tell you." He fumbled with a wine flask on a strap over his shoulder. "Thirsty?"

"Where is she?" I turned and swept my eyes along the column. Placidus peered from atop his bay mare. It was his cart that had transported me. In the vanguard of the troop: Praetorians, mailed and armed. Behind: re-mounts. Pack mules. Gallic cavalry, their ensign limp on its standard.

"Where is she?"

It ripped out of me with a rage that made Cleon retreat a step. I lunged at him, seizing a fistful of his tunic front. "*Where is she?*"

"Aquilo!" A peremptory bark. "Back off."

Valerius Secundus, once my second in command, glared down from his saddle. Next to him one of the Gallic troopers aimed a javelin at me.

Missing the swing of my hair, I fingered my bristly scalp. "What is..." I wanted to sound fierce and authoritative, but my voice caught in my throat. "What is going on?"

Lamia brought his horse up beside Secundus's. "Get back in the cart."

The sun was far to the west, casting long shadows across the road. "Lamia, what have you done?"

"Do not force me to make it an order. I would rather not bind you, but I will."

Why such delicacy from a man who had sanctioned my murder by barbarians? I spat out a last belch of acid. "Why am I here? Where is Aurima?"

"Do as I say, and you will find out."

Damn Vannaz to eternal hell! He had let Lamia have me after all.

"Cleon, tell me." I tried to hold his gaze. "What has become of her and the baby?"

"Better talk to the prefect." He slouched back to his place in the column.

If Vannaz had ordered her to stay in Bruna, she and the infant would be safe until I came for them. Assuming this was the day after I had been drugged, Bruna could not be far away. Somehow I must escape.

I looked around once more, dizzy and confused. This time I saw Dio's pale face turned toward me. Had he and Cleon protested when Lamia abducted me from Bruna? Did they worry that the old woman might have done me in with her sleeping potion?

Aurima was not here. Careful of my footing, I shambled past the two officers to the cart.

"I thought you were dead," Placidus said. He placed a silver cup against my chest and stooped down with his ear against it. "Cough."

"Tell me where my wife is. You must know."

"Either cough or shut up; I cannot hear a thing."

I held back the obscenities I wanted to spit at him. "What excuse did Glabrio give you for abducting her?"

The surgeon straightened, blocking my view of the tent entrance and the camp outside. "Aquilo, I am a soldier and a follower of Mithras. I obey orders. She had to be taken back to Rome. Without a hostage—"

"Aurima is my wife, Placidus! Her child is my son! Did you think it was right to drag off a woman barely out of childbed?"

He said stiffly, "I did not let her leave with us until she was able to travel."

"By Mithras's Dog! Don't you understand? It's part of a plot against me. Lamia and fucking Glabrio betrayed me to Berinhard of Grozhauga."

Placidus's face tightened. I thought the Mithraic oath that slipped out in my fury had startled him, but his voice was crusty with disbelief: "It was your idea to go there. When a bear attacks because you have entered its den, it is not a conspiracy."

"Lamia is wearing my belt. Does that seem like my imagination?"

"Cough for me. Maybe I can tell him you are dying of a weak heart." He leaned down with the cup again.

I coughed. Placidus listened, eyes distant.

Exhaustion drained my rage. "What am I doing here?" I croaked.

He unbent again and moved behind me. "The king gave his permission to take you back for trial. Carnuntum, Rome: I don't know." The rim of the cup pressed through the back of my tunic. "Cough."

"And Aurima, my wife?" If I kept saying *wife*, surely it would make a difference.

"I know nothing about what has become of her."

I twisted to glare at him.

"I swear by Mithras." He tossed the auscultation cup to his assistant, a wiry biscuit-colored Syrian. "Hold still; I am going to look at your arm."

Would Aurima have been told what Vannaz had done? At least she could be sure I had not left of my own will. She knew I loved her. *Beloved*, I had said, the first words I spoke when we were alone, *I came for you.*

I had freed myself once. I could do it again. This time I had Cleon and Dio to help. This time it would be me she embraced fiercely, not an ale-sozzled dwarf; me she thanked as many times as the sky had stars.

"More light," the surgeon growled, unreeling a sodden bandage. Was my troublesome left arm less swollen than before? Its pomegranate ripeness seemed to be less vivid, but perhaps that was an illusion. The tent's opening faced east for morning sick call, and at this hour the daylight that remained was diffuse, colors fading.

"This wound should have been cleaned out sooner." Placidus pitched away the balled-up bandage. "I found a shred of your tunic festering in it."

His assistant poked a tin-backed candlestick between us. Exposed at last, the gash had split open, and—gods help me!—a long yellow worm had stuck its head inside the cut. Nauseated with horror, I groped for it.

"Leave it alone," Placidus said. "It's linen, to draw out the bad humors." He pressed hard on both sides of the cut. Blood and thick bile oozed out. "You may still lose the arm, you fool. Why didn't you send for me in Bruna?"

Salt tears of pain trickled into my mouth. I whispered, "Aurima treated it."

"Whatever she poured into you must have slowed the inflammation. But if I hadn't opened it this morning, you'd have been dead in days." He bent and sniffed.

"I don't . . . remember." Not the surgery, not the clumsy barbering.

"Of course not. Best kind of patient, a man insensate. Clean this up, Epicadus."

Placidus turned away as his assistant moved in to blot up the mess. I heard small noises: a gush of liquid, the tap of a stirring-stick circling, the *tink* of pottery on glass. "Did you hear about Julia Drusilla?" he went on. "They say Caesar is mad with grief."

"Sir." A voice from the tent's entrance. "The prefect says to bring Aquilo now."

Finally. My heart jumped into the base of my throat. Lamia had made me wait to find out what he planned, yet suddenly I was afraid to hear it. It was one thing to face whatever he had in mind for me, but if he intended harm to Aurima and Beran . . .

Placidus ignored the summons. "Some Senator, I forget the name, swears he saw her rising to heaven. We will soon be told to worship her as a goddess, I expect." He returned to my side, agitating a pear-shaped glass *ampulla* with his thumb over the top. "Lie back. This will smart. Gag."

I stared dully, my mind wandering like a fly on a breadcrust. Epicadus lowered me with an arm under my shoulder, then thrust a stick between my teeth. Placidus poured something into the open wound that burned like a hot poker. Even biting hard on the gag, I could not suppress a groan.

He set down the vial and sponged my arm with remarkable gentleness. "This would make a neater scar if I stitched it, but the foul humors need to keep draining. Be sure it stays clean." He pitched the sponge into the basin. "You can sit up now."

I accepted a hand from Epicadus. When I came upright, my head spun. My arm throbbed so fiercely I expected to see it dilating and deflating.

Placidus folded a pad over the cut. As he held out his hand to Epicadus for a bandage, I murmured, "Help me. All I need is a horse."

His gaze flickered up to me, then returned to the bandage whose split ends he was tying together. "I saw you kill Glabrio."

I slid off the treatment table onto my feet. For an instant everything went dark.

"Aquilo." His big hand gripped my good arm. "Man, you are enamored of death."

"Oh, no," I said. I felt my mouth twitch in a crooked smile. "Not yet. I have vows to keep." *LAMIA. INGIOMAR. MAELO.*

I wavered toward the tent entrance. "Wait," Placidus said. "Take off that stinking rag. Epicadus, dig out a clean tunic of mine."

Outside, Cleon handed me my stave. We walked slowly to Lamia's tent, not far.

Stars sparkled in the evening heat-haze. I smelled trodden grass, sweat and porridge and campfire smoke. Heard spatters of conversation, the clink of mess tins, the rustle of picketed horses and mules.

Aurima, where are you? Beran, why can I not hear you cry?

Lamia's adjutant waited by the flap of the prefect's tent. He ducked inside to announce us, then emerged with a nod. I followed Placidus in. Cleon followed me.

Two torches lit the tent's large anteroom. Lamia lounged on a camp stool. Behind him, against the tent's dividing screen, Dio crouched on a tree stump with a note tablet on his knees. He stared at me, his face drawn. Pressed into Lamia's service again.

Like Lamia, Secundus had stripped to his tunic. A cup rested on his knee. Lamia's adjutant pushed in behind Cleon. The decurion commanding the Praetorian cavalry stood to one side, sweating in his cloak and chain mail. He might have headed the detachment that captured Aurima; I had not noticed in the tumult of the ambush.

I steadied myself on the tent pole. "Where are my wife and son?"

Lamia held up a temporizing hand. He seemed relaxed, perhaps because he had five men protecting him. "Surgeon Placidus, what is Aquilo's physical condition?"

"I operated only this morning, Prefect. His arm is still badly inflamed, and he is debilitated from wound fever."

"But I see him walking. You speak as if he had one foot on Charon's ferry."

The words floated inside my head. I sagged down on a large chest and watched the end of Dio's stylus wiggle as he wrote them down for the Special Cohort's records.

Placidus said, "He certainly cannot march, or even ride a horse. I said yesterday that he was too ill to be moved. He should be taken back to Bruna."

Hope sprang up in me: he would tell them that there was no justification for holding me, that I had slain Glabrio only to save Aurima and our child.

"That is not an option," Lamia said.

The surgeon grunted in displeasure. He was used to his advice being obeyed. "Then he must travel in my cart. He will need medical attention and extra rations of food and drink. Even then, I guarantee nothing."

"We are all in the hands of the gods, are we not? Good night, then. Thank you."

Placidus glanced at me as he departed. I could not read the look in his eyes.

Lamia inspected me as if I were a dog that might bite, then smiled at the others. "I think we are overcrowded. Secundus, remain. And Dio. Everyone else is dismissed."

Cleon looked at me questioningly. I hesitated a moment before nodding. Placidus's treatment had depleted my modest strength; I could have slept where I sat. But I had to know about Aurima.

The tent seemed vast and stuffy when the others had left. Flies cruised in a drowsy circle under its peak. The prefect began, "For the record, are you Marcus Licinius Carinna, known as Marcus Licinius Aquilo?"

The anger I had thought extinguished flared up again. It must have showed in my face, but I did not move. He could legitimately have me bound if I became violent.

"Well," he began, and stopped. "Perhaps you will want something to drink before you hear this. Dio, old fellow, pour him a cup of wine." He nodded at a pitcher on the ground between him and Secundus.

Dio—my own freedman, my father's get—stood up. I heard the wine gurgle, but did not look away from Lamia. When Dio held out the cup, I ignored it. He put it beside me on the chest and retreated to his tablet.

Fear started to twine around the hot core of my anger. "I am listening," I said.

Lamia sipped from his own cup, then set it down. "Vannius pointed out that the woman Aurima is one of his people, a priestess and the greatniece of a king." He began to thumb his equestrian ring around his finger. "Since she did not go to Rome of her own will, he claims she is not bound by our law and may not be compelled to leave the Mark." He paused. "I must accept that. It is not my purpose to antagonize an ally."

"So she is still in Bruna? Will he keep her safe from her father?"

He went on as if he had not heard, "You, on the other hand, are a Roman who killed a Praetorian officer. The king has decided he cannot offer you his protection." His ring glinted in the torchlight as it revolved around his finger.

"Even though I am the husband of a Marcomanni king's great-niece?"

Lamia reached for his cup. "Actually, no," he said, and drank again.

"*What?*" I shouted, although my voice was no louder than a whisper.

I was not aware of having risen until Secundus snapped, "Sit down, Aquilo."

Lamia cleared his throat. "Who can blame her? You tried to murder her brother and threatened her father. Since—"

"No! She said—"

He talked over me: "—'rescuing' her, you have scorned her attempts to nurse you. You told her, in fact, to go away. To leave you alone."

"That was— I was—"

"Then, in spite of no longer desiring her, you accused her of betraying you with another man."

"Ridiculous! Who told you that?"

"You even tried, gods forgive you, to drown your infant son."

"What? No, that was an accident." How could he know—

Aurima must have told him. Or Thancmar . . . ?

Lamia's handsome face was a mask of mock sympathy. "Your 'wife' wants no more to do with you, Aquilo." His thumb began to stroke the side of his cup.

"No," I said vehemently. "Let me hear it from her own mouth."

"Sit down," Secundus roared, "or I will call the guards."

The chest rose up behind my legs. I fell onto it.

Lamia went on, "Which made it easier for Vannius to decide your fate."

"You're lying," I said, but the heat had gone out of me again. I tried to recall what I had said to her, how I had acted. How could she possibly believe I no longer loved her? I had risked my life for her. I had tried to protect her and the child . . .

"Cheer up," Lamia said. "Imagine how it will ease your noble father's spirit. You intended to claim a half-barbarian brat as his grandson. Surely he will be glad your family's honor is not thus sullied." There was a sneer in his voice. "What's left of it."

The insult grazed me, but did not draw blood. I was too numb.

The prefect continued, suavely disdainful: "She has friends. The king himself, for one, and his nephew Vangio. So do not worry; she will land on her feet." He lifted his cup. "Or her back," he added, and drank.

My head was full of chaos. Could she really have left me? Not wanted me?

Impossible. It was impossible.

"So you are mine." Lamia set down his cup. "In Carnuntum we will learn whether Caesar orders you executed there, or wants you brought to Rome." He might have been comparing choices for breakfast.

"And you will obey willingly. You will not try to escape." He leaned forward. "Do you know why?"

After a moment I refocused my eyes to meet the intensity of his glare.

"Because whether you succeed or fail"—he reached to the side, clutched a fistful of Dio's hair, and hauled him forward, tablet and stylus cascading to the ground—"Licinius Dio here will have a fatal accident."

My secretary stared back at me, his eyes wide with shock and horror.

"Do you understand?"

I looked from Dio's face to Lamia's in dull disorientation, like a bull dazed by the first blow of a sacrificial ax.

The prefect bared his teeth in a grin. He patted Dio's hair back into place. "Forgive me, there's a good fellow. You'll keep an eye on your old master, won't you?"

"Yes, P-Prefect," Dio stammered, gathering his writing tools.

"You do not need to threaten him." My voice sounded like an old iron gate scraping open. "I will not try to escape."

Lamia's eyebrows went up. He leaned back, the savagery of his smile relaxing into surprised gratification.

"Just promise . . . Aurima and my son will not be harmed or molested again."

"Really?" He glanced sideways. "Perhaps he misheard what I said about her, Secundus? Very well, Aquilo; I promise."

"No. Swear it in daylight before the entire vexillation."

The prefect gazed at me blankly for several heartbeats. Then his hovering smile stretched into a grin. "So be it. I will take an oath after the morning sacrifice."

I needed to be alone. I cantilevered myself up and stumbled toward the tent's open flap, hanging onto my stave.

"I would rather have you in my net than the child, anyway," he said.

I stopped.

"A homely little creature, the *medicus* said. As yellow as a quince, and hairy. I doubt Caesar would have been pleased with him, after all."

"Caesar?" I turned.

"You thought she attacked him as soon as he came to bed, didn't you? Of course she wouldn't have told you, you poor young fool. He fucked her." He stressed each of his next words: "He. Put. His. Seed. In. Her."

I had never asked her. She had never said. I had just assumed . . .

Secundus looked at Lamia, brows lifted in surprise.

"The baby was the reason I sent Glabrio to get her." The prefect gave a sigh. "It would have been an achievement to bring Caesar his first living son. And not difficult, I reckon, to find a suitable lady who would claim to have birthed it. For the traditionalists."

"How did you know . . ." I struggled, but could not get past that part of the question. Even I myself had not been aware Aurima was pregnant. "How . . . ?"

"Glabrio has a number of informers in the Mark. Or had, rest his shade."

That was why Lamia had been in Carnuntum when Vannaz's message came. He was waiting for Glabrio to bring him Aurima and the baby.

His voice dwindled as I pushed out past the tent flap and went away. Away from firelight. Away from people. Away from anything of human making.

I would have walked into the forest, but a sentry turned me back. Someone pointed me to a tent. I stooped inside and crawled into the hot leather darkness until there was nowhere farther to go. Then I sank down and put my head in my hands.

It could be so. She could have hidden her pregnancy from me because she knew Beran was not my son. He had been fathered by Caligula, a man who had destroyed my family.

It could be that when we parted in Carnuntum, she had meant never to see me again. She planned to forget what had happened in Rome and raise the boy as a German. Then I had blundered into the Mark after her, nearly dying for her sake, so she felt obliged to let me claim her and the child she had borne.

But in Bruna she had glimpsed the life her kinship to a king would give her, if she were not wasting time with a bitter Roman who belonged nowhere.

She had left me. She did not want me.

She was gone.

33: FORSAKEN

Lamia swore his oath in the morning. He wanted me to do the same, but I refused. I had already pledged not to escape; there was no need for witnessing by gods or men.

Placidus had examined my arm wound. "Better," he said. But the pain deep inside was worse than any sword-slash. I closed myself around it, breaking apart every memory of Aurima, pawing through the shards, trying to reassemble them into something different. Seated beside the driver of Placidus's medical cart, I watched the miles rumble by in a blur.

The troops made camp. Cleon told me to wait for him to bring food. I sat on a fallen tree as dusk crept in from the woods, watching flames writhe in a firepit.

Dio came, luminous in his white tunic. "Marcus," he said. "I knew nothing about it. Lamia did not take me to his meeting with the king."

"No matter," I said. "He pays well."

He covered the silver bracelet with his free hand. "I . . . Permit me to say . . . Well, never mind; it will make no difference to you."

I looked back at the fire.

He sighed. "You must put her from your mind." He dropped down beside me. "When we reach Carnuntum, Lamia will charge you with murder." The words came quickly, in a half whisper. "Cleon and I need to know your plan."

"Plan?"

"What do you want us to do? Cleon is ready to take a message to the governor. I can ask Leonnatus to get word to the patron in Rome. Even though Julia Drusilla— Even if the patron is still grieving for his wife, he will intervene for you, will he not?"

Still grieving for his wife. But at least Lepidus knew Drusilla had loved him.

"Bring me wine," I said. "Real wine, not *posca*. Or ale. I am allowed as much as I want, so bring me a lot of it."

He looked at me. It was nearly dark, and his eyes seemed to be all black.

I turned my head away, toward the flames. "Go."

At first light the vexillation broke camp. Now that Lamia had what he wanted, he was in haste to reach Roman jurisdiction. How many days until we would arrive at the Danube? I had lost count. Not that it mattered.

The sun was high when I woke in the bed of the cart, sprawled in dusty straw. Cleon was walking alongside. "Remember anything about last night?" He passed me his wine flask.

I drank deeply. My mouth was parched, and my head pounded. "Shouting." I held out the flask to him in an unsteady hand.

"Two men, maybe three. Praetorians. Tried to get in the tent."

"Why?"

"They had knives." He grimaced.

The driver cocked his head. Cleon snarled, "Mind your business, maggot."

One of the wheels dropped into a hole. Wincing, I grabbed the side of the cart.

"Maybe they loved Bat-Ears," he suggested. "Or someone put them up to it."

I slumped back into the straw, uncaring.

"Get out of that cart. Walk with me. You've been sick long enough."

I gazed up at the ribbon of sky between the forest's edges. Why exert myself?

"Marcus." His voice sharpened. "Whose torc are you wearing?"

"Fuck you."

At the next rest break, he rummaged in the straw and found my wooden stave. Trying to walk was less annoying than being harangued, so I shambled beside him when the column set off again.

"That's better," he said. "Dio told me that's what you needed, a ... what did he call it, a *dorytorus hippus*?" He mangled the Greek.

"*Dourateios hippos*," I muttered. "Wooden horse."

He thought it was a joke. "The walking stick?"

Dourateios hippos was also Homeric Greek for the infamous trick that had undone Troy. *You can be my Trojan horse,* I had told Dio. If that was what his message had meant, let him continue playing Lamia's obsequious secretary.

Cleon cleared his throat. "The Senate has voted Drusilla an arch in the Forum."

"Ridiculous." Arches were for victorious generals and heads of state.

"They're falling over themselves trying to pander to Caligula."

I watched road dust puff around my toes. "He does not like hypocrisy."

"They're in a panic." Cleon sauntered along. "He's left Rome. Gone to Sicilia."

The Praetorians ambled on, black helmet-plumes bobbing. Lamia turned in his saddle, presumably to make sure I was still there.

"Cleon," I said, "do something for me."

He made a noise low in his throat.

"Go back to Bruna." I spoke quickly, overriding his protest. "Find Aurima."

"Of course, nothing easier." Heavy sarcasm. "Is that all?"

"It is the last thing I will ask of you."

"You're still drunk. You are dreaming." He lengthened his stride to pull ahead.

I caught his arm and stopped him. "I need to know."

"Know what?"

"About my ... About the child."

"Whether he's yours? Why? What can you do about it?"

"I need to know," I repeated stubbornly.

"Forget it. Forget her."

"You two," yelled the Praetorian decurion. "Move along!"

I paid no attention. "Tell Lamia ... you are finished with me. You want ... to go back ... to train your German gladiators." I was panting now, out of breath.

A trooper rode between us. "Keep going. You're holding up the column."

"He can't walk," Cleon shouted back. "The man's barely over wound fever."

"Back in the cart, then," the trooper barked. "Move it!"

Heat flamed through the layer of ash that numbed me. I let the stave fall, seized his foot in both hands, and heaved him out of the saddle.

Shouts and curses erupted. A score of cavalrymen broke ranks and plunged toward me. Long swords flashed through billows of dust.

"Fifth Gallica, hold!" an officer bawled. Secundus.

"Praetorians, stand down!" their decurion bellowed.

The agitated horse reared, forcing its unseated rider to roll away from its hooves. Across the angry sea of black-crested helmets I saw Lamia shake his head, smiling.

"Leave at daybreak," I said. "I will help you steal one of the remounts."

The darkness was almost solid with the pungency of sweat and hot ammonia-tanned goathide. Cleon said, "Do you want me to bring her to you?"

"No!" It was almost a shout. Hastily I lowered my voice. "No."

Two troopers passed outside the tent, talking about a horse's irritated eye.

I waited until they were gone. "I want her to know I am not angry with her."

"Diana's tits! She's a barbarian; you're a Roman. Who cares what she thinks?"

What was the answer to that? Would it diminish the crater she had left beneath my ribs? "Just tell her—"

"Just tell her she has stirred your brains with a frying pan?" Cleon rolled closer. His breath gusted at me, heavy with garlic and vinegary wine. "Marcus, I didn't want to say this. But I reckon she'd rather be a king's bed-warmer than yours."

I said nothing. If I could have stopped my ears like a child, I would have done it.

"When you were sick, I went with her to talk to Vannius. You should have seen how he looked at her." A pause. "Maybe you didn't know: his wife died a while ago."

He might have been watching me, but I could not make out his expression. In the night we were little more than shapes.

Cleon said, "Now that I think of it, he said he had a boundary dispute to settle. Could be she went with him. So Bruna would be a waste of time, anyway."

I could not breathe deeply enough of the hot, congested air.

He went on, "Listen. She was a good fuck, I understand that. But it's time you forgot her and started figuring how to get out of the Silver Sheep's clutches."

"One more word and I will kill you," I said hoarsely. I got up and pushed myself out of the tent.

This night a blanket of darkness smothered the familiar constellations of the sky. I walked through the camp, finding my way by the ember-glow of fires. Horses whickered sleepily. A few guards flung challenges, but I made no reply.

From the driver's seat of an empty cart I looked out at the blazing torches that limited my freedom. Their light glinted distantly on sentries' helmets and their horses' bits, on scabbard lockets and shield rims. If I had not given Lamia my word, I could run between them and keep running until I vanished into the forest or they cut me down.

Rather be a king's bedwarmer . . . I pictured her bringing in his morning ale, Vannaz embracing her as she entered, his battered boxer's face pressed against her milk-swollen breasts. Inconvenient little Beran far away, handed over to a wet nurse.

In my memory the small mouth gummed the end of my nose, the tiny fingers clenched my thumb. My throat swelled so that for several moments I could not swallow.

Even though I had been no sort of father, I wanted him to have been my son. I wanted to have made my own family of the woman and child I had fought for. I longed for her, for them, so deeply I could have howled.

All for nothing. Ollius, a good man, dead for nothing. Four warriors from Hoheneih slaughtered in cold blood. Chlothar murdered in his son's presence. Glabrio hunted down and killed, who should have been brought to justice. And Rufus—if he still lived—lost to barbarism.

How basely I had rewarded my father's self-sacrifice! Yearning to restore our honor, I had only dragged it deeper in the mud.

With elbows on knees I stared dry-eyed into the night. If there were splinters of delusion in the yarns from which I wove this fabric of despair, I was too engaged in despising myself to notice them.

At change of watch, three troopers coming off duty stopped to insult me and piss against the cart. I looked them in the face, but did not respond to their abuse. They were Gauls, still inflamed by their decurion Licnos's contempt for me.

The night cooled. The camp quieted, men at last comfortable enough to sleep. I mulled returning to my rumpled cloak in the tent, but could not bear Cleon's presence.

My spirits began to cool too. I had been betrayed by Caligula, by Lamia, and now by Vannaz and Aurima. Everyone drove his own chariot, intent on success for himself—or herself, although few women had Aurima's independence and courage.

And I, like an inept charioteer, had been run over. I ought to have learned from my father's example that there was no profit in sacrifice for the sake of a dream; all it had gained him was a dead son. He would have done better to let Caligula kill me as well. He could have taken a new wife and sired more sons.

So be it. From now on I would keep my heart to myself. I would wrap myself in impassivity as tight as a bandage.

I dozed on the cart's seat, shivering, until woken by sounds of activity. A heavy mist lay over the encampment. Troopers were wraiths, fading in and out of sight as they wiped off weapons, saddled horses, spaded dirt over fire rings.

As slaves unlaced one side of the prefect's tent, Dio came out carrying the small chest of his secretarial paraphernalia. With a mumbled greeting to me, he passed the chest to the soldier packing the prefect's cart.

Lamia stepped outside the tent, fastening his cloak pin. He cast his eyes around the fog-shrouded camp. "What a gods-forsaken wilderness." He turned to a groom bringing up two saddled horses.

"Your mount." He gestured to one of them, a wall-eyed brown mare. "You see how well you are being treated, Aquilo. I am confident that you are a man of your word."

He had grasped his own reins to mount when hoofbeats thudded through the mist. One of the troopers burst into sight, his horse's hooves flinging up clods of earth. He pulled up so close that dirt showered over our feet.

"Germans," he gasped.

34: THE BRIDGE ON THE THAYA

The Marcomanni stretched in a solid wall across the Amber Road, blocking the advance toward Carnuntum. There were at least two score of them, long-haired and bearded, some mounted, others rising from a crouch. They carried Roman swords and shields, either stripped from my vexillation's casualties the year before or battle gear of their own disbanded auxiliary cohort. Many of them would have been trained by Army instructors.

Ingiomar dominated the front line astride his white-faced chestnut. Like his men he wore no helmet; a topknot held back his long hair, as pale as a flame in daylight. He carried an oval blue shield of the First Hispanic Aravacians on his arm, and wore a sheathed *spatha* on a shoulder belt.

I had burned the hall where those shields were hung. But they were his prized trophies, proof of his defiance of Rome. Of course he would have rescued them.

Between us and the Germans lay the Thaya River bridge, too narrow to admit a massed attack from either side. Its wooden deck, over which Thancmar and I had galloped a few weeks earlier, seemed now to float on billows of river mist.

The scout's news had spread quickly throughout the camp. Since our campsite was indefensible, Secundus made the same decision I would have: to advance, prepared to engage. In moments the mist echoed with the urgent voices of unseen men, the whinnies of uneasy horses, the *clack* of hastily swung weapons against shields. Ghostly figures moved through the fog, sometimes headless, sometimes legless, hauling rolled-up tents to baggage wagons. Drivers cursed, trying to hitch complaining mules.

Other troopers Secundus sent to reconnoiter reported that the Germans merely waited on the far side of the bridge with no howling or clashing of weapons, no battle cries. "Like toll-takers?" Lamia joked as his orderly hoisted his armor over his shoulders.

Secundus had spotted me sitting on a stump next to the wall-eyed mare. "Aquilo, you speak Germanic. Get a spare helmet and mail shirt and ride with me."

Lamia declared, "I am sure they will understand Roman steel." He looked around for someone to record this martial sentiment, but Dio was busy directing the stowing of his tent. Two slaves lugged out a chest on its carrying poles and slid it into a waiting cart.

I reckoned the Germans, whether Marcomanni or Quadi, would make it clear enough that they were looking for me, but I got up and grasped the mare's bridle anyway. Secundus was announcing the order of march. Lamia interrupted, saying the troops would expect a prayer. While mist and commotion were disorienting the sentries, I could await my chance and slip away. Who expected a murderer to keep his word?

Cleon loomed up out of the fog with a mess tin in his hand. "Marcus." He sucked porridge off his fingers. "What's going on?"

I could not leave him and Dio to face Lamia's revenge. Though I had vowed to care for no one but myself, they were still hostages for my obedience.

Suddenly famished after a day and a half without appetite, I seized his dish and finished the porridge with my fingers. "I am riding with Secundus. Look after Dio."

The mist was still so dense that the first troopers had vanished with Lamia before Secundus and I followed the rear guard out of the encampment. A low-browed cavalry helmet with broad cheek guards hid much of my face. The hilt of a sheathed *spatha* bobbed between my mail shirt and the inside of my arm, and javelins rattled in a sling against my knee.

Secundus was not pleased that I had armed myself, but he had too much else to be concerned about. I followed him along the column, past a dozen Fifth Gallica troopers in red horsetail-crested helmets. The two feathers of rank fluttered in Licnos's crest as he turned his head and scowled at me.

"Stay alert," Secundus called as we rode past. "We don't know what to expect."

Day had broken, but the tunnel between the trees was still dim, and thick with fog. Overhanging foliage dripped on helmets, shoulders, knees, down the backs of necks.

This constrained defile reminded me of the distant trail on which Varus's three legions had been ambushed. No doubt Secundus would be thinking the same. In places where trees had been felled and we could see deeper into the forest's ragged edge, my straining eyes tried to pick out human shapes lurking amid the hazy stockade of trunks.

We passed the five carts, the string of pack mules, the remounts. The cart drivers and servants leading the animals were tense and twitchy-eyed, for our forces were too lean to provide flanking cover.

As usual, Dio sat beside the driver of the prefect's baggage cart. I had a mere glimpse of his face before he was out of sight. Next came Cleon walking behind the surgeon's cart with my stave on his shoulder, Placidus riding ahead on his bay mare.

"Don't give me any work to do," the surgeon growled as we rode past.

"With two tribunes in the lead, what is there to fear?" Cleon yelled behind us.

We came upon the second section of Gauls, their red *V GALL* flag hanging sodden on its boar-topped staff. Heads swiveled toward us. I kept my expression blank.

"*The broad-striper.*" It rustled from one man to another like the sound of rain.

No curses aimed at me? No evil gestures? Perhaps they were more nervous about the Germans than I had reckoned.

"Stay alert," Secundus shouted again. "We do not know their intentions." Probably not to thank us for our visit and wish us safe travels.

At the column's head, black-plumed Praetorians in their somber cloaks rode behind their medallioned *signum.* We fell in beside Lamia, who led the troops as self-importantly as if he were the Divine Julius back from conquering Gaul.

He gestured ahead, where the Amber Road wound emptily through the fog. "The scouts say we are only two hundred paces from the river. No movement among the Germans, as far as they can tell." He leaned past Secundus to glower at me. "You will not speak or stir an inch after we halt. Is that understood, Aquilo?"

"Yes, Prefect," I said, stirred by a mix of excitement and fatalism.

A thin slash in the forest passed to our left: the animal track that Thancmar, Aurima, and I had turned onto. A quick twitch of the reins and I could be on my way to the meadow where we had camped just a few weeks ago . . .

The fire crackling and hissing. Thancmar sucking on a pheasant's leg. Beautiful Aurima sitting beside me, her long legs drawn up beneath her skirts, the baby's tiny fingers clutching her coppery hair as he nursed. Firelight licked her breast and then her cheek as she raised her head, eyes shining at me.

Gone, gone.

I snapped my attention out of the past. Lamia had pulled ahead. Looking imperious with his heavy cloak and helmet plumes, he kneaded his reins.

The forest thinned and shrank back as we reached the Thaya's boggy floodplain. A small hamlet there was deserted, even its chickens and dogs snatched away from the possibility of a battle between Germans and Romans.

The shape of a waiting scout materialized in the mist. Secundus halted the troops, and Lamia rode forward. Secundus and I accompanied him.

Fog swelling from the river veiled the bridge, though it must be close. Low guttural voices and the huffing and stamping of restless horses carried in the saturated air.

Lamia called out to the unseen Germans, "I will advance alone until we can see each other." His downturned palm signaled us to stay back.

Some might have called this brave, but I thought it foolhardy. His cosseting by Vannaz must have led him to expect a warm welcome from every chieftain in the Mark.

Secundus's bunched jaw muscles showed his own doubts, but he obeyed the prefect's command. Lamia had authority in political matters, after all.

Lamia walked his gray horse forward until he and it had almost dissolved into the mist. For a few heartbeats he stared silently at nothing we could see. Then, filling his lungs, he shouted, "I am Decimus Aelius Lamia, regional prefect of the Special Cohort of the Praetorian Guard. Who are you, and why do you bar our way?"

I thought I heard chuckles. Then Ingiomar roared back, "I am Ingiomar whom you call Inguiomerus, known as Ironhand for the Roman murderers I killed with bare hands. I bar your way because you have another murderer I seek."

"I warn you not to hinder the passage of a Praetorian prefect."

Secundus jogged my elbow and jerked his thumb back toward the waiting vexillation. It was an order to conceal myself among the other Fifth Gallica troopers. I answered him just as silently by clamping my hand on my sword hilt.

"We are returning to Carnuntum after a peaceful meeting with your king, Vannius." Lamia spoke loudly for all to hear. "We do not seek to harm or trouble you."

"Nor do we," Ingiomar shot back, "if you surrender the man I want. His name was Carinna. Now it is Aquilo."

"I cannot give him to you."

The prefect's tone was unruffled, but Ingiomar must have heard the faint rustling murmur from the troops behind us. With malevolent triumph he shouted in Germanic, "Do you hear me, turd? I know from a little miller that you killed Chlothar, after telling others I sent you."

Thancmar. The dwarf had spilled the truth, perhaps in his cups. Or, to be fair, perhaps under torture.

"Aquilo is still in Bruna," Lamia lied. "You must ask the king for him."

I kicked the mare forward. Secundus spurred his own horse after me, and we rode up on either side of Lamia. The narrow bridge lay ahead of us. On its far side Ingiomar waited on his chestnut horse with his warriors massed around him, their hair twisted into war knots stiffened with butter.

Maelo, lean and russet-bearded, leaned over to speak to the *fraujaz*. Behind them Maelo's half-grown son Odo thumped the butt of a heavy *framea* between his feet. A youth stood beside him with both hands braced on his own spear: Rufus.

Secundus bent his helmeted head toward the prefect, murmuring too quietly for even me to hear. Lamia shook his head.

The first to recognize me was Maelo, who had become used to seeing me in a helmet when I escorted Aurima to Rome as a hostage. He pointed.

Ingiomar's mustaches lifted in a fanged grin. "*Merda*," said Lamia softly.

Heat flushed into my face. It was not the same rage with which I had murdered Chlothar in his son's presence and thrown myself at Glabrio. But it was good enough.

The javelin was not an officer's weapon and I had no great skill with it, but skill mattered less if I was close enough. If offered a clear shot, I would aim for Ingiomar. Once the fight was fully engaged, I would grab Lamia's cloak and cut his throat with his own Hispanic longknife. There was no need to plan beyond that, since I expected to be dead.

"This is my land, Prefect, and Aquilo killed four of my men. I demand that you give him to us." The *fraujaz* looked from side to side. "What do you say, my brothers?"

Maelo and the other warriors roared ferociously and shook their weapons.

When the uproar died down, Lamia said, "Aquilo is a Roman citizen from a Senatorial family. If you come to Carnuntum and make your case, I will see to it—"

The Marcomanni cut him off with hoots and whistles. Ingiomar said, "We are not afraid to fight you to get him. And if we fight, I warn you, some of your men will die. Many others will wish they were dead and call you a fool."

"Advice?" Lamia muttered to us.

If he sought an excuse to hand me over, this demand provided one. Otherwise the vexillation would have to cross a bridge wide enough for only two troopers abreast, whom the Germans could cut down on the far side like pigs in a slaughterhouse chute.

"Look for a ford upriver," Secundus said. The banks were too steep here.

"Waste of time," I said. "We need Vannius's help." I did not think the king would let a renegade chieftain jeopardize his alliance with Rome.

Ingiomar demanded, "Is it so hard a choice, to surrender a murderer?" He leaned over to hear Maelo. Straightening in his saddle, he shouted, "Do you need time to think? Give him to us by midday tomorrow, and I let you pass safely. Is that not fair, Prefect?"

"Or hand him over now," Maelo shouted, "and get back to your barracks sooner." More hoots and catcalls from warriors who understood Latin.

Lamia tried again: "He will be fairly judged under Roman law—"

"I shit on Roman law!" the *fraujaz* bellowed, so savagely that mist droplets seemed to shiver in the air.

"You god-cursed fool, Aquilo," Lamia fumed as we rode back to the column. "What have you brought on us?"

"He already knew I was here, Prefect. We should withdraw toward Bruna and send to Vannius for support." As soon as the words were out, I remembered that Vannaz might be away settling a border dispute. With Aurima.

"And have it known that my vexillation required a native escort to feel safe? There will be no retreat as long as I am in command."

"Then we must expect to be attacked."

"Inguiomerus is too sensible to attack a peaceful Roman delegation," the prefect snapped. "We will withdraw to our previous camp and wait him out." He squinted. The sun had risen high enough to burn off the ceiling of fog, exposing a whey-colored sky that promised more heat to come.

Our debate had ratcheted up the apprehension of others who heard Ingiomar's ultimatum. Men dried their fingers on the edges of cloaks and saddlecloths, kissed amulets, mumbled to gods. Horses fidgeted, stamping and rattling their harnesses. Axles creaked as impatient mules surged forward and were reined back.

I glanced at Secundus. He cleared his throat. "Last night's camp is not a secure location, Prefect. We need a site on high ground."

Lamia rubbed his reins between thumb and forefinger. "Listen, both of you." He spoke slowly, as if trying to educate lackwits. "I realize you have dealt with this man before. But let us credit him with having learned a lesson. He knows an attack will be severely punished both by us and, I predict, by his king. This is only a threat."

He looked from my face to Secundus's. No doubt our skepticism was evident. "Our men have the rest of the day to dig a ditch and put up a palisade, if that reassures you. But everyone knows barbarians are easily bored. Mark my words, by morning they will have lost patience and dispersed." His voice turned cold. "Let me remind you that I am of prefectorial rank and expect you to follow orders. Understood?"

Secundus gave in. "Aquilo?" He wheeled his horse around.

I ignored him. "Is your notion of risking men's lives meant to shame me, Lamia? Am I supposed to say, 'Give me up, so Inguiomerus will not kill everyone else'?"

Lamia's face darkened. His upper lip quivered in suppressed rage. "You think highly of yourself, Aquilo! No, you are going to Carnuntum to face Caesar's justice."

I shifted the reins to my left hand, ignoring the spike of pain from my wound. The fingers of my other hand curled, anticipating the bone grip of the *spatha*; my arm and shoulder tensed to draw the blade from its scabbard. I could have killed him at that moment and spun around to rush the German line, but for all my zeal I could not foresee surviving long enough to strike at Ingiomar. And dying while the *fraujaz* still lived was not a satisfactory outcome.

Lamia saw murder in my eyes. "Secundus, I want Aquilo disarmed immediately."

"What if we're attacked, Prefect?"

I paused to hear the answer. The prefect said, "Put him in the front line."

35: HEAT LIGHTNING

A hunting owl's cry pierced the night. Or perhaps a German, mimicking an owl. Secundus had set double watches, even though I told him the Marcomanni would be too fearful of spirits to attack. Could Ingiomar, trained by pragmatic Romans, have persuaded his warriors that striking at night would not expose them to tree goblins?

The morning mist had given way to stifling heat. After the confrontation with Ingiomar and return to our previous camp, troopers in sweat-soaked tunics had cut and piled sods in a large square, while others hewed slim trees that would become palings. The resulting fortifications were unimpressive, but weary cavalrymen could do no more. Now the camp looked like a battlefield where sprawled bodies had been stripped of everything but their tunics, and sometimes of those. A few restless men muttered over dying cook-fires.

I lay in a patch of meadow behind the carts, searching the night sky for a scheme to elude or defeat Ingiomar. So far, all my imagined schemes had had dead ends.

While Cleon snored an arm's length away, I daydreamed of teaching a fair-haired boy to ride. The horse was my cherished Boss, who became Pegasus. The boy flew away, shouting, "Look at me, Papa! Look at me!"

Dry grass rustled a few paces away. Cleon jerked awake. And the dream shattered like a reflection in a disturbed pool.

Dio dropped down between us. "Do you still think they will attack tomorrow?"

I sighed. "Yes. Early, perhaps. Inguiomerus likes to surprise his foes at dawn."

"Where's your sandglass?" Cleon asked. As Lamia's secretary Dio was responsible for the timepiece, which would tell us all when to rouse ourselves.

"I just turned it. So I cannot stay long."

I said, "I saw Rufus among the Marcomanni."

"Will he try to kill us?" Dio asked.

I rolled a blade of grass between my fingers. "I don't know. Perhaps he doesn't know either."

"Will you try to kill him?" His voice was hesitant. He was fond of the Thracian boy, whom he had taught to read and write on the journey from Rome.

I did not answer. Cleon rumbled, "If I see him with anything in his hand except his cock, he's dead."

There was a silence. The owl screamed again.

I felt Dio shudder. "I came to ask a favor," he said abruptly.

"Diana's tits," Cleon growled. "You will not die tomorrow, Dio. Have a little faith."

"Gladiators do not pray before a bout, I suppose?"

I intervened wearily: "What is the favor?"

"Will you tell your mother I tried to serve our family well?"

"See to that, Cleon."

"See to it yourself," my bodyguard muttered without animation.

"And," Dio began. He trailed off.

I did not prompt him. When he did speak, his words were a surprise: "Marcus, you once told me that when the Spartan king Leonidas was asked the supreme virtue of a warrior, he said, 'Indifference to death.'"

"Yes."

"I . . . ah . . ." He contrived a smile. "I fear I will never be a Spartan."

Hoarse laughter burst from a couple of men dicing by a fire's glow. He flinched, although there was no way they could have overheard.

"Because of sensible men like you, Dio, the human race survives."

Cleon chuckled, but Dio said nothing. I supposed he thought I was mocking him.

"I need to keep an eye on the glass. The prefect insists that watch changes must be on time." He got up.

"Dio." Tipping my head back to see him, I stretched out my arm.

He reached down. I clasped his hand, feeling the pliancy of his palm, the scribe's callus on his middle finger. Then, quickly, he let go. His steps faded.

"Poor bastard," Cleon said. He took a deep breath and blew it out noisily. "For fuck's sake, Marcus, do not leave us alone in this fucking wilderness."

A few hours earlier, Placidus too had admonished me: "You once dedicated your life to Mithras. Do you think throwing it away will aid the fight against darkness?"

I had made no reply, just rubbed an itch beneath my bandage.

"When I first met you, you were a new officer with a head full of antique virtues and no gods you had faith in." He gazed at a trooper chopping turf with a mattock; then the silver eyes arrowed back to me. "I said to myself: Here is a young man who could make his life matter in the battle between good and evil."

"Worry about your own life, Placidus. By noon tomorrow we will be spitting Marcomanni topknots out of our teeth."

We had stood outside the medical tent, sweating in the sunless heat. The surgeon set down his sausage roll of instruments on a tree stump that still oozed fragrant resin. Propped on my stave, I closed my eyes, breathed, and was transported to a pine grove outside Rome where a red-haired hostage priestess bravely defied me to kill her.

"Very well." He untied the bandage. "Let's see what is happening with your arm."

I was impatient with his lecturing, and tired of having my ugly injury poked at. "There's no need of this." I backed away. "Leave me alone. Go amputate something."

"Hold still," Placidus said in a different voice. A surgeon's command.

I stared at a Praetorian patrolling the camp perimeter. This was useless, all of it. Once Lamia tasted Ingiomar's ferocity, he would make some excuse to give me up. For Aurima's sake, should I slay the prefect before then, ending his fantasy of taking her and her child to Caligula, or save my vengeance for her father, who would otherwise keep persecuting her?

Placidus stripped off the last of the bandage. "By the seven planets!" he said, staring. "You may think you have abandoned Mithras, my brother, but it seems he has not abandoned you." He pressed on the wound. "Does that hurt?"

"When you do that, yes. Wrap it up tight; I will be fine."

"Aquilo, this is uncanny. Look at it."

I looked. The sword cut, which a couple of days earlier had been crusted and oozing in a lava field of bloated red flesh, was scabbed over, its margins smooth and pink. Almost healed.

"Why so surprised?" I said. "Isn't that why the Army pays you like a prince?"

"I do pray for Mithras to guide my hands, but I did not reckon he favored me so much."

Zoubar, I had almost told him. But it could have been a delayed effect of Aurima's nostrums. Or an outcome of my rage, burning out the foulness.

Cleon's voice pulled me from this memory. "Remember how good it feels, Marcus, having the sweat scraped off? And then the cold pool . . ." He scratched his scalp. "Diana witness me, I'd give a year of my life to jump in the pool at the Spartan Baths."

The night sky lit up.

For an instant it was almost day, a day without color. Then night plunged down like a pot lid, but in eerie silence.

Men leaped to their feet, exclaiming to their gods. Startled horses yanked at their tethers, whinnying, and mules uttered their hair-raising squeals.

Cleon sat bolt upright. "Sweet goddess," he blurted, "I didn't mean for you to take it right this minute!"

Another bright flash dissolved the darkness, freezing the shapes of people and animals. Lamia proclaimed that the heat lightning was a good omen: Jupiter's message that he was watching over his Romans and would grant us good fortune. But maybe the Germans reckoned it showed the favor of their sky god, Thunraz, who had his own plans.

"Gone!" the scout shouted, before his horse had stopped. "They're gone, Prefect."

"All of them?" Lamia's black plumes bobbed in the torchlight as he strode closer.

"They do not like the lightnings, *ja*?" The man grinned broadly. He was Boldt, one of the treacherous Quadi scouts who had arranged for Berinhard to kill me.

The prefect ducked his head and pulled off his helmet and cap. Despite the early hour, his silver hair was already plastered to his skull with sweat. "Or perhaps we called their bluff," he said, smirking at me. Without waiting for a response, he began to speak with Secundus about getting the vexillation underway.

I had woken from sleep prepared to test myself against Ingiomar, knowing that if the encounter killed me, or both of us, Aurima would hear of it. No matter how badly I had behaved to her, she would surely grieve a little for the man who loved her and had become tangled in the derangement of her mother's murder.

Call it pride, self-pity, defiance; indifference to death has more than one root.

Cheers erupted as word of the Germans' departure spread among the troops. I should have felt relieved, for a battle would have cost the lives of men who did not deserve to die. But my first reaction was *Now it will have to be Lamia instead.*

Or perhaps not. In the misty darkness on a road edged with thick forest, was it wishful thinking that Ingiomar had given up and withdrawn? I said, "We can't be sure—"

Rough hands seized my elbows and pulled them behind my back. I struggled, yelling. "Steady," said the gruff voice of Luccius, Lamia's adjutant. "Prefect's orders."

"I am a Roman citizen. I demand to be treated with respect!"

Cleon had been similarly overpowered by a couple of Praetorians. "Bind their wrists," Lamia ordered. He added to me, "Just a temporary precaution, Aquilo." Which, I guessed in impotent rage, would turn out to be a lie. Like so much else he had said.

We sat side by side on Lamia's campaign chest with our outer wrists lashed to its carrying handles, facing backward as the cart jolted over the Thaya bridge. The sun had not yet crested the rim of the world, and fog brooding on the river soaked us to the skin.

Cleon was furious. After cursing Lamia, Secundus, and their ancestors, he called to the guards riding behind us, "You'll cut us free if the barbarians attack, won't you?"

"Maybe." One of them grinned. "How fast can you run?"

"Hey, Aquilo," yelled Licnos from farther back in line. "The Germans have no letters, right? So what do they brand a runaway with—a picture of a foot?"

Howls of laughter.

It was not easy to hold up my head. Never had I been as humiliated as Lamia made me feel, bound like a criminal or a slave, jeered at by men I had once commanded. Battus, head of the Praetorian detachment, avoided my eye. Licnos—short, weather-wrinkled, hard-sinewed—shot me a glare that held the grudge he had never overcome.

Past the rise where the Marcomanni had blocked the road, Secundus increased the pace. No menacing war growl rumbled through the trees. No Germans leaped upon us.

"This is where Thancmar and I rescued Aurima," I told Cleon a short time later. A great churned area of hoofprints extended into the battered woods on both sides of the road. Dark patches still showed where Glabrio had bled, and Friduric, and others. At the knoll overlooking where Friduric and his companions had camped, I thought of *TE AMO* scratched on a pottery shard and wished I could retrieve it.

We met a northbound caravan of ox-drawn wagons laden with straw-packed amphoras: wine to trade for furs or amber in the hinterlands. Warned by a scout, they had pulled off the road to let us go by. When Secundus questioned them, I saw heads shake: no marauding Germans ahead. The troops' spirits rose, along with the oppressive heat. It was four hours before noon.

Cleon and I were allowed to stretch our legs during the next rest stop. When we plodded back to the cart, Dio was waiting with watered wine. As we gulped thirstily, he said, "Secundus says we can reach the Danube tomorrow night in two long marches."

Cleon brightened. "We're as close as that?"

Junior officers were yelling all along the line for men to mount up. I felt an icy prickle of foreboding. "We are not supposed to make a long march today. We're going to dig in early and prepare for an attack."

Dio made a face. "The prefect thinks Inguiomerus has backed down."

I shouted for Secundus. He arrived on horseback, eager to get the column underway. I argued that the man who had promised to disembowel me would not slink away without a fight.

"Perhaps he has decided to make his case in Carnuntum, after all."

"Didn't you listen yesterday? He does not give a fig for Roman law."

"My decision is made, Aquilo."

We glared at each other. Anxiety had drawn lines in Secundus's tanned cheeks and hung pouches beneath his eyes; one would think him at least a decade older than he was. I had not guessed that Ingiomar's ambush last fall had left such deep scars in him.

Perhaps he and Lamia were right that Ingiomar had withdrawn. Had I been frightened so badly that I imagined the *fraujaz* behind every tree, in every shadow? Had I lost confidence that Roman cavalry deserved the Germans' respect?

"Up you go," ordered a Praetorian by the cart, dangling our bonds.

I looked at the narrow-stripe tribune. "Quintus Valerius Secundus, do not do this."

Addressed as a fellow Roman citizen, Secundus had the decency to blink. He looked at the Praetorian. "Leave them unbound."

The column resumed alternately walking and trotting, but every mile after the bridge was hard-won. The harder our animals were pushed through the heat, the more often they needed water and rest. The morning hours seemed to evaporate, the sun to fly upward.

As midday approached, my belly cramped into knots. The campsite Secundus wanted to reach had good natural defenses, but we were not going to get there in time to prepare for an assault.

Lamia appeared beside the cart on his gray horse. Instead of objecting to our lack of wrist bindings, he said, "Well, Aquilo! Still think we have underrated Inguiomerus?"

The cart jounced, throwing me against Cleon. I said, "You don't know the kind of man he is. He commanded the First Marcomannians, an auxiliary cohort he'd raised. They trained for a few summers with the Fifteenth, and then were posted to Siscia."

Lamia wiped his face with his neck-cloth. "I know the story. His wife was killed."

"Murdered," I corrected. "The soldiers who did it earned a slap on the wrist. You know why: the legions were fractious; everyone feared mutiny. Inguiomerus was a citizen, so he appealed to the governor of Pannonia. Sabinus refused to hear him."

"Why?"

"Why take the risk? If he reversed the judgment, the legion might rebel. Uphold it, and the barbarians might rise." I had explained this to Aurima, but she had wept in such rage and frustration that I wished I had not tried. "And so Inguiomerus hates Rome."

"Above all," Lamia said, "he hates the Roman who was stupid enough to fuck his virgin daughter." His laugh was a sudden thunderclap. Troops around us chuckled.

"You are merry for a man who may not live out the day," I said.

"I find it amusing that all your efforts were for a woman who has rejected you."

"Laugh, then. Ironhand does not give up. If not for your pigheaded vanity, we would have withdrawn to a more defensible location and sent word to Bruna for support."

"You think I'm a fool, do you?" A tiny sweat-slug crawled down Lamia's cheek. "At least I have a father who kept his oath to Caesar, and a wife of good family whose children I know are mine."

Cleon cursed and lunged at him across me. His sudden movement startled Lamia's horse, which bolted forward. The two mules swerved away from the horse, squealing. The driver yelled. A wheel lurched into a hole, something cracked, and the cart stopped abruptly, listing like a ship that had hit a reef. Cleon and I grabbed frantically for handholds to avoid toppling out onto the road. "Careful of my chest!" Lamia cried.

We were stumbling out of the cart when Secundus rode back to investigate. He scowled at the broken spokes. "Vexillation, halt," he shouted. "Dismount. Water and rest the beasts."

We were not far from the ruined tavern. A perfect time and place for an ambush, I thought: the column strung out with men milling around on foot, servants running to fetch water, and a jacked-up cart blocking most of the roadway. Yet there were still no war cries; no spears pelted at us from the trees.

Men swarmed around to survey the wreckage. "A two-day pass if you replace that wheel within the hour," Secundus told the transport specialist.

Lamia's campaign chest was hauled out of the cart. To cool Cleon's temper, I sent him in search of a drink while the prefect examined his precious box for damage. At last he nodded sourly, remounted, and rode off with Secundus to inspect the rest of the column.

Once they were out of earshot, the onlookers became talkative, interrupted by loud *bang*s from beneath the cart as the broken wheel was hammered off its axle.

"It's holding us, brothers." *Bang, bang.* "This forest don't want us to get home."

"Listen, I've felt this prickling at the back of my—"

"Shut your trap about the damned forest." *Bang, bang.*

"Aquilo thinks the Hairies will hit us."

"Shut up about your fucking broad-striper, too." As if I were not sitting on the prefect's box nearby.

"Oh aye? Let's see you princesses get your hands dirty with a *dolabra*."

"The Praetorian Guard"—*bang, bang*—"does not dig ditches, you mustached clod."

"Enough of that," I snapped, before they began to brawl.

Cleon pushed himself onto the chest beside me. Passing me a wine flask, he muttered, "Not looking good, is it?"

I took a swig of the lukewarm *posca*. "If we are attacked, grab a weapon and hide in the woods across the road. Dio and I will find you."

"Right." Which meant he would use his own judgment, no matter what I said.

At last the carpenter pounded the iron-socketed hub off the axle. I looked up to gauge the time, but bands of cloud like unwashed wool hid the sun.

Since it would be impossible to dig in at the preferred campsite before midday, Secundus would have to decide whether to risk an ambush by keeping the column marching into the afternoon, or to make camp at a nearer and less secure location—one we both misliked for its evil memories.

With grunts and curses, the sweating men fitted a new wheel onto the axle. Secundus came back as the cart's contents were being reloaded. Looking grim, he shouted, "Hear me now."

Others in the vexillation straggled closer to listen. He said, "We will make camp a few miles south of here, where, if you remember, there is a low hill in a boggy meadow. The Marus runs on its far side." He glanced at me. "Aquilo and I encamped there with our troops last fall."

So that was his decision. I kept my face expressionless. That meadow, then dry enough to be fortified, was where Ingiomar's rebels had attacked us. I had revisited it many times in nightmares, standing with my feet nailed to the ground and my voice frozen in my throat as wild-haired men hurtled through the mist toward my troops.

"Mount up! And stay alert." Secundus swept his gaze around. "We do not want to take unnecessary risks so close to home."

Bravely said, I thought. And tried to guess how close it was to noon.

36: STYX BAIT

The terrain was just as I recalled it. Over there, across the road, the Marco-manni had flooded out of the forest. There the centurions had formed up the battle line. I had sent cavalry to flank the enemy there, and there. And I had been standing by that mossy stump when two soldiers brought me Ingiomar's captured daughter.

She was unconscious, knocked out as she ran with an ax into the thick of combat. I first saw her rump, wrapped in a flea-brown cloak rucked up by the lack of ceremony with which she had been hoisted onto a legionary's shoulder—Maturras's, that rogue—exposing one long dirty leg. When he and his comrade propped her up before me with the hope of promotion in their doggish grins, her thick coppery hair flopped out of its binding, draggled with mud and grass. Beneath her grimy tunic she was as lean and smooth-muscled as a hunting fox, no prize for a man who liked comfort in his bed.

I had looked into her face, stained with rain-washed dirt. Her slitted eyes showed a glimpse of white, and her pale mouth, cracked ajar, bared blood-rimmed lower teeth. It gave me the notion that her stubborn defenses could be pried open.

I had brushed a shred of grass from her cheek. "The witch-girl," Maturras prompted impatiently, as if I did not know. "Old Ironhand's daughter."

At that moment, I was not thinking of what a gift Fortuna had given me to end the rebellion. Even then I recognized the spirit that burned in her and wanted to feel it, to make it mine.

Then her eyes had opened . . .

To Secundus's credit, he had fast-marched the vexillation to this site. Our detachment was small enough to deploy on the wedge-shaped hill, but there had been no order to wall off the camp.

Indeed, the hilltop around us lay as quiet as if everyone in it were drugged. Insects buzzed in the grass. Men moved slowly at their duties, wearied by the heat, or sprawled half-naked under makeshift canopies. No one shouted. No mess tins clattered. Above stacked armor and weapons that thrust up like wheat-stooks rose the peaks of Placidus's medical tent and La-mia's praetorium.

I intercepted Secundus on his way back from the latrine trench. "I believe you are the man who said, 'Let us not take unnecessary risks'? We need walls and ditches."

His short brown hair stood up in sweaty bristles. "Aquilo, it is midday and there is no sign of your Germans." He kept his voice low, although no one was near.

I was furious, apprehensive, and out of patience. "Are you afraid of being criticized for excessive prudence? Or do you fear Lamia will fault you for heeding me?"

"Lamia has nothing to do with it! The men are exhausted." He walked faster, slashing short angry strides through the grass.

I increased my own pace. "You were right to get us off the road, Secundus. But we are still exposed to attack."

He stopped. "How would you rather face an enemy: with soldiers who have enough breath and sinew to fight, or with overtaxed men behind inadequate defenses?"

I saw the jaws of the trap he was in. "I am sorry," I said. "You are not to blame."

"If anyone is to be faulted, look to yourself." His voice grew heated, as if my fury had bled into him. "You riled Inguiomerus until he is like a bull with its tail afire. You allowed Lamia to think he can saunter into the Mark without infantry support. And because of you, our Gallic troopers are quarreling with his Praetorians."

It was true: I had been so eager to lead Lamia's detachment that I had let him silence my objections to its vulnerability. As for Ingiomar's rage, that was foredoomed from the day I fell in love with his daughter. But what had I to do with animosity between the cavalry units?

Too late to ask. Secundus was on his way to give the watchword to the quartermaster, our acting camp commandant.

I unknotted the sweat-drenched strip of cloth around my forehead and wrung it out. The road lay about a thousand feet away, bone-white in the sun, at the bottom of a sloping field where our horses, mules, and donkeys grazed. The hill's other sides were steeper, falling to a meadow where marsh grass and reeds clumped between channels of spongy muck. A couple of troopers led their horses along a path through the tussocks toward the river.

"Let's go for a swim." Cleon rose from an old stump. He had knotted the top of his tunic on one shoulder, baring the other. "Gods send us a break in this weather. I swear I'm growing moss." He ran his hand through his hair.

Darkening clouds to the west warned of rain. A bad sign for the next day's travel, assuming we were lucky enough to escape being killed in the meantime. I looked around for Dio.

"He's in with the Silver Sheep," Cleon said.

"Let's go, then," I said recklessly, surfeited with useless tension. We started down the steep hillside.

"Did Secundus tell you about the scouts?" he asked over his shoulder.

"Those two weasels of Glabrio's? What about them?"

"The Sheep just sent them north with a message for the king." He ran down the last of the slope and jumped onto a grassy hummock. A *calo* leading two wet horses back to camp had to restrain them when they jibbed in alarm.

"To ask for reinforcements?" I leaped down beside him.

Beasts led back and forth to water had churned the path into dung-larded mud. Cleon sidestepped a clump of manure. "According to Dio, to tell him Inguiomerus was menacing travelers."

Which Vannaz might, or might not, take as a request to lend a hand. In any case, we were a good forty miles from Bruna, and . . .

I said, "Vannius may not be in Bruna." He might not get the message for days.

After slogging across the marsh-meadow, we passed through a trampled gap in the scrim of brush and saplings that screened the river, past piles of dropped baldrics and scabbards, saddles and harnesses. Stripped to their tunics, men were washing horses belly-deep in the water while mounted guards watched for threats. Towering trees cast ragged shadows over the far bank, a javelin-cast away.

Troopers glanced up at me, then stared. I was overcome by a wave of discomfort, a reluctance to intrude on men who held me responsible for our predicament.

I fought my way upstream along the bank, ducking under branches and brushing away flies. Gradually the voices and splashing faded, and the loudest noise was Cleon stubbornly thrashing through the brush after me. The going was treacherous, with furrows and den holes hidden by nettles and vine-choked deadfalls. Small creatures rustled away through the undergrowth. A turtle splashed off a rock.

Finally I reached a place where the green river glided smooth and untroubled. I hoisted myself onto the mossy trunk of a toppled ash whose branches combed the water. Cleon halted, scratching nettle-rash on his thigh.

I studied the stream's languid flow. This was the Marus, in whose lazy waters my tiny son had nearly disappeared a few weeks ago.

Not your son. Caligula's.

No.

A heartbeat later the world of anger and shame vanished. I sank into the cool slippery embrace of the river, sliding through brown depths flecked with shredded rushes and tiny things that floated like snowflakes. Reaching down, I stirred a slow billow of silt from grass undulating on the bottom. If I stayed here, I could drift all the way to the Danube. And perhaps at length into the Euxine Sea, although there were surely enough hungry fish on the way to consume everything but bones.

I glided up. Cleon's head broke the surface a few feet away, dark curls hanging in his face. Air rushed into my lungs again. No escape, I thought.

"Styx bait," he choked.

He had not called me that since I was a youth obsessed with racing chariots. It made me laugh. Something in the absurdity of the situation infected him. Splashing to stay afloat, we sniggered and guffawed like moonstruck drunkards.

Until we heard the shriek.

I reckoned it was horseplay downriver, but amusement vanished from Cleon's face. He motioned me to stillness, his head cocked to listen.

Another scream: a horse's. Then a torrent of shouting, confused and panicky.

The attack had begun.

37: UNDER ATTACK

The peaceful scene of moments earlier had exploded into a melee. Horses scattered as men flung themselves toward the shore, thrashing and floundering in great brown geysers of water.

Across the river, the trees seemed to bellow like wild beasts. Spears hurtled through the air. A cavalryman wallowing toward safety was struck in the back and folded beneath the surface.

My bare feet slipped on the broad muddy ramp that men and animals had gouged in the bank, but I managed to catch the halter of a leopard-spotted horse bolting from the river. "Withdraw," I roared. "Withdraw to the camp!"

With a fistful of mane I hauled myself atop the horse. Kicking it back into the water, I leaned down where I had seen the wounded man disappear. That movement was my salvation, for a spear that would have pierced me struck my mount instead. The horse squealed and reared, blood slatting from its shoulder as the spearhead tore out.

My searching fingers closed on sodden cloth. I yanked the man up by the neck of his tunic. Fortunately, the Germans were too far away for their weapons to pierce deeply, and the spear in his back came free when I kicked it. Its haft bobbed as the heavy iron point sank into the river.

Something flashed in the air. I ducked, and another *framea* grazed my shoulder. A distant voice bellowed something in Germanic about "Ingiomar's Roman."

A horse plunged past me spraying water, its rider clinging as it scrabbled up the slimy bank. Other troopers were still wading toward shore, some tugging their horses by the halter, others trying to mount.

"Marcus, get back," Cleon yelled over the frantic splashing. "You're in range."

"Return to camp," I shouted back. "Raise the alarm." I pulled the rescued trooper through the shallows by his tunic. "Get him to the surgeon." I shoved him toward Cleon.

More spears flew from the trees on the opposite bank. I kneed my leopard horse deeper into the stream, yelling, "Romans, to me!"

No armor, no weapon, no shield. Only anger.

Then the far trees spewed howling men whose beards bristled down their naked chests. They threw away their shields and waded into the stream with swords held high. Ingiomar was not among them, nor Maelo.

Sherry Christie

Nor, as far as I could tell, Rufus.

One of the two sentries had ridden into the water, holding his shield over the men closest to the assault. A trooper supporting a wounded comrade stumbled, and both plunged into the water. The sentry rode between them and the Germans, then turned his black mare to confront the attackers with his sword.

I reached the injured man and his companion. One caught my outstretched hand, the other my ankle, and I towed them to the shore where others pulled them to safety.

The tumult must have been audible in the camp. Was no one coming to our relief?

I looked for stragglers. The foremost German had grabbed the sentry's reins. Crouched under the black mare's neck, he hammered upward with his sword. The sentry blocked the strikes on his shield, thrusting cautiously with his *spatha* instead of chopping at his assailant. The fool would rather risk being struck down than kill his own horse.

I glanced around for a weapon. Troopers were wrestling swords from piled scabbards farther up the bank. Too far away.

The beleaguered sentry made the mistake of glancing around at the other Marcomanni splashing toward him. His attacker's next blow glanced off his shield rim and struck him in the chest. Although he wore chain mail, the impact knocked him backward in the four-horned saddle.

The German rose to his full height, clutching the sentry's reins. It was flat-nosed Cotto, one of the men who had escorted Aurima to Rome. He hauled back his sword arm for a mighty swing.

I urged my leopard horse back into the water. "Cotto," I shouted.

Cotto wrenched his head around, recognized me, and dropped the reins. As he began to flounder toward me, blade raised, the sentry's mare reared. Flinching away from her hooves, he lost his balance.

The sentry had a clear strike. His *spatha* cleaved Cotto's shoulder to the armpit.

The other Marcomanni were almost upon us. The man in the lead was an old enemy: weasel-eyed Radulf, whose favorite sport had been clubbing my ravaged back. As I veered toward the shore, Radulf seized my horse's tail. His sword flicked out. Ducking to evade it, I kicked my mount hard. But the man was too close; unarmed, I could not escape him.

A spear hurled from our side of the river breezed past my thigh. I felt the shock as Radulf jerked back. A brief ghastly view of shattered white bone and blood where his face had been; then my horse kicked backward and he was gone.

It was madness to continue offering myself as a target. As I kneed my mount toward the shore, it stumbled over something. Its bare back canted under me, and I fell into the water.

"Grab my saddle horn," the sentry yelled as I thrashed to the surface. He dragged me to shore, and Cleon's big hands pulled me up onto the bank.

From the direction of the camp a horn blared the urgent call that meant "Under attack, form up on commander."

The Marcomanni wallowed and splashed across the river behind us, all on foot. What had become of their mounted comrades? Where were Ingiomar and Maelo?

The leopard horse sloshed ashore behind me. I grabbed its halter, and Cleon threw me onto its back again. I hauled him up behind me as the sentry wheeled around to cover our retreat. We were the last to leave the churned riverbank.

No, not quite the last. A dapple gray, speared in the throat, had struggled ashore before collapsing. "Save yourself," I shouted to the dripping trooper who knelt beside it.

He thrust himself to his feet, swiping an arm across his eyes. Without haste he twisted the *framea* from the dead horse's neck, took careful aim, and launched it at the nearest of the oncoming Marcomanni. Impaled between the collarbones, Friduric's companion One Eye flung out his arms and toppled backward into the river.

The spear-thrower clutched the girth strap of the sentry's black mare and gasped, "Go!" He stumbled alongside as the sentry and I kicked our mounts over the bank.

As we emerged from the screen of undergrowth, the question of the missing Germans was answered. A score of screaming warriors were galloping up the slope toward our encampment, long hair aflutter, spears high. Startled mules, horses, and asses scattered as the pair of guards who had overseen their grazing bolted toward the camp. A few troopers on foot had braced to repel the attack, oval shields locked and javelins spiking, while other men hastily dragged carts into a barricade behind them.

Riders fleeing the river ambush streamed through a gap between the shields. "Faster!" voices bawled. We were the last, the stragglers. My horse checked at sight of the shrieking Marcomanni on course to cut us off, but it lunged obediently upward under the pressure of my knees. Cleon nearly crushed my ribs as he hung on, cursing steadily.

The Fifth Gallica's shield wall came closer. We were outrunning the warriors' ponies. But perhaps not their spears.

The sentry fell back between us and the Germans. When he pulled the trooper from the riverbank aboard behind him, he must have had to cast his shield away. "Go, Tribune!" he yelled.

Amid heart-tripping fear of being brought down by a German spear, I thought, That man merits an award for valor.

"Daft bastard," Cleon panted.

We spurted through the gap in the defensive line, with the sentry and his passenger racing in on our heels. Someone ordered, "Shields up!"

I pushed Cleon off the horse's back. "Get down!"

We threw ourselves flat. I buried my nose in matted grass, waiting for a blow between my shoulder blades that would be the last thing I felt.

The ragged flight of iron-tipped *frameae* banged against shields, thumped into turf. "Belenos," someone cried, in anger or in shock.

"Fifth Gallica, javelins ready," Secundus shouted. "On my command . . . launch!"

"Diana save me," muttered Cleon, cheek to the ground.

I peered through the palisade of troopers' knees. A belly-spitted German toppled off his mount. Another threw down a javelin-spiked shield. A pony nosedived, spilling its rider. Down the slope, was that Ingiomar on his white-faced chestnut?

The line of defenders shifted then, and I could not see past their hairy shins. "Withdraw and rearm," Secundus ordered. The line disintegrated, troopers jostling past tailgates and jumping over cart shafts. I crawled under the nearest vehicle, trying to keep clear of cavalry boots and mud-clotted hooves.

Armloads of javelins rattled together. "Here! Give them here," men yelled.

"Ready," Secundus shouted. "Launch at will!"

When the supply of missiles was gone, the fighting would be hand to hand. Cleon had the same thought: "Marcus, I need a sword."

There was a crash. The cart above us jolted. Something showered over my legs.

A voice yelled in Germanic, "Forward, my sword-brothers!"

I crabbed out from under the cart just as a warrior bounded onto it. Rings glittered in his beard as he bellowed defiance, sword scything. A trooper caught the blow on his shield and stabbed up beneath it. When the blade twisted and withdrew, the German fell forward. His chin hit the wall of the cart, and his head snapped back at a freakish angle.

Secundus was standing on a wagon seat to see over the Gallic troopers' helmeted heads. "Aquilo," he shouted to me. "We need the Praetorians! Find out why the prefect is holding them back."

I pulled myself into the cart to get my own view. Beyond the dozen or so warriors whose onslaught our men were fighting off, another hundred or more waited on horseback at the foot of the slope.

They would be Ingiomar's main force. The attackers charging wildly uphill to batter us one by one were the hotheads, the young men who had not trained in his First Marcomannians cohort. The more disciplined fighters were biding their time.

For how long?

"Understood," I said, and jumped down to head for Lamia's tent.

A muddle of splayed saddles, packs, collapsed canopies, loose horses, and hurrying servants betrayed the surprise of the assault. The quartermaster stood in the weapons cart, heaving armloads of javelins down to a couple of slaves. "Swords," Cleon shouted to him. "Shields."

I dodged through the commotion toward the red flag hanging in front of Lamia's tent. "Prepare for battle," it meant—as if anyone could be unaware that the attack had already begun.

A handful of Praetorians stood at attention in front of the tent, helmeted and armored, shields and javelins braced as if on crowd duty at a Triumph. Yet for all their panoply they were tight-faced and white-eyed, hearing the din of the Fifth Gallica fighting only a spear-cast away.

Other Praetorian troopers rushed to fall into line, shrugging armor onto their shoulders as servants chased them with belts and baldrics, plumed helmets and weapons. "Where is your officer?" I barked.

"In with the prefect," said the next-senior man, the *duplicarius*. But when I tried to enter the tent, two of the guards blocked the way with their javelins.

"Stand aside," I snarled, in no mood for games of power. The *duplicarius* hesitated, then nodded, and the crossed javelins fell back.

The tent's interior was dim and sweltering with the hide walls rolled down. Why would a leader under attack not want better visibility?

Only one of the four men within looked up when I entered: Battus, the Praetorian decurion, edgily gripping his dagger's hilt. Lamia's orderly was buckling him into his breastplate and backplate while the prefect dictated to Dio: "—without warning, and with the intent of causing serious loss of life—"

"Prefect, your men are needed," I broke in.

Anxiety swept over Dio's face. He stopped writing.

Lamia crooked an arm to let his orderly lace up the sides of his armor. "Stay calm, Aquilo. More haste, less speed."

I thought haste ought not to be disdained at the moment. "Why are you holding back your troops?"

"Oaf! That pinches." He glowered at the orderly, then said calmly to me, "I must make a report. Your Inguiomerus will not get away with this."

"The main attack has not taken place yet. When it comes, the Praetorians may be able to flank the Marcomanni and fall on them from behind." I looked at Battus. "Any of your men without mounts can relieve the Gauls in the front line."

"Without mounts?" he echoed, frowning.

How long had the Special Cohort prefect kept him shut away here? "The horses you put out to graze have scattered into the marshes."

"*Merda!*" He whirled toward Lamia. "Permission to go, Prefect?"

"Easy, Decurion. We must keep our heads." He tugged the knot of his commander's sash a little tighter. "I will join Secundus as soon as I finish my dispatch. In the meantime—"

I fought an urge to grab him by the confounded sash. "In the meantime, Inguiomerus is holding back four or five score mounted warriors. Come and see for yourself."

"I thought as much." He nodded in satisfaction. "This preliminary skirmishing is just to get our attention. He will throw all his men against us only if we force it on him."

The ignorant fool thought the Marcomanni needed to be prodded into annihilating us! Six years had not diminished Ingiomar's lust for vengeance on Romans. "Lamia, men are dying! We need to strengthen our defenses."

"Prefect," Battus interrupted in agitation. "Sir, I must see to my troops."

"One moment," Lamia insisted. His orderly laid the black cloak on his shoulders and began to adjust its folds.

Enough wasted time. I needed to see how the Fifth Gallica was faring, inform Secundus of the prefect's notions, and find out what had become of Cleon.

"Aquilo," Lamia called. But I was already out in the steamy afternoon.

Cleon, now armed with a shield and sword, fell into stride with me. Loudly enough for the Praetorians to hear, he drawled, "Weak in the knee, eh? Needs a taste of hot iron," which is the goad used to drive reluctant fighters into the arena.

I just grunted. Although I too believe that Fortuna favors the bold, I had no desire to become a bound prisoner again for trying to countermand the prefect.

Despite Lamia's dallying, order was being restored in the camp. Soldiers and servants moved with purpose, piling loose baggage and supplies beside the praetorium, picketing horses out of the way. Only the crash and clamor of battle still spoke of chaos and death.

A roar erupted from ahead. I broke into a run. One of the Marcomanni had leaped from a cart into the line of defenders.

"Wait," I said hastily, as Cleon would have rushed ahead. Accustomed to fighting on his own, he would disrupt the troopers' coordination.

Then a second warrior bounded into the cart, hoisting a spear over his shoulder.

Secundus was a perfect target, scarcely ten feet away. The heavy *framea* hit him high on the breast and punched through his segmented armor. He fell out of sight among the fighters. As someone bellowed for a medic, the warrior who had cast the lethal spear sprang back onto his pony and raced away, yelling in triumph.

"Strike that man down," I roared, pointing.

A tall trooper farther down the line grabbed a javelin and hurled it, transfixing the fugitive in his broad pale back. He slumped forward and tumbled off his horse.

The Gauls cheered. They had felled the other German and pushed his body outside the ring of wagons. For the moment at least, no one else was attacking.

In the lull, Cleon and I dragged Secundus into a clear space. I loosened his neckcloth. His helmet was half off; one cheek guard flapped open with the chin lace dangling. Shock bleached his face.

Hurled from such short range, the spear had pierced the steel bands of his armor. Its butt sprouted from the front of his shoulder like an obscene sapling, and the conical head protruded a finger's length from his back. As yet there was not much blood, but I knew there would be.

"Carinna." He strained upward to speak. "L-Lah . . ."

For an instant I relived holding my father as life bled from him. Nausea burned in my throat. I bent lower. "I hear you, Quintus. What is it?"

"L-Lamia . . . nev' . . . f-figh'."

He meant what my visit to the praetorium had already confirmed: that Lamia—a schemer, a man who moved game pieces to his liking—had no experience commanding troops in combat.

And he had used my old name as the Fifteenth Legion's senior tribune.

I said, "Fear not, brother."

He gave me the ghost of a smile. His eyes closed.

"Oh, gods. Sweet Apollo." It was Placidus's orderly, gaping stark-eyed at the projecting spear shaft. "Is he dead?"

Once Secundus had been borne off to the surgeon's tent, the heart went out of the Gauls as visibly as steam rising from a quenched fire. "Fuck it, this is hopeless," muttered one, wiping blood-spatter out of his eyes. Another, the *turma*'s standardbearer, lowered his gashed shield. "Where are the buggering Praetorians, Tribune?"

Yes, and where was Lamia?

Although I had only as much authority as these soldiers would grant me, I could not stand aside while the prefect dallied in his tent writing reports. I sent slaves to fetch drink for the sweating fighters, ordered a count of able fighting men and weapons, and saw that the wounded were attended to.

Then, with a deep breath, I picked up Secundus's helmet and seated it on my own head. The leather liner was hot and sweaty, and the fit and balance were different, but none of that mattered. "Decurion, front and center," I said.

"Here, Tribune." Licnos stepped back from the battle line. His sword arm and right leg were as red as the two feathers cresting his helmet.

He eyed me when I directed that all available mounts be bridled and saddled. "Are we counterattacking?"

"We must be ready for anything," I said.

Licnos scratched his sweaty scalp, then clapped his helmet back on his head. "Get the horses ready," he told his second-in-command.

Cleon did not like being superfluous. "Why don't I have a nap while you sort things out?"

I glanced at him sharply. He scowled and shut up.

A few of the Marcomanni were picking their way through the tussocky marsh-meadow in pursuit of our scattered animals, but most remained bunched at the foot of the hill. I doubted that we had disheartened them.

Whatever Ingiomar was planning, the cunning old boar's greatest advantage was that his Roman-trained warriors would follow his orders. I decided to take that control away from him. "Cleon," I said. "Here is a task for you, if you are willing."

He listened and grinned. "Done," he said, unknotting his loincloth.

Lamia arrived at last with several of his Praetorians. He looked around haughtily, his plumed helmet crest wobbling like a drunken crow. A medical orderly was splinting a trooper's broken forearm. The other Gauls slouched at ease behind the carts, sharpening their swords between swigs of ale, while slaves gathered spent javelins and German weapons from the field. Nine of the compact Gallic horses chewed on their bits as they were saddled.

"Ah, Prefect," I said pleasantly. "Kind of you to join us."

He addressed himself to the Gauls' decurion. "Report."

Licnos slid me an expressionless glance. It seemed that he considered me the senior officer present. I said, "Fifteen men of the Fifth Gallica fit for duty, three injured, none killed. Tribune Secundus has been seriously wounded. Five of the enemy killed, an estimated eleven wounded."

"And the meaning of this?" Lamia gestured beyond the barricade.

Cleon had walked out to one of the German corpses. Taunting the warriors massed below the hill, he lifted his sword and shouted, "*Roma Victrix!*" Like the champion gladiator he had been, he strutted around the slain fighter, flourishing his sword with another triumphant yell that ensured all eyes were on him. Then he bent over, flipped up his tunic, and showed the Marcomanni his bare bottom.

Our troops howled with glee. Over the derisive whoops and piercing whistles, Lamia huffed, "By Hercules! How will we treat with them if we desecrate their dead?"

The insult was beyond remedy now. The group of Marcomanni burst apart with bellows of outrage. If I had reckoned rightly, they would charge us in a disorderly mob, forgetting whatever discipline they had learned.

I signaled Cleon to return to the encampment. "Work around them and attack from behind," I told Licnos.

"Hold!" Lamia commanded. "Decurion, stand your men away from those horses. I must stop this madness. Praetorians, mount up."

The Gauls' jeers turned to yelps of shock and protest at this commandeering of their horses. Cavalry mounts are not livery nags to be passed on to any rider; each man and his beast are a trained unit. But since most of the Praetorians' own steeds had scattered into the marshes, there was no other choice.

I said, "What do you mean to do?" The Marcomanni had already launched themselves toward us. Racing uphill would slow their momentum, but in moments the first of them would be upon us.

"Repair what you have done, damn you." He took the reins of his gray horse from a servant and climbed into the saddle from the man's bent back.

"Praetorians, on me!"

Riding into the teeth of a barbarian assault takes extreme courage. Or absolute idiocy. A Praetorian led the troop with a strip of white cloth fluttering from his javelin. Behind him, our trumpeter blew a brave signal: *Hail to the commander*. Trotting forward with their unfamiliar riders, the horses skittered and tossed their heads.

"Fifth Gallica, stand ready to repel attack," I shouted, silencing the Gauls' imprecations.

"Close formation. Shields front! Javelins front," Licnos bawled, clouting a laggard with the flat of his sword. When he glanced at me, his eyes were apprehensive.

The double row of Praetorians spread out in front of us. Lamia, in the middle behind the man with the truce flag, raised his hand and shouted something inaudible above the din of hooves and yells.

The earth trembled. Crows flurried, squawking, from the bodies of the dead.

The Marcomanni were not slowing.

38: APOLLO AND MARS

At the last moment the Praetorians couched their javelins. But the Germans were moving fast and had had time to mark their targets. Some of their horses veered aside; others plunged into gaps between the troopers. The Praetorians' ranks convulsed into pandemonium. Javelins splintered; blades crashed on shields. Men and beasts shoved and bawled, breast to breast in dust and carnage.

We onlookers roared in horror and fury. The troopers with me surged forward, some smacking into the barricades as if blind to them, a few trying to climb the carts to rush onto the field. "Fifth Gallica, steady," I shouted. "Hold the line!" They would accomplish nothing except to increase the casualty list. And without their meager line of defense, everyone else in our camp was doomed.

The white banner toppled into the heaving mass. Lamia's black plumes bobbed amid horsehair crests as his men clustered around, trying to guard him. They were outnumbered ten to one, a dark islet in a sea of fair-haired giants.

Then a score of Marcomanni broke away to attack the barricades, and there was no more time to bemoan the Praetorians' plight.

"Get back." Cleon butted me aside, shoving his way into the front rank with a *spatha* in one hand and a shield on his other arm.

"Ready javelins," Licnos roared. "Launch at will. Make it count!"

Fifteen fighting men. Twenty-one javelins among them.

I heard grunts of effort. Sweat flew with the irregular volley. Too much commotion to see the result. Horses neighing, men screaming. What had become of Lamia? If I leaped onto the cart where Secundus had stood—

"Fifth Gallica, close ranks, shields up!" Licnos bawled.

The words had barely escaped his mouth when spears slammed into the front line. Two of them hit him, one on the boss of his shield, the other on the brow of his helmet. He crumpled, opening a space that revealed more warriors charging us. Beyond them, Lamia's plumes had vanished in a tumult of rearing horses and slashing swords.

Two other defenders were down, a third dazed and reeling, a fourth clutching his neck. Cleon yelled obscenities at the Germans. I wrested the shield off the forearm of the nearest casualty and snatched up his sword. There was no point in staying behind the lines to command a crumbling defense.

Perhaps this seems selfless and heroic. It was the Gauls who were truly heroic. They fought on despite their losses, fueled by rage at the attack on the Praetorians—or on their own cherished horses, more likely. Although I had good reason to want revenge for what Ingiomar had done to me, I could not summon the same fear-obliterating fury. The Marcomanni had erased my ardor when they smashed into Lamia and his troops.

When you are making a decision that may cost men's lives, think hard before you choose, Father had once told me. He was referring to the hubris that had led to Varus's fifteen thousand men dying in a German ambush, but he might have been warning me against taunting the Marcomanni by dishonoring their dead comrades.

Of course I had not known that Lamia intended a suicidal sortie from the camp. I had meant only to disrupt whatever sinister plan Ingiomar was hatching.

I had not thought hard enough.

So it was not heroism that prompted me to pick up a sword. It was a need to make amends for lives lost and others endangered, including Cleon's and Dio's. Far from roaring with battle wrath, I gulped with fear of disgracing my father.

In the moment before I edged into the line, the scene stood still before me: amphoras caught in midspill as a cart tipped under the press of attackers; a horse's head with blood-rimmed nostrils flaring and one eye astare; the straw-stiff hair of a German who had drawn back his ax, muscles bulging around a gold *armilla*.

Cleon smashed his shield into the ax-wielder's elbow, then lunged forward with his sword. "Charon take you," he panted as the German fell across a wagon tongue.

Another warrior jumped from his horse onto the cart, his sword scything at my neck. I flung up my shield. His blade sliced through its iron rim with a force that numbed my arm and drove me back. His sword snagged in the layers of birch. As I staggered, he leaned forward, trying to free it. I stabbed up beneath the shield as Ollius and Cleon had taught me.

My *spatha* punched into his stomach. He looked surprised. "Harder," yelled Cleon, looking up as he yanked the gold arm-ring off the man he had killed. "Twist."

I pushed harder. Twisted the sword.

The man glared, blue eyes blazing. When I pulled out my blade, he opened his mouth in a bloody-toothed snarl. He tried to take a step toward me, but his knees buckled and he fell backward out of the cart.

My shield weighed twice as much with his sword planted in it. After trying stupidly to shake it free, I came to my senses and threw the shield down. Someone gave me another.

It was Dio. "Gods of our family guard you," he said quickly, and slipped back into a scatter of men behind us. The quartermaster, engineer, muleteers, and other special-duty soldiers stood in armor with swords drawn.

Behind them hovered servants and slaves, armed with knives and mattocks and even tent poles. Only the surgeon and his assistants were not there.

The trooper whose weapons I had taken was carried away. The quartermaster Aprilis, a gray-haired *evocatus*, pushed into the gap bellowing the Fifteenth's war cry, "Apollo and Mars!"

A russet-haired youth jumped his pony over a cart tongue and chopped down at me with an ancient bronze sword. For a terrible moment I thought he was Rufus. Uncertainty slowed my reactions, and I escaped his blade only by dropping to one knee. I managed to raise my shield high enough to block his blow. Then I lunged under the shield and stabbed him beneath the arm.

He was not Rufus.

One of the Gallic troopers reeled into me. The dent in his helmet was deep enough to cook an egg in. "By ram-horned Camulus," he spluttered, and stumbled back to smash his own shield into a warrior hacking through the cart's splintered side.

On the field below us, a lone Praetorian broke away from the chaos of screaming Germans, of tumbling bodies and riderless horses. The gray-haired veteran was first to spot him racing toward us. "Friend," he shouted, pointing with his sword. The man's helmet crest was sheared off, his armor and his horse's chest splashed with blood. Half a dozen Marcomanni dashed after him.

We roared encouragement. Eager hands dragged a cart aside to make an opening.

The Praetorian was only a few horse lengths from the barricade when a flung spear struck him. He slumped over his mount's neck, held in the saddle by its horns, as the horse burst through the gap.

"Look out!" someone shouted as the cart was being pushed back into place. A second horse with a *V GALL* brand, this one riderless, galloped into the camp. A slave caught its reins and brought it to a trembling halt.

One of the troopers flung a knife end over end at the spear-thrower—we had long ago run out of javelins—but I did not see what came of it. I was squatting beside the Praetorian, who had been lowered gently to the ground.

The *framea* had not embedded itself, so he might survive. Questionable good luck, if the Germans exercised their renowned cruelty after overrunning us.

I eased off his helmet. Blood striped the dust on his narrow face. "Tribune," he gasped. "Decurion's dead. *Duplicarius* too. Took his head off with an ax." His eyes reddened. He wept, mucus from his nostrils smearing the blood.

"What of the prefect?" I demanded.

"Dragged him away." He tried to wet his chalky lips. "O gods . . . I couldn't . . ."

As slaves took him off to Placidus, I spared a moment to wonder if Ingiomar had some use for a prefect of the Praetorian Guard. Or could he have mistaken Lamia for me in his plumed helmet and shiny breastplate?

Nothing to be done about it. I rubbed away sweat leaking under my cheek guards, and pushed into the front rank of fighters again.

Time and memory blurred. Some of the Germans tried to come around the end of the line. I gathered the engineer and one of the remaining Praetorians and we threw them back, shouting the legion battle cry in cracking voices. We were raspy with thirst, and as sweat-drenched as if the stubborn heavens had yielded and let down their rain.

Finally a horn blatted from down the hill. Once, then twice, and a third time.

After battering at us for so long, the Marcomanni too must have been tired. They withdrew, howling threats. We shouted back. A few men copied the Germanic taunts I was hurling, which had been spat at me in Hoheneih: *shitten-legs, rabbit-heart, milk-liver.* Unlike our worst insults, which are about unnatural sex, it is cowardice the Germans most despise.

On our side there was loud cheering and relieved backslaps. I posted lookouts, then stood down all the fighting men.

Most sagged to the ground, heads drooping. A few feet away Cleon sat asprawl with his sword across his splayed knees. I shouted hoarsely for slaves to bring water. "Well done," I croaked to the exhausted troopers. "We held them."

"Not bad for donkey-wallopers," Cleon rasped.

"You," I said, still short of breath. "Not bad with a spear, for an old trident man."

He grinned. "At the river? I wasn't sure you noticed."

Seeing the gleam of his eye whites, I realized it was nearly dusk. Had we been fighting all afternoon?

But neither sun, moon, nor stars hung overhead, just an ominous wallow of heavy and humid bruise-colored clouds. Rain clouds. Storm clouds. Gods of Rome, let it rain soon! Let it rain long and hard, with thunder and lightning. While the Marcomanni cowered fearing the wrath of Thunraz, we could rebuild the barricades and retrieve more of our scattered horses.

In the meantime, there was much to be done. Both Licnos and his second-in-command were badly wounded, and the Praetorians had lost both of their officers in the calamitous sortie. In the absence of Lamia and Secundus, I seemed to be in command.

While the others drank, I pulled off my helmet and wrung out the saturated browcloth again. Thanks to Fortuna or my family's gods I had not been badly hurt, but my sweat-sodden tunic rubbed salt into every cut and scrape. No wonder the ancient Greeks had used to fight naked.

Cleon guzzled water, dunked the gourd in the slave's bucket, and drank again, slobbering water over his chin. I made a note to check on our stock of potables.

He noticed I had squeezed out the headband one-handed. Beneath its filthy bandage, my left arm throbbed viciously. "The *medicus* should look at that," he said.

I dismissed the notion, seeing no need to add to Placidus's chores. Crows flapped into the air as soldiers and slaves retrieved our casualties and the Germans hauled off as many of their fallen as they could reach. A weary trooper stumbled out to a thrashing horse whose leg was caught in its own entrails. He cut its throat, slumped to his knees, and vomited.

The bodies must be burned at once, tonight. I would have Dio collect the men's identification tags and record the deaths. Would any of us survive to deliver a report?

Maybe the scouts would encounter armed travelers between here and Bruna who would help us. Or even the king himself. Ha. Why not wish for Hercules or Mars?

My eye was caught by one of the troopers who had tipped water into his upturned helmet so his horse could drink. The black mare's shoulders were rimed with sweat. It was, in fact, the very horse that had followed the fleeing Praetorian into the camp. No need to ask if it was his own. "You were on sentry duty at the river," I said.

He ladled more water into the helmet as his horse slurped noisily. To forestall a rebuke, for I had not yet ordered that the animals be taken care of, he said, "It is my own ration I am giving her."

"Your name?"

"Trooper First Class Caturix, Tribune."

I was sure now that I recognized him. "Stand at attention, Trooper."

He shoved the helmet into the serving slave's hand and straightened wearily.

I took a deep breath. "Caturix, I appoint you acting decurion of Turma, er..."

"Sixteen, sir."

"Turma Sixteen, Fifth Ala Gallica." I added, "For your courage, I will do all I can to make the promotion permanent."

Faces turned toward me, then to the new junior officer. I realized I had done this backward. "Hear me now, men of the Fifth Ala Gallica, the Tenth Praetorian Cohort, and support forces! I am resuming my position as commander of this vexillation. Until we recover the prefect, you will take orders from me. Is that clear?"

There was no dissent. Better an ex-tribune than none, they must have thought.

The server offered me the gourd. I had told him earlier not to come to me until everyone else had drunk. An officer must attend to his men's well-being before his own, as I had learned from a short-spoken centurion when I was new to the legion.

"Decurion Caturix," I said. "I think you have not had your ration of water yet."

The medical tent was a horrible place, as steamy as a *sudatorium* despite the rolled-up walls, aswarm with flies and mosquitoes, and stinking of everything that is usually inside a man. Casualties lay side to side like floor tiles.

Placidus was sewing up a thigh wound with quick, looping stitches. A sort of turban kept sweat out of his eyes. Without looking up he replied, "Secundus? Outside."

Where the corpses were.

An unexpected flush of grief swelled my eyes. I heard Placidus say, "Sorry." But that was inadequate for the loss of a brave and reliable man, a soldier from a family of soldiers who had hoped for promotion to the Guard in Rome, then retirement one day to a magistracy in his hometown. Arelate, was it? Or Nemausus?

This attempt at self-distraction failed, and I felt tears slide down my cheeks. Not just for Secundus, but the others whose life threads had been cut today.

If I had not fallen in love with Aurima. If I had surrendered her to Caligula's jealousy.

"Do not weep for the living," Placidus muttered.

I untied my browband to wipe my face. "What is the tally?"

"Ask your man Dio." He knotted the thread and reached for a knife to cut it. Almost soundlessly he added, "What hope, brother?"

"We have the high ground," I said loudly, so others could hear. "We have killed or wounded scores of them. We have time to regroup." I did not say, *And it may rain*, because we had wished it so often without success. Instead I said, "And we are Romans."

Placidus's patient spat out the stick he had bitten on. "Fuckin' right, Tribune!"

I smiled.

"Not yet," the surgeon said, and stuck the peg between the man's teeth again. Dousing his stitchery with vinegar, he said softly over the patient's squalling, "Find a way to get us back to Carnuntum soon. I can do nothing more than patchwork here."

As he had enjoined, I did not weep among the wounded. Instead, as I moved through the tent I offered each of them praise and reassurance, if only a firm hand on a man's shoulder. The great generals assert in their memoirs the value to morale of this practice. Yet it was one of the hardest things I have ever done, acting confident and resolute when all I wanted was to lay my body beside theirs and abandon them in sleep.

Dio sat on a chest he had dragged outside Lamia's tent, ripping spare tunics into bandages. "Will it rain?" he inquired eagerly, as if I were a sibyl.

I advised him to ask Jupiter Pluvius. We were talking about the tasks I wanted done when two burly mule drivers appeared. "Need that box for the barricade, clerk."

"Impossible." Dio jumped up, then stooped to gather the fallen rags. He spread his arms to protect the chest behind him. "This holds the prefect's private and classified documents."

One of the muleteers ducked into the tent. "Another one in here, Suellius."

"No! Those are the prefect's personal effects."

"Dio," I said, "if the prefect were here and needed persuading, I would persuade him. We must strengthen our defenses."

"But ..." He edged closer and whispered into my ear in Greek, "Marcus, his money is in there too, and his gift goods."

"The chests are locked, are they not? Let the men take them." It crossed my mind that Lamia's documents would make interesting reading, but that could be attended to later. If there was a "later."

A loud groan brayed through the heavy air, ending in a spatter of breathy honks like a fat man's farts. Dio snickered nervously. It was our own captured horn, sounding the end of this brief lull.

A red-faced lookout pushed past the mule drivers. "Sir, the Germans are moving."

39: *HALJO DUNKARA*

Maelo reined in when he, Odo, and Rufus were a little more than a spear-cast from the barricade. "Romans," he shouted in Latin. "Are you hearing?"

His horse danced, unsettled by the boom of his voice and the stench of death. The two boys, riding bareback, ranged back and forth behind him like hunting dogs. The gloom made Rufus's red hair as dark as dried blood, and turned all three of them into faded specters on the pale field.

"Your prefect and three of his men are our prisoners," Maelo yelled. "They are going to die. I promise, they are not going to die well." He wheeled his restless mount in a circle. "Do you wish to save them? Eh? Do you?"

Over muttering in the ranks, I shouted, "Rome does not bargain with snakes."

His face turned toward me. "But Rome is not stupid! It is sensible to trade one bad man so four good men can live. Not so?"

No one asked the obvious question. They knew who was meant to be traded.

Maelo shook his shield. "Give us Marcus Aquilo, who murdered our brothers!"

No one stirred.

"You do not believe me, eh? You think they are not going to die?"

He turned to the boys and gestured. Rufus and Odo trotted forward on their ponies, each with a sort of sack at his side. Odo hurled his, then Rufus. The shaggy heads of the two Quadi scouts hit the ground in little puffs of dust and rolled toward us.

Which meant that Ingiomar had men to the north of us. And that they could join the others to our south whenever they wished.

Over the gasps and curses, I shouted, "Who are the murderers now?"

He pretended not to hear me. "So! Here is what happens. At the rise of the sun we kill one of your troopers. You are going to hear him die in much pain, unless you give up Aquilo before. At the third hour, the other two troopers—*ja?* And at midday, we burn your prefect alive where you can see." He drew his sword and pointed at the trees bordering the road. "All because of stupidity, if you do not give up Aquilo to us."

Rage flooded me. I vaulted atop a battered cart. "There is no need of this coward's game, Maelo. Where is the so-brave Inguiomerus—licking his balls like a dog? Let him come and fight me man-to-man, and free our comrades if he kills me!"

From the depths of the battle line I heard Cleon growl, "Gods above." Then he aimed his sword point at Maelo, shouting in bad Germanic, "Shit-leg!"

Someone else leveled his own blade and yelled, "Rabbit-heart!" Then they all pointed their weapons at Maelo, front ranks and rear, bellowing defiance in three languages that fused into a wordless roar.

He yanked on the reins so hard his horse half reared, spun around, and galloped down the slope with the boys tagging behind. For a moment of vanity—well, longer than a moment, actually—I hoped my father smiled, if he was watching from the other world.

Still there was no rain. At this rate, we would soon boil like lobsters.

The dense heat muffled the bang of hammers nailing barricade vehicles together with a hodgepodge of cart shafts, wagon tongues, tailgates, and tent poles. In the last of the light I sent slaves out to scavenge stones, while men who had hunted in boyhood showed others how to make and use slings. The bodiless heads of Tudrus and Boldt were added to the unlit pyre without a shred of regret on my part.

Everyone was busy. Too busy, I hoped, to brood about the fate of Ingiomar's four captives.

There was no hope of mounting a rescue mission. The seventy-four-man vexillation that had set out from Carnuntum was now reduced to seventeen fighting men and six senior staff fit for duty, ten walking wounded, fifteen incapacitated, nine dead, four missing, and twelve Army servants and slaves.

The numbers darted through my mind like a swirl of sparrows. "Surely that is seventy-three, not seventy-four," I said to Dio.

"I did not count Glabrio, since you killed him weeks ago." He folded his tablet. "Marcus, you have told me what to do. You need not also do it yourself."

We had food, *posca*, and ale for three more days. Even if it failed to rain, there was enough water to last our three remaining horses and two mules for a day and a half. Sooner or later, the blockage of traffic would prompt an investigation from Bruna or Carnuntum. This was the Amber Road, after all, not the untrodden Hercynian Forest.

"If you will not rest, at least let me make you a sling for your arm," Dio said.

"I am fine." I changed the subject. "Did you see Rufus?"

"Yes, gods damn him." For Dio to curse revealed how deeply he felt the Thracian boy's betrayal. "I must see if the pyre is ready. We have plenty of dry grass and oil, at least." He clasped the tablet to his chest. "Perhaps I am the only one not praying for rain."

I was so preoccupied with other thoughts that I almost missed the weak joke. Dio, jesting in the midst of a siege? Had his fears succumbed to fatalism?

It was I who should be resigning myself to death. My will was written. My ring—well, I would die with my signet ring on; I was my father's son. But I did not want some greedy minion of Ingiomar's taking Father's torc to flaunt on his tattooed biceps.

I said, "Dio, this neck-ring makes me a target for every barbarian lusty for gold. Keep it for me until this is all over." I put my hand to the torc.

"Wait," he said at once. "It is how you are recognized as commander. It . . . Seeing it makes me feel . . ." He blinked and looked away. "Give it to me later, if you still wish." The engineer and the Gauls' acting decurion, Caturix, were waiting to talk, so I let him leave for the rocky spur where our dead would be burned.

A little while after inspecting the strengthened barricades, I paused by the Fifth Gallica's unit flag. A torch streamed smoke, as straight as a pillar. What a different tale this would have been, had we only brought a few centuries of legionaries! With their digging tools and experienced labor, the hilltop could have been fortified properly with a ditch and a head-high palisade.

Behind me Cleon crunched into a rusk of twice-baked bread. "Get some sleep," I told him. "No one here is going to throw me over the barricades to Inguiomerus."

"Wait till they've heard enough pretty music of men being tortured," he said.

But the evening was quiet except for the buzz of crickets, and the group of men gathered at the barricades seemed to have no interest in capitulating to Maelo's threat. Far from weeping and praying for their lives, they regaled each other with recalled experiences of the day. I heard excitement—"*Whap!* Like a butcher chopping a brisket!"—scoffing retorts, even laughter. What god had instilled in them this reckless elation? Did they really think I could save them?

Standing alone behind a cart toppled on its side, I looked down the slope of the field. At its foot moved the barely visible shapes of mounted German sentinels. Farther to the south, at the edge of the trees, winked the campfires of Ingiomar's main force. I did not need to imagine the terror the captives there must be enduring; I remembered it myself, all too well.

If I stayed and fought beside the men whom I now thought of as mine, and by my leading them they defeated Ingiomar, some would surely die. So, probably, would Lamia and the three other hostages. Yet I might live—and with Lamia dead, I could keep my vow to reunite my *familia*.

My *familia*. No longer the woman I had chosen for my wife. Or her child—our child, *my* child, whatever Lamia claimed. But my father's old body-slave Turtle, Turtle's mouthy little grandson Astyanax, Father's chief secretary Nicander, the stablemaster's boy Thalus, the other secretaries and stablemen, the kitchen staff and servers, housemaids and seamstresses, guards and messenger boys, litter bearers and laundrywomen . . . all the slaves of our household, now the property of the State, hoping I would redeem my pledge to gather them again.

I will come back one day and find you all, every one, no matter where you are, I had declared, and had sworn it with my own blood. *If I prove false, may Father Jupiter and the other gods of Rome, and the* di manēs *of this house, cause my blood to be spilled in the wilderness and there cause me to die.*

Or the other choice: to give myself up . . .

There was no shame in surrendering to an honorable enemy. Once Ingiomar had what he wanted, there was a fair chance he would honor Maelo's promise and free Lamia and the other hostages. Nor would he have any reason to resume his attack on the men waiting with steel and stones on the hilltop.

Yet the *fraujaz*'s honor could not be relied on. He might decide to kill as many Romans as he could, starting with me. Which meant I would die for nothing.

What is the right choice, Father? Should I take my chances in battle, and risk the lives of more brave men? Or surrender to Ingiomar my wretched carcass, stained with blood guilt, in the hope of saving others? Faithful Phormio, how would you counsel me? Publius, my courageous brother, what would you do?

All three of them had sacrificed themselves for the sake of others. Did I, bitter and betrayed, hold my life so much dearer than they had theirs?

There is another choice, whispered a little voice. *Run in the night, away from the Germans, away from this flimsy hill fort, and live . . .*

I must choose before daybreak. Which meant that this sweaty, oppressive night in the wilderness might be my last.

The notion came to me of leaving a message for Aurima. I said, "Cleon?"

A glug: he had scavenged something to wash down his hardbread. "Aye?"

I changed my mind about asking him to find Dio. The impulse to write a farewell was only self-pity. I said, "Got another crust of that tooth-breaker? I could eat a bite."

Faraway lightning flickered. Someone shouted, "Jupiter is with us."

"Rain," cried another man. "Jupiter Pluvius, bring us rain!"

Rain would force a delay in cremating our dead. Still, if I chose the coward's way out, it would be a better cloak for a solitary escape than flickering torchlight.

"It's only a tease," Cleon grumbled. "Just like last . . ." He broke off. His eyes widened, glazed with surprise. The hand extended toward me with a piece of hardbread fell as if his strength had been sapped.

I stood up to see what had drawn his attention. "What in buggering Hades is that?" someone else said.

A ghostly green light was moving toward us, appearing and disappearing behind trees that screened the northern end of the road.

Others began to notice. Men rose to their feet, staring. Down the road, one of the Marcomanni lookouts let out a hoarse cry.

The eerie glow drifted closer. Blinded by the lights at our perimeter, I could not at first make out what was approaching. Some kind of animal?

The Marcomanni fled from the apparition. Who could blame them? Our torchlight glimmered distantly on a monstrous creature of bony curves and spikes, long hoofed legs, huge vacant eyes.

Hair stood up on the back of my neck.

The creature stopped. The green light rose until it glowed high in the air.

The man next to me fell to his knees, babbling in Gaulish to Cernunnos, their antlered god of life and death.

As my sight continued to sharpen, I discerned a dark arm beneath the lofty radiance. But by my soul, where were the body and head?

Cleon gripped my shoulder hard, as if to keep from falling down. His other hand clutched the phallus amulet at his throat.

Distant lightning flashed, faded, and flashed again. From the spine of the silvery horned beast grew a woman's body, clad in dark robes. The green light glowed from a staff in her upraised hand. Serpents, not hair, tangled on her head. Her face—I could not help gasping with the others who saw it— was horribly deformed, a black chaos of ruts and pustules. Light gleamed on empty eye sockets shaped like tears.

The Marcomanni clustered in their encampment like terrified sheep. Clutching each other, they gaped from their insignificant sparks of fire.

The dark goddess. I knew her name: Haljo Dunkara, queen of death.

In Germanic, pausing after each inexorable word, she shouted in a deep voice, "I seek the one who is owed to me. Let him come forth!"

No man who saw her could speak. Gaul, Roman, German, all stared spellbound.

Again she bellowed, now in Latin: "Where is the one who belongs to me? Give me him!"

Whispered incantations and a flurry of protective gestures filled the awful night. Someone said under his breath, "The dead. She wants the dead."

The green light descended to the level of the beast's horns. The air was so thick I had to open my mouth to breathe.

"Who does she want?" another man whispered.

"Me," I said. I pulled myself onto a pole connecting two carts.

Cleon stuttered, "What— Marcus, what are you doing?"

The bloody ground on the far side of the barricade squelched when I landed on it. "Look after Dio," I told him, and ran down the slope toward her.

"Tribune, no!" a voice shouted behind me.

Lightning flashed. The goddess sat upon her horned steed, her terrible face toward me. Thunder smote the night with a *crack!* like a great sword striking a shield of bronze.

I kept running. My helmet fell from the crook of my arm and rolled away.

When I was a horse length from her, the voice of iron commanded, "Stop."

I dragged in a deep gulp of air.

"I have come for you," she said.

A cold wind rushed upon me, heavy with threat. My heart pounded as if it would explode.

She swept her dark cloak aside. Taking her offered hand, I vaulted onto the antlered beast and pulled her cloak over my own shoulder.

A burst of lightning splashed blood-red against my eyelids. Then thunder boomed, and the silver beast beneath us leaped into flight with a surge of strength, leaving behind the living and the dead.

Trees rushed past, their leaves and branches blown back by her headlong speed. She soared toward the storm, her green fire shredding in the wind. Tattered bits peeled from her face and pelted me. The heavy snakes untwined from the crown of her head.

A goddess of the underworld ought to be an icy and skeletal wraith, but that was not what I felt against me. My thighs pressed against hers, and her mount's muscular haunches flexed beneath my legs. My blood throbbed, echoing the thud of hooves.

When I could stand it no longer, I reached around her and pulled on the reins. Her mount slowed. I slid off before it stopped and reached up my arms.

The dark mask, fissured and partly disintegrated by the wind, tipped down toward me from her height atop the huffing steed.

"Come," I said gutturally.

From somewhere in the forest swelled the roar of onrushing rain. She slipped down against me, and I cleared the dry mud from her face. Then we were rolling in the soft leaf mold under a tree, and as the first raindrops spat down on my back I was deep in my wife's embrace, telling her over and over that I loved her.

40: TWICE-FERMENTED WINE

I slept. Morpheus and Nyx, how I slept! Aurima tried to rouse me.

"Magnificent," I mumbled, smearing the dirt on her cheek. "You. Goddess."

"Wake up," she said. "We must go. I need my baby."

It was still dark, but the rain had stopped. As Maelo's ultimatum came back to me, I struggled to sit up. Sore muscles clamored in my arms, back, and neck, which had not hurt while my lust burned. It had been too long since I worked with my bodyguards on sword skills.

Spider shoved his head against my chest—the antlers now gone from his bridle—and nuzzled his wet face against mine. I held his head and rubbed my cheek against his, and we communed affectionately for a few moments.

Clutching his mane, I pulled myself to my feet. Aurima was letting out milk from her breasts. Hearing my groan, she said with mock humor, "Have I destroyed you?"

I would have embraced her from behind, if her tone had not discouraged it. Instead I went around the tree to relieve myself. "How did you know I was in danger, my heart?"

"It is Thancmar's doing. When my father learned where you were, he summoned his warriors to hunt you down. Thancmar rode like the wind to Bruna to warn you."

I thought of responding with equal dryness that I had not known the dwarf held me in such esteem. Perhaps he was atoning for having been Ingiomar's source, but I would not force the sister who loved him to admit it.

"Of course you were not in Bruna," she went on matter-of-factly.

My disquiet deepened into unease. Our lovemaking had been hot and hungry. Why was she now so distant?

"So I left word for Vannaz and Vangio and came to find you."

"By yourself?" I ducked under a tree limb to face her.

"With Thancmar." Her booted foot scuffed dry leaves. "I did not mean to . . ." A pause, then she cleared her throat. "I must go."

"Go where?"

"No matter." She lifted her chin. "My father now thinks the Dark Goddess took you, may she forgive me. When he is gone, you can follow your friends to Carnuntum."

As she turned away I caught her by the arm, forceful in my urgency.

"They are not my friends, beloved. They are taking me to trial for killing Glabrio, the whoreson who captured you."

"Is that ... That is true?"

I wished I could see her eyes. There was moonlight, but it did not penetrate under the massive tree. "Did Vannaz not tell you?"

Rainwater dripped around us. Spider shuffled through leaves, nosing for grass.

At last Aurima said in a more subdued voice, "Gisila said you did not want me anymore. She said you wished to go back to Rome."

"That was a lie," I growled. "Gisila helped Lamia. She made me sleep"—I did not know how to say "drugged"—"and when I awoke, I was his prisoner."

"She told me not to grieve for you. She said that if I wish to please Austro, I must raise my son among his own people."

"Lamia made me think you hated me. He knew things. He even knew about the baby falling in the river."

"But how . . ." She stopped. So quietly that I barely heard her, she said, "When I could not bear it, I opened my heart to Gisila. I asked for her counsel."

So it was the old woman who had done this damage. "He also said I was not your husband." I forced out the next words: "Nor your child's father."

"You did not believe that, did you?"

I could not answer. I was too ashamed of having doubted her.

"My love, who else would I want as husband?" She grasped my bearded jaw to draw my face toward hers. "There has been no man but you. Who else could have fathered so handsome a son?"

Feeling the wetness on my cheeks, she caught her breath in a sob. We held fast to each other as the tree shed fat cold tears on us.

No other man. No one else's son.

The whole shape of my future altered. There was now another choice: to stay with my own tiny family, my wife and child. If we went away in secret, perhaps to one of the villages in Illyricum that had given us shelter last winter, superstitious men would reckon I had been carried off to the underworld, and Roman investigators would suppose mine was one of the bodies burned on the hilltop.

Furthermore, Caligula Caesar would not rule forever—indeed, might have already been unseated. We could then return to Rome, or perhaps to a country town if Aurima refused the city, and I would rebuild my *familia* so my boy grew up as truly a Licinius Carinna as I could make him.

Oh, it was a lovely dream. Its only costs were the deaths of Lamia, who had tried to murder me to advance his career, of three soldiers who had dutifully followed his orders, and perhaps a few others, or many others, in the hill fort if Ingiomar did not believe I had fled. Cleon, Dio, brave Caturix, Placidus, Aprilis who had reenlisted to follow the Eagles ... the fighters and followers and all the wounded who would succumb without a legion hospital's care.

Amid the gloom of *ifs* and *shoulds*, of wishes and needs, it was the light of happiness that showed me my choice at last. I felt its justice with perfect certainty—not in my mind or heart, which wanted desperately to protest, but in my soul.

But how could I tell Aurima?

I was searching for words when she said, "We need to go. I must feed my baby."

"Where is he? Is he well, my Beran?"

"Yes, Goddess be praised." She rummaged in the leaves for her dark cloak. "Thancmar waits with him a short way from here." She clicked her tongue to call Spider. "In two days we can be safe in Bruna."

"I must join you later." I spoke as casually as I could. "Your father and your uncle have hostages, and they are going to start sacrificing them at dawn unless I am there."

"Roman hostages?"

"Lamia and three of his troopers."

"You owe nothing to that man." She gathered the stallion's reins, about to mount. "Let them meet their fate."

"I am sorry, *frijdila*." I interposed myself between her and Spider. "Let us go together to Beran. But then I need the horse."

"No." She held on to the reins. "Have I done all this, daring the terrible anger of the Dark Goddess by using her likeness"—she touched her cheek with her free hand—"for you to give yourself into the hands of my father? No. I am not allowing it."

Only the weakest of men lets any woman but his mother tell him what to do. Once I would have reacted with astonishment, disbelief, and displeasure, but this was Aurima, who had fought Roman troops with an ax, who had stabbed Caligula Caesar to avenge my brother's death. She was not "any woman," and never would be.

"It gives me joy to have a wife who loves me so much." I clasped her face in my palms. "How can I say I must go, and not have you think I love you too little?"

She stepped back. "Is it because they are Romans, and I am not?"

"No, my heart. It is because you are safe, and they are in danger."

Her glare pierced me. "Your son is in danger of having no father."

I labored to explain myself, to voice a reason she would accept. *It is my duty*, I would have told her, but did not know the right words in Germanic.

Aurima let the reins fall and seized my wrists, gripping hard as if I might try to escape. "I am not letting go," she threatened.

"I do not want you to let me go," I said. "I want you to send me."

Her hands clamped even tighter. I knew she wanted to confront her father with me or instead of me, and because the baby prevented it she was in agony.

A swell of emotion nearly choked me: tenderness, awe, a fierce protectiveness. I said, "Aurima, I must end it with Ingiomar. Until he is rid of the hunger for revenge that poisons him, we are never going to be safe."

She sighed. The stiffness in her shoulders eased, and she released my wrists. "Then I send you, my poor husband who chose a woman of great trouble. May Austro keep you safe."

I was about to speak when she silenced me with a finger on my lips. The stallion had raised his head, ears cocked. I stooped for my sword belt.

In a moment I heard it too: the slow thump of a horse's footfalls on the road. Spider's nostrils distended; he was about to whinny a challenge. I held his muzzle down.

And then: a faint humming, the way a man might idly croon as he honed a knife or carved a tent peg.

"Rufus," Aurima cried.

"Wait," I warned. Before I could hold her back, she burst out from under the tree.

He slid off his horse, and she flung her arms around his neck. In the moon's cold light the young Thracian was all bones and stringy sinew, hair to his shoulders, his chest bare and his legs in ragged trousers. A knife rode in a sheath at his hip, but his hands were on her shoulders, not on the hilt.

His dirty face cracked in a broad white grin. "Au'ima," he said.

I drew my sword from its scabbard. "Rufus."

Hastily he let her go and moved aside so that he had a clear approach to me. Or I to him, as Fortuna chose.

"Mar's," he said, the smile gone.

I swallowed, but my voice was still thick. "It took you long enough to find me."

Aurima stayed me with a hand on my wrist. "You do not mean harm, Rufus?"

Rufus shook his head. He unsheathed his knife and held it on his palm toward me, hilt foremost. "I help," he said, looking from me to Aurima.

I relaxed a fraction. Her mud-distorted face and hair, the mussel shells that had shammed blindly gaping eyes, the staff tipped with green swamp fire, and the horns fastened to the crownpiece of Spider's bridle had somehow not deceived him.

I asked if our hill fort was still safe, if Ingiomar was still resolved to kill the hostages. A nod. Another nod.

"Then I must go now." I was proud that I could speak calmly. "The two of you take Spider; I will ride Rufus's horse." Ingiomar would not get a second chance at my roan stallion.

"Do you mean to fight beside your Romans?"

"I mean"—and here, regrettably, my voice did falter—"to save them."

"No," Rufus said insistently, shaking his head. "Bu'n." He pointed at me. "Bu'n."

It was no surprise that Ingiomar thought to change the manner of my death. Burning alive would be slower than drowning, gutted, in a bog. But if

I could not kill the bastard and escape alive, I would cheat him with a sharp knife for myself.

Another woman might have clutched me, crying, *Do you not love me?* But Aurima, daughter and sister of warriors, simply looked at me in the moonlight.

"You came here to be free," she said, though not reproachfully.

"I am free," I said. "But I am still myself." And then I said, "*Basia me,*" a catchphrase between us that I thought might spark a smile.

I meant the kiss to be a quick one that would not weaken my resolve, but both of us, trying for valor, were betrayed by anguish and desire. When at last we broke apart, she said breathlessly, "I am going to find Vannaz."

I did not think his aid could possibly come in time. Some impulse made me lie, "Fear not; I have a plan."

I gripped Rufus's shoulder in farewell, bidding him to keep her and the child safe. Then I heaved myself atop his horse, and was a quarter of a mile down the road before remembering that I had meant to give Aurima my father's torc.

My blood fizzed like twice-fermented wine, and my thoughts drifted like summer clouds. She still loved me. Did she know, had I made it clear, how much I loved her?

I almost turned back to make certain, but she would already be on her way in the other direction with Rufus. Moonlight masked so many stars that I could not see how much time remained until sunrise, when the first trooper would be slain.

Get serious, man. How to confront Ingiomar? How to make him free the captives?

A pity it was not Lamia who would be first; I would gladly wait until they were done with him. Perfidious toad! Spewing poison about Aurima spurning me for Vangio or Vannaz, about Caligula lying with her. He could not have heard any of that from old Gisila. He had invented it to torment me.

Ingiomar's camp could not be far. Knife against my anklebone, hidden by boot lacings. Don't try for the throat. Remember the mistake with Chlothar's beard. Maybe the eye socket.

Fool, this may be the last hour of your life. Do not waste it.

There was little to sense, other than the gray loom of trees like a barrier against the sinking moon. I inhaled wet horse, the cool heady musk of sodden forest, a wisp of smoke. Listened to the patter of raindrops spilling on lower leaves, the glutinous thump of hooves in mud. Reached within myself and felt pain in my arm, aching, weariness and need of sleep, yet still that mindless exhilaration...

I felt her bravery. Confidence. Pride.

Indifference to death? asked Leonidas, leader of the Spartans at Thermopylae.

Not that, great king. But as you told the Persian invader Xerxes when he offered to spare you if you gave up your sword: *Come and take it.*

No matter what happened this day, the governor of Pannonia would learn Romans were killed. Ingiomar had been lightly punished last fall with the surrender of a hostage, but this time Sabinus would exact the standard revenge for treachery. Warriors would be butchered, women and children sold into slavery.

I halted again. I should have warned Aurima. But she and our child would be safe in Bruna, protected by Vannaz.

Yet harsh reprisals could spark a rebellion among the Marcomanni and Quadi. Then Sabinus would have a war on his hands: the Mark in flames, Pannonia overrun.

A pity he would never understand that this blood enmity was his fault. Instead of sending Ingiomar away unheard when the man came seeking justice, he could have listened and made reparations, as I myself had later urged Caligula to do.

Some while later I realized I was staring blankly into the darkness. The horse had stopped and was browsing at the roadside. And an idea had come to me, after all.

41: THERMOPYLAE

Even before torch flames atop the hill came into view, I heard the singing. It sounded Gaulish, lighter and more melodious than the Germans' hoarse warbles. An attempt to ward off the Dark Goddess, perhaps. Or just to stay heartened.

Night had not yet loosened its grip on the sky, and the chill brought by the storm had teased ribbons of mist from the water meadow's serpentine channels. I saw no sentries, either theirs or ours. Muzzling Rufus's horse with my headband, I led it up through the swirling fog that swathed the foot of the hill.

The Gaulish tune ended. Someone started a marching song, "Germanicus's Legs." In a pause between verses, I called out the watchword, *Vis Romana*—Roman Strength—that Secundus had chosen an eternity earlier.

Silence fell. Then an unsteady voice shouted, "Are you man, or other?"

I tried not to smile at the memory of the ghostly queen on her steed. "A man."

"Show yourself, then, or you are dead."

When I surfaced from the mist, glad to have been challenged instead of summarily speared, it took some time before everyone realized I was not a shade or a lemur. "What happened?" they asked. "Who was she? Where did you go?"

A Gaul pointed to the shoulder brand on Rufus's horse. "How did you get one of our mounts?" I had not noticed the brand. The boy must have acquired one of the animals that had strayed or lost its rider in the cavalry melee.

"Did you go and fight that bastard Inguiomerus without me?" Cleon demanded.

One of the Praetorians pressed: "Will he free my comrades? And the prefect?"

None of them asked, "Why have you come back?" Obviously it was not the wrenching decision I had thought it to be.

I raised a hand for silence. It was still dark beyond the torchlight, actually darker than before since the moon was setting. Gray mist humped across the landscape beneath us. There was no sound from the Marcomanni camp. What a pleasant surprise if Dunkara's appearance had unnerved them enough to flee, leaving the hostages alive.

"Where I was, and who took me there, I cannot say," I began. "However, I must tell you honestly that we cannot expect reinforcements, either human or divine."

A moan grated from their throats, like the plaint of earth stressed by upheaval.

"But I have a plan," I went on, low-voiced lest the words carry in the fog. Then I stopped, struck by the look on Dio's face. He hung back on the fringes of the crowd with an expression that seemed accusatory.

"A plan," voices murmured. "He has a plan … The tribune has a plan."

"The odds of success are no better than one in two," I cautioned. "We must still be prepared to defend against attack." I paused again to let this warning sink in. The faces in the firelight gazed back with faith and resolve.

All at once I was absurdly happy to be among these men. "Right. First, I need volunteers for quick work here in the camp. Two carpenters. Two mule handlers. Two men with strong backs. Step forward."

The resultant jostling almost knocked down the torch. I chose from the willing and waved them to one side.

"I also need a man to accompany me to the Marcomanni camp. Someone who can drive a mule cart. Listen well!" I had to speak louder over the comments and questions. "If the plan fails, I will not return. Nor will whoever comes with me."

The enthusiasm died away. Putting one's head on a chopping block was a different matter. I looked around, reluctant to plead or to command. "I would not ask any man to risk his life unless it—"

"Diana's tits! Cut the gabble," Cleon broke in. "Let's get on with it."

Before the mist closed around the five of us, I glanced up at a flock of small birds wheeling above the treetops. The luminous green of the early sky reminded me of Aurima's eyes in sunlight.

Even if I did not see her again, she and the baby would be safe. She had Rufus and Thancmar to protect her, and her formidable grandmother Hroswitha.

That thought did little to calm my nerves. But most of my life had been a matter of feigning confidence I did not have, so I made myself ignore the bellyful of bees.

The wet fog thickened, muffling the thump of hooves, clink of harness, and creak of the laden cart. Treetops and sky faded into gray, until there was nothing to see but torn-up turf passing beneath us. Light cast by a torch fastened to the cart's side was so wan that it cast no shadows.

"Think they'll go for it, Tribune?" the mule driver, Cato, asked quietly. He shifted the reins and goad to his other hand and wiped his palm on his tunic.

"Inguiomerus knows that if he murders the prefect in cold blood, Rome will destroy him and his whole clan," I assured him. "We are offering him a way out with dignity."

"More than he deserves, the filthy renegade," muttered Aprilis. The quartermaster had not been eager to come, but I wanted a credible witness from the Fifteenth Legion. He rode in his still bloody and dented armor, with a black-scabbed gash across his nose and cheek from a blow that had split his helmet's cheek guard.

"Take care; many of the Germans understand Latin," Dio warned from his seat beside the mule driver. I had tried to veto his joining us, but he had pointed out that as Lamia's secretary he would lend the mission more official legitimacy.

His dour face had brightened when I told him privately of Aurima, and learning of Rufus's change of heart had lifted his spirits even more. By contrast, the news had muted Cleon's normal good cheer. He rode beside me now in somber silence, a shield on his left arm and a drawn sword laid across the pommel of his saddle.

Pale patchy cobwebs splotched the turf here and there. Austro's promises that sunlight would burn off the haze, Aurima had once told me.

Was that a long-haired man looming in the mist? Or my tired eyes making shapes out of nothing?

I swallowed. Although I had swilled a good half *congius* of water before we left, my mouth was as dry as a freshly sand-strewn arena.

If things did not go well, Aprilis was to hoist Cato onto his horse, Cleon would take Dio, and I would cover our retreat. Provided that the fog held, there was a fair chance of making it back to the fort. For some of us, at least.

"Anybody sees a riverbank and a ferryman up ahead, I'm gone." Cato's uneasy chuckle at his own joke shot up into a yelp when the cart splashed into a rut. We had reached the Amber Road.

"Halt," a sharp voice ordered. A dozen mounted warriors materialized out of the silvery half-light, trapping us in a hedge of spears.

One of them lifted a twisted aurochs horn to his lips. A melancholy *boo-ooo* shuddered through the mist.

Distant shouts. Cleon began to lift his sword. "Down," I hissed to him.

"You are late; it is almost sunrise," one of the Marcomanni said in Latin. His smirk was nearly hidden by his bushy gray beard, the reason I had not known him at once. He was another of the men Maelo had taken to Rome in Aurima's guard of honor.

"Still here, Segomo?" I said in his own language. "Did you not understand the Dark Goddess's warning?"

The reminder caused a stir of unease. "She took the man she wanted," another warrior said defiantly. Anso, I thought: a cousin of Friduric's. "We saw it. A Roman."

"One of us? Do you think so?" I glanced around at my companions. "Perhaps it was me. Yet I am here." I smiled at the Germans' disquiet. "We have come to see your *fraujaz*. Where is he?"

Anso tried out his own Latin: "Give your swords."

Come and take them. "We are not your prisoners," I said. "We are envoys of Rome who wish to speak with Inguiomerus." Riders were coming fast, hooves thudding.

Anso scowled. I stared back. My left hand lay on a horn of my saddle, holding the reins; the other rested near the hilt of my sword.

In the next moment more Marcomanni on hot-breathed, scuffling horses swarmed around us. Anso declared hastily, "I have Aquilo!"

Ingiomar was not among them. Instead, Maelo pushed his way forward. He said to Aprilis, no doubt viewing him as senior among us, "This is the right thing you do. We give you our captives for this worthless one." He jabbed a thumb at me.

"Are you Inguiomerus?" Aprilis barked.

Maelo's roan beard jutted out as he expanded his bare chest. "I am Maelo, sister's son of the great king Marbodo."

"Then you are not the man we want. Take us to him." Army quartermasters are not easily cowed.

"When I am ready," Maelo snapped. He turned his glare on Anso. "Why are they still armed?"

Anso nudged his horse closer until his spearhead touched the topmost lacing of my steel corselet. Sparkles of mist glinted in his grease-stiffened hair, twisted up at the temples like ram's horns. "I told you your sword to give."

"And I told you, I wish to speak with Inguiomerus." I nodded at the cart. "We carry weapons to protect what we bring him."

"He said they are *legati* of Rome," Segomo explained to Maelo.

Three or four others began to talk. This is characteristic of Germans, few of whom have a sense of discipline or urgency.

"Are a few Romans such a threat to you?" Maelo jeered at Anso, and then scowled at the others. "You sound like women chattering over the wash! Why are you not keeping watch on the road?" He flung a hand to south and north. "Do you want traders to be wandering through with their donkeys and stinking cowhides?"

A couple of disgruntled warriors rode off in each direction. Authority reasserted, Maelo nodded to us and turned his horse. "Come, then."

42: BLOOD AND JUSTICE

"Look, they are giving him up," someone crowed.

Resourceful travelers, perhaps even a Roman detachment, had long ago swamped this clearing out of the edge of the woods. The mist, furling and unfurling, revealed a scatter of lean-tos. A dozen horses grazed in a brush-fenced corral. And over the heads of the warriors thronging around us rose a tree from which a body hung.

I caught my breath. Then a ribbon of mist swirled aside, and I saw it was a deer hanging by its hind legs.

The Marcomanni jeered and poked their weapons at us, trying to provoke a reaction. Cleon's snarled oaths suggested he was near exploding. "Patience," I muttered.

Maelo's broad shoulders blocked the view directly ahead. "Ingiomar," he announced, "they bring Aquilo to us."

"No," I corrected, nudging my mount past him. "I brought them—"

Shock froze my tongue. Ingiomar was grinning at me from atop a big sorrel horse.

My horse. Boss, my warhorse, whom I had thought dead and mutilated.

The stallion's head was bent, his eyes downcast and his mouth agape, for he had been bridled with a savage bit used only with the most unruly of mounts. When the reins are pulled, this bit gouges the roof of the horse's mouth and crushes his lower jaw, while yanking the headstall against the tender area behind his ears. Boss's reins were drawn so tight that his neck arched and his ears splayed in misery.

I stifled an impulse to call to him, for Ingiomar would probably respond with a vicious jerk on the bit. Trying to empty my face of expression, I looked up at the *fraujaz*.

The mist that had matted his long pale hair glittered on the rings plaited in his beard. His eyes were narrowed—with satisfaction, I thought. Well might the bastard gloat; he had truly shocked me.

I steadied my voice enough to introduce my companions. Maelo murmured to Ingiomar, pointing to Cleon and Dio, whom he had met in Rome. Ingiomar ignored Cato, the muleteer; his gaze lingered on the veteran, Aprilis.

"I brought them to guard what is owed to you," I said. I turned my cavalry horse aside, making room for Cato to drive the cart forward.

"I do not believe I am owed anything," Ingiomar replied in a gravelly voice. "Except you."

As the cart trundled closer, the Marcomanni realized that something lay under the crumpled goatskin within it. "A box, is it?"

"It must be full of gold to buy the turd's life."

"It is big enough to hold swords."

"Maybe it is the bones of Caesar." Laughter.

I said loudly, "I will explain after we see that our men are still alive."

"Throw down your weapons first," Maelo insisted.

"We did not come here to fight."

"Then you do not need them."

"We will not give up our swords." I glanced at Cleon and Aprilis, whose blades were drawn. My own was still in its scabbard. "But we will put them away if you bring us the prefect and his men, alive and well."

Ingiomar shrugged. "Segomo, get the Romans."

Although it was too soon to relax, I was surprised by how smoothly everything was going. It seemed absurd that I had agonized over the decision to come here. That I had nerved myself to be worthy of Aurima's dry-eyed farewell, as brave as that of any Spartan wife seeing her man off to war. That I had even imagined someone telling Beran one day of his father's courage in giving his life for the sake of honor.

We waited for the hostages. Birds twittered in the trees. The horses cropped grass. Some of the Marcomanni dismounted. Slaves brought them strips of meat, nuts, horns of ale. The fog grew thinner, and the day brightened.

"Where are they bringing the poor buggers from?" Aprilis grumbled. "Scythia?"

Ingiomar merely chewed his lip with fanged teeth, his eyes distant. I had hoped he would dismount too, but at least he eased the reins, letting Boss lift his head.

I will have my horse back from you, you serpent.

The stallion's nostrils flared. He probably scented me, but I avoided his eye. This was not the time to incite him.

Yet without meaning to, I must have nudged my mount forward. It was a mistake. Ingiomar hauled on the reins and Boss flinched back, pink saliva foaming around his jaw.

Beneath the mist-enhanced smells of campfire smoke, cooked meat, and dung I caught a whiff of something foul. A coarse plaid cloak flung across Boss's withers blocked my head-on view of his barrel and flanks. Did it hide a festering wound?

Ingiomar rasped, "Your rusty armor does no credit to Caesar, Tribune." As if my sweaty corselet's original owner would have had the opportunity to scour it.

"I looked for you in the battle line," I retorted. "Are the Marcomanni content to follow a leader who does not fight?"

He stared at me for an instant; then his tawny mustaches lifted in a malevolent smile. "Tonight, boy, it is you that Haljo Dunkara comes to fetch."

"Here they are," Dio interrupted, high-voiced with nerves.

The hostages staggered out of the forest, escorted by Segomo and several others. All four had been stripped of their armor. Lamia shuffled along in the lead, leaning on his men's broken standard. Behind him two Praetorian troopers in bloody tunics carried the third, naked and limp, with their arms under his shoulders.

"Your swords," Maelo prompted.

"I bargained for four living men, not three," I snapped.

The captives saw us. "Merciful gods," one gasped.

The second trooper's face contorted. "They came." Tears spilled down his cheeks.

"Wake up, Gnaeus!" They shook their insensible burden. "Gnaeus, we're saved!"

Lamia scuffed closer, panting with the exertion. Black blood crusted the side of his head. "Come to save my life, Aquilo?" he croaked.

"Is that man dead?"

He turned to look at the naked soldier being lowered to the ground by his comrades. "He was about to be impaled through the anus on a stake, and probably set on fire. I think the prospect unsettled him."

I felt my face tighten. Dio gagged. "God-cursed savages," Aprilis blurted out.

Even those Marcomanni who had no Latin understood what the prefect was saying. They thumbed obscenely at their own buttocks, hooting at our horror and disgust.

Unless I could persuade Ingiomar otherwise, that would be my fate. Fear reached down my throat and clenched my heart in an icy fist. For a moment I could not speak, could hear nothing except blood hammering in my ears.

My father's voice cut through the panic: *Do you practice your voice exercises daily, Marcus? . . . There is nothing more ludicrous than when a man rises to speak on some important issue, a man whose opinion should be weighed, and from his lips comes the squeak of a mouse or the honk of a goose.*

With my life in danger, it seemed useless advice to recall.

Except that it was not. I took a long deep breath, exhaled slowly, and took another. "Enough!" I shouted.

In the brief lull I breathed in and out again. The law courts. The floor of the Senate. A legion assembled beneath the sky. *I am Titus Carinna's son; I will be heard.*

"Maelo vowed they would be freed if I came," I told Ingiomar. "Here I am. But we have a matter of justice to discuss."

"In the meantime"—Lamia limped toward the cart—"Dio, old fellow, make room for me on the seat. Loyal of you to come along to find me. You too, Aprilis."

"Wait," I said.

He stopped abruptly. I had used my father's voice.

"Clear a space." I pointed to the patch of ground in front of Ingiomar. "Anso, you are strong. You and the man next to you, set the box there."

"Is it too big for you?" Anso mocked. But he could not miss the chance of being first to see what lay under the hide cover. The two Germans threw off the old piece of tenting and dragged out the cedarwood chest beneath it.

"By Hercules!" As it was carried past him, Lamia made a grab for it and nearly fell. "That is my ... Aquilo! What are you ... ?"

"Get in the back of the cart," I said. "With the others."

"That is my chest! There are important things in it . . . private . . . valuable!"

"More valuable than your skin? Then stay and look after it, if you like."

He did not protest further. The two troopers lifted the third. The poor wretch screamed, flailing his arms; in his fear he had fouled himself.

All four finally crammed themselves into the bed of the cart. Lamia tried to squeeze away from the witless man, but the two other troopers stretched their limbs to fill the space. A small revenge.

"Sheathe your swords," I told Cleon and Aprilis, and waited until they had done so. Most of the Marcomanni were eyeing the chest that now sat on stubby feet before their *fraujaz*. Every German I have known loves a story, and they are as curious as cats when they think one is about to be told.

"Get moving, Cato." I tipped my chin toward our camp. "I will follow later."

Before the driver could flick his switch at the mules, Maelo rumbled, "You do not go until we say, Romans."

"That was not your promise," I shot back. "Your gods heard you swear, as ours did, that these men would be freed."

"Maelo." Ingiomar breathed hard. "Let them go. All but him." He nodded at me.

"Not going," Cleon said curtly. As I had hoped. No, expected.

I told Aprilis, "You must return to camp with them. For the Fifteenth." To help defend the hill, I meant. And, if he should survive, to report to the legion commander.

The quartermaster nodded gravely. "Yes, Tribune."

Cato was eager to go. That left only Dio. Dio who tried to meet my eyes, who, as much as he wished to, could not manage to say, "Not going," as boldly as Cleon had. Should I honor the manliness he yearned for by asking him to stay with me, or send him away and probably save his life?

I hesitated too long. Lamia blurted out, "You are not thinking of staying, Dio? By Hercules, I need you to write this up!"

"Yes," I said. "Go, all of you."

Cato had to wheel the mule team around in a half circle, which caused such a stir that I almost missed Maelo and his son Odo moving to Boss's side. The stallion put his ears back, but could not move his head because of Ingiomar's stranglehold on the reins. Instead, he tried to back away. "*Rôva*," Ingiomar spat. *Stay.*

I stopped myself from commanding the stallion to pitch him off. Not while Aprilis and the cartload of men he escorted were still in danger.

Their faces looked back at me as Cato goaded the two mules into a trot. The wheels spun up mud from the wet road, and spray bounced alongside from the hooves of Aprilis's cantering horse.

The journey would take half an hour, I reckoned. Plenty of time for Ingiomar to catch up with them, if he changed his mind.

Far beyond them, above the fort that rose from a wreath of mist, smoke streamed into the pearly sky. The pyre of the dead had been lit. *Farewell, Secundus,* I thought, but had no time to say a prayer for his soul.

"Marcus," Cleon said. When I turned, he gestured toward Ingiomar.

"Where is Rudra?" Odo was saying. "The beast does better with him." Warily he grasped the reins to hold Boss steady. As Ingiomar eased himself sideways out of the saddle, he leaned on Maelo's shoulder for support. When he lifted his other leg to clear the horse's back, it came free of the plaid cloak that had covered it.

The reek of wound-rot hit me like a blow. Stained bandages wrapped his foot and shin, swollen beyond normal size. So that was why he had not taken part in the fighting.

"Diana's tits," Cleon said under his breath. When an untreated wound —be it sword cut, thorn prick, or even a torn blister—swells and begins to shoot poison toward the heart, it is almost always mortal. If not for Aurima and Placidus, that fate could have been my own.

Ingiomar kept his eyes on me through glinting tears of torment. He sucked air between his teeth as Maelo set him down on his good foot. "Odo," Maelo barked, and the boy let go of the reins to help his father seat their chieftain on a log.

"I did not know you were injured," I said neutrally.

Ingiomar lifted his thigh with both hands, then let it down so that a smaller log set upright supported his knee. He caught his breath. "Fortuna is a whore." He forced a grin. Sweat darkened the fair strands at his hairline. "It was your horse who stepped on my foot."

"I can ask our surgeon to treat you." Yes, I wanted the man to die badly and become ashes in the wind. But if Aurima asked me, I could tell her I had offered help.

"Hah! To cut off my leg? No. When I go to the Warriors' Hall, I go on two feet."

His men called out their approval. I said nothing. I knew former soldiers who had survived amputation of a limb. Not many of them would have preferred to die.

"See how he likes it, Uncle," young Odo said brightly. "Cut off his legs one at a time."

No wonder I had never cared for the little cockroach. Amid a chorus of appreciative comments, I dismounted. Although the early morning was still cool, fear-sweat itched under my helmet. Beneath the leather cuirass to which the corselet's steel strips were fastened, my tunic was pasted to my skin.

I drew my sword with a flourish. The nearest warriors sprang back in surprise. Hands flew to sword hilts, but before anyone could lift a weapon I plunged my blade into the ground next to the cedar chest. If Father had taught me anything, it was that a dramatic gesture compelled attention.

I said, "It is time to talk about the matter of justice." I looked into Ingiomar's eyes. "First I will take an oath."

Their harsh muttering and guttural whispers enveloped me like the drone of flies around fresh meat. I expanded the power of my voice to silence them.

"Hear me, almighty Jupiter," I called to the sky, "and you who are known to the Marcomanni as Tiwaz, if you are not the same. Hear me too, grim Mars who grants victory in war, and Wodunaz of the battlefield, if you are not the same."

I touched my fingers to the pommel of my sword. "On this sacred iron I swear that what I say shall be true, as far as I know it. If I speak false, may this sword turn on me and wreak vengeance on me. This oath I call you to witness, great gods on high." Senators' sons learn to pray fluently in public, a proficiency often put to use later as a *paterfamilias*, a military officer, and perhaps a member of a pontifical brotherhood.

The Germans' eyes stilled with respect.

I took off my helmet. The new day, transparent and airy, opened its embrace to my senses. Now came the difficult part: I must argue for my life.

Another deep, slow breath. My audience—my jury and its judge—quieted themselves in anticipation.

"Six years ago," I began, "there was a man who commanded soldiers in Siscia, many days' travel to the south of here." I spoke slowly, with simple words. "This man, whose courage and honor were widely known, had a wife he loved greatly. A woman of spirit. Although she did not like Siscia, which is a garrison town of the Ninth Legion, she remained for the sake of her husband." I paused. "Are you hearing me?"

Heads nodded. Ingiomar and Maelo regarded me stonily, brows lowered.

"One night, this woman did a bold but foolish thing"—I softened my voice—"and it caused her to die."

Unbroken silence surrounded me now. I said, "When her husband learned of her death, it robbed him of his wits. He wept and howled and cursed the gods." I looked around somberly. "You do not know this woman's name."

"Ammisia," the Germans told me. "Ammisia, she was Ammisia."

"No." I shook my head. "Her name was Valentia. Her husband was commander of the Ninth Legion."

"What?" Maelo lunged up from his seat beside Ingiomar. "Do you insult my sister?"

"Bind him," Ingiomar growled.

Anso grabbed my left arm, sore from the hours of shield-bearing. A bolt of pain transfixed me, and despite myself I cried out.

"Hands off!" Cleon lofted his sword.

A large dark shape appeared behind Anso. It grew larger, and larger yet. By the time I realized it was Boss rearing on his hind legs, I could only gasp, "Look out."

Someone yanked Anso backward an instant before the stallion's hooves thudded down where he had been.

I caught the flying reins and pulled Boss's head toward me. "Quiet," I murmured, still short-breathed from the throbbing pain.

He shivered with agitation, eyes staring, nostrils wide, froth dripping from his jaw. When I touched his face, he jibbed and tried to bite. I spoke softly to him and let him breathe the scent of my hand. When he calmed, I cut through his bridle and withdrew the cruel bit from his mouth.

For a moment I imagined leaping astride him and racing toward our camp with Cleon, but it was too soon for the cart to have reached safety. The mission would end in disaster if we were all overtaken or cut down.

Boss can outrun the others, the vile little voice whispered to me. *You, at least, would not be overtaken.*

The Marcomanni were arguing among themselves, but Cleon's sword and the horse's teeth had deterred anyone else from laying hands on me. I clambered atop Lamia's chest.

The voices died, one by one. "Odo, take away the horse," Ingiomar snapped.

I would have objected, but this was not the time. As the boy shut the stallion into the horse pen, I said from my height, "I have no wish to offend Ammisia's spirit, may the gods give her peace. Will you hear what else I have to say?"

"Speak," a few men yelled. But Anso roared, "Cut him down, the butter-tongued liar," and Segomo shouted, "Who is the leader here?"

"Listen, then!" I made my voice crack like a whiplash. "When Valentia fell ill, not even the commander's own physician could make her well. Her husband sent for a native healer from the settlement, a woman of whose skill someone had heard.

"It was long after curfew on a black night. He did not know that the healer's husband was on a hunting trip with most of his men, and that none but an old warrior was left to accompany her to the fortress. If she had asked, he would have sent guards to protect her. But since it was to save a life, she came without waiting for guards."

Maelo nodded. "Ammisia did not refuse to anyone the Goddess's gift," he said hoarsely.

"The man who loved Valentia hoped she would be saved. But the thread of her life was nearly at an end, and all the healer's skill could not stay the hand of fate." Gods, I was falling into my father's orotund style.

"In his grief at his wife's death, perhaps he paid no heed that a body was found in the Savus River the next day. Perhaps no one told him. So I think he did not know the murdered woman was the healer who had tried to save his wife."

Ingiomar ground out, "I could not speak with him. Only with the camp commandant. He told me to prove that soldiers killed her, or he could do nothing. I spoke to the town officials, the *duumviri*. They said the same: find the killers."

"And you found them, the men who murdered your wife."

"Soldiers. Four soldiers she marked for me with her teeth and hands."

"And did the Army put them on trial?"

Maelo broke in, "Already you know! These murderers of an *auxilia* commander's wife, these . . . barbarous violators of a holy priestess, are told to march for three days on the parade ground. They are not being beaten, they are not being discharged in disgrace, they are not even"—his words exploded in a spray of spittle—"losing any pay!"

The warriors roared their anger. Knife points jabbed at me, the representative of Rome's injustice.

Cleon muttered something about a barbarian calling Romans barbarous. "Better calm this crowd, Marcus, or you'll be spiked like a hedgehog."

"It was shameful," I shouted. "Shame on the legion commander, then."

"It was a boy who judged them." Maelo's eyes gleamed in fury. "A tribune."

I pretended I had not been aware of it. The commander had taken his wife's ashes to Rome, leaving his broad-stripe tribune to conduct the court-martial. I knew, too, that at that time the Pannonian legions were on the verge of revolt. If the four guilty men had been as severely punished as they deserved, the Ninth might have mutinied.

But that was not something to admit to rebellious Germans. Instead I said, "A tribune? A young officer, then, with much to learn. So you made your own justice, Ingiomar, did you not? You and Maelo and Friduric killed the four soldiers yourselves. The blood debt was paid."

Ingiomar snapped, "Rome paid nothing!"

"Nothing?" I looked hard at him. "Was it nothing that your daughter Aurima stabbed Caligula Caesar to avenge her mother's murder, and nearly killed him?"

His lips disappeared between mustache and beard. Any muleteer would have recognized the obstinacy in his eyes.

"Maelo told you, did he not? And others. And still you sent her away in shame."

"In shame because of you, Roman!"

"And you, *svehra*, never told me I had a son."

The taunt of "father-in-law" stung. He tried to lunge upright, but his swollen foot would not hold him. He fell back on the log with a gasp, his face white.

"You rape her," Anso fired at me.

"Is that what your *fraujaz* told you? Segomo, did she ever say I raped her? Odo, did she not willingly free me of a curse? Maelo, did I not bring her safely home to the Mark?"

No one denied my words. "I name her my wife," I said, "and her child is my son."

"Romans," Anso sneered. "They are as false as birds that lead away from the nest."

"You killed Adalwulf and Fulco," Segomo charged.

"And Egino," someone added.

"And Wido!"

I retorted, "Are you saying now that a wronged man cannot make his own justice?"

That produced an uneasy silence. They muttered to each other, combed their beards with their fingers, shifted position. "Where is Aurima?" a querulous voice asked. "Let Aurima speak."

I would not let her be drawn into this. Knowing that she and the baby were safe was my only solace. "Look, here is what else Rome gives to repay the blood debt." I jumped down, managing not to stagger. Dio had not possessed the key to Lamia's chest, so I was denied the grand gesture of unlocking it and flinging it open. "Odo," I said, "you have gained much strength this summer. I am sure you can break this lock."

Though made of stout iron, the lock was no match for a youth who knew grown men were gauging his brawn. He forced open the hasp at the cost of his sword's edges.

The lid squeaked on its hinges. Fortuna grant that the prefect had hidden away items valuable enough to serve as reparations . . .

Spread across the top of the chest's interior was a swath of fine wool dyed an extremely expensive crimson. An auspicious start. I lifted a fold of the cloth, uncovering a hem embroidered in gold thread. "Cleon, help me unpack this."

Though it clearly did not please him to give up his weapons and his superior height, he sheathed his sword, dismounted, and hung his shield on the saddle horn. "Hold it up so all can see," I instructed. "Careful, man; it is worth a fortune."

To judge by the absence of pinholes, the heavy crimson cloak had never been worn. As brazen as a huckster of luxuries in the Saepta Julia, I praised the intricacy of the embroidery, the density of the weaving, and the uniform hue. "A handsome gift for a former auxiliary commander. Cleon, will you present it to the *fraujaz*?"

Cleon marched forward like a street-sweeper holding a dead dog on a shovel. He let the cloak fall into Ingiomar's lap.

The chest now revealed an ebony box holding a pair of silver drinking cups embossed with scenes from *The Iliad*: the duel between Hector and Ajax, and Achilles killing Hector. Highly suitable gifts for warriors. I described the Trojan War, until Ingiomar let out a rumble of impatience. The ebony box was laid with slightly more style beside him.

Then appeared, enveloped in folds of emerald silk, a score of gold arm-rings and torcs tied with a silk cord, which I gave Ingiomar for distribution to his followers. These were followed by a soft hide bag holding a leather belt studded with gold plaques depicting bears, bulls, crocodiles, camels, lions, and other wild beasts, which drew many greedy eyes away from the *armillae*. I caught Ingiomar's eye and nodded slightly at Maelo. He blinked slowly, which I took for approval to award it to his brother-in-law.

Next came a handsome dagger in a jeweled scabbard. This I also gave to Maelo, on the principle of not adding to Ingiomar's weaponry.

The Marcomanni elbowed each other like children, exclaiming as each new item came to light. Still Cleon had not yet plumbed half the depth of the chest. Who in Hades' name had Lamia intended these presents for?

Cleon pulled out a flat panel perhaps a foot and a half long. The red cloth swathing it was embroidered all over with golden phoenixes—a device on Augustus's imperial signet ring lately adopted by his great-grandson Caligula, who no doubt appreciated the symbolism of rising from the ashes.

A portrait. I might have known.

He looked out at me from a forearm's length away, his face the size it would be in life. His beautifully shaped lips curled slightly at the corners, given menace by the brows scowling over his staring eyes.

"This will remind you that your daughter, too, has extracted payment for the blood debt." I held out the painting to Ingiomar. He let it drop, and it landed upside down against the ebony box by his foot.

Maelo picked it up. He smiled faintly. "Caligula Caesar."

"What's this, a dead goat?" Cleon growled. He wrestled out of the chest a huge, gamy bundle of white fur tied with a colorful woolen band. "We've hit bottom, at least."

Had Dio not said the chest also held Lamia's money? I had been distracted at the time. Perhaps he had meant the other chest, the one I left behind.

When I untied the wool binding, the hairy bundle seemed to expand in Cleon's arms until it resembled a smothering beast. His question was muffled: "What is it?"

"A bear," I told him, from the feel of the fur. But no kind of bear that I had ever seen. It was as white as mares' milk, with long-clawed paws each larger than a man's head.

"An albino?"

"No." Suddenly I knew. "Hold it up." I raised my voice to quell the surrounding jabber. "Last, Rome offers a very rare treasure." Cleon stretched his arms high to display the pelt, but it was so vast that most of it still puddled at his feet. "From the icy lands of Hyperborea far to the north, we bring you the coat of a snow bear, killed with great danger by the bravest of hunters."

It took both of us to carry the thing to Ingiomar. He rubbed and sniffed it, then jerked his head for us to heap it beside him. The claws clicked together like dry bones.

I leaned over the chest. There was no bag of coins, but it was not quite empty. Something lay in the bottom: a long flat object wrapped in a piece of deer hide.

I tugged on the wrapping, and my old longknife tumbled into my hand. Lamia had had it, after all. "Gifts for everyone, it seems," I murmured, thrusting the knife into the back of my belt.

It was a sign that all would go well. Ingiomar would accept these presents to repay the blood debt owed for his wife's murder. Recognizing that I had not dishonored Aurima, he, Maelo, and the others would release me and abandon their attack on the hill fort. I would rejoin my wife and child, leaving Lamia to limp back to Carnuntum and explain how his decisions had led to so many Roman deaths. Rufus was with us again, and Cleon would bring Dio to me.

My shadow jumped across the grass as I stepped forward. The last of the mist had vanished, and bright sun was edging over the tall treetops. My gift-giving had taken us well past dawn, perhaps into the second hour.

Ingiomar appeared to be studying Maelo's animal-plated belt, but his eyes showed that his thoughts were deep within himself. Maelo slid the dagger admiringly in and out of its ornate scabbard. Tracery swirled over the steel blade. Spanish, perhaps?

No use putting it off. I had no more to offer.

I exchanged glances with Cleon. He unsheathed his sword and whacked it against the shield hanging from his horse's saddle. The animal whinnied and shied, and might have bolted had the crowd been less thick.

The crash caught everyone's attention. I lifted my hands, palms down, to show peaceful intent and bellowed, "Men of the Mark!"

Ingiomar raised his head slowly. He would have known the reckoning was coming. Maelo handed the golden belt to his son Odo, stood up, and drew his own sword.

I shut the chest, and Cleon gave me a boost atop it. Once more I could see over the helmets and tawny heads into the sprawling camp. Cooking fires expired in threads of smoke. A slave gave drink to a wounded man. A woman gathered a pot from beneath the deer carcass. Boss stretched his neck toward grass outside the enclosure. Birds pecked at the turf beside a brushy shelter.

"Men of the Mark," I repeated, looking from one to another of them. "On behalf of the Senate and the people of Rome, I, the cousin of Caligula Caesar, have explained that Roman justice failed to avenge Ammisia's death because of a mistake, because of a grieving commander and a young officer without experience. It was not meant to offend the powerful Marcomanni, who for many years have been Rome's allies, or to insult the family of Ammisia."

Ingiomar and Maelo gave no indication of being convinced. My lips were dry, but licking them would signal weakness. "Have I spoken fairly?" I challenged the assembled warriors. "What do you say?"

Silence. Then a few grumbles. A grudging nod. Someone said, "*Ja,*" the word dragging with reluctance. Another few nods. "*Ja,*" others muttered.

"But Romans it was who killed her," persisted Segomo.

"There are men from everywhere in the legion," I replied. "Most fear the gods and obey the law. Some bad men do not." I paused. "When I was a tribune, I kept watch on such men. If they broke the law, I punished them."

More mutters. I waited for Ingiomar's response, trying to appear unworried, but the *fraujaz* did not speak.

Finally Maelo announced, "We are saying that we understand the mistake. We understand that Rome did not mean to make so little of the murder of a priestess of Austro." He looked around. "Is that so, my brothers?"

The *jas* were more willing this time.

"Much blood has been spilled to settle this debt," I went on, encouraged. "Roman blood; Marcomanni blood. Even the blood of Caligula Caesar himself." I let my gaze linger on Ingiomar. "With these rare and costly gifts for Ammisia's husband and her brother, it is the wish of Caesar, the Senate, and the people of Rome that the blood debt be forgiven and that there be peace again between us."

I was sweating with earnestness. The *rhetors* never warn that making an impassioned speech will cause you to drip like a fountain. Father had always seemed as cool as a citron when he railed against an opponent in court.

I turned to Maelo. There was a better chance of earning his consent, which might then influence Ingiomar's. "Maelo, son of Hroswitha, do you agree before the gods that the blood debt is paid and you are willing to live at peace with Rome?"

Maelo glanced again at the impassive Ingiomar, then swelled his chest with air. "From the day when the gods made the first man and woman, we of the Mark lived between the two great rivers of the North." He pointed in that direction. "In the time of our grandfathers' grandfathers' grandfathers, Rome forced us to move so to make a milk cow of our homeland. Belgica you call it now, *ja?*"

I said nothing. One is not expected to respond to a harangue.

"To find land here we fought other tribes, the Boii, Daesitiatae, and others—"

"Coletiani," someone added.

"Now this is ours," Maelo continued evenly. "My brothers and sisters are true to the gods in these forests and rivers, these meadows and mountains." He raised his brows at me to make sure I understood.

I nodded silently.

"We see Rome move over the land like the dark shadow of a death spirit, seizing everything—trees, crops, beasts, men—to feed that city, that great stinking wound in the earth. But not here. You tell Caesar: not here. Let Rome not cast its shadow over us, and we are willing to live at peace." He paused again, glaring at me, then threw his head back. "What do you say, my brothers?"

This time there was not just a rumble of approval but a roar. Boss lifted his head from grazing, ears flattened.

Cleon knocked the pommel of his *spatha* against the chest. When I glanced down, he looked pointedly at my own weapon, still planted in the ground.

I shook my head and took a deep breath, trying to gaze firmly into every beard-furzed, shout-swollen face. As if it did not matter to me what these men thought of Rome.

The clamor went on. And on.

Like the dark shadow of a death spirit. Yes, it did matter.

Maelo flourished his sword high. "If Rome gives us peace"—he reversed the blade and drove it into the earth beside mine—"then I say the blood debt is paid."

Relief flooded through me, so overwhelming that my legs threatened to crumble.

Maelo smiled at the shouts of approval. He wanted to be the new leader, I saw. Ingiomar was going to die, and the warriors would need to choose a new *fraujaz*.

He stepped toward me to seal the agreement. I jumped off the chest, and we clasped hands over the two swords. His palm was hard with callus. The overstrained sinews of my hand and arm ached when I gripped it.

"It is done," he said in satisfaction.

"No, it is not done," Ingiomar said in a scraping voice.

Men turned back who had started to drift away without waiting for his opinion. A lesson in the impermanence of power, I thought. Did Ingiomar resent it enough to oppose the truce that Maelo had accepted?

A loyal dozen or so, including Segomo the graybeard, hotheaded Anso, and Maelo's son Odo, clustered around him. "The governor refused to hear!" Segomo cried.

My apprehension grew. In recounting the miscarriage of justice in Siscia, I had purposely omitted the Pannonian governor's role. It was best not brought to light.

I broke in, raising my voice: "Inguiomerus called Ironhand, husband of Ammisia!"

He looked up, eyes sharp in the tangle of his beard and bristling hair. I was reminded of a lion in the arena, wounded but far from finished off.

I coughed to ease my dry throat. "It is the desire of the Princeps, the Senate, and the people of Rome to end bloodshed between the Marcomanni and Rome." *Now flatter him.* "You have been a good and valued friend and ally, honored by Tiberius Caesar with Roman citizenship." *And might be a citizen still, had you not ambushed a Roman vexillation last year.* "Do you understand that in the handling of Ammisia's wrongful death, no insult to you or your people was meant?"

His face wavered. I blinked away the blur. Without waiting for his answer, I indicated the gifts with a sweep of my hand. "Insofar as the loss of your wife can be requited, Rome wishes to make amends." *"Requited"? Who here will know that word?*

He might have read my thoughts. "Insofar as her loss can be requited? Fine language, Carinna called Aquilo. Language to go with"—his own hand waved—"gold and silver and the fur of snow bears."

I tried to remember the formula I had used with Maelo. "Then do you agree before the gods that the blood debt is settled and that you will make peace with Rome?"

"No," he said.

43: SACRIFICE

A murmur like a gust of wind passed through the field of men. Segomo cackled gleefully, and Odo buffeted Anso's shoulder. Maelo stared at Ingiomar.

"Why do you refuse?" I said, once I knew my tongue would not trip on the words.

Ingiomar leaned over and murmured to Odo. The youth trotted off.

He rocked upright on his log. "You have learned well, turd. All men of my people like to talk." He glanced skyward. "Why not? It lacks some time to midday, when I am going to kill you."

Maelo began to protest, "My brother, we—"

Cleon sprang. Catching the blur of his movement in the corner of my eye, I snatched up my own sword. Ingiomar shouted a command. Before either of us could complete a stride, we were buried in a pile of attackers.

Something struck me in the head—maybe Cleon's flailing fist, gripping his sword hilt. A crushing weight bore me down. My face slammed into the ground, and my teeth mashed into grass and dirt.

Must fight. Last chance. Kill him. Kill Ironhand. Knife in belt.

But I could not breathe. The world revolved ponderously around and around. I was a moon in the sky. I was a corpse in the earth.

Farewell, beloved. Better than burning...

I slithered down into a dark whirlpool, rolled and tumbled. Then nothing.

Brightness. A razor-edged groan.

Everything hurt. From end to end I was a sack of pain.

A fly walked on my forearm, an inch from my slitted eyes. I stared blearily. My lashes brushed grass blades.

More flies minced across my back. My bare back.

No armor. No tunic. No boots.

I moved my eyes, searching for Cleon.

I saw Anso. He wore my segmented corselet and was defending with lazy strokes against an assault by Odo. Odo's sword cracked again and again on the steel armor. They were laughing. A group of men watched, squatting on their haunches. "You must cut off the turtle's head, Odo," one of them

Sherry Christie

called.

Beneath me the ground shook with pounding hooves. A voice called something about riders from the north. "Stop them," someone else said carelessly, and the hoofbeats faded into the distance.

Midday, when I am going to kill you. But the assembled warriors had agreed to peace with Rome, forgiveness and freedom for me. Ingiomar could not do this against their will.

I heard more voices. To see who spoke I had to twist my neck, sharpening a pulse that stabbed behind my eyes.

Ingiomar sat on a large deadfall with his bad leg propped up alongside. Flat mushrooms projected from the rough bark beneath him. A rotten tree. A rotting man.

"They did not know where he was before," Maelo was arguing in Germanic. "Now all those Romans"—he pointed into the distance—"know we have him! If you insist on this, you are going to bring the legions on us."

"The Romans are not going to tell anyone," Ingiomar said. "They are going to die." He tipped a horn to his lips, closing his eyes as he drank.

"You think it ends there, woodenhead?" Maelo snarled.

Ingiomar licked his lips. I saw him smile.

"But you do not care, I see. You expect Wodunaz to welcome you to his feast hall, the great killer of Romans, while here below we fight for our land and our lives?"

"Once you were not such an old woman, Maelo. I want to die with a prick between my legs, not a shriveled slit." He looked beyond Maelo. "Bring the turd. He is awake now."

Since there was no further need to lie low, I pushed myself up on my knees. "Cleon!" I spat mud and shredded grass from my mouth. "Cleon!"

Two warriors closed in on me as I peered around. Digging their fingers like crane-hooks into my armpits, they dragged me across the clearing.

This was not the same place. There were no lean-tos, no firepits, no horse pen. Trees towered on all sides, combing meager strands of sunlight through a thick canopy of foliage. Shadows lay deep in a jumble of half-toppled trunks and blowdowns.

I spotted Cleon, tied face-first to a dead tree with his head drooping to one side. He did not respond to my call. In my hasty glance, it was impossible to know if he was alive. I could not even tell whether the blood on his tunic was new or old.

The two men pushed me at Ingiomar. I fell onto my knees in the bed of a little stream that ran over roots and stones. When I tried to catch myself with my hands, my bad arm buckled and I went down like a peasant bowing to a pharaoh.

Ingiomar chuckled. "Turn him around, Adalfuns. He did not see why he is here."

One of the men spun me through a clumsy half circle. I righted myself, and then beheld the worst horror I could have imagined.

The oak was monstrous. From root to crown, it was higher than the distance from the Forum pavement to the gold chariot atop Jupiter's Capitoline temple. Not that I was measuring its size. I was staring aghast at its branches.

Bodies hung there, some gray and rotting amid the dark leaves, others decayed to white bones that curved in graceful arcs like wind chimes. Many were animals: stags and boars, a horse whose tail was snarled in its femur, an aurochs knowable by the great spread of its horns. So huge was the tree that the remains of these large beasts looked like the little amulets people hang on potted plants for the new year.

But some were smaller. Roe deer. A dog or wolf. And men whose beardless skulls bore wisps of short hair. Romans.

In front of the tree stood a six-foot post as big around as my wrist. It was freshly cut and stripped, the cambium still glistening. The end had been whittled to a point.

Terror crashed around inside my head like a caged bear. I shat myself.

At last an inner voice pierced the blind panic. It told me this was what he wanted; he would delight in telling Aurima how badly I had died. As if I, of the blood of Licinii and Antonii, had no more courage than that poor demented Praetorian, a common soldier.

My senses trickled back. I was slumped on my heels, head hanging. The icy streamlet gurgled around and over my bent legs. Men stood around, but I heard no taunting or laughter.

"Maelo wished me to see how brave you are," Ingiomar's voice said.

I stared down at the crooked roots, dead branches, and glistening pebbles over which the brook tumbled. Slowly I dipped a hand and scrubbed my face with clean water. Then, squatting deeper, I splashed the backs of my thighs.

Shitten-legs. How superior I had felt when yelling that insult.

Without looking up I croaked, "Give me back my father's torc."

I did not really expect it, but after a moment the golden ring landed in the water, spattering my forearm. I reached toward it. Took a breath. Then rose and hurled with all my might the stone I had seized from the streambed.

Unluckily my bare foot slid on a slippery root, diminishing the force of the blow. Still, it hit Ingiomar square in the chest.

He toppled backward off the tree trunk, his bandaged foot lifting into the air. I snatched up two more stones in the same sweep, awaiting a shot at his head.

Segomo dived at me. I swung around, aiming a missile at him, and he stopped.

"Leave him," Maelo shouted, running to Ingiomar's side.

Anso charged at me with his sword raised, the segmented armor rattling. A tall warrior halted him with an outstretched arm, shaking his head.

Maelo and Adalfuns scrambled over the fallen tree, crouched behind

Ingiomar, and with care for his bad foot hoisted him onto the trunk again. I had hurt more than just his dignity; the *fraujaz*'s chest heaved, and he clamped a hand beneath his plaited beard. But I cursed, for the damned beard had cushioned what I had meant to be a heart-shot.

I threw the two stones in quick succession. Someone yelled a warning. Ingiomar ducked behind Maelo's shoulder, and the stones sailed uselessly into the woods.

"Stop, or your guard dies now!" Maelo pointed at Cleon.

I stood in the brook, feet apart, fingers stretched to scoop up another stone. "Is your oath before the gods worth nothing?" My shout came out as a raw-throated bark.

"*Fraujaz*," said the tall man who had stopped Anso, "I think we do not please Tiwaz by sacrificing this Roman. Aurima is of our own people—the child also. If we take his life, I fear Tiwaz makes us weak in battle."

"Me, I say it is not wise to anger a priestess who can curse a man," volunteered a man with grease-spiked hair.

Another warrior nodded. "This Roman did not kill Ammisia, *fraujaz*."

Maelo said, "You have had your revenge, Ingiomar. This is enough."

"Who else wants to let him live?" Ingiomar snapped. He paused, wheezing. "Who else among you has the heart of a rabbit?"

"When the warriors of the Mark say yes," I rasped, "how can one man say it means no?"

Two or three others began to speak. Ingiomar outshouted them: "You think I have had my vengeance? You want peace with Rome? Here is something this turd did not tell you in his fine language." He dragged in a deep breath, wincing.

I crouched and grasped another stone but did not throw it, for Cleon had turned his head toward me. The tip of Anso's sword touched the back of his neck.

"Ammisia could not heal the Roman woman," Ingiomar declared. "Do you know why? Because the woman was with child and tried to kill it. Yes, my brothers, we know the Romans do such unholy things. This time, Nerthuz took her revenge: the Roman woman died. And her husband, not wishing it known why she died, had his men kill Ammisia because she knew the truth."

"No," I blurted out. "That is not so!"

"No? Then why, after your so-young coward of a tribune gives the killers a kiss on the hand, does the governor of Pannonia refuse to hear my *appellatio*?"

My legs quivered with strain, and I went down on one knee. Sabinus had feared that if he overturned the young officer's lenient ruling, the legion would rebel. But how could I say that? These men must not be allowed to think our army lacked discipline.

Ingiomar was not waiting for me to sort out my loyalties. "You, Theothelm, you say to me that Aquilo did not kill Ammisia. But it is because of him that my son Friduric can no longer walk on two feet. Cannot hunt a boar, or fight a man, or lie with a woman."

He has injuries, Aurima had told me. *One leg is badly hurt.*

"I pray that the child Helle carries is a son," the *fraujaz* went on. "But so shocked was she when she saw his wounds, the Goddess alone knows what she is going to birth."

His hearers drew in their breath. An intimation of disaster swept over me.

He raised his voice. "Do you see now, my brothers, why a few playthings cannot pay the blood debt? I demand this man's death! I demand that he feel the pain that my son feels! I demand that he be unmanned, as my son has been unmanned!"

Maelo protested, "It was the wolf who did it, Thancmar's wolf! You saw it, Ermenric."

"No, it was the Roman," insisted the sparse-bearded man I had nicknamed Mangy Face. "His magic turned him into a wolf."

"In Rome I saw the wolf they worship," Segomo put in. "By day it is of bronze, but at night it comes alive and hunts in the city. A terrible thing, ugly and glaring! With these eyes I saw it in the place they call the Old Forum."

The men closest to me shuffled back a step or two.

Roaring, I exploded out of my crouch and threw myself at Anso, who had become distracted from guarding Cleon. He backed away, tripped on a root, and went down with a clatter of his ill-fitting armor. "Cleon," I shouted. "Turn so I can cut you free."

I was reaching for the sword Anso had dropped when my arms were pinned to my sides in a muscular vise. Some kind of cloth fell over my head, and the world disappeared in reddish light.

"God-cursed savages," Cleon yelled. "Rot in Tartarus!"

I struggled wildly to free myself. "Boss, to me," I shouted at the top of my lungs. My warhorse might be a hundred paces away or thousands; impossible to know how far they had taken me from their camp. But I had no other hope.

Ingiomar's voice said, "Well done, Adalfuns. Not on the head! I want him awake to enjoy this."

Adalfuns lifted me bodily into the air. As I dangled in his grip, someone pulled a noose around my left leg. I kicked out frantically.

Cleon kept bellowing abuse. I was still roaring, half in rage and half in agony at the crushing of my sore arm. Adalfuns clamped me tighter. "Be still, Roman," he said grimly. "I am the brother of Adalwulf, whom you killed."

Too short of breath to keep yelling, I heard Ingiomar say, "We have no priestess, but I am sure the Terrible One still welcomes this sacrifice. Hold his legs apart."

My strength was ebbing, despite my great fear. "No," I gasped.

My heart thundered—*thud thud, thud thud.*

Hooves?

Whipping my head from side to side, I managed to dislodge what blinded me: my own tunic. "Boss," I cried out.

Leaves and branches rustled and snapped.

"Give him to me," Ingiomar snarled.

With my head turned toward the intruder's crashing approach, I was unprepared when Adalfuns shoved me. My feet tangled and I pitched forward, colliding with the trunk of the fallen tree. Ingiomar grabbed a fistful of my hair and hauled my head back. A knife in his other hand dug into my throat.

"We are just beginning, turd," he panted. His harsh hot breath ruffled my hair. "Be ready to scream loudly. I want your friends to hear."

I rolled my eyes to see him, but he was directly behind me. If I moved hand or foot, I knew the next breath I drew would be of my own blood.

"Kill me, and Haljo Dunkara sends you into darkness," I wheezed.

"So you know Haljo. Last night she came to warn you of your death, *ja?*" His fingers tensed on the blade, and he inhaled deeply. Not to cut my throat—but to hold me tighter while the post was pulled out of the ground and dragged closer.

Boss smashed into the clearing like a boulder launched from an *onager.* In the instant when Ingiomar's attention flickered, I seized his wrist and yanked it away from my neck. He hauled back against my grip, but the blade glanced off my torc. I bit into the meat of his thumb with my jaws' full force.

He bayed in pain and fury. The knife dropped. I lurched away so hastily that I fell over backward, shouting again, "Boss!"

Expecting to be attacked from all sides, I scrambled for the knife. But when I struggled to my knees, my sorrel stallion was looming protectively over me, as I had trained him to do if I was unhorsed in battle.

The Marcomanni had scattered, gaping at us. At him. Boss stamped his huge hooves, his eyes wide and bloodshot. Bloody froth spilled over his bared teeth.

Then riders burst through the gap between the trees. First among them, astride a silvery roan, was a woman with copper-colored hair. Close on her quarter rode Vannaz, king of the Marcomanni and Quadi, with his nephew Vangio. Behind them came Caturix, acting decurion of the Fifth Gallica. And Rufus with Dio up behind him, and Thancmar, and Aprilis, and more, more.

"What goes on in this sacred grove of Tiwaz?" the king bellowed.

"Father, what are you doing?" Aurima cried. From a bundle tied against her heart surged an infant squall of displeasure and protest.

Ingiomar looked up long enough to shoot them a murderous glare, then continued to bind his bloody thumb, gripping in his teeth one end of a strip torn from my tunic.

Aurima slid down from Spider. I pulled myself to my feet by Boss's saddle horn, wanting to embrace her. But suddenly I was on my knees again, then sitting on my heels, and it was she who had her arms around me with Beran howling between us.

I smiled, or meant to. "Help Cleon," I said.

44: TO THE HEROES

"As soon as the king returned to Bruna and they gave him my message, he and his guard rode all day and much of the night." Aurima wiped blood from my throat. "When we met them on the road this morning, I told him you expected another attack. Never have I seen Vannaz so angry."

She wetted the cloth again and dabbed a scrape on my chin. "At the little fort, the soldiers thought at first that we were more enemies. Then Dio said you and Cleon had not returned from my father's camp."

I lay with my head pillowed in her lap, adrift in the pleasure of being alive. Sunlight made rosy patterns on the insides of my eyelids.

Her fingers brushed tangled hair off my forehead. "So we go there, but I see only women." She paused, swallowing. "I shout, 'Where is he?' Then I hear a big *crash!* and a horse breaks out of the pen and runs into the forest."

My eyes popped open. Aurima grimaced self-consciously at the loudness of her interjection and glanced down at the baby sleeping in her shadow. More quietly she went on, "I thought it was Boss, but you told me Boss was dead. So I knew the Goddess must have made that horse look like Boss, and I said to Vannaz, 'Follow him!'"

At the sound of his name the sorrel stallion looked up. He was hungry, I saw, but was eating little. Spider grazed nearby, his black tail flapping away flies. He had smelled Boss all over, Boss had nipped him, and peace reigned for the moment.

"You will make something to heal Boss's mouth?" I asked. Caturix had promised to have a barley mash sent down from the camp.

"Once already I have said yes."

I heard a drag of weariness in her voice. After long hours of riding hard, she had slept less than I had. "Lie down," I said. "Let us rest together."

We had made our own little camp in an open space far from Tiwaz's sacred grove. Cleon was moodily occupied in getting drunk on wine that Aprilis had brought, while Dio and Rufus exchanged animated words and gestures. Voices rose and fell in an undulating mumble from Ingiomar's encampment down the road, where Vannaz was talking with the *fraujaz's* people.

Aurima lay against me in the dappled shade of a lean-to, her head on my shoulder. I ran my fingers through her coppery hair, raking out the last bits of clay. Once everything settled down, I thought, I would marry her according to her people's customs.

I was daydreaming about it when Aurima said, "Well," with a drawly intonation just like mine. "I cannot lie here all day. Let me get up."

"My Amazon," I said, wagging my head in drowsy wonder. "My Antiope."

"Husband, you . . ." She paused, her gray-green eyes steady on my face. "When I saw you there, saw how they repaid your courage . . ."

I gazed at her, marveling. The sun had brought out her freckles in a pattern I knew as well as the stars.

"I wanted to kill them all," she said.

Her ferocity was as eloquent as a hundred kisses. I smiled crookedly. I was marrying Medea.

"It is true," Aurima said. "Watch the baby. I must look for my father."

Could she slow the wound rot with magic, or whatever she had used on me? Would she wish to? "Do not kill him."

She frowned.

I said, "Leave it to Nemesis."

As soon as she had gone, Beran opened his eyes. I feared he was about to wail for something I could not provide, but instead he crooned like a pigeon and waved his fists.

"You cannot see down there, can you?" I lifted him onto my chest so we were face-to-face. He was a more normal pink now, as Aurima had predicted, with blue eyes, and the tawny silk on his head was all the hair that remained. When I told him he was better-looking than before, he watched my mouth move and drooled on my tunic.

An urge to keep him safe rose within me, more immense and painful than I could have imagined. Hardly able to breathe, I kissed his forehead.

My child.

My son.

Beran's tiny hand gripped one end of my torc. With remarkable strength he tugged on it and began to suck on a terminal.

My friend Silius liked to say, *Fatherhood is a shudder and a sigh; all the rest is money.* He was wrong. I would never surrender my child to the customs of patrician Rome, where a family's next generation is raised by slaves.

The baby's eyes closed. I held him on my chest with a hand clasping his small back, and before long I too was asleep.

When his howling woke me, Aurima was standing a dozen feet away with Vannaz. They stopped talking, and she scooped up the infant, who quieted at once and sought her breast.

I pushed myself to my feet. Vannaz scratched his chin through the ginger-colored beard. "You are well?" he asked at last, his pale prominent eyes scanning up and down.

"I will be all right," I said.

He grunted. "What do you wish to happen?"

"For myself?"

He nodded.

Instead of blurting out my thoughts, I said, "I must talk about it with Aurima." I was learning.

He toed aside a drift of dry leaves. "And those who wronged you?"

I looked off into the trees, contemplating the names I had written in the earthen floor of the cave: *INGIOMAR, GLABRIO, MAELO, FRIDURIC, CHLOTHAR, LAMIA.*

"I must deal with Lamia myself," I said at last. "The other scores are settled."

Vannaz looked relieved. "You do not seek revenge on any of our people?"

"If they do not harm me, I will not harm them."

In the silence I heard a trumpet call from the distant hill fort. Aprilis must have recovered the instrument. It blared again and again like a demented cock. Not an official signal, just high spirits.

Cradling the nursing baby, Aurima moved sideways as if to block the sound. "There is a problem," she said.

"What is it?" I wanted to joke but did not, so somber did she and Vannaz look.

"For the injury to Friduric and the killing of Egino and the others, my father and some of his men still demand your death."

Our companions had drawn closer to listen. "Diana's tiss!" Cleon slurred, brandishing a half-full aleskin. "Was he s'posed to let hisself be sacrificed?"

Dio declared, "A man is not a murderer if he fights to save his own life."

"Here it is not so simple," Vannaz said. "Who is to feed the wives and children of these men? Helewidis is to birth a child soon, may the Goddess protect her. How can Friduric hunt for them?" His arched eyebrow quirked higher.

"They will not eat better if my master is put to death," Dio shot back.

"But your master has made their life hard. So even when a killing has a good reason, we say the family must be paid. Often it is cattle or a promise to hunt for the family for some years. This is more fair, I think, than your law."

"I have no cattle," I said.

Vannaz's eyes went to Aurima. Her stony face did not change.

He cleared his throat. "When the man who has killed cannot pay the debt, another can pay it for him. But then the man who pays has ... I do not know how to say it, a hold?"—he clenched his fist—"on the man who cannot pay."

I understood. "Inguiomerus would pay my debts. And if I could not repay him, he would demand—what? My child? My freedom? My life?"

"That's fucked," Cleon erupted. "Where's the bassard? I'll take care of 'im."

Aurima said in Germanic, "Vannaz, I think we must call a Council of Women."

He was not happy about it. "Your father must agree, but ... yes, you are right."

"Six days from now. When the Moon God turns his face to us."

"Ach, so. In Bruna." He took a step. Then, as if he had almost forgotten it was my fate at issue, he asked in Latin, "Do you accept what the Council of Women says?"

I hesitated. How could I—a man, a Roman patrician, and an accused murderer—trust my future to a gaggle of illiterate Germanic females?

Aurima might have guessed that I was about to refuse. She took me aside. "Why must I be judged again?" I protested. "When Maelo asked the warriors, they said yes."

"But some say no, my heart. If all do not agree, you are in danger. Anyone can capture you and take you to my father."

If he still lives.

She guessed what I was thinking. "Only Tiwaz knows how long he is going to stay in this world. But those like Adalfuns, whose brother you killed: they do not forget."

"Then let us leave the Mark now." If it came to a choice, I would rather gamble on Roman law.

"I have promised your comrades free passage to the Great River," Vannaz put in helpfully. "They go tomorrow."

Aurima said nothing, but a shadow of melancholy crossed her face. If I became a fugitive from her people, she might never again see her brothers, her grandmother, her friend Helle. Yet she turned, clutching the baby, and said bravely to Vannaz, "There is no need of a council, then. We go to the Romelands."

I, who had lost so much of my family, could not deny her what was left of hers. I said, "I have thought again. I will wait for the judgment of the Council of Women. If Ingiomar is of the same mind."

"Good," Vannaz said. He disappeared into the trees with some subordinates.

I asked Aurima, "Will you tell my story to this council?"

"Yes." She laid Beran against her shoulder and rubbed his back. "Do not worry. My *amma* will be there, of course, and the king's mother, Gisila, who is the leader."

My heart sank. The sly old woman who had drugged me? Hardly news for hope.

"There are men in my father's camp who are hurt worse than you and

Cleon," Aurima said. "Rest here, and I will come to you as soon as I can." She tucked the baby into his sling, picked up her healer's bundle, and followed Vannaz.

It would have been paradise to relax as she had commanded. But if Lamia's vexillation was to leave in the morning, I must somehow force him to withdraw the murder charge against me.

"Counshil o' Women?" Cleon leered. He added an obscene boast that Aurima fortunately could not hear. Rufus grabbed the aleskin from him and emptied the rest of its contents over his head.

I straightened myself, trying not to totter. "I am going to say farewell to our comrades in arms. Who comes with me?"

Rufus mouthed his eagerness as soon as I finished speaking.

I shook my head. He looked so much like the young warriors the troopers had been fighting that he might come to grief in Lamia's camp. "I have another task for you. Make a count of how many horses and mules with Army brands are held here. I am sure Lamia will need some of them back."

Cleon broke in, "I'm your bo'yguar' . . . bo'yguard. Wha' 'bout me?"

I shook my head gravely. "Rest your bones, old fellow."

"Old? Who's old?" He reeled against Dio.

"Why, man, wait till you see yourself," I said. "This morning's fright has turned your hair as white as snow."

"What?" he bleated, clutching his ale-drenched head. "Truly?"

He staggered around, tugging vainly on curls too short to see, until our laughter gave away the joke. With a roar of indignation, he took a punch at me that missed. He overbalanced, flopped down suddenly, and began to snore.

"Well, Dio," I said, "I guess it is just the two of us."

Dio coughed. "Er, Marcus . . ."

I paused a moment, looking down on Cleon. My loyal guard slept noisily with his mouth open, the small bulge of a second chin showing beneath his unshaven jaw.

Warmth filled me, milder but not unlike the emotion I had felt for Beran. Odd: with all this hardship, I, who had thought to become more ruthless and unsentimental, had instead grown more tender of heart.

I turned back to Dio. What was on his clerkly mind? Rosters and reports, numbers and letters? "What is it?"

"Before you speak to the prefect, there is something you should know," he said. Diffidently, he told me what it was.

He looked astonished when I hugged him. "Well done! Oh, well done!"

Dio blushed. "I thought it might be useful," he said modestly, and almost grinned.

When I paused to tell Vannaz where we were going, he stepped away from Maelo and said quietly, "Ingiomar agrees to the council if it meets at Hoheneih. Helewidis must take part, but she is too close to her birthing time to travel."

I had no liking for the stronghold where the *fraujaz* had held me prisoner. But when I sought Aurima's opinion of the change in venue, she was busy bandaging her father's leg on the far side of the encampment. So I told Vannaz he had my consent.

Traffic on the Amber Road had resumed. As I rode with Dio toward the fort on the hill, we followed a train of donkeys carrying baskets of Samian ware packed in straw. Hoping we might be customers, the trader showed us a sample. I thought that Aurima might like to have such a bowl, red with a glazed interior, its rim prettily incised with olive leaves, someday when we need not fear strangers who appeared at our door.

Aprilis was standing beside one of the sentries when we reached the top of the hill. They snapped off parade-ground salutes, and Aprilis said, "An honor to welcome you back, Tribune." His greeting sounded wholehearted, even though fatigue deepened the seams around his eyes.

An honor? To greet a man whose presence had incited a deadly barbarian attack? "As you were," I said, knowing I did not resemble the impressively uniformed officer who had left the fort before daybreak. My boots, belt, knife, and torc had been returned to me, but my tunic was tattered and stained, and my armor had disappeared.

Surprisingly, the stockade was still in place and manned. I said, "The threat is contained, Aprilis. Why have the barricades not been dismantled and the men stood down?" The carts would need to be repaired if Lamia intended to march in the morning.

"Permission to take that as an order, sir?"

"Let it be so."

The quartermaster faced away as if to bellow the command. Instead he said in a sideways mutter too low for the sentries to hear, "When I asked the prefect for orders, he told me to be gone. Hasn't stirred from his tent since we got back."

This too was strange, considering the remarkable coolness with which Lamia had behaved during his rescue. Sometimes a shock could have delayed effects, of course. "Has Placidus examined him?"

"Not sure, sir. Maybe you'll be speaking with the surgeon?" He was telling me what he could not say outright: I needed to find out why the prefect was behaving so strangely.

I jerked my chin for Dio to follow me to the medical tent. Aprilis added, "One other thing, Tribune: about the orders you left to light the pyre at sunrise."

"Yes. I saw the smoke." It was still rising, a gray plume slanting northeast.

"No one's given the funeral oration."

"The prefect . . . ?" It was an act of shocking disrespect to cremate the dead like a heap of trash, their sacrifice uncommended to their comrades, to Rome, or to the gods. I had been sure Lamia would make the funeral speech when he returned to camp.

The quartermaster shook his head.

I considered. There was no denying that I wanted to shake Lamia into recognition of his duty. Yet he had not fought beside these men, as I had. He had not seen the vigor and tenacity with which a handful of dismounted cavalrymen had grappled with scores of howling enemies. He had not witnessed Secundus's bravery or Licnos's steadiness. With no experience of combat, he did not know the importance of honoring the living as well as the dead.

"Have the men fall in beside the pyre in half an hour," I said. "The wounded too, all those who can walk or be carried."

Aprilis saluted again and shouted the order to stand down as I continued on with Dio. Men groaned with weariness and stumbled back to their units, hardly noticing the two of us. Lamia must have been told that Ingiomar's hostilities were at an end. Why had he kept exhausted troops at their battle posts?

We reached the small promontory where the funeral pyre still smoldered. No mitigating spices or incense fragranced the air; it reeked of burned meat and wet smoke. A soldier sat on a chest, head in hands, while another poked despondently at embers.

At Aprilis's bellowed command to form up by the pyre, the sitting man heaved himself to his feet. "Hear that?"

"About fucking time," the other said sourly. Turning, he saw us. "You're back, sir!" The surprise on his face slackened into relief. "Suellius, the Tribune's back!"

Cleon should have been here. I ought to have made him come with us. He too should be hearing men say to him *You're back!* and *An honor to welcome you.*

"I will be giving the funeral oration," I said. The chest that had served as a seat was familiar from Lamia's tent. "Where did that chest come from?"

Suellius glanced at Dio, then quickly averted his eyes. "It showed up last night, sir. Empty. We reckoned to use it for the casualties' belongings. Is that all right, sir?"

"Fine," I said, not looking at Dio. "Once their effects are delivered in Carnuntum, sell it and use the money for a sacrifice to Jupiter Invictus."

"Sir!" They saluted.

"I will find you in a few minutes," Dio murmured.

"I'll be with the surgeon," I called after him.

Placidus was asleep on a cot at the back of his tent, oblivious to the flies circling overhead. To reach him I would have had to step over his chief assistant, Epicadus, who startled awake at the sound of wounded men's greetings.

"Tribune, gods bless you."

"Tribune, thank you, sir."

"Never forget what you did, sir."

It seemed to me that I had merely made myself obnoxious to Ingiomar until being rescued by my wife and an annoyed king. "You men, you did it," I said. "From now on, recruits will look on you veterans with awe."

I clasped grimy hands, asking small questions—where they came from, how many years they had served. "What's the first thing you'll do when we reach Carnuntum, Tribune?" someone inquired, expecting an answer they could all envy.

No one had told them my situation was unresolved, so I pretended to give the question weighty thought. "First? I'll take my wife to bed. Second, I'll go to the baths. Or, depending on what she says, the other way round." There was a rustling of chuckles.

"What's this racket?" grumbled Placidus, now on his feet with a blood-stained tunic thrown over his bulk. "You disturbing my patients, Aquilo?"

"They need stirring up." I let my gaze flit around. "Dozy lot." A small ripple of mordant amusement. "Do you have a few minutes?"

"Just hoping for a nap before the funeral oration. Are you speaking?" He followed me outside, yawning. "You look suited to it. Like you've been to Hades and back."

Why had I not asked Dio to find me decent clothes? I put aside the misgiving. "How are the hostages? I have not seen any of them."

"I returned two of them to duty." Placidus fingered a flake of dry blood off his lip. "The third . . ."

"The one who cracked?"

"Unfortunately, he found a knife before I could examine him."

I stared at the ground, thinking about the man's fear, about the memory of it breaking through my own panic. Had his departing soul spoken to mine?

"I hear you were an eyeblink away from becoming pork on a skewer yourself."

"I would not care to go through it again," I said, in the way men admit abject terror to each other.

From a distance came banging and grinding as the barricade was pulled apart. I voiced the question I had come to ask: "How is Lamia?"

"Do you plan to see him? Well, you will find out." He ran his fingers through his brush of hair. "I reckon he can make it to Carnuntum. And being inside the frontier again may be all he needs. How's the arm?"

"My arm is fine. Placidus, how would you treat a man whose foot was stepped on by a horse, and whose lower leg has bloated greatly?"

"How does it smell?"

"It stinks."

"Then I would take off the leg, probably above the knee. And cauterize it. He might survive. Or not."

A *calo* trudged past with a cavalry horse, both of them plastered to the eyes in mud. I said, "And if he will not allow you to take his leg?"

He yawned. "Then the poison will keep spreading, and that will be the end of him. You are talking about the leader of those Marcomanni, are you not? Inguiomerus?"

"How long will he live?"

"Hard to tell. A couple of days or, if he has no fever yet, as long as a week."

The Council of Women was to meet in six days. If Ingiomar died before then, perhaps they would cancel it.

Placidus yawned again and turned back toward the tent. "Hungry? Epicadus can find something for us."

"No time," I said, though my belly growled in protest.

"A few moments will make no difference." He ducked under a drawn-back flap to his own quarters at the back of the tent, and I followed. "So where does this leave you? Still wanted for killing that streak of slime, Glabrio? Or"—he picked up a ewer from a folding table and peered into it—"will Lamia forget the charge since you saved his rosy pink bottom?"

"I am here to find out."

"Well, until then . . ." He splashed something into a cup, handed it to me, and held up another. "Let us honor Mithras, Lord of Light, who has delivered us from evil."

I was too grateful to refuse. "To Mithras, Lord of Light." We drained the wine.

A smile cut furrows in Placidus's long face. "Do you still think he is not watching over you?"

I made a noncommittal grimace. "Eh!" he said with a shrug. "We will talk about it in Carnuntum."

It was the moment to tell my surgeon friend about the judgment I would soon face from the Council of Women, but I held my tongue. He would laugh, reminding me I was a cousin of the governor and of Caligula himself. If I told him I had given my word, he might say that a broken promise to barbarians meant little to Mithras, God of Truth.

The wedge of sunlight falling past the tent flap shrank as Dio appeared outside. I helped myself to a disk of hardbread from Placidus's table. "I must prepare my speech. Thank you, Lucius Verginius."

"I see Dio has brought you another tunic. You are hard on your clothes, Marcus Licinius. Be well." He pushed into the main part of the tent, where slaves were helping some of the wounded to stand and hoisting others onto stretchers. As I put on the new tunic, I heard him bellow, "Easy there! You are lifting a man, not rattling dice in a cup."

I tipped my face to the smoky sky above the pyre. "Jupiter, Mars, and Apollo, hear me! Hear me, you other gods, in whatever realm you rule, who are friendly to the Roman people! We who stand here bear witness to the valor of our comrades who died fulfilling their sacred duty to Rome and to you. May you look with favor upon them and upon us."

Aprilis handed me a tablet, and I read aloud the roster of the dead. First by seniority was Quintus Valerius Secundus, narrow-stripe tribune of the Fifteenth Legion. His name caught in my throat, forcing me to swallow before I could continue. Among the nine other names I read out was that of the rescued captive tormented by fear and shame into killing himself. No one here would have denied him the right to be honored.

I closed the tablet, gave it back to the quartermaster, and concluded: "We pray you will grant peace to their spirits."

No sound came from the remainder of the detachment formed up behind me. I turned to face them.

The standards of the Fifth Gallica and Tenth Praetorian cohorts stood in the front lines, their flags limp in the late-afternoon stillness. In the ranks beyond, black plumes and red horsetail crests lifted resolutely from the bowls of troopers' helmets. Only a closer look would reveal the holes and rips in chain-mail shirts, the dents and sprung segments in steel cuirasses. And only a turn of the head would disclose Placidus and Epicadus at one side, next to the wounded who lay on stretchers or braced themselves upright.

Where was Lamia? The prefect should have been here.

I spoke with force to carry across the hilltop. "The gods have spared those of us who gather before this pyre. We are grateful to be here, for life is dear to us. So we grieve all the more deeply for our comrades, who gave up their own lives to save ours. We will miss them. We will weep for them. And we will never forget the sacrifice they made.

"That sacrifice raises these brave men to a rank higher than any they ever held on earth. They are heroes of Rome. Join me in saluting our fallen comrades. To the heroes!"

I turned back and saluted the pyre. Voices thundered behind me, "To the heroes!"

As the crowd melted away, I fought an urge to sink to my knees and move no more. But if I did not confront Lamia now, what mischief would he wreak in Carnuntum? "One last task, Dio," I said. "We must shear the Silver Sheep."

45: BALANCING THE SCALES

The command tent looked as if it had been put up by blind men. The kingpost, sawn in half to serve more usefully in the barricades, had been awkwardly splinted so that the peak of the tent sagged to one side. The left wall was gone, cut up for slings, stretchers, and shield patches. The entrance canopy had been rigged with poles of unequal length, so that it too canted sideways.

I was dismayed to recognize one of the ransomed Praetorians on duty outside Lamia's headquarters. A man who had passed through hell ought to be granted immunity from ordinary duties for at least a day or two.

The man recognized me. "Sir, are you in command now?" he hissed.

It was not the greeting I expected. "I cannot say," I told him.

"Who's there?" Lamia demanded from inside the tent. "Who speaks?"

"Tribune Aquilo to see you, Prefect."

No answer. I said, "Prefect?"

A different voice said, "The prefect asks that you come back later."

Without bothering to argue, I entered through the missing side of the tent. Lamia's orderly was first to spot Dio and me. A look came over his face that I was beginning to recognize as mixed relief and entreaty.

The prefect sprang up from a box that had held javelins. His brow was bandaged, and his silver hair tufted up like a potful of dead grass. "What has become of my chest?"

"I traded it for your release. Don't you remember?"

"What was in it?"

"Silver cups, a gold belt, a bearskin—"

"Not that chest! The other one."

"What other chest?" I asked obtusely.

"Dio, you remember it! The chest with my papers. My private papers."

"Is it not here?" Dio looked around.

"It's missing! And look, my bed is gone, my table, my wine set, my chairs . . ." Eyes wild, he thrust his open palms here and there at the empty spaces.

"There was a good deal of turmoil after you were captured," I said apologetically. "Our men looked everywhere for materials to strengthen the barricades."

"And, apparently, to steal whatever they could find! They did not leave me so much as a cot to sleep on, or a stool to sit down on. And those infernal b-barbarians took my best armor, my weapons, and my horse!" He strode over and flung up the lid of the box. "Look, there is nothing left to pack but my parade boots and my astrology chart!"

I glanced at the orderly. "No ideas, Sabellus?"

"Sorry, Tribune. I was running around to build up the defenses. Everybody was."

"You did not give both chests to the Germans, did you?" Lamia pressed.

"Only the one you saw," I said.

He leveled a shaky finger at Dio. "I blame you, Dio. It was your responsibility to look after my confidential files. You were derelict in your duty!"

This had gone far enough. I said, "Lamia, I need a private word with you. Dio, Sabellus, leave us and tell the guard to admit no one."

"Yes, Tribune," Sabellus said, as if I, not the prefect, were his superior. Dio picked up his satchel and followed him out.

My aches thrummed with every heartbeat. I shut the top of the weapons box and sat, reckoning I needed repose more than Lamia did.

He rubbed the back of his neck, ill at ease now that we were alone. "I did not mean you were wrong to take my chest of gift goods, Aquilo. Obviously it bought our freedom—mine and my men's."

"Saving your life nearly cost me mine."

"So Aprilis told me." He turned away, picking at the binding on the broken tent post. "I suppose you want me to withdraw the charges against you."

"Yes."

He swung back to me. "I can arrange it. Once we reach Carnuntum."

Did he think I trusted him enough to finish the trip with him? Once across the Danube, he could have me bound and transported to Rome. After his past treachery, I would not believe the man if he swore the sea was wet.

I said, "Well, listen, Decimus Aelius. I have a better offer for you."

"Oh?" He raised his brows, then winced and put a hand to his bandage.

"Your missing chest," I said. "I know where it is."

"You do?" His eyes lit with eagerness. "Where is it?"

"Near the pyre. I saw it as I was arriving."

"Damn the idiots! If they tampered with the lock . . ." He shouted, "Sabellus!"

I lifted a hand to forestall him. "It now holds the casualties' personal effects."

"What?"

His orderly appeared. "Yes, Prefect?"

"Never mind. I will call again if I need you." The man was barely out of earshot when Lamia hissed, "What about the papers that were in it? Where are they?"

"They are being kept for me."

"Kept for you? What do you mean?"

"I have put them in a safe place."

Color drained from his face. "Where?"

I was glad to see how badly the news alarmed him. "Out of your reach. Perhaps with my wife's kinfolk. Perhaps with the king of the Marcomanni and Quadi."

He steadied himself on the tent post. I went on, "I will not use them, provided you and the Special Cohort never again harass or harm me or anyone in my *familia*."

"Prove what you say."

"There is no need to prove it. You do not know where to find them, and I do."

"You're bluffing," Lamia sneered. "You were not even here." He crossed his arms, then uncrossed them. "In all the panic, someone must have used them to light the pyre."

"Very well, I will send one of the documents to provincial headquarters in Poetovio. I'm sure you will hear from the governor after he reads it."

His face purpled. "You arrogant prick, do you think you can intimidate me? I am a senior officer of the Praetorian Guard's Special Cohort." Saliva foamed in the corner of his mouth. "I don't care if you're related to Jupiter himself, you'll pay for what you've done. I'll see you deported so fucking far from Rome, your slaves will be hairy apes!"

"Try it," I said flatly, "and I will expose you."

Lamia's fists clenched. "Turn yourself over to Aprilis. You're still under arrest."

An obscenity burned on my tongue. After abandoning me to a horrible death, did he think my vow of docility still held? "Don't be a fool," I snapped, and stalked out.

Dio joined me outside, slinging his satchel strap over his shoulder. The camp was shutting down. Carts were being reassembled and weapons counted; half the latrine trench was already filled in. Slaves led in animals retrieved from the marshes. Anyone without a task slept where they could.

We walked on. I seethed silently, my fury at Lamia's stubbornness chilled by his threat of deportation. Dio murmured, "Did you notice anything?"

"What? Oh." I had forgotten to look. "I hope they are as watertight as you think."

"I used plenty of wax."

"Still, they will stink."

"Truth does not always smell sweet," he countered, which sounded like a quotation from Lamia and possibly was.

A trooper stopped me to ask about Cleon. Regaining my dignity, I told him that the best bodyguard a man could have was now asleep with a bellyful of ale.

Caturix, the Gallica's new decurion, had heard that I killed Ingiomar. "No," I said. "He is a sick man, unbalanced by his wife's murder. Not all Germans are like him."

Dio nudged me. "We need to leave the camp."

"Are we in a hurry?" Anger at Lamia had given me a second wind.

"Yes," he said quietly. "A courier rode in while you were with the surgeon. I put his new dispatches in my satchel."

Caligula had returned to Rome from his grief-stricken flight. Great joy in the city. All Army units were to offer sacrifices of thanksgiving.

Once more the wreath of supremacy had been snatched from Lepidus's grasp. I wondered for a few moments if my patron would take it tamely. But there were more urgent matters to deal with, closer to home.

46: SUNSET SKY

The underbrush rustled. A wild pig emerged in the dusk, heavy-shouldered, black as soot. A sow, without the upthrust tusks of a boar.

The sow's long snout wrinkled as she snuffled noisily, ears pricked. I quieted my breathing. Wild pigs have poor sight, but they can smell and hear better than men can.

She lunged down the bank on her delicate legs, waded into the water, and swam toward the other side. A second sow followed. A third. A fourth. Behind the seventh came a parade of squeakers, still wearing their piglet stripes. One after another they swam the stream, clambered up the other bank, and disappeared into the forest.

The ripples faded, streaks of silver and coral smoothing to reflect a sunset sky.

Aurima hugged her knees against her chest. We had sat silent and motionless beside the watercourse long enough to have become part of the forest. Beran slept between the two of us, swaddled in Aurima's cloak.

In bringing her to this private spot, I had hoped to find her disposed to affection. But she was distant and withdrawn, and would not even touch me.

I ventured, "Are you still angry about the boys fighting?" After learning that Rufus had not given up his attachment to us, Odo had attacked him. The brawl had been stopped before much damage was done—a clump of Odo's hair yanked out and a knee-blow to the balls, while Rufus had lost an earlobe and been slashed down the ribs—but Aurima thought I should not have left the Thracian youth in the Marcomanni camp.

She shook her head. It was more serious than Odo's feelings of betrayal.

A few moments later I asked, "How is your father?"

Her breath caught. She was weeping.

I had no idea what to say. I could not regret that death hovered over her blighted madman of a sire. Finally I picked up the baby and settled him in her lap, then hitched over beside her and drew her against me. "I love you," I said.

Aurima gulped. Her tears fell faster; the gasps became sobs.

"Do not grieve so, my heart." I wanted to stop this brave woman from crying, and it alarmed me that I did not know how. "Hush, you are waking Beran."

She rocked the whimpering infant in her arms, looking away from me. "You think ... You think ..." Her tears fell on his cheek, frightening him. He bawled.

With my good hand I turned her wet face toward me. "What do I think?"

"I almost lost you ... again ... and s-so many men are dead ... injured ... because of me."

"No, *carissima*. Because of your father." I thumbed hair off her hot brow. And without knowing where the thought had come from, I said, "He must have loved your mother very much."

She tried to smile. Her silver eyes glittered at me.

The baby howled. Distractedly she pushed down the shoulder of her tunic and put him to her breast. He quieted into murmurs of contentment.

If she were murdered, would I not be as enraged as Ingiomar? Most likely, I would not wait for a foreign justice system to exact punishment. But if I did, and the killers were set free ...

"Aurima, what will the council do?"

The new subject stilled her weeping, as I had hoped. She wiped her face with her sleeve. "When there is ... no agreed choice, they"—a deep breath—"sometimes let Tiwaz decide. The two men fight each other until one surrenders or dies."

"Your father cannot fight me." My stomach shrank at the possibility that he could name someone else to take his place. I did not want to face single combat with a stranger. And I would not ask Cleon to fight for me.

"No ... I think they will not say that." She sniffled. "But they may say he owes you a payment. Or you owe him one."

"I have already given him gifts: an embroidered cloak, silver drinking cups, many gold arm-rings. A white bearskin. Will those not count for me?"

"Yes. I have told my *amma*."

That reminded me of Gisila, the senior priestess. "Vannaz said his mother leads the council. Will she be against me, if she thinks I blame her for parting the two of us?"

"Do not worry," she said. "There are many wise women on the council. It is not like the Senate of Rome, where men vote according to the side they are on."

I leaned my face against the top of her head. The smell of her, pine and grassy herbs and baby milk, intoxicated me.

Her breath eddied out, warm on my throat. "Afterward, where will we go?"

"I know you would be happy to stay in the Mark. But I promised ..."

"You promised to bring back the lost Eagle."

"I no longer have so much ambition. I will be content with reuniting my *familia* and living an honorable life. Away from politics. Away from Rome."

"Husband, you speak like an old man."

"I was much younger before I met you," I said. "Say that again: 'husband.'"

She smiled. "*Basia me, mi amor.*"

"Close enough," I said.

47: DISAGREEABLE WORK

The Roman vexillation departed as soon as it was light enough to see, so eager were they to return to Carnuntum. It was a sad sight, the troopers on horseback barely half the number they had been before, the carts crowded with wounded, the pack mules overladen with tents and weapons and all the other impedimenta of the march. Placidus rode close behind Lamia, as if to be on hand in case of need.

I watched for a few minutes, yearning to be with these men whose lives had twined with mine. In a few days they would be back amid the barracks, baths, and familiar duties of a legion fortress linked by paved roads to Rome.

The prefect had made no attempt to recapture me. Perhaps the continuing presence of a hundred restless Germanic warriors and their king discouraged him. But I hoped it was my warning that had persuaded him to leave me alone. As a spymaster who thrived on scheming and lying, he could not risk his private correspondence becoming public.

"I should have asked Placidus to take a letter for Mother," I muttered. My poor mother, who must have wept over the ashes she thought were mine.

"You will have more to tell her after the council meeting," Dio reminded me.

I nodded glumly. The Germans had already sent messengers to convene the council, and were readying themselves to leave for Hoheneih. Once they had gone, I would rally my own small force to retrieve the documents Dio had hidden in the latrine trench. Not a task to anticipate.

"Marcus." Cleon squinted painfully from the effects of his drinking bout. "This Council of Women is important, eh? They might throw us out of this wilderness." He added in a growl, "And none too soon."

"So what?" My mood was tindery.

"Before then . . . Will we have time . . ." He rubbed a hand over his bearded face, then said in a rush, "Ollius wants his bones buried."

"Of course." I was ashamed not to have thought of it. The journey to Ingiomar's stronghold, where the council would meet, would be interrupted for a night at Grozhauga. I did not know what luck we would have in finding Ollius's remains, but we could try.

In the meantime, there was something I looked forward to even less. Aurima had asked me to visit Ingiomar.

Maelo, Anso, and a third man were constructing a horse litter for him.

The *fraujaz* lay on a bed of pine boughs, cushioned by the white bearskin and covered by the red cloak. Aurima knelt beside him with Beran peeping out of the sling on her back.

She was combing her father's pale gold beard, holding each lock in her free hand so the bone teeth did not pull too hard. I traced with my eyes the curves of her bowed head, her neck and shoulder, the insinuated S of her spine, her captivating bottom, the boot toes barely showing beneath her tunic hem. I was tempted to lift her to her feet and say, *Tend to this wreck of a man later; come with me.*

Ingiomar's arm shot up and knocked her hand away. "Enough, girl! Stop poking at me. You cannot make me prettier, so let me be!"

Beran let out a wail, startled by the bellow.

"And take that puling bastard away!"

Aurima snapped to her feet. Frightened, the baby began to yowl in earnest.

Anso strode over, plucked him from his sling, and bounced him in his scarred hands. Beran stopped crying, bemused by the comic grimaces being made for his benefit.

Ingiomar saw me staring aghast at this adversary dandling my son. He grinned maliciously. "Soon Friduric gives me a true grandson. His boy is going to grow tall and strong, fierce as a cave bear. And a killer of Romans."

My jaw tensed. But there was no point in cursing a man who was already cursed.

Anso laid the baby in my hands. I saw a look in the man's eyes that might have been amusement. He knew I had not expected such gentleness.

"Come away," I said to Aurima, making up an excuse: "You need to look at Rufus's ear." I could hardly bear the stench of decay from Ingiomar's wound.

"Could you not have asked your *medicus* for the juice that brings sleep without pain?" In the edginess of her voice, I heard the stress of dealing with her father.

"Am I a milk-livered coward?" Ingiomar lifted a *spatha* that lay beside him and pounded its pommel on the ground. "I must meet the gods with a sword in my hand."

That hand, the one I had bitten, was puffy and red. It must have hurt like blazes to grip the sword hilt. "There is no more you can do," I told Aurima. "Leave him." *And let him rot,* I added silently.

Her uncertain gaze flickered around. Beran, who had been sucking on the end of my torc, began to wriggle and fuss.

Brush rustled and hurrying footsteps thumped on the path that led from the larger camp below. Then came the terrible panting of some animal rushing closer.

Aurima snatched the infant. I pulled my knife. The others seized their own weapons, and we all yelled as a wolf bounded into the clearing.

The shouting should have driven the beast away, but instead it merely stopped and stared. Then its eerie yellow eyes fixed on Aurima, and it wagged its tail.

"Tig," she gasped, half laughing in relief.

Thancmar stumbled in after his pet she-wolf. "Riemy," he puffed. His scowl wavered around at the rest of us and settled on Ingiomar, propped up on one elbow amid his exotic bedding. "So!" He marched over on his short legs, teetered, and nearly fell on top of the injured man.

Apparently he had been on a drunken spree—the reason why I had not seen him to offer my thanks for alerting Aurima in Bruna.

"Little Thancmar! What dead log have you been hiding under?" Ingiomar rasped.

"I am here to settle a matter with you, my *fraujaz*," the dwarf retorted. He spread his legs and planted his fists on his hips. "All these y-years . . ." He stopped, then started again. "All these years, you fought Romans. You made Friduric fight Romans. You sent Riemy away because she l-lay with a Roman. All to avenge the death of Ammisia. Yes?"

"Do not puke on me, little man."

"I am her son!" Thancmar burst out. "But you never explained my mother's death to me! Who left her alone in Sis-Siscia? You did! Your wife, your daughter of thirteen summers, and a slave—you left the three of them with old Bodico, because he was too lame to ride on the hunt with you. Did you really think he was going to keep them safe?"

Ingiomar reached for his sword. "No," Aurima cried, pulling her half brother backward by the neck of his tunic. The blade swept out in a horizontal arc that could have severed a foot.

Thancmar tumbled onto his rear. Sitting dazed on the ground, he seemed to realize at last that something was wrong. "What ails you?" he faltered.

"Let me show you," Ingiomar answered with a savage grin. He flipped back the fold of cloak covering his right leg.

The poison had risen nearly to his knee, marked by an edge of bright red. The calf below it, swollen and blistered as if burned, wept a foul-smelling pus. His ankle had become as dark as bronze. And his foot, from the arch to the toes, was charcoal black.

Boss had caused that, perhaps with the very foreleg Ingiomar had wanted me to believe he severed. *Eironeia*, the Greeks call that.

Instead of standing up as he had been about to do, Thancmar plopped on his rump again and fell over backward. His eyes rolled up in his head.

Tig nosed at him, then licked his face. He blinked and moaned.

"Father, there must be—" Aurima began.

"Go away, girl! And take your moon-mad Roman with you."

I made a step forward, anger rising. Aurima spun and thrust the howling baby into my arms. Fisting her hands on her hips, she shouted at her father, "Do you think it pleases my mother's spirit to see what you do in her name—the women you make widows, the children who are fatherless?" A hank of hair fell across her cheek. She tossed her head furiously to displace it. "You are sick with vengeance, Father. Let her spirit be at peace!"

"How do you know what would please your mother?" Ingiomar snarled. "Be gone! You too, you fainting fool, take your drooling beast before I have it killed. Let me not see any of you again." He sagged back on his bedding.

We returned silently to our little camp. Someone brought ale and venison. Aurima spoke little, busying herself with changing the baby's breechcloth. Cleon sharpened all our blades. Rufus tended to our horses and the donkey he and Dio had acquired from a trader. I did not know what had become of Thancmar and his she-wolf, and did not much care. Yet his accusation returned to me: *Who left her alone in Siscia?* If Ingiomar held himself to blame, perhaps no amount of revenge would ever satisfy him.

Dio came over to me, the ever-present satchel hanging from his shoulder. "I went through the other new dispatches this morning. Do you wish to know about them?"

I saw red scrapes on his jaw, a scab beneath his nose: unlike Cleon and me, he tried to shave every day. "Yes, cheer me up." I made room for him to sit on the grass beside me. "Tell me the Special Cohort is being replaced by Numidian tomb-cleaners."

"Nothing quite so picturesque," he said. Since our narrow escape from death, he was developing a mild sense of humor. "You can read the decrypted messages yourself, or I will summarize the most important news for you."

"Go ahead." I began to scrub my teeth with a broken twig. Meat-eating demands constant cleaning; I have met Germans whose breath reeked worse than Ingiomar's leg.

"In Caesar's absence, a plot against him took root." Unable to see me roll my eyes, he continued, "Tribune Saxa lists several suspects."

"I am not going to like his list, am I?"

"Gaius Silius is on it," he said, and I sighed. "But there is worse, Marcus. Saxa thinks Caesar's sister Julia Livilla is involved."

Would Livilla never learn? She had narrowly escaped banishment for her role in her cousin Gemellus's assassination plot.

"There is no proof." He kept his voice low. "But Saxa is keeping an eye on her."

"Has Caligula been told?" I asked, and guessed the answer before he said it. Of course not. Caligula's fragile balance had nearly shattered last fall when he was twice betrayed—first by the cousin he had adopted and indulged, and then by my father, his closest adviser. With his cherished Drusilla now gone, his sanity might be destroyed for good by the treachery of his youngest sister, whom he had already forgiven of so much.

I smiled without amusement. "Poor Icarus."

"Icarus?"

"That is what Nina called him: the boy who flew too high and fell to earth." I got up, trying not to groan as my aching limbs protested.

"There is one more thing, if you care to know it."

"I suppose you will tell me anyway."

"There have been riots in Alexandria. The local Greeks are trying to drive out the Jews by assaulting them, burning their shops and houses, and tearing down their temples."

This was appalling news. Without shipments of grain from Egypt's primary port, thousands of Romans on the bread dole would become hungry —and angry—this winter.

"Where was Roman law while this was going on?"

Dio clicked his tongue. "Marcus, you look like your father when you ... Never mind. Yes, that is a good question. The prefect of Egypt is being recalled."

It was a machine of many parts, this world encompassed by our *imperium*. Like a catapult or a mill, one malfunctioning part could bring the whole to a standstill.

As worrisome as such news of conspiracy and massacre might be, acting on these matters was no longer my concern. I intended to disappear into the countryside, well below the notice of the imperial eagle. If the Council of Women said I must send Friduric fifty *modii* of grain or a mare in foal every year, so be it.

So I forced the apprehension away. It was time to tell Cleon of his unattractive task on the morrow. Since Rufus would be spared because of his wounds, perhaps I would round up Thancmar to help. At least it would keep him out of the ale.

No need to describe the unpleasantness of digging two clay amphoras out of a soupy, smelly latrine trench. Cleon said he needed no tipsy dwarf to help with the disagreeable work. Up came the treasure at last: a squatty jar formerly filled with *garum* and a taller one that had held wine.

Dio and I took a few steps back as Cleon flung himself on the ground, naked and dripping muck. "If that big one's full of rocks, you poxy scribbler, I'll throw you in with it," he snarled.

I caught a hint of a grin on Dio's face. He said, "Marcus, did you notice something missing from the chest you took to the Germans?"

Lamia's money.

His grin twisted slyly. "Eight thousand denarii, I estimate."

I stared at him. Had I corrupted an honest man?

"He would have paid it, would he not, to save his life?" Dio said pragmatically.

For once Cleon did not offer a jibe. He lay flat in the grass, not even brushing off the flies. "Go wash yourself," I told him. "This crafty felon and I will fill in the ditch."

"No." He clambered to his feet. "I'll do it."

After the amphoras had been scrubbed, Dio chipped away the wax seal, pried out one of the stoppers, and drew out a crumpled roll of papyrus. "Dry," he crowed. He straightened the furled document and began to read it.

I was thinking of the freedom eight thousand denarii would buy. It was far from a fortune, but a good stake for settling down in some remote area.

Dio handed me the scroll. "Perhaps this will show the prefect you are serious."

It was a message to Saxa in Rome, written in an unfamiliar hand. "You did not scribe this," I guessed.

"His regular secretary did, the one I replaced. This is Lamia's own copy."

The message began by suggesting Pannonia's strategic importance as a staging area for the campaign two years away. Instead of launching fifty legions against Britannia, as currently planned, Lamia proposed enlisting Vannaz's Marcomanni and Quadi to pacify the Lugii tribes north of the Mark. That done, the legions would subdue the Mark itself. From this new Roman province, which he grandly named Marcomannia, troops could move east against the Iazyges and eventually secure the expanse of Dacia all the way to the Euxine Sea.

I rolled up the papyrus and passed it back to Dio. "Vannius would declare war on us if he knew this. How many more like it are there?"

"I stuffed as many as I could into the amphoras," he said apologetically. "The rest I wrapped in bloody rags and threw on the pyre. All the tablets, too. There was not enough time to read them."

"No matter. This letter alone will make him regret leaving you a key to his chest."

"Oh, he was too careful to do that." He shrugged. "The mistress asked me once to open a jewel box whose key was lost. It is not so difficult, really."

"You picked the lock? Licinius Dio, you astonish me!"

The tip of his sharp nose turned red.

"You may have saved us all," I added, and his blush deepened with pleasure.

48: THE HALL OF WARRIORS

"What is in those jars?" the boy asked Rufus, who sat on a stump working on the donkey's pack frame.

We had reached Grozhauga the day before, the stronghold that had been Berinhard's and then his brother Chlothar's, and now was held by the tattooed man named Haimo. Although the track continued on through the drowned forest to Thancmar's mill and Hoheneih, Vannaz's retinue had stopped here, crowding the palisaded settlement and meadow, for Ingiomar was in too much pain to travel farther.

That morning, the fourth before the council would meet, Aurima and Thancmar had gone to inform Haimo that we intended to look for Ollius's bones. I asked her also to find out if Chlothar's son had died with his father, a possibility that still troubled me. Luckily the boy, Ivo, turned out to be alive and well. Less luckily, he had followed Aurima back to our small camp. And now wanted to know what our amphoras contained.

Pinning down the end of a willow strip with one hand, Rufus pointed with the other at Dio's careful lettering of Garum on each vessel.

"What does that mean?" Ivo persisted.

Rufus twitched his chin toward the amphoras and sniffed noisily. The boy stepped closer, caught a good whiff, and retreated with a scowl. Several washings had not rid the pottery jars of their reek. A German might easily confuse that with the odor of a favorite Roman condiment, fermented fish sauce.

Ivo inspected me as I groomed Boss's flank with a fistful of straw. Other than the shortness of my hair and beard-stubble, I must not have looked very different from before.

"You killed my father," he said.

I faced him, letting my hand fall near the hilt of my longknife. "I came into his hall in friendship. He murdered my companion, and only by the Goddess's favor did I live." I stared down at him. "A man who murders must expect vengeance."

"A murderer should not let his victim's son live," he replied evenly.

I met his blue glare, glad he was nearly a decade from manhood.

"I am going to tell the Council of Women about you."

I shrugged. "I did not want to kill you."

"Soon you are going to wish you had," Ivo said, and stalked away.

Aurima and Rufus had both heard the exchange. Rufus half drew his knife with a questioning look. I shook my head quickly. "Curry the horse for me, you cutthroat."

I walked a little distance away with Aurima. "Must I pay another blood price for avenging Ollius?"

"It may be," she said. "Killing a guest is very bad. You should have told the council and let them decide on Chlothar's punishment. If I can make them understand that you did not know our custom, then they may agree that he earned his own death."

She must have just fed Beran. The baby dozed in his sling with milk on his lips, his face as lustrous and innocent as an oleander blossom.

I was gazing pensively at him when she added, "My *amma* is here."

"Here? Not at Hoheneih?"

"The council will meet here instead." She bit her lip, but her voice was steady. "My father fights, yet still Haljo's serpent swallows his leg."

She had slept badly these past nights, distressed by his slow death. I slid my hand into the mass of her coppery hair and pressed her soft cheek against mine. "The gods take men in their own time."

"What god would have taken you, Marcus Aquilo?"

I drew back uncertainly.

"Once you prayed to Mithras to keep you brave and true. For you he was the god of light, not so? The god who fights for Rome against the darkness that is not Rome."

"All that I thought was light is not light," I said. "And all that I thought was darkness is not dark."

"So for you there are no gods?"

"I think each of us has different gods." With my thumb I touched my father's ring. "This is what I believe in. Honor. Courage. Loyalty. You." I nodded at Beran. "Him."

As the words hung in the air, I seemed to hear Placidus say, *A young man with a head full of antique virtues and no gods you had faith in.*

Aurima wet her lips with her tongue. "Helle's baby is born," she said. "A girl."

Cleon refused to let anyone help him. He spaded through the midden with a neck-scarf tied over his nose and mouth, mumbling prayers or curses, I knew not which. A cloud of flies assailed him, and crows peered from the gable of the ruined shed. Dogs prowled, sniffing. Curious Germans muttered to each other.

I watched silently. I could do no less for a man who had died to save my life.

Aurima had wished to watch with me, to honor Ollius. I persuaded her instead to show off Beran to the many people she knew here, hoping it would lift her spirits.

Heat and scavengers had hastened the process of decay. If not for severed bones protruding from the left forearm, the melting, worm-ridden flesh might not have been recognizable as my bodyguard's. I gagged, hiding my face in the crook of my elbow. Cleon ripped off the scarf, stumbled back, and vomited.

The crowd around us fell silent as Cleon lifted Ollius's remains gently onto a deerskin, using the spade and his hands. Silver tears slid down his cheeks into his beard.

Finished, he folded the stiff hide carefully over the ruins. Rufus had found a handcart. Together, youth and man, they transferred the deer hide onto it.

I became aware that Aurima stood nearby. "My *amma* asks for you," she said.

"Later." I blinked away my own tears. "After we are finished with this."

The sad bundle was lifted onto a pyre that Dio and Rufus had built at the end of the meadow. Dead branches cracked beneath its weight, settling it into a prickly nest.

I picked up a jar of river water that stood ready. "With this cleansing, we wash away any offenses that Ollius Capaneus committed against any of us." I poured water over everyone's hands, then rinsed my own. "We pray that his spirit will forgive us if we offended him in any way."

As *paterfamilias* I ought to have led the farewells, commending Ollius's spirit to the gods as I had done with the Army dead. That valedictory had flowed easily, but now my mind and tongue ceased to work. "Ollius," I began, and broke off. I saw him before me: shaven-headed, strong-shouldered, barrel-bellied, a grin baring uneven teeth framed by a trim mustache and chin beard.

I gestured inarticulately to Cleon, who took over with a halting account of Ollius's record in the arena. I was elsewhere, in the entrance to Berinhard's *halla*, pinned down by enemies as Ollius fought three opponents and Berinhard unsheathed the sword that I had unwisely told my bodyguard to surrender . . .

After killing Chlothar I had shut this memory behind a door, as if I had paid a bill. I had not been haunted by his spirit, or by those of the others: Adalwulf and Fulco; Wido and Egino; Glabrio. I had been a different man, without remorse, with nothing in my mind except getting to Aurima and savaging those who betrayed me in my search for her.

In the span of a few days, that blind brutality was draining away. Now that I had found her, I no longer thirsted to kill anyone, not Lamia or even Ingiomar. The *fraujaz* was dying; the prefect was disarmed; and the Council of Women seemed likely to assess a fine I could pay with pillaged coins.

Dio held out a peeled beech wand to me. The others had finished their farewells. Gruffly I said, "Ollius, my friend, may you be welcomed by the gods with as much respect as we hold in our hearts for you." I dipped the wand into Dio's firepot, then stepped forward and touched its flaring tip to the pyre.

The fire burned quickly and hot. My thoughts wandered to Ollius's early attempts to train me in using a sword ("I don't know where his mind is, Senator, but it ain't on the blade"), his lurid tales of the brothel where he had been a guard before his owner rented him to a gladiator trainer, his fondness for Fox Tail, a Vesuvian wine. I would pour him a drink, I vowed, when we set up his tombstone.

By the time I remembered that Aurima was waiting, Dio and Rufus had already gone. Only Cleon waited by the pyre, his head bent. Without turning he said in a muffled voice, "Don't wait for me." He flung another piece of wood on the fire.

We were only a few steps away when he groaned, "Fuck it, Ollius! It should have been me."

I hesitated. Proud as he was, he would not wish to be seen unmanned by grief. Yet if he was blaming Ollius's death on my judgment, I could not ignore it. I told Aurima I would find her in a few minutes.

Cleon hurled something small and hard into the flames. He must have heard my approach, but did not acknowledge it. I said, "Are you accusing me, him, or yourself?"

He swung toward me, his face streaked with tears and smoke. "I'd have gotten you out of that hall on your feet."

It should have been easy for me to refute him. I was his patron, the head of the family that had fed, housed, and commanded him since he left the arena. But he was a legend, a fifty-win champion with net and trident, a man who had broken legs for gang lords before Father made him choose between gladiator training or execution as a criminal. I trusted and respected him too much to chastise him.

"Nine years I guarded your father from street gangs and cutthroats." He glared, red-eyed. "I promised to do the same for you." He brought his clenched fist to his chest.

I eyed the fist warily, having felt its force when I was a boy. "Ollius killed Berinhard. I killed Chlothar. There is nothing to reproach yourself for."

"Nothing? Would that bastard Inguiomerus have tried to impale you if I hadn't jumped him? And then, tied to that tree, I . . . could not . . . do . . . a fucking . . . thing." He shoved out the words between his teeth. "When you quit resisting because they threatened to kill me, I cried for shame."

I managed to follow his leap from Berinhard's betrayal to Ingiomar's attempted sacrifice. "Cleon, you have saved me a hundred times—"

"A horse! A fucking horse saved you!"

He drew back his arm. Bright objects with strings and chains showered from his opened fist into the fire: Ollius's amulets.

His anguish arrowed into me. He thought he was unneeded. Worse: a liability.

"Are you going to leave me?" I asked, disbelieving.

He turned his back and stared into the smoking coals of the pyre.

The words I sought tangled themselves in brambles. I dared not appear to patronize him or belittle his pride.

"Cleon, we would not have reached Carnuntum if not for Ollius and you," I said at last. "The pirates who tried to rob us, the mountain bandits ... How could I have defended us with nothing but nerve and a noble name?"

I tried a thin smile, which made no difference since he could not see it. "Since then I have done things I never expected to do. And hope never to do again."

He turned his head sideways, profiled by the flames. "He was sure you'd find the Eagle of the Eighteenth."

We stood in silence. The fire hissed as it devoured something that once had lived.

I raised my eyes from it, tracing a churn of smoke into the deep-blue sky. "I thought if I could do some great thing for Rome, it would erase what happened to my father. To our family. I imagined what that would be like." I paused, his outline by the fire blurring as a different scene took shape. "Standing at the top of the steps of Jupiter's temple with you and the others. The Senate and people applauding and cheering as I presented the lost Eagle to Caesar. Mother and Nina weeping for joy."

"Aye," Cleon said softly, as if he had imagined the moment too.

"But when we were ... there, with that tree, and I reckoned I was going to die, I never once thought of the Eagle or Rome or restoring our family's honor. It was Aurima and Beran—they were why I wanted to live."

I rubbed my thumb over my scarred signet ring. "I am going to find a place where we can live in peace. Somewhere that is Roman, but not Rome. And where I can someday become known as a man of influence and *honestas*." I looked up. "That will not be easy with enemies like Lamia and Saxa, and perhaps Caesar himself. So I need you, Cleon. I need your strength. Your experience." I essayed the smile again. "Your bronze balls."

He grunted. Looked away. "Sounds boring," he said.

The last of the pyre collapsed in a shower of sparks.

"Regular pay. Decent food. Real beds. Women of easy virtue. Though I can't promise they will pay attention to you, you ugly son of a bitch."

He looked back at me. "Let's get ourselves out of this fucking wilderness, then."

Contentment and relief flooded me. "On winged feet," I assured him.

How could I not have noticed his frustration? I had supposed he would shrug off the ordeal in the sacred grove, since he was accustomed to mortal danger. But that was self-deception. In truth, I had avoided the subject out of shame that he had seen me in such an abyss of terror.

At least everything I had told him now was true. I would have given all Lamia's silver to be able to pack up and head for Carnuntum in the morning.

But it would hardly improve Rome's precarious relations with the Germans for me to break my word.

I looked for my wife among the tents and shelters spread across the meadow. Perhaps Hroswitha's summons meant Ingiomar was dead. That cheered me up.

There she was, her coppery hair like a beacon among the drab-dyed clothing and bleached late-summer grass. I felt a smile start as I walked toward her. This beautiful, determined, mettlesome woman, who could have her choice of men, called me *husband*. I must find out if we could marry formally before the gathering dispersed.

She uncrossed her arms as I came near. "Did you forget that my grandmother wishes to see you?"

"I remembered." The harshness in her voice surprised me. "Where is the baby?"

"I left him with *Amma*. Come with me."

"What is the matter? Slow down. Let me ask you something."

Aurima did not answer. Her anger radiated from strides so vigorous that I had to stretch my legs to keep up. I forgot about discussing a wedding. What was this about? If her father had succumbed at last, I would have expected melancholy.

Hroswitha sat beneath a high-crowned beech tree, her amber-tipped staff leaning against its trunk. A small girl of perhaps ten squatted on her heels beside her—a pupil or apprentice, perhaps, as Aurima once had been. People wandering in and out of the *halla* glanced at them, but no one came near.

The old woman peered up at Aurima and me. More than ever she had the air of a creature from the spirit world, with her thistledown hair, gaunt features, and long dark robes. On her knees slept a tiny Cupid with his thumb in his mouth.

I said politely, "The Goddess's greetings to you, Hroswitha."

Her heavy-lidded eyes, as gray as concrete, opened wider. "No longer do you call me *Amma*?" she asked, also in Germanic.

"I do not know what to call the grandmother of my son's mother."

"*Amma* will do." She smiled without showing her teeth. "You are stronger now. That is good. Aurima, take your child and Linza, and leave your man with me."

"*Amma*, please do not do this." Aurima's voice was low and strained.

Hroswitha's response was to hold out the sleeping baby. Without another word Aurima picked up Beran, took the girl by the hand, and vanished behind the *halla*.

Her grandmother studied me carefully. My legs were bare beneath the faded red tunic, for I was still Roman enough to find breeches hot and itchy. "Sit," she said, gesturing to the bench beside her.

I obeyed. Remembering the uncanny way my hands had been healed for as long as I needed to use a weapon, I wondered if she would tell me what she had done. But I did not ask. I was not ready to admit that I believed in magic.

The old priestess laid her staff slantwise in her lap, fingering the luminous amber. Without looking up she asked, "When you die, what becomes of you?"

Suspicion sharpened my curiosity. Was this to do with Ammisia? With Ollius's bones? With Aurima's question about my gods? The steadiness of Hroswitha's white-lashed eyes gave no hint.

"I believe there is another place after I die," I said.

She nodded. "Just as we do. But we think there are many places." Her knob-knuckled hands swayed and spread to hold numbers of imagined afterworlds. "For brave men there is the hall of Wodunaz with fighting and feasting, drinking and telling of tales, all the great warriors together. Do you understand this?"

I said I did. The Hall of Warriors might be a paradise for men like Ingiomar and Maelo, but it was not mine. Where was the old stork going with this? She did not need to have sent Aurima away in order to have an eschatological discussion with a Roman.

She stroked her staff again. "To reach this place, one must die fighting."

That, too, I understood. Aurima had once baited me to attack her so that she might die a warrior's death.

"Ingiomar is dying," she went on. "It is not a good death."

I said nothing. She must know how much I hated him.

"He fears being unable to hold a sword when the Sky Maidens come."

Her eyes probed my face as if expecting a revelation to burst across it, but I was still in the dark.

"He wishes you to kill him," Hroswitha said.

Horror exploded through me. "No." I sprang to my feet.

Her face was calm. She did not seem to know the enormity of what she had said.

"Why should I give him a good death? Let him kill himself."

She shook her ghostly cloud of hair.

"If he has too little courage, one of his companions can do it," I argued.

"He does not lack courage. Do you?"

"My courage is not what we are talking about."

She stood up. "I do not ask this for Ingiomar," she said. "I ask it for Aurima."

I turned away.

"His blood will not be on your head." She began to say something about the gods.

"Did Aurima suggest this?" I interrupted, not looking at her.

"No, I told you. It is the wish of Ingiomar, husband of my murdered daughter."

At last I understood. He wanted to die fighting a Roman.

No wonder Aurima had been angry. How dare Hroswitha ask me to slay Ingiomar, my bitterest enemy, so he could go to the Hall of the Warriors?

There was nothing more to say. I walked until I found our camp. As the day darkened, I sat by my companions' cooking fire and drank ale. Ollius's funeral pyre settled into a bed of ash and bone, embers and char, smoking into the pallid sky.

Aurima glanced at me but said nothing about her father, nor did I speak of him. In a shameful mingling of resentment and cowardice, I hoped he would die in the night.

The ale failed to choke off dreams. Hroswitha hovered over my sleep, mantling me with her robes like an owl's great wings. Trees swayed around me, hung with rattling bones and rotting carcasses. Far away, someone I loved cried for help—my mother or my sister, or perhaps Aurima—but I could not find her.

No scream came in the night, no sad wail that the *fraujaz* of Hoheneih had gone to his gods. As soon as it was light enough to see, I untied and mounted Spider without speaking to anyone. Eyes watering in the new day, I galloped him away from Grozhauga, toward the Amber Road.

49: DEATH COMES

It was absurd. To die was to die. You could have a sword in your hand or a cup of wine or a whore's tit, and it would make no difference. Ingiomar was no more likely to go to Wodunaz's feast hall if he died fighting than if he opened his veins in a warm bath.

But he believed it. And Aurima believed it.

And how could I, who thought myself rational, be so sure that each man's soul did not have its own afterlife? I had been visited by my brother's spirit seeking vindication. On behalf of soldiers cremated on a pyre, I had prayed sincerely to gods I did not believe in. I had promised to splash a man's favorite wine on his tomb.

It did not really matter, did it, what Ingiomar thought would happen when his life ended? What mattered was whether I was willing to take it from him.

I relived all the wrongs he had done me: the torments and humiliations, the burden of innocent men's deaths, the terror of expecting my own hideous end. And the cruelty with which he had torn Aurima away from me, kept her a virtual prisoner, and sold her child—his own grandchild—to a Special Cohort double-dealer.

Yes, anger helped. Before the injury to his foot, I would willingly have killed him. Then I was glad I had not had the opportunity, since blood poison was slower and more agonizing. I would not offer him a faster, easier death. He did not deserve one.

Cleon would have no reservations about slaying him. Would gladly take on the duty, I was sure. But the threads that bound me to Ingiomar were stitched into my soul. Since the fraujaz had asked for me, he must feel them too.

I asked the counsel of my father's and brother's spirits. But the only response was from Spider, who regarded me with a dark intelligent eye as he munched grass.

"How difficult your decisions are," I said. "Will this tuft or that one better fill your belly?" I flicked a piece of bark at him.

His ears swiveled, and he lifted his head. A few moments later I heard it too: the rumble of wheels on the track. Around a bend bumped a two-horse cart carrying four women. A youth drove, and two armed men rode as escorts. After a pause when they spotted me, they must have decided I was no threat. I was sitting under a tree at the old campsite where Thancmar and I had stopped, the morning after I killed Chlothar. We had been on our way to intercept Glabrio's detachment, and the murder I had just committed had seemed of little importance compared with the urgency of rescuing Aurima.

Thancmar had told me then how happy she was as the baby grew in her, and how she looked forward to bringing him to me in Carnuntum. *She said you had lost so much, but here was something found.*

The voices rose like the twitter of birds, diminishing as they jolted on toward Grozhauga. Sensing my disquiet, Spider ambled over and dribbled slobbery grass on me. I rubbed his head and sweet-talked him, and felt calmer. It came to me then that with all my dithering, it was a horse who knew the right question.

What could I not live without?

"Yes," Ingiomar gasped. "Yes, it is my wish."

His bed was laid in a thatch-covered shelter with no walls. Despite the sweet fragrance of firewood stacked there, it was impossible to ignore the smell of his rotting leg. "When?" I asked, keeping my eyes on the piled logs.

"Soon as . . . you are ready."

Turning to leave, I recalled what Hroswitha had told me to ask. I swung back, forgetting not to look at him.

Bloody saliva streaked his thick blond beard. His cheeks and forehead burned red, and his sunken eyes shone with fever. Pain whined in every wheezing breath.

"Do you forgive me for bringing you death?" I said gruffly.

He grimaced and shut his eyes.

Let the bastard die with his malevolence, then. "So be it. Do it yourself."

"Wait . . . Tiwaz the Just . . . be my witness, I . . . forgive you for . . . what you do." His head turned on the mat of his sweat-stringy mane, and those agony-bright eyes fixed on me.

I heard myself say in Latin, "It will be quick," and was annoyed to have let that small condolence slip past.

I insisted on one condition: that Maelo be the sole witness. The deed was pathetic enough without having a crowd of onlookers. Far too many knew already; eyes followed me as I walked to Haimo's longhouse, where Aurima's uncle was waiting.

In a pile at his feet was the armor I had been wearing the day I was captured: my crested helmet and liner, the backplate and figured breastplate, the padded waistcoat with its leather strips at shoulder and thigh, my sword, scabbard, and baldric.

I said thunderously, "No." But I had already gone too far to refuse.

There was not a sound, not a child's yelp or a dog's bark, not a cough or a whisper, only the jingle of belt rings and the crunch of my boot nails on the sandy path. My left hand gripped the hilt of my sheathed sword. My face was frozen in sternness, my jaw set, my eyes fixed. I must have passed Aurima, Dio and Cleon, Rufus, and dozens of familiar Germans, but saw none of them.

Someday my son would be told that his father had killed his grandfather. He might not understand. Might despise me.

The lowering sun poured into the wood shelter, turning the log butts into coins stacked edge to edge. Maelo watched me from the entrance, his brightly lit hair flaming.

I reached the shelter. Maelo and I met each other's eyes. He nodded once, and I ducked my helmeted head to pass under the thatch.

The bed was gone. Ingiomar lay on the ground amid scattered wood chips, his head pillowed on the white bearskin. His face was turned to the sun, which struck gleams from finger-rings in his beard and gold *armillas* on his wrists and upper arms. He wore long striped breeches, and a wolf-fur vest that bared his strong torso.

"Is that you, Roman?" His voice was shaky, slurred with fever.

I went closer without speaking.

"I see him again, Maelo." He tried to lift his arm. A strip of cloth bound his sword hilt to his swollen hand. "The ghost . . ."

Maelo cleared his throat. "Not a ghost this time, brother. Are you ready?"

"Maybe you are . . . a ghost too . . . ?" His chuckle broke off in a wheeze.

"Ingiomar," Maelo said sharply. "Wake up. Your death is here."

The *fraujaz* stared up at me. I had not moved.

He lifted his head. "Maelo, stand me up." His brother-in-law bent down, slid an arm under his shoulders, and raised him to a sitting position. "Is it really . . . you, turd?"

Holding the throat of my scabbard, I drew my sword.

"Not yet! . . . Maelo, let me . . . lean on you."

Maelo hauled him upright. Ingiomar shouted, "Thunraz!," a yell of anguish. He fell against the stacked firewood, his own blade dangling uselessly from his hand. A few logs rolled off with meaty *clonks*. The breeches slit around his poisoned leg flapped open.

My gorge rose. I could not do this.

I stepped back. Ingiomar straightened, propping himself on his good leg against the bank of log-ends. "Fight me, coward!" He swung his long *spatha* in an uneven arc, then aimed the blade at me. "I challenge you, Roman! . . . Fight me!"

From somewhere he found breath to revile me, my parents, and my offspring. I knew his intent was to kindle my temper, but I was frozen with horror and pity.

With a furious oath he lunged and swatted his sword against mine, a blow that drove my blade down. Off balance, he would have fallen had Maelo not caught his arm.

"For the love of your gods, Aquilo, do it!" Maelo gasped.

There was no need to think about where to strike, so experienced had I become. I touched my sword to Ingiomar's chest, just below where I reckoned his breastbone to be. "Your wife waits for you," I said, and thrust upward with all my might.

Maelo had only time to cry, "Sky Maidens, come!" before Ingiomar crumpled, blood gouting over his vest and legs. More logs tumbled as he fell against them.

I ought to have tugged the sword free, but could not manage it. My hand and forearm dripped scarlet on the white bear's fur.

Crouched over a body all askew, Maelo tried to speak. Only a crow's caw came from his throat.

I pulled off my helmet and cap and dropped them beside him. Awkwardly I lifted off the baldric and scabbard and tossed them down. Unfastened the buckles and let the breastplate and backplate fall. Unlaced the padded waistcoat, tugged it off, flung it aside.

I walked into slanting rays of sunlight that turned the faces I passed into backlit blurs. Out through the overlapping gates, across the long-shadowed meadow, to the spot where we were camped. I sat down in the grass, legs crossed, looking at nothing.

In a little while Aurima came and sat beside me, not speaking. I tried not to hear the distant lamentation for her father, but to listen only to the soft snuffly breaths of our sleeping child. She did not move as the sun sank, leaning against my back when I wept.

50: THE HALCYON BIRD

They burned him the next day. I think they slew his horse too, the white-faced chestnut, so he would have a mount in the next life. But I was not there to see if they did. I went upriver, riding Boss through chest-high water as mud churned and spiraled around his hooves, until we came upon a dark tree-hung pool. There I washed and washed, trying to scrub away a stain of retribution that held no release, of mercy that stung like guilt.

A long-skirted man with a crooked back had publicly sacrificed a wretched dog to Nerthuz to absolve me of the murder. It did not seem to have done me any good.

Finally I hoisted myself out of the water into a tattered patch of sun. As insects danced over the river, I tried to lose my grief and anger in watching its languid flow.

I had wanted for a long time to kill Ingiomar. Did it torment me that he had gone where I could no longer find him? That I had given him an easier death than he deserved? Or that, even at the end, he did not acknowledge my courage, my honor?

There were too many strands to make sense. It was like Nina's first attempt to weave, with twists of wool straggling here and there in disarray.

A glittering blue jewel caught my eye, flashing from one bank to the other. A halcyon bird, symbol of peace.

Foliage rustled in the thicket behind me, and Boss snorted. It was his "What's that? I don't like it" snort. I rose to my feet, reaching for my longknife.

"Aquilo? It's Thancmar. Tig, no!"

My warhorse squealed and thrashed violently, bucking and kicking. Unlike Spider, he had not grown accustomed to the she-wolf.

"Send her away," I bellowed, trying to calm the frantic stallion.

The racket must have terrified every creature within miles. At last Thancmar emerged through the brush, leading his own pony. "All is well. She has gone off to hunt."

With Boss quieted at last, I demanded, "What are you doing here?"

"Riemy asked me to find you. I told you, Aquilo, I am good at tracking." He glanced at the sky, veined with rose and lavender. "You are not going back tonight, eh?"

"No," I said curtly. Despite my ache for Aurima, I felt as if I bore a pestilence. Which perhaps I did. After all, the hunchback priest's absolution was a matter of faith.

"Are you thirsty, then?" The dwarf held up a fat aleskin by the neck.

I attended to the horses and kindled a fire while Thancmar waded into the river with his knife. We dined in silence on bony fish, perhaps perch, and barley bread with salted *butyrum*, the milk-grease I had forced myself to tolerate.

Mostly I drank. I would have liked to drink myself into insensibility and not wake until the Council of Women had adjourned, but there was not enough ale.

Thancmar traced a conjure circle around us with his knife and invoked Nerthuz's protection. Asprawl on cloaks as fireflies sparkled in the dusk, we passed the aleskin back and forth. The horses stirred occasionally; a heron croaked; a frog plopped into the river.

I ought to have been thinking about the speech in my defense that I would make to the council in two days. Preparing it should not be difficult; the facts were clear, and I was a trained orator. Semi-trained, at any rate.

Instead, I began to remember why lying exposed under close-crowding trees unsettled me. It was foolish to have remained here. Why not tack up Boss and return to Grozhauga? I had found my way in the dark when escaping Hoheneih, had I not?

I sat up. Thancmar said, "Aquilo, there is something that bothers me."

His company, even just the sound of his voice, seemed better than groping along a forest trail in the night. I reached for the aleskin. Empty. With a sigh I laid my head back on a rolled saddle blanket, expecting him to ask about Ingiomar's death.

"The night Riemy took you away from the fighting . . ."

One of the horses snuffled. We both listened. Nothing.

"When you left her, she wept."

How I love you, frijdila. With me she had been stoical, a true warrior's woman.

"With her you were safe. Maybe safe with your Romans, too. But you put your head into the bear's mouth."

Did that bother him? "I could not abandon my men," I said. "Ingiomar —"

"Sst!" He started up. "Do not say his name." The whites of his eyes gleamed as he peered around. "Call him Ironhand."

I tried to contrive an explanation in my workaday Germanic. "I had to do it."

"To let him kill you?" He looked at me, frowning. Sap popped in the fire.

I shifted to ease my healing arm. "We have a saying in Rome: *Vivit post funera virtus.* It means 'Honor lives on after death.'"

He snorted. "If Ironhand sacrifices you to Tiwaz to avenge my mother's death, he is the one who has honor, not you."

"What does this mean to you, to have honor?"

"Others see that you are a man to be respected. A man the gods favor. Like a warrior who defeats a man of more famous deeds."

Vulthu was the Germanic word we were using for "honor." But in his explanation, the term seemed more akin to "renown" or "glory."

Of course, that was why I had wanted to bring the lost Eagle back to Rome. I had hoped for the esteem of others: acclaim and renown, public recognition of my feat.

But it was not for the sake of glory that I had put my head into the bear's mouth. I said, "Thancmar, how do you say it if you are a man who ..." I fumbled for words, finishing lamely, "... who tries to be a good man?"

That was not what I wanted to say. I meant to describe the idea of honor that we call *virtus*: excellence in valor, resolve, and moral character. The Greeks call it *arête*, and my Athenian-born Phormio considered it the best and most important quality in a man.

I had always had stubbornness and audacity to spare, but as Phormio had tried to drum into me, that is not the same as being a good man. Once, when I gave an insincere apology to a boy I had tripped in a footrace, Phormio had shamed me with a scolding: *It is not enough to seem to have a noble character. You must strive for honor even if no one else is watching.*

Ah, Phormio, how I miss you.

Evidently Thancmar had been waiting for me to expand on my question, for it was a few moments before he said, "A good man? Like a man who rejoices in attacking a fierce enemy, so the gods can see his bravery?"

"That is not what I mean. I mean a man who tries to do what is right."

"But it is right to show bravery when the gods may give you death."

"Then I ask you this: If the fight is over and an enemy asks for mercy, what does a good man do?"

He turned his face to me. "You ask strange questions for a leader of soldiers."

"How do you answer?"

"Well, if the anger of Thunraz roars within you, you kill him."

"Let us say your anger has gone," I said. "Do you still kill him?"

"*Skita!* I am a miller; I do not make such choices." He fell silent. I did not prod him. Then he said, "If the gods have spared his life so far, I say it is for them to take it."

"Do you not decide within yourself?" I wanted to say *in your soul*, but did not know if there was a German equivalent.

"Within myself?" He was surprised. "How do I know the gods' will?"

It is the simplest of philosophies: by attributing everything to divine will, one has no responsibility for what happens. One thanks the gods when life is good, and tries to propitiate them when it is bad.

I could tell Thancmar that I did not believe a man needed the gods' favor to live a good life. *Persuade Aurima that she does not need to serve Austro,* he might say. And I would answer that even though she was dedicated to the goddess of light, she did not wait for the gods to decide what would be done. For which I loved her.

He was so quiet that I reckoned he had fallen asleep. Suddenly he said, "Segomo, who has been to Rome, says that Tig and I can be a big success in the arena at Carnuntum. Do you think so?"

I grunted assent. The soldiers would enjoy seeing a trained wolf take down a deer or wild pig at a dwarf's command.

The dying fire hissed softly. Finally he sighed. "No chance of it, I suppose, if there is going to be a war."

51: WAR

I had not heard such a tumult since Ingiomar humbled me on a leash. The feast hall fairly shuddered with yells, jeers, roars, and pounding on wood.

Riding back across the meadow had been hair-raising enough. Women and girls had swarmed me, so many of them shouting that I could make out only an occasional word amid the collision of voices. *Kill. Warrior. Roman.* Some spat in their palms and drew curse signs in the spittle. A few wept, their hands stretched out to me.

Boss's new hatred of Germans inflamed his warhorse instincts. His frenzied rearing and kicking made it impossible to search for Aurima among the women. Thancmar might have helped pacify the mob, but he had lagged behind, seeking Tig.

Cleon stood by the overlapping gates to the stronghold. Shouldering through the crowd, he shouted, "Where have you been? Everyone's looking for you."

To my relief he was with Rufus, who took Boss's reins as I slid to the ground. I wiped spittle from my cheek. "Where is Aurima?"

"Safe." Cleon pushed forward through the gates. "Come on. King wants you in the ale hall."

I turned to give Rufus instructions about Boss, but he was already riding the horse down toward our campsite. Cleon beckoned impatiently. I slogged after him, hiding my alarm behind the irritation of hunger and thirst. "What's all this madness? The Council of Women isn't supposed to meet until tomorrow."

He did not answer until we neared the open doors of the *halla*. "I keep hearing, '*Krig! Krig!*'" His dark brows drew together. "What does that mean?"

"War," I told him.

The great hall was jammed with men: Haimo's men, Ingiomar's men, the king's men, and others from miles around whose angry womenfolk had way-laid me outside the walls. The sour reek of ale was strong enough to stop a charging bull.

Heads turned. With startling unanimity the uproar diminished and died away, as when a boiling pot is taken off the fire. Even the dogs quit their excited yapping.

I stopped, the hair on my nape prickling at the silent stares. It might have been a ghost who had walked in, not a wind-blown Roman in a patched tunic.

"I'll cover you," Cleon muttered beside me. If I backed out, he meant.

Not a maiden or matron could I see among them; ale was being served by young boys, now stock-still and gaping. At the end of the raftered hall, Vannaz leaned on his arms over a trestle table set crosswise to the others. He sighted me over the shaggy heads between us and straightened, his battered face relaxing.

Vangio lurched to his feet beside his uncle. "See, he did not run away!"

"Then where was he?" rasped tattooed Haimo, Grozhauga's *fraujaz*.

The yammer sprang up again, men shouting over each other. The boys resumed scurrying about with pitchers of drink.

What had these hot-tempered fools stoked themselves up to while I was struggling with Ingiomar's death? "Come away," I told Cleon wearily.

Vannaz hammered the table with the pommel of his knife. "Let him speak," he bellowed. His voice was slurred: *Let him shpeak.*

I had already turned to leave. But as the warriors stilled each other, he called out in Germanic, "Aquilo, where have you been since yestermorn?"

I did not feel obliged to answer. Yet because they had burdened me with killing Ingiomar, I said in a carrying voice, "I talked with spirits, O king."

It became quiet enough to hear the rustle of vermin in the thatch. Then the men nearest me scrambled up, toppling benches, and retreated against the walls, thumbing and muttering to their luck charms: *Tiwaz, guard me. Thunraz, Lord of Battle, be with us. . . .* Spilled ale ran across tables and dripped into the straw-littered dirt.

Maelo pushed himself away from the king's table and squelched across to me. "Tell us, Tribune: Is war coming?" His breath assaulted me, thick and fruity with drink.

"I know nothing about war," I said. Cleon glanced at me sharply, recognizing the word. "I want only to take my family away."

A trickle of sweat ran down Maelo's cheek into his beard. "Ironhand has gone to the gods. You are revenged. Rome is revenged. There is no need to send soldiers."

"Let Caesar come!" someone bawled. "Let him try to defeat us!"

Whoops, cheers, pounding on tabletops. "Who says Rome is going to send soldiers?" I shouted over the din.

Vannaz stretched out his arms. When he could be heard, he said, "Ask my sister's son, who returned from Carnuntum today."

It was news to me that he had dispatched Vangio across the river. Of course, he would have wanted the legion commander to know Ingiomar had been dealt with.

"They stopped us at the guard post where the crossing-boat lands," the dolphin-faced prince began indignantly. "We waited a long time until horse soldiers came over on the boat and crossed the river with us. Guarding us like prisoners!"

Segomo Graybeard broke in, "On the side of Carnuntum, men are shouting at us. Always and again we hear the same, like dogs barking—Rome is going to take revenge; Rome's legions are going to cut down the Marcomanni like trees!" He glared, his face beneath the squirrel's-nest hair as dusky as the redware bowl I had wanted for Aurima.

"Stones and dung they threw at us," snarled a stocky, hay-haired youth.

Maelo crashed a fist on the table. "They spat on us!"

Word of Ingiomar's attack on the vexillation had obviously sped from the fortress to the town and the customs port. "What did the legion commander say to you?" I asked.

Vangio lowered his ale horn, wiping his mustache with the back of his hand. "Lamia said to see him first, so we can talk with Poppaeus together. But—"

"But he was not there!" Maelo interrupted. Specks of saliva sparkled amid the pierced coins and rings in his beard. "And Poppaeus, he brushed us away!" He swept his hand sideways, contorting his face in a mask of disdain.

More hammering of fists. More threats.

I was close enough to see color flaring across the king's broken cheekbones. "That is a bad sign," he said, pitching his voice for my ears. "Before, he had respect for me. For our people. You know that, I think."

I nodded. In private Poppaeus mocked the *hirsuti*—"hairy ones"—as everybody did, but in public he was careful to observe the civilities owed to an allied king. His discourtesy seemed more ominous than the provincials' insults. "Vangio, was there much activity in the fortress? Did he cancel leave for the garrison?"

The doorway darkened. Thancmar stumped in. Someone else reeled out.

Vangio was still nursing his injured pride. "Thunraz witness me"—he raised a fist toward heaven—"never I have been so shamed! He refused to see me—me, son of the king's sister!" Something reminded him of his uncle's foster son. "And Ellanher, grandson of the Hermunduri king!"

"Milk-livered dogs!" Adalfuns, whose gate-guard brother I had killed, drove the point of his knife into the tabletop. "They need to feel the bite of our swords."

"Enough," I protested. "You are making much out of little." Maybe something had prevented Poppaeus from receiving the delegation. Illness, miscommunication . . . Perhaps he had even been away from the camp and Vangio was not told.

Haimo bared his teeth at me in a sardonic grin. "Who trusts a Roman, trusts a viper." Thinking, no doubt, of Chlothar, whom I had lured from this hall to his death.

"Are we going to talk until they march in and slaughter us, brothers?" Maelo exploded. "We must attack them before they come to attack us!"

Above the roar of agreement I shouted, "You see ghosts in the dark. Caesar is looking toward the north. Our generals want peace with the Marcomanni and Quadi."

"Before then, there is time enough for a war," Maelo shot back. We both knew that Caligula's vaunted fifty-legion campaign in farther Germany and Britannia would not start until the spring after next.

I expected Vannaz to act the wise chief, reminding his bloodthirsty warriors that they had no reason to expect an invasion of the Mark. That it made no sense for Rome to launch reprisals that might flare into an unwanted war on the Danube. But he stood at the head of the room with arms crossed, listening to the arguments. *A king does not rule his people*, Aurima had told me. *He is ruled by them.*

Let them deal with it, then. Once the council established my fine, I would be gone with my wife, son, and companions. "Maelo, you foresaw this; you warned Ironhand. Why did you not stop him?"

His drink-glazed blue eyes fixed on me. "Do you not care if we rape Pannonia, while your sheep-witted Romans piss themselves in fear?"

I glared back, remembering his name scrawled among the others. "Do not look to me." I snatched a horn of ale from a passing server and swigged it down.

"You refuse to use your *vulthu*, Roman?" Maelo bellowed. "Then you are our enemy!"

I shouted over the clamor, "If you fear war, it is for you to stop it."

"Yet you are the head of a noble family." Maelo staggered a little as he swung around, a hand lifted to draw attention. "Yes, it is so, my brothers! Caesar is his kinsman, and likewise the governor of Pannonia! Whatever he advises, so they are going to do."

I tensed. Cleon tugged on my knife belt with a finger. "What are they saying?"

I hesitated, knowing he expected a signal to fight or flee. I might calm these drunken hotheads by promising that I would try to appease the legion commander and the governor, even though I doubted they would heed me. My father, and I after him, had lost the influence that Maelo thought I could exert.

Yet the issue was not really *vulthu*. It was honor. *Virtus*. A good man —the man I should be—would do anything possible to keep the frontier secure.

Resentment burned in my throat. All I had wanted since leaving Rome, apart from the grandiose fantasy of finding the lost Eagle, was to be with Aurima. And that was still all I wanted: her and my child.

"Make him disappear, as Ironhand wished," someone yelled nearby. It was Anso, that rash fool. "Nobody is going to hear him facedown in Nerthuz's bog."

"He must pay for my brother. And Fulco, and the rest," Adalfuns howled.

The king pounded the table with his knife hilt. "Aquilo goes before the Council of Women tomorrow. They decide what he must pay."

"He is a *vikkan!*" someone bawled. "I saw him change into a wolf before he bit Ironhand."

I swept my eyes around to find Thancmar. He shook his head in disbelief.

"Is it true?" Haimo blurted. "Do your gods make you a wolf when you are angry?"

I barked a derisive laugh. "Do you see one now?" I said, and strode out.

52: DREAMS AND RUMORS

"The Germans got cursed and spat on?" Cleon said. "What did they expect? Folk in Carnuntum must have thought they'd come to scout for an invasion."

We stood in the shadow of the *halla*, relieved to be out of its fug of sweat and ale. "They think I can persuade the governor not to retaliate," I told him.

He frowned. "No telling what trap the Silver Sheep has laid for you. I reckon it's better to stay out of reach."

"They say Lamia isn't there. Gone back to Hispania, I hope." In fear of my threats.

"Aye, now that he's thrown a torch into the tenement!"

I understood now the fear and anger with which the crowd of women had met me. But here in the stronghold, silence replaced shouting. Slaves and children fetching water and unloading packhorses edged away. Eyes fastened upon us: awed, suspicious, sullen, uneasy. Except for the voices still booming in the feast hall, punctuated with shouts and table-banging, a spell of mute animosity seemed to have fallen on everyone.

Clamping his stave under one arm, Cleon scratched his scalp beneath the wet curls. "What was it you said at the end?"

I told him the "wolf" story—distractedly, for I had just sighted Aurima under the tree where I had spoken with her grandmother. She sat on the grass twirling a spray of leaves above Beran, who tried to grab them. He chortled happily.

"A wolf man!" Cleon grinned. "I'll tell them I've seen the fur and the fangs."

"No, thanks." I could not take my eyes from my wife crooning to the baby.

"Look, I traded a pair of boots for some new ale. To help you sleep tonight."

I did not want to know where the boots came from. "Fine. Just leave me here."

"Later, then." He smirked and ambled away, swinging his cudgel. "'Wolf.'"

As I walked around the tree, I discovered a woman nursing another baby on the bench near Aurima. Beside them sat a strange man with a crutch propped by his knee.

Not so strange after all. He was Aurima's wounded brother.

315

Friduric was no longer the handsome young giant he had once been. His face was marred by a red gash torn in one side of his mouth. One hand lacked two fingers, and the other three were bent into talons. Puckered scars the size of a wolf's jaws spread over his other wrist and forearm. Since he wore a tunic and breeches, I could not see what further damage Tig had done, though the crutch was hint enough.

Aurima rose with Beran against her shoulder, her expression warm with welcome. Being Aurima, she did not say, *Where have you been?* or *I was worried about you*, but only "Husband, here is Friduric."

I half expected him to abuse me, but he merely studied me with his golden-lashed eyes, so like his sister's. For her sake I tried to swallow my rancor, but I could hardly tell him I was pleased to see him again, or condole on his father's death.

"And see who else has come: Helle, his wife! I have told you of her."

A familiar young woman with yellow braids looked up from her baby, and a rosy bloom mounted her throat into her cheeks. She glanced at Friduric from the corners of her eyes. I was not to let him know that she had smuggled drink to me once, when I was thirsty enough to lick dirt.

"The Goddess's greetings," I said to her, as if we had never met. "I hope you and your child are well."

A relieved smile lit up Helle's round face and blue eyes. "Austro has blessed us both with good health." Beaming, she picked up her infant, even tinier and redder than Beran had been, and held it up to be admired.

"What a little sweetling." Aurima simpered at the homely newborn, as women do.

Friduric's misshapen mouth stretched in a grimace. "Only a girl."

"'Only a girl'?" his sister mocked. "Born in a bird's nest, were you?"

He flushed. I remembered Ingiomar saying that his son would sire no more children. No boys, then, for this haughty warrior.

"I am naming her Ammisia," he said, the words distorted by the notch in his lower lip. "For our mother." He touched Helle's shoulder. "Come, wife; *Amma* wishes to see the baby."

"Wait, Fridi." Aurima held Beran toward him. "Take him, just for a moment. No, lay him on your arm. There, see? Is this not a treasure to be protected, a child so small? That is how you are going to feel about your daughter."

Beran wailed in his uncle's grasp. "Take him back," Friduric said brusquely.

I interrupted, "My heart, I am tired and hungry." The ordeal in the feast hall had been grueling. And I disliked seeing him cradle my son, no doubt as much as he disliked holding the child of a man who had corrupted his sister, maimed him, and slain his father.

Aurima plucked the baby from her brother's arms. "Eat with us tonight. Helle and I have much to tell each other."

Friduric said, "Not tonight," and the glow faded from Helle's face. "I must join the warriors' assembly." He nodded toward the *halla*.

"Try to talk sense into those shouting for war," I said.

"What do you know of it?" He wiped spittle from the corner of his torn mouth.

I shrugged. "That they are probably going to drink and talk until the Council of Women meets." I glanced wryly at Helle. "I hope you are on my side."

Friduric stiffened like a drawn bow. This innocent request must have reminded him of the lewd boasts I had invented.

Aurima explained to her brother, "In Rome one must have friends at a trial, especially powerful men, and many *clientes*. You remember what our teacher said: *clientes* are like companions owing help to one person or one family." She turned to me. "But here, we women decide what is best for all." The lift of her chin encompassed the stronghold and the forests outside it.

I was unconvinced. "Not just for the Marcomanni and Quadi, but for a Roman?"

"For all," she repeated, but the emphasis was lost when Friduric spoke over her.

"Even for you," he said. If his lips had been able to curl, he would have snarled it.

Helle said hastily, "We must meet later, Riemy." Cradling their newborn, she followed her husband as he limped off.

As we walked toward the gates, I asked Aurima, "What is a *vikkan*?"

"It is a ... dangerous thing. Do you know what *zoubar* means?"

I nodded. *Magic.*

"What you named, it is a magic creature. An animal that becomes a man, or a man that becomes an animal. You call it *monstrum* in Latin, I think?"

I did not feel like laughing now. "Am I a monster for having killed your father?"

Hearing the bitterness, she looked at me. "No. You were the hand of Tiwaz."

I kept quiet. Beran peeped wide-eyed at me from the sling on his mother's back.

The palisade's shadow was a long black bar across our path. My bare arms tingled in the chill as we traversed it. Summer was ending. Before long, there would be snow in the Alpine passes.

Outside the overlapping gates, the mob of screaming maenads had transformed into innocuous clusters of mothers and grandmothers tending cooking fires. They scowled but did not trouble us. Shrieking children dashed around the meadow, waving sticks while dogs yapped at their heels. One lad rapped a smaller boy on the arm, yelling, "You are dead, Roman!"

The victim screamed and fell dramatically.

Romans and barbarians. The old game, never ending.

A fire-eating juggler who had set up by the gate ramp was packing away his torches for the night. The gathering had also attracted a tinker with a cart of hardware and pots, a dealer in rags and scraps, and a horse trader with a pen of ponies. My trial had become the occasion for a country fair.

Aurima went on, "There is talk that once we return to Carnuntum, you will demand revenge on my people."

"You know I will not."

"Tell me, then, that the legions are not coming against us."

"My *vulthu* is not as great as you and Maelo think. The governor will decide on reprisals, not me."

She stepped over horse dung. "Did you know our men chose Maelo as *fraujaz*?"

No wonder he had been so vociferous in the *halla*. "Maelo and Vannaz both knew of your father's hatred," I said. "Now they must deal with what he did."

Dogs barked as a new caravan splashed through the river at the ford: two horse-drawn carts carrying several women, an escort of mounted warriors, a scatter of children, a tethered cow and calf. Here to see judgment pronounced on me.

I went on, "Once the council meeting is finished, I have thought of taking Rufus home to Thracia. Would you like that?"

"Rufus wants to marry a girl of Hoheneih," Aurima said—smugly, I thought.

"He's much too young!" Probably only fifteen. Sixteen, perhaps.

"He is a good hunter. And has proved himself as a fighter." She kept her eyes on her footing. "It is too soon for him to take a wife, but they are promised to each other."

I had to swallow my indignation. He did not need permission from me; I had told him he owed me nothing. "Will he stay here, then? Not come with us?"

Instead of answering, she looked across the meadow at scythe-horned cattle being rounded up for milking. "Do you no longer believe your *Pax Romana* is important, or the many people who are going to die if there is war? Mothers? Children?"

"Of course they are important. But you and Beran matter more to me."

"So," she said, sounding very German. She blinked fiercely, eyes bright. "You asked me once if I could desire a man who breaks his sacred oath."

My jaw loosened in shock. "What do you mean by that?"

She turned away so I could not see her expression.

"Do you think me a coward for wanting to keep you safe?" But I was talking to the air.

In a dark mood I plodded through the grass after her. Smoke from Ingiomar's pyre draggled upward on the far side of the river, ghostly pale against the trees beyond.

Perdition, I was sick of pyres.

My roan stallion and the donkey grazed placidly. They had cropped great swatches around their tethers, and were fattening up like jarred dormice. I saw Boss hobbled at a distance with some ponies, far enough from Spider to avert any quarrels. Our saddlebags, the amphorae, the cask with Ollius's ashes: all safe. Once we were allowed to depart, it would take less than an hour to pack up.

Rufus's feelings for the girl might be only puppy love. Perhaps I could change his mind. He could even bring the girl, if she wished, to help Aurima with Beran.

Dio and Cleon, sitting cross-legged outside our slanted shelter, saluted my arrival with sloshing cups. Clearly they had started on the new ale without me. I forced a cheerful smile. "Well, my lads, one more day and we should be on our way out of here."

I glanced at Aurima, who had knelt to unwrap a dirty clout from between Beran's small fat legs. If she responded to my joviality about leaving, it was hard to tell.

Cleon filled another wooden cup from his keg and handed it to me. Dio lifted his flushed face. Seldom did he drink more than a few swallows of ale, but he seemed to be breaking that habit this evening. "I saw the women swarm you," he said. "*Roma Dea*—and I thought it was the men who were dangerous!"

Cleon fished a fly out of his ale cup. "You should've been in the beer hall, old cock." He belched. "Watching them roar, '*Krig! Krig!*' and wave their knives around."

Aurima frowned at him. "Don't worry," he assured her. "Our Wolf stood up to 'em. Didn't turn a hair." He cackled at his own joke.

Dio looked into his cup. "One more day . . ."

"One more day!" Cleon lifted his own cup in a toast. They swilled ale together.

I drank too, but the taste nauseated me. I put down the cup and tried to catch Aurima's eye. The talk of war had set me on edge; I wanted to draw her under our lean-to and hold her and Beran safe in my arms, imagining a life without belligerent Germans or treacherous Praetorians.

The baby giggled as Aurima stroked ointment over his bottom and tiny phallus. "Messy little goose," she teased, tickling his belly.

Two girls from Haimo's household brought us a bowl of stew and coals in a firepot. As we gathered hungrily around the meat and beans, I realized that Aurima had pinned on her cloak. She stooped down beside me, cradling Beran in his sling. "Husband, all of us who serve Austro must prepare before she appears in the morning. So we are going to be together tonight."

I reared back, startled. "May the gods give you good sleep," she said, and kissed my cheek. "*Ana morgan.*"

I caught her arm, preventing her from rising. *Until tomorrow* was no way to part. "Aurima, wait. Stay with me."

"Do you not understand? I am going to ask her to smile on you in the new day."

"*Frijdila,* I long for you." My eyes were hot with need.

She weighed the possibility of staying, or I thought she did. Then she shook her head. "I must be there with *Amma* and the others. It is necessary."

I watched her stride long-skirted across the meadow with the baby clasped tightly to her cloaked breast. The lowering sun struck sparks in her coppery hair, fluttering like flames about her head and shoulders.

"Wish I could see the Roman Games," Cleon was saying. "Ollius and I had a bet on a *mirmillo* from Apollonia." He leaned over and tapped the cask that held Ollius's ashes. "If that fat Apollonian bugger wins, old friend, I'll buy you a drink when we bury you."

He and Dio began to talk as they ate, reminiscing about people and places in Rome: friends, gladiators, poets, booksellers, bathhouses, wineshops, harlots. And about those who were gone: my brother, my old tutor Phormio, Ollius, my father.

I rose and paced around in the twilight, making sure none of the other journeyers had moved too close, cosseting Spider with a handful of beans, testing the donkey's tether. Was Aurima even now discussing how to guide the council's ruling with her grandmother Hroswitha, the ruthless old sow Gisila, and other priestesses I did not know?

I could not dismiss a growing unease. Yet what reason had I to dread the morrow? Aurima thought I need not fear a sentence of personal combat. I was willing to pay a fine in silver, even though I had not killed wantonly. If the council's judgment was truly fair, we too would receive payment for our suffering; but that seemed implausible.

Perhaps I feared this night without her. My father surely had never yearned for my mother when battered by malevolence or ill fortune. He would have gone off alone, as he had done among the bones of Varus's massacred legions, cursed or wept, and emerged with iron resolve to see the matter through.

Very well, curse or weep later. In the meantime, concentrate on the likelihood that by this time tomorrow, we would be free to leave the Mark.

Which reminded me that I needed to talk with Rufus. Was he off courting, or had he joined the warriors in the *halla*?

I returned to our campfire in time to hear Dio sigh, "How I wish we were home." Reaching for his cup, he knocked it over. A rill of ale snaked into the firepit and sizzled in the embers.

I picked up my cloak and wrapped it around myself, for the day's heat was fading. "Get some sleep, both of you. I am going to check on Boss."

Rufus leaned on his elbow beside a small fire. With a tasseled stem of grass, he was tickling the bare arm of a girl who sat talking with Thancmar.

Tig was first to notice me; she leaped up from under the dwarf's hand, growling. Boss and Thancmar's pony jerked at their tethers in alarm, and I stopped short. "No, Tig," Thancmar called to the wolf. "It is Aquilo."

Cautiously I took the last dozen paces to my sorrel stallion. I talked to him, scratched his withers, and let him smell me all over, until finally his hide stopped twitching and his ears relaxed.

Rufus had scrambled up. "Come here," I said, more brusquely than I had intended. To make amends I nodded politely to Thancmar, who was hugging Tig under his arm, and the girl, who was rising to her feet. Tall and sturdy with flaxen hair, she gazed at me in curiosity tinged with suspicion.

When Rufus reached me, I asked him what her name was. He shook his long red-gold hair away from his face. "Bal'ha."

Baltha: "brave." A good name. "Are you bedding her?"

His eyebrows drew together. "No," he said, affronted.

Germanic girls were usually chaste, but I had not been sure about him. "And you are promised to each other? You want to marry her?"

Rufus's nod was meditative. He tapped the "R" that shone silver on my left wrist and looked a question at me.

"Not to Rome. But yes, we are leaving the Mark."

He held up a fist, then a clutch of curled fingers: his signs for Cleon the fighter and Dio the writer. "Of course they are," I said. "I want you to come, too."

His face stilled, and I read on it what I was asking him: to return to a society that had made him a slave, had robbed him of speech, and would always consider him a barbarian.

"You have learned to read and write," I argued. "What use is that here? And when you are eighteen, I will free you."

He smiled and shrugged. He was free now.

My spirits sank. He was part of my past, a link to Caligula, to Phormio, to my father. I tried once more: "When you saved my life, I said you would always be part of my *familia*."

Rufus touched his heart. "*Immo*," he said, quite clearly. *Yes, indeed.*

Mist rose in a serpentine bulge along the river. Campfires twinkled all around like fallen stars, and the perfume of woodsmoke sweetened the rankness of dung and trodden grass.

A dog yapped as I crossed the meadow, and others took up the alarm. From Army fortress to metropolis to Germanic outpost, there were always dogs barking in the night.

Recognizing me, the gate guards were equally unwelcoming. I told them I was looking for Haimo, which I was not, and obeyed the demand to surrender my sword.

The warriors' assembly had ended. Muffled in my cloak, I threaded past men stumbling into each other, bellowing raucous war chants, banging swords and shields in mock combat, crawling into or under wagons to sleep, snoring in a heap at the base of walls. Noble warriors, appointed by their tribes to decide on peace or war. The variety of their behavior confirmed that no decision had been reached.

Guessing that the most esteemed guests would have been given the home of the *fraujaz*, I sauntered to the longhouse I had been told was Haimo's. Light peeped through seams and cracks. Women were talking inside, but I could not distinguish voices.

Not wishing to be caught lurking by the closed doors, I ambled on. Picked up a flat stone, tossed it away. Bent over a scrap of wood: too rough. Crouched by a smashed pottery bowl and separated the pieces.

Moments later I tapped quietly on a door of the longhouse. The voices stilled.

"Who is it?" asked a girl's voice.

I hoped I had found the right place. "A friend of the Goddess."

Whispers within.

"What do you want?"

"Is Aurima here, the daughter of Ammisia?"

More whispers.

A grudging reply: "And if she is?" With so many drunken men roaming around from different tribes, they would not call her to the door for a stranger.

"Give her this."

The inner bar lifted. A spear of light fell across my feet. I saw a suspicious eye, then an extended hand.

"What is this?"

"Just give it to her," I said. The door shut; the bar dropped into its brackets.

I waited. A stray dog paused, snuffled at the threshold, and went on its way.

"What are you doing here?" a voice hissed in Latin.

I put my nose to the chink between the double doors. "Come outside."

"I told you, we cannot meet until morning!"

"Did you read what I wrote?"

"I love you too, husband, but—"

"I will lie down here in front of the doors until you come out."

She drew in her breath harshly. Finally she whispered, "Wait at the back. And keep quiet."

I walked around the house. Moonshine warned me of a sawbuck adrift in chips, a scatter of cow dung, a heap of rubbish. Startled birds flew off the thatched roof in a noisy flapping of wings.

The hill fell away at the other end of the house, so the back door was reached by steps up to a narrow platform. A basket outside the door held someone's unremembered shawl.

Perching on the top step, I looked over the serried tips of the palisade to the mist-marbled field. From here Berinhard and his brother Chlothar might have watched my small troop set up under the chestnut tree, gloating over their plan to entrap and murder the self-important young tribune who headed it.

The night grew quieter and colder. Fragments of disquiet roiled through my head. Segomo Graybeard's warning: *Rome's legions are going to cut down the Marcomanni like trees.* Aurima's demand: *Do you not believe your Pax Romana is important?* And Thancmar's confused query: *How do I know the gods' will?*

I moved back to lean against the house wall, sheltered by a roof overhang. From the silence within, they might all have gone to bed. But sleep did not weigh upon me, and I was sure Aurima would come.

When a soft thump and creak finally heralded the back door opening, my heart leaped. I pushed myself to my feet, stiffened by the chilly vigil, as she slipped through a narrow gap and drew the portal shut behind her.

"Hush," she whispered.

I brushed my lips against her jaw and found her mouth, mindful of the warm lump of Beran in his sling.

Aurima pulled back. "What is it you want?" she said, the words barely distinct.

I kicked the basket aside and slid down again, cradling her in my lap. "This," I said, dragging my cloak around the three of us.

"You are an animal," she scolded. But she did not resist.

"Didn't you hear? I am a wolf." I gnawed a mouthful of her hair, growling softly.

She gave a little chirp of a giggle.

I sighed and leaned my cheek on the crown of her head, breathing the scent of the flowers and herbs she washed her hair with.

She wriggled comfortably. As we curled into each other with the baby between us, the warm zephyr of her breath pulsed against my throat. The shards of worry dissolved. Peace settled on me, as soft as silk.

Beran squirmed and mewed. "Hungry, little bear?" Aurima murmured, fishing him out of her sling. "Mama aches to feed you."

Her exhalation of relief and the infant's eager suckling roused me from my contentment. "Are you c—" I began. But as I looked at my wife and son, something swelled so intensely within me that it stopped my voice and my breath. Violent and overpowering, it happened again. And a third time.

They were mine, these treasures. I would die to keep them safe.

When I could breathe, I rasped, "Are you cold?"

"Ach! Not so fierce, Beran." Aurima broke the seal of the baby's lips with her finger. As he resumed sucking, she guided my hand under the hot swell of her breast so that I felt the rhythms of both mother and child. Its effect was magic—more intoxicating, indeed, than when Hroswitha had bewitched my mutilated fingers.

"My husband," she said softly, "I ask your pardon for what I said about oath-breaking. I was not thinking about Lamia. If you go to Carnuntum, he can make trouble for you. For us."

"I think I frightened him enough to keep him quiet."

"But if he calls you a murderer, who is going to listen to you?"

I would not admit my fear of being clapped into a barred carriage and sent to trial in Rome for Glabrio's murder. "Before we cross the river, I will send Dio and Cleon ahead to see how the wind blows," I promised.

Aurima pried the nursling free and transferred him to her other breast. "Anyway, I have told my sisters that . . . that Caesar is angry with you and your family, and will not listen to your counsel about peace."

"Well done, my love. But in truth, I do not believe your people will be punished for your father's madness."

"Is it madness when a man cannot forgive?"

"Sometimes," I said. Then I thought of myself. And my own father.

The meadow was smothered in mist now, tents and wagons hidden as if beneath a thick fall of snow. But here on the islanded hilltop, the moon still glowed in the night sky.

"Marcus," she whispered. Not "husband," this time. "Will we ever return?"

"Yes, someday we will return," I said recklessly. "Shall I make a vow for you? I have another wrist."

Aurima smiled. "There is no need." She detached the drowsy baby from her nipple and laid him in my hand.

I cradled my son's small warm body against my chest. He clamped one fist on the neck of my tunic, the other on my torc, and drooled back to sleep.

"I think we should live in southern Gaul," I said. "By the sea."

"The sea!" Sailing across the Adriatic, out of sight of land, had unnerved her.

"A warm and pleasant sea. I will teach you to swim. We will be fish together."

"How— How far away is Gaul? As far as Aquileia?"

"A little farther," I said evasively.

"Do they speak Gaulish? Will I understand them?"

"I am sure people speak Latin, my love. It has been a province for many years."

"Is Austro known there?"

"I cannot say. But we would not be among strangers. Nina lives there, and her husband has a large farm, a *latifundium*, where they grow grapes and olives and flowers."

"Flowers? Why?"

"For garlands. And, uh, perfume. Things like that. And they make wine." Inspiration struck me. "You shall have a cat."

"Are there many trees?"

"I have not been there, *carissima*. It cannot be just like here, if they grow grapes."

She cleared her throat in a small husky rasp. "How will it be for Beran?"

"I will teach him to ride when he is old enough." I caressed her cheek. "He will hunt rabbits in the hills and bring them home for dinner. Swimming in the sea will make him strong. He will learn Latin and Germanic and Gaulish. And maybe Greek, if his father does not forget how to speak it." I twisted a curl around my finger and tugged gently on it. "And girls will fight each other for his favor."

After a moment she turned her head aside. "Because of me you have endured so much."

"Not because of you, *carissima mea*. For you." I hooked the basket with a foot and settled Beran on the rumpled shawl within it.

Disturbingly loud, a man's voice one or two houses away bellowed, "Death to them all!"

I folded my hands around Aurima's cold fingers. Softly, perhaps shyly, she whispered, "I am sorry I said how hard it was to wait for you." She met my eyes. "You have never complained about how hard it was to come for me."

"I love you," I murmured, sliding a hand under her skirts to her thigh. *Te amo.* Scratched on the fragment of bowl I had sent in to her.

Higher.

She gasped. "Hush ... the baby ..."

"Don't worry," I said, raising myself above her. "I reckon he already knows."

Before me was a faded mural of Hercules clubbing a fire-breathing giant. I had fallen asleep in my brother's small bedroom.

I was at home. I closed my eyes again.

There was a sound. Heavy breathing. Hercules stepped off the wall, club in hand.

Not Hercules. A trousered man with a long braided beard as pale as winter sun. Below one knee he had a horse's foreleg.

Impossible. I was at home. I was safe here.

He lurched toward me, limping on the pale hoof. *Jerk-clunk, jerk-clunk.*

I hauled myself up in bed, scrabbling desperately for something to throw.

Clunk, jerk-clunk. With every step the room elongated. Still he advanced, huffing like a fire bellows with every uneven stride.

I crabbed backward, voiceless with terror. With a fanged grin he lifted his sword.

Not a sword. A pole with a sharpened end.

My back hit the wall. I screamed.

The room swelled with other screams, as shrill as Furies'. In heightened panic I thrashed to escape jaws that seized and shook me. Then it all fell away and I was tumbling down, down to the underworld ...

"Marcus, come back!" Aurima shrieked.

Thus ended the stealthy tryst with my beloved. Chirping women in disheveled sleeping tunics helped me right myself from a headfirst sprawl down the steps. Babies and small children howled in fright inside the house. Gisila, a thundercloud presence by the door, demanded to know what had happened.

My throat was so dry I could not speak. Hroswitha fetched me a drink while Aurima stammered an excuse: while waiting on the steps to greet her at daybreak, I had been attacked by an evil tree-spirit.

The eyes surrounding me said they knew why I had been attacked. Humiliated, I tried to retreat before the entire settlement awoke. No, I had no broken bones. No, Aurima must stay with her sisters. No, I did not need help to find our campsite. No, no, no, until I was out of sight and sound at last and plunged into the mist, shaky with fright.

53: THE PRICE OF A LIFE

I was to be judged not once, but twice. So I discovered the next day outside the *halla*, where Chlothar's son Ivo was whispering to a bone-thin woman who clutched the hand of a child just old enough to walk. Ivo glared at me. So did the woman, likely his mother.

I had woken to bright sunlight lancing through a rip in the lean-to, my mind still adrift. "Aurima told us not to wake you," Dio said, holding out a cup. He squinted, pain lines radiating around his eyebrows. Last evening's drink had evidently given him an infernal headache.

Cleon had aimed his thumb at a girl who stood close by, hands clasped together. Blinking nervously, she said, "Lady Aurima wishes for you at the *halla*. Come with me."

I climbed to my feet, took the cup, and sucked ale down my parched throat in a couple of gulps. The sun hung half a handspan west of midday. Around us lay deserted tents and lifeless campsites. No customers beset the vendors or entertainers, and the horse pen was nearly empty. The only signs of life were crop-haired servants tending a score of big carcasses spitted over smoky fires. The feast to follow roasting the Roman.

The men had gone hunting to let the women palaver in peace, Cleon said. Somehow I had missed all the clamor, the barking and earthshaking hoofbeats. Had I been given another sleeping draught, to have stayed dead to the world for so long?

"You should have woken me up," I muttered, looking around for my sword. Rattled by the terrible nightmare, I had forgotten to retrieve it from the gate guards. "Am I late for the council?"

The girl fled when I peeled off my stained and dirty tunic. Dio handed me the one he had ferreted out in our vexillation's camp, newly washed and mended for this occasion. "You missed the opening ceremonies."

"A lot of singing," Cleon said. "The king's mother cracked an egg, and doves flew from it." He rolled his eyes upward and waggled his head in a parody of awe.

"Charming salute to a deity," Dio muttered. "From the same people who would butcher a man as a sacrifice."

He agreed to stay with our little camp. Although none of our possessions had been bothered so far, some of the natives might be unhappy with the council's judgment. "If there is trouble," I told him, "give them anything they want. The money. Even the horses. Don't risk your life, do you understand?"

Dio mimed shock. "'Even the horses'?"

"As a last resort," I clarified. Cleon popped him solemnly on the shoulder.

Riding back from the river the day before, I had carefully devised a speech in my defense. Yet as I walked across the meadow with my guard, the unease returned. Just a tiny doubt, really, like a speck of granite between heel and sandal. I reminded myself that there was nothing to fear. The Council of Women would not forbid us to leave. If anything, they would be glad to rid the Mark of a Roman haunted by a dead man's ghost.

Had they been a male jury, I would have been more confident. But expecting women to act like men was a mistake. Aurima had boldly exposed herself to degradation and death to sully the honor of Rome. My sister Nina had risked divorce and exile to voice notions that women are not supposed to speak. Even my mother, in public a loyal and dutiful matron, had for years nursed rage as searing as the heart of a volcano.

Savory smoke from the roasting pits drifted past us at the foot of the gateway ramp. Except for a few elderly women and men, young girls looking after small children and animals, the entire settlement was as empty as if a great wave had washed through it. As we passed through the stockade, the scuff of running footsteps had made me turn: Rufus was joining us.

So I thought myself prepared for anything when I came upon Aurima by the closed doors of the *halla*, the sling under her breasts heavy with a torpid baby. Friduric leaned on his crutch beside her, his hair straggly with sweat. Helle gave me a tired smile from a bench where she cuddled her newborn. And Ivo and his mother glared.

I ignored their hostility. Chlothar's treachery and my act of vengeance had left nothing combustible in me, neither anger nor pity. "What is happening?" I asked Aurima.

As if in answer, voices chorused within the hall in an uneven declaration that might have been "*Ja.*"

Aurima plucked leaf fragments out of my hair. "They are deciding," she said.

The doors were thrust open from inside. Women straggled out, chattering to each other. They fell silent as they caught sight of us.

"Is it finished?"

She shook her head. "Just a rest. Then they say what they have decided." She shifted from one foot to the other. Wisps of coppery hair stuck to the curve of her jaw.

"Why do you not sit with Helle, *frijdila*?" I said softly. "The sun is hot."

Friduric spoke for the first time: "For a powerful Roman, you have few companions." His disdainful glower touched on Cleon and lingered on Rufus, who sat on his heels with a spear across his knees. "And one of them has two faces."

Rufus uncoiled like a hooded snake. I said, "I trust these men with my life."

Friduric grunted. He seemed in greater need of a seat than his wife. His knuckles shone white on the crutch's hand grip, and above the yellow beard his cheeks were ashen. Although I had vowed to make him pay for his brutal efforts to keep me from Aurima, I wished I could have killed him cleanly. Only after my failure had the wolf attacked him.

For distraction I said, "The gifts I gave your father—the arm-rings and silver cups and all the rest. Where are they now?"

He looked at his sister. "I heard you wrapped him in the white bear-skin, to give him a noble arrival to the feast of Wodunaz."

Aurima's mouth tightened. She did not speak.

More women emerged from the *halla*: young, old, slim, stout, lithe, stiff-jointed. The king's mother glided toward us like a rain cloud in her dingy white garments. She murmured to Aurima, then moved off.

"What did she say?" I demanded.

"When you are summoned with Ivo and his mother, bring no companions."

"But you can come with me, yes?"

"No. The matter is between you and Chlothar's family."

I frowned; I had counted on her. Aurima said gently, "It is our way, husband."

The women who had left the hall were everywhere, nattering in clusters, tucking infants into fresh wrappings, reuniting with older children, as if they had no care for the sinking sun. Some paused to dip a cup into the apprentices' buckets of milk. Most went some distance away, lifted their skirts, and squatted. At this rate judgment would not be delivered until tomorrow, when I wanted to be packed and gone.

I turned to tell Cleon and Rufus that they must remain outside. "And you cannot wear a weapon," Aurima added. I had been thoughtlessly stroking the finger grooves in my knife's bone grip.

A monstrous flat metallic *crack* rent the air, as dead and doomful as a split in the circle of the heavens. Heads jerked up; conversations broke off.

Hroswitha hauled back a battered bronze sword and for the second time whacked an old shield hanging by the door. "Come, sisters," she called. "Austro cannot wait, and your men are returning soon from the hunt."

Women trudged back into the hall. Not with eagerness, I thought. Perhaps if I offered right now to pay Chlothar's widow whatever she wanted, I would not have to enter this ill-omened place?

"*Svert*," Ivo's tiny brother cried, pointing to the sword Hroswitha had propped beneath the shield. "*Ek svert!*"

His mother bent and whispered sternly. "Me sword!" the tot insisted, pulling on her arm. The mother glanced up at me in mixed vexation and anger, as if I were at fault for witnessing this misbehavior.

"*Svert, Mamaaa . . .*" The protest rose into a howl.

Ivo's face reddened. "Shut up, little pig," he hissed.

The small one yelled louder. Despite the gravity of the occasion, I was amused to see the fierce avenger plagued with an unmanageable sibling.

My smile was no more than a flicker, but Ivo launched himself at me, knife in hand, like a gull attacking an eagle. Or a sitting duck, more aptly, for I was caught off guard and slow to move.

Cleon barged past, knocking me sideways. "Whoa there!" His hand reached out as I toppled. By the time I rolled onto my feet again, he had seized the boy in a bear hug. The fallen knife skittered across to my boot.

Ivo's mother was screaming as loudly now as both of her sons. So were Aurima and Helle. The babies began to wail.

Another sky-shattering *crack* struck everyone mute, except the shrilling infants.

Hroswitha lowered the heavy sword. Cleon released Ivo, putting his foot on the boy's knife. I looked at Aurima, who met my eyes silently. No one spoke.

The old priestess said, "Is anyone hurt?"

No one replied.

"Emma. Come inside with your boys."

Ivo glared down at his knife until Cleon casually moved aside. The boy picked it up, and after a sullen moment surrendered it to the maiden at the door. His mother hoisted the goggle-eyed toddler onto her hip, where he clung with a thumb in his mouth. All three followed Hroswitha into the feast hall.

Cleon grinned as I went past. "Good luck, Wolf," he said. "We'll be waiting."

Standing an arm's length from sulky Ivo, I heard him and his mother swear by the Three Gods to be bound by the council's decision.

The place still stank of ale and piss, but the tables had been put away. We who were parties in this matter stood next to a fire ring, beneath a ragged circle of blue showing through a sooty smokehole. I noticed shields and spears hanging from the rafters beside massive antler racks and sickle-sharp boar tusks, details unheeded in the turmoil of the warriors' assembly. Justice would be served beneath a dozen ways to skewer a foe.

Finally I contemplated the jury: perhaps threescore women, from wrinkled grandams to bright-eyed maidens. The eldest sat in front; the youngest stood behind. Hroswitha completed the left end of the arc; Gisila, the right.

The king's mother overflowed the bench she sat on. Dull light from the doorway picked out the gold beads on her shoes. In her toothless slur she said, "Aquilo of Rome, can you understand me?"

"Yes, if you speak slowly."

"You must swear by light-bringing Austro, life-giving Nerthuz, and justice-loving Tiwaz that you agree to be bound by our judgment."

Although I had weighed this since the boy and his mother had made their vows, I was still undecided on my response. I was here out of courtesy to my wife's beliefs. Germanic ideas of justice could not bind me, a Roman. If I truly wished to bind myself, I would swear by the spirits of my own ancestors instead of her gods.

In honesty I should confess this to the king's mother. But how much longer would that prolong this ordeal? Hours? Days?

"Aquilo?" prompted Hroswitha from the other end of the arc.

I spat into my right palm as I had seen the others do. "I swear by Austro"—raising my hand to the circle of daylight—"by Nerthuz"—stamping my right foot on the earthen floor—"and by Tiwaz"—touching my fist to my heart—"to be bound by this council's judgment."

"I understand Latin now!" croaked an old woman, as seamed as a walnut meat.

"Magic." Her neighbor brandished crossed fingers to block my sorcery.

"He is speaking our tongue, aunties," a plump girl at the back told them.

Hroswitha rose, dark robes rippling, and raised her staff to the sky beyond the smokehole. After a dozen heartbeats she grounded the staff and faced Ivo and his mother. "Emma, widow of Chlothar of the Quadi; Ivo, son of Chlothar: you ask this council to decide if Aquilo the Roman owes you *wergelt* for the death of Chlothar."

She bent toward me, her eyes hawkish and fierce. For an instant I feared she would rip out of me the truth that I had sworn by gods I did not believe in. "Aquilo of Rome, you are accused by Chlothar's son Ivo of causing his father's death. Is it true?"

"It is true," I said, "but—"

"We know the reasons. It was wrong to take revenge instead of asking the king for justice."

"I was hunted by Ing— by Ironhand. I had no time for the king's justice."

"That does not matter," Aurima's grandmother said implacably.

I glared. Had she not known me as a wretched, starving fugitive from Ingiomar?

"Since then Emma and her children have no hunter, no protector," she went on. "Therefore, the council says you owe forty cows to his family and twenty to the king."

What was the cost of a cow? German cattle were scrawny and small, but say it was twenty silver denarii a head. Sixty cows would come to well over a thousand denarii. A thousand, to pay for slaying a man who had killed Ollius and nearly killed me! "I am not sure I heard you correctly," I said.

Yes, sixty cows. "Or," she added, "the king agrees to take two good horses for his share."

Of course he would. He knew I had two good horses.

"Emma, do you accept forty cows to pay for your man's death?" Hros-witha asked.

"It is not enough," Ivo burst out. "The Roman killed him by treachery!" He scowled at the council members. "Father had no time to draw his knife. So I must live knowing he does not feast with the gods!"

That cursed notion again. A diffuse mutter greeted his outcry.

"Ivo."

He whirled. Gisila had floated to her feet opposite Hroswitha. "Another Roman gave Berinhard and his brother, your father, fifty silver coins to kill Aquilo."

The boy's mouth fell open. Gisila continued, "So you must consider that your family already has received five and twenty pieces of silver."

Emma set her free hand on Ivo's shoulder. "We accept forty cows, honored ones."

"Aquilo, do you agree to pay Emma forty cows, and twenty more to the king?"

I watched a swallow that had flown in through the smokehole as it darted around the hall and perched on a rafter. "Honored ones," I said, letting my gaze travel along their ranks, "my life as a hunter and protector for my wife and son was worth five and twenty silver denarii to Chlothar. Is it not right for that to be the price of his life to me?"

54: JUDGMENT

"They thought a rich Roman would pay anything," I told Aurima. It would not be seemly to grin, but I was bursting with self-satisfaction. "Emma agreed to a hundred and fifty denarii. Let her buy as many cattle as she can."

After the council recessed, I had sent Cleon with instructions for Dio to extract payment from Lamia's hoard for Emma, plus fifty denarii more for the king. That added up to almost a year's pay for a legionary, although I did not say so.

Aurima frowned. "That is not much. You told me once that you paid ten hundreds for a horse."

"For Spider as a colt, yes. But I do not think I owe anything to a murderer's family." I saw disapproval in her eyes, but she said nothing more. Beran slept on her shoulder, his bottom cradled in her spread fingers.

Ivo's departing scowl was even more poisonous. In eight or ten years I would have a deadly enemy. However, I did not intend to be here to tempt him.

The lowering sun turned the trees a rusty gold as if it were already fall. There was still no sign of the hunting party. Hroswitha pushed past a couple of women trailing back into the hall. "Aurima, are you ready?"

"Yes, *Amma*." Aurima hoisted the baby more firmly against her shoulder.

"Friduric and Helewidis, it is time." Her thistledown hair glowed white in the shadow of the entrance.

Helle sighed to her feet, hugging her tiny infant. Pushing himself off the seat beside her, Friduric swayed, then recovered his balance against the wall. The four of us followed Hroswitha into the *halla*.

The arc of jurors showed gaps now. Tired women had abandoned the meeting, I reckoned, to prepare supper or retrieve children. Or did they not want to witness delivery of the judgment they had already reached?

Gisila again oversaw the oath-taking. Friduric was hoarse with pain and Helle's voice quivered with nerves, but Aurima gave her word without hesitation.

In the momentary silence that followed, the two old priestesses studied each other across the half circle. Was I, the defendant, supposed to state my case now? I stirred, about to open my mouth, but Aurima nudged me to be quiet.

Then hooves thudded. The stillness fractured into barking, whinnying, shouting, cries of welcome. From outside Maelo roared, "By the one eye of Wodunaz! Are they still yammering in there?" Guffaws.

A few of the women began to stir. The king's mother commanded, "Do not fail Austro after all our work." They settled again, unhappily.

Two blood-spattered hounds ran in. A man outside whistled and called for them, but a girl had to haul one dog out by the scruff of its neck before they were both gone.

Get this done, I wanted to shout. *Let it be over with!*

There was no advantage to losing my temper. I forced down the impatience, but could not withhold a huff of exasperation.

The noise had woken Helle's baby. The infant scrunched up its red face and yelled, fists churning like a washerwoman.

"She is hungry . . ." Helle faltered.

"Feed her, then." Gisila waved at an empty mat. When the child quieted, she resumed, "Friduric, son of Ammisia, may her spirit rest; and Aquilo of Rome: you ask the Council of Women to judge whether one of you, or both, owe *wergelt* to the other."

The hunters' nearby clamor almost overpowered her toothless mumble. When she added, "The decision was not easy," saliva in her mouth muddied the words.

"Ironhand, who now feasts with the gods, said that you, Aquilo"—and she spoke an unfamiliar word—"Aurima, and thus—"

I interrupted, "I do not know what that means."

"It means to spoil," Aurima murmured in Latin. "To ruin."

"I ruined you? No! No, that is not true."

"Quiet. You speak later." Gisila wiped her lips with an edge of her robe. "Thus you broke the agreement of peace made between the Marcomanni and Rome."

Which Ingiomar had necessitated in the first place with his ambush last year.

Gisila continued, "He said he saved you from being killed by Chlothar. Then you killed four of his warriors and fled. Others were injured, including Friduric." Her words became garbled again. She stopped and spat on the ground. "Sister, help me."

Hroswitha climbed slowly to her feet. Unable to keep quiet any longer, I burst out, "His hate for Romans caused everything. He could not believe I love his daughter. And he was not willing to forgive his wife's death, even though he accepted the gifts I gave him to pay Rome's debt."

"Do you bear guilt for the death of his wife?" Hroswitha asked dispassionately, as if her murdered daughter were no kin to her.

"Of course not. Six summers ago I was still a boy in my father's house in Rome."

"Yet it is because of you that the agreement of peace is broken."

I opened my mouth, then closed it. There was no denying that Ingiomar might have honored the treaty as long as Aurima remained a hostage.

"You admit it?"

"But I have not said how Friduric dragged me behind his horse until the skin came off my back, how Ingiomar enslaved me—"

The others gasped, and Hroswitha stopped me. I had uttered the dead man's name. Gisila called out to his spirit: it might resume fighting and feasting in the Hall of the Warriors, for it had been accidentally invoked, not summoned. I bit back my frustration.

"What you have said is known," Hroswitha resumed. "We have spoken to others."

Many of the council members looked stern. A woman was weeping, perhaps for someone who had died, or for my perfidy.

"Aquilo of Rome, Ironhand said also that you joined the prefect and his soldiers to fight our people. Many more were killed."

As if I had initiated Ingiomar's attacks! I shook my head angrily.

Hroswitha said, "He called on Tiwaz to aid us against Roman treachery. But for a long time we did not give the god the blood of an enemy, and Ironhand wished to show that we still honor him." She hammered the butt of her staff on the ground three times. "Since our people are not at war with Rome, it was not allowed for you to be sacrificed."

Did she mean that if the warriors' assembly voted for war, the sacrifice could be resumed? Surely not. Not if they were already concerned about Roman reprisals.

"Thus said Ironhand before he went to the gods. Do I speak truly?"

"What I said is also true," I insisted.

"Aurima, what say you?"

Aurima drew herself up with Beran in the crook of her arm. She met my eyes briefly, then looked away. Her eyelids were pink with unshed tears. "That is what my father told me."

In that instant the suspicions that Lamia had sowed burst into life all over again, like dragon's teeth sprouting into armies. Many a daughter would choose to uphold her father, particularly since his telling showed him in a better light than mine did.

Aurima went on, "But what my husband says, I know that to be true."

The dragon's teeth in my heart exploded like puffballs. I wanted to tell her, *Everything I have done, I did for love of you*, but Friduric's yell cut me off.

"No!" he shouted. "He— He—" He wiped spittle off his mustache. "He made the men of Grozhauga believe it was my father who ordered Chlothar's death, so they attacked us. Then he and that cursed runt Thancmar led us all into a Roman ambush on the road—"

A muscular woman with a coronet of mouse-brown hair rose to her feet. "Honored ones," she declared in a voice loud enough to silence Friduric, "some of the council wish to reconsider the judgment."

The two old priestesses turned to each other. Hroswitha tapped twice with the butt of her staff.

Gisila heaved herself up. "The council has already discussed its decision." She swiveled her head, dominating the others with her clouded glare. "The truth is important. But what is right for our people is more important."

From outside erupted a frenzy of snarling and snapping, wet gobbling growls, squealing and scuffling: the racket of hunting dogs fighting for offal. Friduric's face twitched with pain or memory, or both. Helle returned to his side, clasping her infant to her shoulder.

Gisila said above the dogs' noise, "A Roman has been injured here in our lands. An important man, the kinsman of Caesar. When Rome decides whether to seek revenge, he is going to be listened to."

"I do not want revenge," I protested.

The king's mother paid no heed. "There is anger among us, too. All agree that you caused deaths. Many still blame Rome for the murder of Ammisia, blessed of Austro."

"As I do." Friduric thumped his crutch on the ground.

"When peace is desired between proud families of two nations"—Gisila wet her lips—"there is an ancient way."

Helle drew in her breath audibly. Aurima tightened her arms around Beran.

"What is the matter?" I thought I had missed something the old priestess had said.

Hroswitha raised her staff to the sky, as if the amber tip might pull up the sinking sun. Gisila lifted her own staff with its circular green headpiece. "She has cast her light on the judgment of this council," they chanted together. "All praise to Austro."

"All praise to Austro," echoed the rest of the council.

Gisila announced, "It is the council's judgment that Aurima and Aquilo must take the daughter of Helewidis and Friduric with them into the Romelands."

"No!" Helle screamed.

"The son of Aurima and Aquilo must stay here with Helle and Friduric."

I was sure I had not understood correctly. I turned to Aurima.

Her freckles blazed like pox marks on her chalk-white cheeks. I knew then that I had heard aright, and I seemed to go outside myself as in a dream. Her lips formed my name, but I did not hear it.

"Riemy," Helle wailed.

"Helle." They flew together and clutched each other, keening. The squeezed infants began to cry, their screams overlapping the clamor of the fighting hounds.

"Children are given as hostages for peace," Gisila said. "We wish the Mark and Rome to be tied by a desire for peace and brotherhood."

She looked from me to Friduric. Neither of us uttered a word. His pale eyes were fixed on the baby in his wife's arms.

Within me someone was shouting with unbearable urgency, roaring curses and calling on Cleon and Dio and Rufus to run in with their weapons, to seize Aurima and my child and escape this madness.

Helle lifted her face, red with weeping. "Riemy. Stay here. Here with your son."

Aurima's cheeks were pale but dry. "Yes, then I am not parted from him ..."

Ice speared down through me. So cold did I feel that when I opened my mouth, vapor should have spewed from it. "Aurima," I said. "I am not going to stay in the Mark."

She was too dazed to grasp the choice at first. Then anguish kindled in her swollen eyes. *Surely you do not still mean that*, her gaze entreated.

I would not remain here. I could not. This vast and dangerous land was too hostile to me and to the vows I had made.

Weeping, she pressed Beran's cheek against hers. "I cannot leave him."

"We will not leave him," I said in a growl. "He will come with us."

We Romans are accustomed to fostering foreign leaders' heirs, partly to ensure their parents' good behavior and partly to indoctrinate them in our ways. But we do not trade them our own children.

Gisila might speak no Latin, but she understood my tone. She shuffled toward us, so bent-backed that her steely braids swung against her robe. "You are a wolf, Aquilo." She peered up at me. "Of course you want to guard your young."

My glare could not penetrate her opalescent eyes. "But it is more serious," she went on, her mumble so soft that no one else could hear over the babies' howls. "Many of the younger warriors already want to attack the Romelands. After so long a peace, they are greedy for glory. They itch to kill and burn, to capture women and horses. Most of all, to face the famous Roman Army." She wagged her head, jowls wobbling. "If you agree to give a hostage, Vannaz can perhaps calm them. If you refuse, they are going to think Rome plans to go to war."

"I do not know what Rome plans." My voice cracked.

Gisila sniffed. Turning, she murmured to Hroswitha, who had come up beside her.

I tried to speak more calmly. "I am not a king. Nor is Friduric. Our children cannot make a difference in preventing war."

Hroswitha caressed Beran's hair, then stroked the brow of Helle's baby. The two infants stopped crying. Calmly she said, "When two nations give hostages to each other, both have a reason to keep the peace."

"*Amma*, these are the grandchildren of your daughter," Aurima pleaded.

"*Frijdila*, we made this judgment because all of us want our children to live." Hroswitha tilted her staff toward the council members. "Gisila and I reminded them of the war against Rome when my brother was king—Marbodo, may he feast with the gods. When the Cherusci asked the Marcomanni to join them, my brother said no. The Romans took vengeance later on all those who fought. Entire tribes are gone now, their men dead, their women and children slaves in the Romelands."

"Rome's vengeance is reason enough to avoid war," I argued. "You do not need our son."

Friduric's eyes were on me. What did he think? Was he willing to trade the only child he would ever sire for the offspring of an enemy? I reckoned the council's decision would be law to him. He would not fight to keep her.

I interrupted a lament from Helle: "Did the king approve this? Did Maelo?"

Gisila's brows rose, then twisted in a frown.

Friduric explained scornfully, "Among the Romans, men decide such things."

"What foolishness," said the muscular woman. "Men only want war."

Gisila's clouded gaze had not left me. "You are thinking you can say yes and change your mind later."

I hoped I did not show that she had guessed right.

"When you agree before the gods to give a hostage but then take him away, it is oath-breaking. That does not please the gods. Or our people." She paused meaningfully. "Our warriors."

I repeated doggedly, "He cannot make a difference."

The features of her face seemed to wilt, eyes and nose and chin sagging toward a mouth that had lost its bite. She said, "But perhaps he can."

Perhaps he can. Perhaps the warriors' assembly would see an exchange of hostages as a sign of Rome's goodwill. Perhaps they would decide not to call for war. Perhaps townsfolk and farmers and half-civilized tribespeople on the Roman side of the Danube would not be slaughtered, and men of the Fifteenth Legion would not die in a battle line or under torture. Perhaps the northeastern frontier of the *Pax Romana* would remain intact—the Roman Peace, that perishable construct of law and order that enabled invention and enterprise and prosperity throughout the world . . .

My throat tightened. I tugged with an unsteady hand on my father's torc. He too must have thought, *Perhaps he can. Perhaps he can keep the Republic from falling apart.*

That "perhaps" had cost a life. This one cost only . . .

This one, like the other, cost love.

Beran looked up from the crook of Aurima's arm, his eyes bright and curious. I saw him as a small boy, barefoot and dirty, perched unsteadily on a scruffy pony; as a youth, long-haired and trousered, hunting and raiding cattle, growing his first whiskers; as a scarred, tattooed man with unshorn hair and beard, living in a thatched hut, illiterate and ignorant of the world . . .

"No," I said. I tried not to weep, but tears gathered on my eyelids and spilled onto my cheeks. I reached blindly for my son and nosed his small wet-hot, milky-sweet face. He wriggled away from the prickles of my beard.

Through a glaze of grief I met Aurima's wide imploring eyes. To her, as

Sherry Christie

to Friduric, the council's decision could not be questioned.

It was my choice. Surrender my child, or sanction war on the frontier.

Although there was no sound to mark it, I felt what I had always thought to be a poet's fancy: the cracking of a heart.

55: AS LONG AS THE SUN SHINES

Jerk-clunk. Jerk-clunk.

Mist rising from the river might have been carrying the sound, or perhaps I felt the vibration underfoot. My heart began to hammer, and I turned so quickly that Cleon grabbed to keep me from overbalancing.

Friduric limped toward us on his crutch. His striped trousers seemed borrowed from a shorter man, for a handspan of bare calf protruded above each bony ankle. An intricate tattoo swirled across his bare chest. Most noticeable in the firelight was his gold: a torc around his neck, arm-rings above one elbow, a thick cuff on each wrist.

Helle could have been one of Vesta's virgins beside him, all in pale linen with her fair hair braided up on her head. But of course a Vestal would not be carrying a baby.

I blinked prickles of mist off my eyelids. As the crowd shifted in the early half-light, I glimpsed Dio between our laden donkey and the saddled roan. Boss would be farther away, kept from misbehaving by Rufus.

Aurima swayed. I put my arm around her shoulders. "Just a little longer," I murmured, though in truth I had no idea how much time the ceremony would take. "Then we will be on our way."

She hugged Beran to her breast. He was drowsy-eyed but awake. More awake than I felt.

My wrist throbbed in time with my head. An old man had marked my skin with a bone needle and oak gall. It ought to have been painful, but I had been past caring. Still was.

I shut my eyes. The noise went on: somber mutters, eager chatter, sharp exclamations, harsh arguments. The yelps of excited children in the meadow. Axles squealing, horses neighing, wheels grumbling, oxen groaning. Others too were ready to depart, although no one had left yet. Who would miss a ritual of this significance, a fostering ceremony between nations that might not be seen again for a generation?

A hand rocked me awake. Cleon jerked his bearded chin toward the fire, where Gisila was speaking an invocation. My eyes were drawn to the serpentine ring at the top of her staff.

Yesterday, that green circle had bobbed like an Army standard over a throng of women enveloping Aurima and Helle. Gisila might have been speaking to them, but I had heard only a roar in my ears.

Frantic with incredulity at what I was agreeing to do, I had headed for Aurima. Vannaz blocked the way. What was he doing in this group of Harpies, these snatchers of babes, these hounds of Haljo?

Come with me, the king had said.

"Come with me," Gisila said now, guiding Aurima and me to a place across the fire from Friduric and Helle.

The crowd's noise stilled. Daylight was strengthening beyond the thinning mist.

Hroswitha sang in a high voice that splintered with age. Gisila accompanied her in a mellow croon. The young apprentices added their sweet fluting voices. When the sun's rim flashed through the trees, all the women in the crowd joined the priestesses' song.

The brightness pounded in my skull. *Charming salute to a deity,* Dio had said. *From the same people who would butcher a man as a sacrifice.*

I held out my hands to Aurima. "Let me hold him."

As the mist melted, larks swooped and darted in the pale blue sky. The sun climbed free of the forest. Light gilded the thatched gables of Grozhauga and spilled down the hill. Now men too gave tongue, deeper-voiced, as the women's harmony soared. Lifted hands cast stripes of shadow across impassioned faces.

Beran dozed in the curve of my arm. He had already grown from a hand's length to a hand and a half. Would his hair be red, like his mother's? A young patrician with copper-colored hair would be a sensation among the noble ladies of Rome.

I must not think about what might have been. I nudged his little hand with my knuckle, hoping he would reach up and clutch my torc. Would cling to me one last time.

O gods, Mithras, Apollo, Jupiter and Juno, Austro, Fortuna, any others who hear me, take care of my son. Let him grow up strong and healthy, honest and brave. Let him see his mother in the rivers and birds and trees. Let him be proud of his father.

I had overthrown my gods. But if they did not exist, how else could we hope to create virtue out of shapeless time?

The baby sighed and turned his head. For the first time I noticed a small patch of cloth, no more than an inch square, behind his ear.

I fumbled one-handed to peel off the cloth, which was stuck down with ointment. Beran squirmed and mewled. Had he been injured? Why had Aurima not told me?

Beneath the patch a black mark showed in reddened skin. "What is this?" I hissed.

Aurima tapped my wrist, where I bore the same symbol: something like a "B," with two triangles stacked on a vertical line. We had both been tattooed.

She took back the baby and smoothed down the patch behind his ear. Poor Beran, had he cried when they needled him? Still, I felt a gleam of pleasure, tiny and fleeting, that to the gods, or the Fates, or whoever might seek either of us, we were marked as father and son.

Vannaz and his retinue were gathering around the two priestesses and us parents. Spears pricked up behind a wall of shields blazoned with boar's heads, wolf's masks, horned circles, triple spirals. Many of the men looked young and grim. Still lusting for war.

The king shouted about *muot*, courage. My gaze drifted to the fire in front of him, burning almost invisibly in the sunlight.

In the deserted smithy last night, glowing embers on a hearth had made dark menaces of an anvil, a workbench, a half-mended wheel. *Where is Aurima? Where is my child?* I had raged, fearing they would whisk Beran away while I was confined here.

Both fathers must agree, as both mothers agree, Vannaz had said. And then added, looking at Friduric, *To avoid war, this must be settled here. Tonight.*

Fathers must agree. It must be settled. Or chaos.

Beside me now, Aurima breathed deeply and stepped forward. Hroswitha was beckoning us with her amber-headed staff. Hroswitha, who had bewitched my damaged hands. Why could she not bewitch all these people to believe they could live at peace with Rome, without a need for hostages?

I followed across the beaten grass. Sunlight stabbed my eyes; my belly writhed queasily below my heart. But this was a moment to look like a Roman, dignified and stoical. To equal, if I could, the dignity of my wife, who had not wept since we rejoined each other at cockcrow. I had expected to find her in shock, bewildered and anguished, but she had remained pale and calm all this time.

Gisila brought Friduric and Helle closer to us. While Helle cuddled her baby girl, Friduric glowered at me. *What do I care of peace? Let Tiwaz take me in battle with my enemies!* he had exploded, raking his wolf-clawed cheek with the hand that was no longer a hand.

Those fiery nail gouges now crossed the claw marks, but he had washed his face so that dried blood no longer straggled down it. His lips were clamped so tightly together that they were only a line between mustache and beard.

"... so that there may be brotherhood and peace between the people of Rome and the Marcomanni and Quadi tribes," Vannaz was shouting. "The son of Ironhand's daughter is to be fostered by Friduric and Helewidis, and the daughter of Ironhand's son by Aquilo and Aurima. To this the two fathers agree."

The priestesses beckoned to Friduric and me. A young apprentice filled cups from a pitcher for each of us.

Friduric held out his cup. I did the same, not sure what was expected.

Gisila gestured us closer together. "The brotherhood drink."

Pressed hip to hip, we hooked our cup-arms together. Friduric gave me a bloodshot glare. "Do not make my daughter a fat heifer in a marble barn."

"Do not make my son the killer of Romans your father wanted," I snarled back.

Each of us swilled from his own cup. The taste of ale nearly turned my stomach after last night's surfeit of drink, but I forced it down.

The throng shouted approval as we untangled and stepped back. Next Aurima and Helle embraced and kissed, coppery hair against gold, sisterly in their pale gowns. A spurt of dread froze me, fear that the terrible moment had come.

"Each mother—" Gisila cried, her thin voice inaudible over the crowd.

Vannaz amplified her words: "Each mother and father vow to raise their foster child as their own. They promise to keep this vow as long as the sun shines, the water runs, and the earth endures."

A flurry of dust scattered from the old priestess's hand into the fire. With a *whoof*, flames flared higher than our heads. "If the ill will of any man or woman harms either child," the king shouted, "may fire never again warm that person.

"If the ill will of any man or woman causes either child to die, may Austro no longer shine her light on that person."

Freeze to death in darkness, Friduric, if you hurt my son.

Confined by the king's order in that dark smithy, dense with iron, ash, and smoke, we had drunk ale until we were stuporous and weeping. Humiliated by his dreadful injuries, Friduric wanted to die in combat. Roman troops would gladly oblige, I said; but when he was feasting in the Hall of the Warriors, would it please him to know that his wife had become a soldiers' whore and his baby daughter lay dead? In the end he had pulled two thick gold rings off his arm for Ammisia's future dowry, and agreed to give my father's signet ring to Beran when the boy was old enough.

Gisila's green-crowned staff tipped toward Friduric and Helle. "Who stands with this father and mother to protect their foster son?"

Who among Friduric's companions could be trusted to protect the child of a man they had tried to kill? I muttered to Aurima, "Did you know about this?"

Aurima did not answer. She stood stern-faced and immobile beside me, like a caryatid bearing the weight of a temple roof.

If no one spoke up as a protector, maybe the ceremony would be halted until somebody could be found. We would have Beran a little longer. We would have the crushing anticipation of his absence a little longer.

Vannaz cleared his throat. Perhaps to stop the proceedings. Or to offer himself.

"I stand as the child's protector." A stocky young man stepped from the ranks of the king's escort, lifting high his spear and shield. "I am Ellanher, foster son of Vannaz. Before all the gods I promise the boy my protection and the good will of the Hermunduri."

A murmur from the spectators.

"I, too, swear to protect this child." A familiar voice. Thancmar stumped forward from the crowd. He looked up boldly at Vannaz, nearly twice his height, and then at Gisila. "I am Thancmar, son of Ammisia, may her spirit rest. As Austro witnesses me, I promise all my power to keep the boy safe."

All my power. A mighty vow for one who lived with a wolf and an enchantress.

Rufus loped toward Thancmar and Ellanher, sunlight sparking in his red-gold hair. "I, Rudra," he announced, and the buzz of comment about Thancmar faded. He touched his chest, then held out a hand toward Beran. "Him," he said, and slid his knife from its sheath. He laid the blade across his palm in a sign of fealty and dipped his head to Aurima and me.

Something unswallowable lodged in my throat. I coughed, eyes watering.

Even though this was all spoken in Germanic, Cleon had understood. "Will they let me stand for the girl, Marcus?"

I hardly heard him, but Aurima did. She gave him a tight nod.

He said, "I'll get Dio."

Gisila led Beran's three guardians through an oath prickly with the names of gods. When Vannaz asked who would protect the infant girl, Cleon and Dio swore the oath that he rendered into serviceable Latin.

I heard but did not listen, closed to everything but the murmur of the river, the whisper of trees on the bank, the cries of birds in the milky sky. A memory of the eagle returned to me, of myself flying over a snowy forest and that dream call: *Ithaca.*

The king's voice deepened. "If we of the Mark do not honor our vow of peace, may the Roman people send this child of Friduric and Helewidis to the darkness of Haljo. If the people of Rome do not honor their vow of peace, then may we send this child of Aquilo and Aurima to that neverending night."

"Aquilo, it is time." Gisila tapped my arm. "Take your child."

I turned to Aurima. If she had begged me at the last minute not to let him go, I might not have had the courage to meet the demands of honor. But her composure was absolute, her cheeks tearless. She lifted Beran gently, kissed his head, and handed him to me.

I looked down at his small snub-nosed face. He blinked at me with long-lashed eyes as blue as a starling's egg, and gave me an open-mouthed rosy smile.

Gisila said, "How is your son called, Aquilo?"

I raised my chin. "He has a Roman name: Titus. But we call him . . ." My voice roughened and ran dry, as if I could not release his name.

I drew a deep breath. And said, "Beran," loudly enough for the crowd to hear.

The king's mother compared the tattoo on the back of my wrist to the mark behind the baby's ear. She nodded toward Friduric, who held his own child. Thrusting out his wrist for her inspection, he rumbled, "Ammisia is her name."

Gisila said, "Give her to Aurima. Aquilo, give him to Helewidis."

I began to walk, carrying my son like a gift for an emperor. Friduric passed me, cradling his daughter.

"We make this sacred agreement in the sight of Austro, that she may bless it," Vannaz boomed out his mother's words, "and beside the River Thayaz, that he may carry it to all the waters of the world."

I put Beran into Helle's arms. "You have my hope," I told her huskily.

Tears glittered on her face. "And you have mine," she whispered, yearning after her husband's small burden. Then her eyes flared wide.

A moan surged from the crowd. Helle ran past me with a cry, clasping Beran.

On the ground, beyond Friduric who still clutched his infant girl, I saw crumpled linen and coppery hair, an outflung arm, a booted foot. Aurima had fainted.

56: THE GOVERNOR'S AIDE

Despite the hot summer and lack of rain, the rosebush that Leonnatus's late wife had planted outside the kitchen door bore flowers as yellow as butter. If all the water hereabouts dried up, the old trader would probably open a vein in his arm to keep the thing alive.

My wicker chair squeaked as I leaned sideways, scratching the watchman's puppy behind the ears. Spicy smells drifted from inside the house. A distinguished guest was expected for dinner—much more distinguished than a former tribune who had returned with his small *familia* after half a year across the Danube.

Leonnatus hobbled into the arbor. "Is there anything you desire, my friend?"

"I am content, thank you," I lied.

It was a brusque reply, but I did not want to encourage more anecdotes about what to expect in wonderful Gallia Narbonensis. A destination we might never reach anyway, unless my uncertain legal status was favorably resolved. That, in turn, would depend on the judgment of Governor Gaius Calvisius Sabinus, the dinner guest.

The old trader paused to pick an ant off a rose leaf. "Your Dio has been useful to you with his cryptography skills. Have you given more thought to letting me hire him?"

"Ask him, by all means," I said. "But I do not think he cares for this part of the world anymore."

The puppy pricked up its ears at a distant commotion in the receiving yard. Leonnatus's eyes brightened. Reminding me, "My house is yours," he excused himself.

Landing at the customs port two days earlier, we had found sleepy little Carnuntum seething with fear of a German invasion. Patrols roamed the riverbanks. Many of the shops and houses were already shuttered, as clots of people trudged toward the imagined security of inner Pannonia with their belongings packed on mules, donkeys, wagons, pushcarts, or their own backs.

Leonnatus had been among the local merchants shipping goods to safety. After learning from me that Vannaz did not plan to attack, he had switched to renting out warehouse space for others to store their valuables. *Salve lucrum.*

My forced smile faded when he disappeared. Anger burned in me all the time, even with those who deserved no reproach.

The puppy wandered off. I took another swallow of my host's crisp white Baeterran and looked down at the wax tablet in my lap.

My will. Written nearly six months earlier, when I had had virtually nothing to bequeath anyone. My family ring, my copy of my father's memoirs, and his torc were to have been sent to my mother along with Rufus, who was to be freed when he was of age. My horses, my armor, and anything else I owned were to be sold and the proceeds shared by Dio, Cleon, and Ollius. There was no mention of Aurima, because I had not known where she was or even if she still lived.

I needed to revise it. I had a wife now, a child.

A child.

As if on cue, a baby screeched elsewhere in the house. Aurima had hardly stirred from our room so far, trying to soothe the endlessly fussing infant. That was her excuse, anyway, although it did not explain her clouded glances, or the brooding reserve that hid her feelings.

In time, I thought—I hoped—she would make peace with the decision to surrender Beran. But the longer we stayed in this outpost of Romanness, the more likely she might conclude that leaving him had been wrong, and choose to leave me instead.

A server brought a plate of hard-boiled egg halves. I lifted one dripping with *garum*, then hesitated. Aurima loathed the reek of pickled fish on my breath. I gulped it quickly, a defiant reward after the ordeal of the Mark. But like other delicacies prepared by Leo's accomplished cook, it had as little savor to me as the Germans' bland fare.

I heard the ominous scrape of nailed boots approaching, along with the scuff of leather-soled sandals. Leonnatus limped back into the arbor, saying to someone else, "Perhaps you two know each other."

The newcomer was shorter than I, with a face hatcheted into flat planes: brow, nose, cheeks, chin. In spite of his civilian tunic and a mantle draped toga-style, his bearing, boots, and thick-crowned haircut all said *Army officer*.

"Arruntius Gratianus," he announced before Leonnatus could introduce us. "Military aide to Governor Sabinus."

Knowing Sabinus would have to be told I was here, I had been apprehensive about this moment. I got up from the chair. "Licinius Aquilo. I remember you, Centurion."

"Of course, Tribune." Gratianus's smile splintered the geometry of his face. He did not comment on my name change or the expiration of my *ad rem* rank.

He let Leonnatus offer him a seat and a cup of wine, and they conversed for a few minutes about the five-day journey from the governor's capital at Poetovio. I sipped my Baeterran and fondled the ears of the puppy, which had trotted back to see what was happening.

Gratianus set down his cup. "I must check security arrangements for the governor's visit."

"Certainly." Leonnatus rose to his feet too. "He is at the fortress now, I suppose?"

"Yes, inspecting the grain stores. May I have a word with you, Tribune?"

My suspicions flamed up. Was I about to be removed from this pleasant villa to a cell in the fortress? Wanting Leonnatus to witness the answer, I asked, "Am I to be charged with a crime?"

Gratianus's brows lifted into dark hooks. "What crime?"

"Murder. *Laesa maiestas*. Inciting war. Or all three."

"Good gods." It was said jocularly, but there was no smile in his eyes.

Leonnatus said, "I must point out that Licinius Aquilo is my guest, and I have the honor of being his friend. His mother Antonia Terentia is also a patron of long standing."

Gratianus looked pained. "Governor Sabinus merely seeks information."

It was not an answer. But I needed one, so when he left the arbor, I went with him.

"I understand you have not made a report to the legate," Gratianus said.

"He has been out of camp," I explained. I did not bother to say that Poppaeus's inspection tour of watchtowers along the river had left the garrison in the hands of the camp commandant, a cynical, oak-hard veteran who would have confined me under guard as soon as I showed myself.

We were walking west along the river road, with a field on one side and a pasture on the other. Gratianus glanced from the corner of his eye at his two guards, trailing us out of earshot. "In Poetovio, we heard only that Prefect Lamia's vexillation was attacked on its way back from a diplomatic mission to the German king. I rode here to investigate, but it has not been easy to put together a clear story for the governor."

"You will not hear the truth from Lamia." According to Leonnatus, the Special Cohort prefect still lurked in the fortress with his Praetorians, agitating for reprisal raids to prevent the Marcomanni from rampaging across the Danube. No doubt that was why he had defaulted on his promise to confer with Vangio—and, perhaps, had poisoned Poppaeus against receiving the German delegation.

"As you evidently know, the prefect is accusing you of murder. Though not of treason or inciting war, as I recall."

It was a pity I had not killed Lamia when I found he had lied to me about Aurima. I should have ransomed only the three soldiers, and told the Marcomanni they could keep him. Too late now; he was trying to sink me in a judicial cesspit for my slaying of Glabrio.

I stopped. "I have some information that will sour Sabinus's opinion of the man." Half of the stolen letters hid beneath a false bottom in the cask holding Ollius's ashes. The others had been left with Rufus, who by now would have concealed the smelly amphora that contained them.

Gratianus frowned at the road as if finding fault with the stonework, whose laying, as it happened, I had overseen myself. "I have questioned others as well: the surgeon, the quartermaster, the senior cavalrymen."

My gaze slid over the silver-gold wheat field, shorn as close as a recruit's scalp. Crows hopped and pecked in the stubble. Far beyond the field the horizon rose to the vast sky, a proper horizon of gentle hills banded with trees.

I inhaled until my chest swelled, willing the harvest-scented air to waken my senses. Lately, my sleep had been torn by dreams of a child who was lost and the howls of the one who was found.

A butterfly fluttered among dusty wildflowers at the roadside: lavender, goldenrod, tall bronze horsetail. Blue cornflowers, as blue as . . .

"So far," Gratianus observed, "the tale seems to involve a dwarf, a lunatic, and a mysterious apparition that may have been Epona, Cernunnos, Proserpina, or a forest-spirit. A baby is also in it somehow, is that right?"

I could not answer. Had I opened my mouth, the rage and pain that spewed from it would have flayed the trees, uprooted the paving stones, and blasted birds and men off the edge of the earth.

After a time he said, "Let us turn around. If your secretary has your report ready, I would like to read it."

Greenish light from the arbor gleamed on Sabinus's bare scalp. In the past four years, he had become as bald as a ballista stone.

The first time I confronted this short, cold-eyed man in an unheated room of his headquarters in Poetovio, I had tried to persuade him that I had lost Father's letter requesting my appointment to his staff. Pretending to believe me, Sabinus had posted me to the Fifteenth as its broad-stripe tribune, junior only to the legion commander. This I considered a great honor, until discovering that the incumbent had been so viciously harassed by the legion's centurions that he was resigning before his term was up. The assignment was meant to teach me obedience to the father I had defied.

Now the governor and I faced each other again in Leonnatus's *tablinum*, richly decorated with fine furniture and colorful murals. This time Dio was with me. Gratianus took up position in front of a frescoed Mercury.

Sabinus lowered himself into a chair behind a goat-legged desk. "Thank you for sparing us your presence at dinner, Carinna. Aquilo." His voice grated like a millstone.

His hostility put me on guard. "I prefer Aquilo. And I did not wish to spoil Leonnatus's tribute to your palate." Aurima had been in no state to endure a formal dinner, and I refused to be the butt of painful questions over boiled parrot and stuffed roast sturgeon.

He did not like my intransigence. "No doubt you have grown unused to decent food. You are certainly looking more barbarous than before."

Leonnatus's barber had trimmed my hair and beard, but I had not let him shave my face. In some corner of my heart lurked a secret fear that Beran would not know me without whiskers—a notion I knew was senseless, and despised myself for harboring.

Dio had brought up a chair for me before moving unobtrusively next to the wall. I turned the chair at an angle to the desk, deflecting Sabinus's dominance, and sat. "Have you read my report, Governor?"

But he was not yet done with pricking me. "My condolences on your father's death. Almost a year now, is it not? How unfortunate that the gods drove him mad."

I glanced away to master a spurt of reflexive anger. My scarred right hand on the chair's arm looked like someone else's, the third finger still indented by a ring that was not there. "He did what he believed to be right."

His smile twisted cruelly at one corner. "It seems you have inherited his derangement." He flipped open a wax tablet on the desk before him, made a show of referring to it, then glared at me. "Murdering a Praetorian officer, one of Prefect Lamia's agents."

Dio had argued against admitting that I had been the aggressor. We had agreed on a short and ambiguous account: *While I was attempting to rescue my wife, a struggle ensued with Special Cohort Agent Glabrio, who was fatally wounded.*

"Have you read the report?"

"Yes, young man, I have read the report!" He lifted the tablet so abruptly that its three leaves clapped together, and smacked it on the desktop. "A great deal of slaughter, ensuing from your attempts to recover your woman."

"My wife," I corrected.

"A sacred hostage—whom you restored to her people in defiance of legal, political, and religious conventions!"

"Am I to be charged with sacrilege as well?"

My challenge hung in silence for a moment. Sabinus tipped his chin toward the arbor, where a girl was humming as she swept up dead leaves. Gratianus closed the folding doors, blocking the vine-sieved streaks of late-day sun. Light grayed in the room.

"You," Sabinus said ominously, "do not seem to realize what your criminal impulsiveness has led to. You have destroyed an alliance sanctioned by the Senate and people of Rome, and have brought us to the brink of war."

"On the contrary, I have restored amity and prevented war. Let me explain."

"A vexillation minding its own business was attacked because of you; cavalry troopers and Praetorians were injured, killed, and offered up for sacrifice." A vein snaked blue on his brow. "If that is not grounds for reprisal, I don't know what is."

I had held back the volcanic news of the hostage exchange, wanting to control the disclosure, but could wait no longer; he was close to dismissing me. I looked him in the eye. "I give you my word, Governor, that reprisals will incite the war you want to avoid."

"Raging Hercules! I have heard enough." He lurched to his feet. "Gratianus, take this presumptuous—"

I raised my voice over his. "And you may tell Prefect Lamia that contrary to his warmongering, the Germans are not about to invade across the river."

Sabinus's gaze became so intense that his eyes seemed to bulge from their sockets. "Oh, you know that, do you?"

I said, "I speak with the authority of Vannius, king of the Marcomanni and Quadi."

He stared at me for a long moment. "Galla," he shouted toward the arbor. "Galla! Fetch me something to drink."

57: RIOT

The governor threw himself back in his chair. "Gratianus, did you know anything of this?" Not waiting for his aide's response, he glowered at the inflamed tattoo on my offered wrist. "What are you showing me?"

For a moment I could not speak, fearing that I would fail to persuade Sabinus against the savage reprisals that were normal Roman policy. That I would fail my son.

"This is my authority," I said.

Cornelia Galla glided through the arbor doors with slaves bearing pitchers and cups. They mixed the wine and left at her finger-flick. Ignoring her husband's scowl, she poured a cup for him and for me, put them before us, and settled into a chair as if invited.

Would my father's cousin be an ally? Or did she, like Sabinus, reckon me "criminally impulsive," deserving to be surrendered to Caligula?

"The tribes agree to maintain a truce, contingent on our own restraint," I began.

Sabinus worked his nutcracker jaw. "The attacks on Lamia's vexillation were brutal. Condoning them would set an intolerable precedent."

"Agreed. But I have listened to an assembly of enraged and distrustful warriors, and I tell you that any attempt at retaliation will stir the Mark into an uproar. Preparations for Caesar's campaign will be disrupted."

A glance flickered between Sabinus and Gratianus. He said, "So what do you propose—you who have restored amity and prevented war?"

"First, we must accept that Inguiomerus's outbreak has been appropriately punished by Vannius himself. He stopped the attacks as soon as he learned of them, and Inguiomerus himself was put to the sword."

"Not harsh enough. What will keep the man's followers, allies, and family from continuing his aggression? Better to obliterate the whole clan."

My gullet clenched. "Sound policy in wartime," I said hoarsely, and cleared my throat. "But not now, when we want to keep the Marcomanni and Quadi friendly. The wiser solution is to give hostages. That is their other condition."

Displeasure or even outrage would not have surprised me. Instead, Sabinus smoothed a hand over his bald head, as if grooming hair that no longer grew. "Hostages," he mused. "Who would they give us?"

"It is already done. They exchanged the only child of Inguiomerus's elder son."

"'Exchanged'? You mean they expect us to provide a hostage, too?"

"Yes, Governor." I tried to keep expression from my voice. "To secure the peace, we have given them the grandchild of a Roman Senator."

Cornelia Galla realized it first: "Your own child?"

"Are you as lunatic as your father?" Sabinus spiked me with the lacerating glare I remembered from four years earlier. "You are not empowered to make treaties. Did they understand that this so-called exchange of hostages was unofficial?"

"On the contrary," I shot back. "I swore on their gods and ours that Rome would honor the agreement, with Vannius the king and two hundred of his people as witnesses."

"You had no authority to make that commitment!"

I stood up, looming over him with my hands braced on the desktop. "Will you repudiate an agreement I made to protect the Republic?"

He lunged to his feet too, mirroring my stance. "I cannot believe you took it on yourself—you, the disgraced son of a dishonored family—to make a promise on behalf of the Senate and the Roman people!"

"The tribes were about to vote for war. There was no time to consult the Senate."

He thrust himself closer, gusting odors of fish and wine into my face. "If I want to take my fucking legions into the Mark, I will, and to Hades with your hostages!"

"Do you reckon the bloodshed will be good for your future, Governor?"

I had hit a nerve. "You arrogant son of a bitch," Sabinus roared. "You presumptuous young ass."

It would have been prudent to drop my gaze and back away from the most powerful man in Pannonia, but submission would mean defeat. We were still eye to furious eye when Gratianus interrupted, "Sorry, sir. Urgent message from the fortress."

The doors from the arbor were just folding shut again. Sabinus straightened himself. Seizing the tablet from his aide's hand, he broke the seal and began to read it.

Cornelia Galla crossed in front of me, compelling me to step back from the desk, and took my wine cup as if to refill it. Turning away from her husband and his aide, she whispered, "Marcus Licinius, you have surprised him. He expected you to beg for pardon and demand revenge on the Germans. Let him think about it."

Surprised or not, his response dismayed me. Unless I could persuade him otherwise, the frontier would burst into flames—and our small son would be lost in neverending night.

Sabinus grabbed his cloak from the back of his chair. "Trouble in the camp." He strode toward the doorway. Gratianus followed, stuffing the tablet into a satchel.

"What kind of trouble?" Galla demanded.

"Riot," her husband said curtly, and disappeared with his aide.

In an Army camp, a riot meant mutiny—the secret fear of senior officers since the days of Augustus. My years as a tribune prompted me to rush
to the fortress too. But if Lamia's tales of his ordeal had made the troops
rabid for vengeance or, worse yet, panicky lest they be ordered into the Mark,
my presence would not improve things.

If mutiny spread to the whole legion, would the hostage exchange
even matter?

Dread hit me like a blow to the stomach. I sagged into my chair, weak-
legged.

Bear up, man! Rufus would not allow a child of Aurima's to be harmed.
Nor would Thancmar. Or Ellanher of the Hermunduri, if he was a man of his
word.

Galla sighed. "Your child is freeborn?"

"Of course he is," I said. Born to a Roman citizen and a free woman,
Beran was not only free but a citizen. Like it or not, Sabinus must accept that
the agreement was...

Binding. For as long as the sun shone, the water ran, and the earth
endured.

"Did they force you to give him up, my dear?"

"No." The word cracked out, as violent as the slam of a door. "I forced
myself."

Shouts from the courtyard. A horse's whinny. Hooves churned gravel.

"Ah," she said in a voice laced with melancholy, "you are your father's
son."

She had known him in a way I could not. Perhaps she guessed at the
great sacrifice he had made, but I could not speak of that with her. Unfolding myself from the chair, I managed a stiff smile.

"You think it unmanly to show grief." Her answering smile was
equally strained.

I saw him in the light of the vigil lamp, an old priest of Apollo had told
me. *He was biting on a fold of his cloak, so his weeping would not wake your
brother.*

"Yet if we did not mourn," Galla went on, "we would not be human."
She coughed roughness from her throat. "Is your wife greatly distressed?"

"She has the other child to care for, the little girl." Regretting the
spitefulness of this reply, I added lamely, "She is much within herself these
days."

Her eyes narrowed in sudden fury. "Oh, you fool. Go and comfort her."
She yanked back one of the folding doors and held it open. "Don't wait another minute."

I began to say that Leonnatus must be warned. If rioters broke out
of the camp, his storehouses full of trading goods would be an irresistible

target.

"Marcus," Galla broke in, "many other people are responsible for taking care of disobedient troops." Her lips tightened into a pale line. "You are the only one responsible for taking care of your wife. Go."

My wife, who had not touched me of her own will since we left Grozhauga. Whose heartache, clutched silently to herself, might already have persuaded her to return to her lost child.

Cleon was waiting for me in the atrium. "Marcus, there's mutiny at the camp." He had shaved off his beard, and the lower half of his ruddy face was as pale as a peeled almond. "They say it's a Hispanic cohort."

Hispanians? Something needled briefly at my mind, then was gone. "Why?"

"Don't know. That's all Zephyrus heard"—he meant my former groom, sold to Leonnatus the year before—"before the governor and his dog pack almost ran over him."

Dio caught up with us. "How serious is it?" He had clamped the writing tablet under his arm and was rubbing bits of wax from his fingers.

"The legionaries will take care of it," I said. I did not want to think it might spread.

"One more thing the governor will hold against you."

"What do you mean?" Cleon scowled at him, then at me. "Does that poxy old knobhead blame you for killing Bat-Ears? Curse him, he owes you for keeping the peace!"

"Let us pack up now," Dio proposed. "We can join the others leaving town. It will spare him from having to make a decision about you."

"I have done enough running and hiding," I said. "You two help Leonnatus get ready in case the rioting spreads. I have something else to do."

"What—?" Cleon stopped himself, but the rest of his question was obvious: *What could be more important?*

The unrest at the fortress vanished from my mind as I came to our room. Through the door curtain I could hear Aurima talking with someone. Disconcerted, I veered through another door into a small garden steeped in dusky shadow, and sank onto a stone bench.

This side of the house was very quiet, away from the kitchens and storehouses. My only company was a frolic of gnats and an array of plantings whose flowers, relieved of the day's heat, gave off a ghostly fragrance.

I stared at moss-edged flagstones, letting my thoughts churn and collide.

To Hades with your hostages, Sabinus ranted in my head.

Children died all the time. Many did not live long enough to be named. My parents had endured their share of losses: a baby stillborn, another dead in the first year.

Simply pretend, then, that our round-faced infant with trusting blue eyes, a daintily fashioned nose, and plump lips the color of his mother's nipples no longer lived.

I had to choose. Don't you understand? The last thing my father had said to me.

Yes, I understood now.

Later, when he learned that the choice he made had averted a civil war, was the value of his sacrifice any consolation to him?

If Sabinus invaded the Mark, mine would never be of solace to me.

A glow blossomed in the corner of my eye. A newly lit lamp inside the house had transformed a window fly-curtain from filmy to sheer. Although I was invisible out in the darkness, my solitude was broken. I got up silently to depart.

Then stopped. Through the diaphanous curtain I saw Aurima sinking to her knees beside her nursing chair. The top of her tunic drooped around her waist, and lamplight burnished the rose gold of her breasts. She reached down out of sight, first one arm, then both, and I heard splashing.

Her hair flashed like polished copper as she shrugged it off her shoulders. With a plump dribbling sponge she bathed one breast, slowly and carefully, stroking the nipple, lifting the sleek globe to wash beneath it. I heard a quiet sigh, then a ripple and plash as she rinsed and wrung out the sponge.

My breath came short. My mouth grew dry.

She drew the sponge along the slope of her other breast. Trickles of molten fire ran around the curve of it. A diamond quivered at its tip.

I hardened in desire. Like a thief peeping in the baths, I could not look away.

Aurima contemplated herself. One long-fingered hand rose, empty now, and cupped a breast. Her lashes sank as she slid her palm around the fullness of it and hefted it. She sighed again.

The matter of a moment: into the house, two or three paces to the door curtain, snatch it aside ...

But I was still rooted to the garden flagstones when she reached to the chair's seat and gathered up her pendant. Twisting on her knees, she raised the golden amber to the lamp flame and gazed into its glinting heart.

"O Austro, have mercy on me. Goddess of light, help me." Her voice was soft, confidential, unlike the peremptory shout with which we Romans address our gods. "My Lady, it is you I serve and honor, like my mother and her mother before her."

More than anything I wanted to barge in, pretending I had just arrived, and scoop her up to relieve an ache of eye-watering proportions. But it would be inexcusable to interrupt her at prayer. I moved across the garden and leaned against the wall beside the window, turning away so the sight of her near-nudity would not stir me even more.

Her voice was so much closer that she might have been speaking into my ear. "O Lady of the Morning, grant me wisdom. I do not know how to hold him...."

Had I misheard? Perhaps she had actually said "hold her"—Helle's daughter?

"He is angry because it is my kindred who took our baby and my father who made it needful. And because I have changed...." Her voice thickened. "Here among his own people, I feel him pulling away from me."

I bit my lip. It was clear now who "he" was.

"Great goddess, I promise to honor you among the tribe of the western lands who grow flowers and make wine. I, your priestess Aurima of the Marcomanni and Quadi, ask you to open my husband's heart to me again. To me and to little Misia." In a half whisper she added, "And make my breasts smaller again, the way he liked them."

I stepped closer. In an aura of golden light hazed by the curtain, I saw her shut her eyes and kiss the amber pendant.

Stealthily I took off my sandals and moved barefoot to the garden door. As I reentered the house, I met a slave lighting a sconce in the corridor. He opened his mouth, startled, but I put a finger to my lips and passed him without a word.

When he had finished his chores and disappeared, I went down the corridor again with my sandals slapping noisily on my heels. Outside the curtained bedroom doorway, I nearly lost my nerve.

Embarrassed. Apprehensive. Unready.

"Aurima?" I shouldered the curtain aside and went in.

She had just risen to her feet. With one hand reflexively lifted to shield her bare breasts and the tunic draping from her hips, she was Venus come to life.

Blushing at her own modesty, she let her hand fall and began to tug at the collapsed top of her garment. "Not so loud," she whispered, with a glance at the fat-faced baby in her basket. "The child is asleep."

"The child must get used to her foster father's voice," I said.

Aurima's eyes, swollen and red-rimmed as always these days, widened as I came nearer. I trapped her hands and lifted them to my mouth. "I have realized," I said, kissing one, "how often on the journey from Rome I longed for a real bed to share with you." I kissed the other. "And how many weeks I spent afterward on fire without you."

I tried to clear the last of the anger and pain from my own eyes. "Now I am an arm's length away from a comfortable bed with the most brave and beautiful woman I have ever known." I lowered her hands to her sides. "It would be shameful to ignore such a gift from the gods."

She stared at me warily. When I slipped my hands under her breasts and caressed them, her lips parted as if she might speak.

"Do you like that?" I teased a nipple with my thumb.

Her green eyes slitted.

Holding her with one arm, I bent, lifted her breast, and let my tongue do the teasing.

Her soft exhalation touched my cheek. She swayed a little.

"I think your husband has neglected you." I kissed my way to the base of her throat, then drew back.

Aurima grasped my ears, dragged me forward, and pressed her mouth on mine. Then recoiled. *"Garum."*

"Sorry," I said, but was not repentant enough to keep my hands off her belt. Her tunic crumpled to the floor, leaving her naked.

I unwound my mantle and unbuckled my own belt. Despite her forwardness with the kiss, I saw she was not yet disposed to loving. Still, need drives out sentiment when men are lustful.

Usually.

Yet I, who had defied family and Princeps and bloodthirsty Germans to win this woman, now hesitated for fear she would refuse me.

She would yield if I pushed myself on her. But she would withhold her heart, leaving me to the worms of my bitterness and self-doubt. And I, perhaps, would do the same to her.

I tried to break the stillness. *I have forgotten how to captivate you,* I might have meant to say.

Aurima shook her head. "My love," she said, looking down at my tunic, "I believe it is your wife who has neglected you."

I lifted her by the waist and sat her on the edge of the mattress. The last clothes were disposed of, and then we wore only each other, at last toppling down onto the bed, its ropes squeaking to the sound of bird cries in a gusty wind.

Often when we made love we were surrounded by other people, so she would muffle her cries in the bedding, or sometimes sink them in the meat of my shoulder. I was charmed to think it maidenly modesty, and did not understand when she said it was to prevent less fortunate men, hearing her, from envying me. Why should they not envy me, well-born and virile and able to please such a spirited woman?

But this time, clenching me tightly, eyes rolling in a riot of hair, she uttered a gut-deep bellow. Only once, when she was cheated of longed-for death, had I heard its like. Perhaps it was the roar with which she had birthed our child.

Something tore loose inside me. And as if I too were swollen with a force desperate to escape, it exploded through its restraints and burst forth.

We held each other, hearts bounding, and grieved.

Aurima whispered, "If the governor chooses, are you going to be judged like the men who killed my mother?"

"I think not, *frijdila*." I stroked damp hair off her brow. "I can say that I am not subject to military justice. When Glabrio and Lamia abandoned me to Berinhard, they took away my rank and authority as tribune." For a time, anyway. Until I took it back.

She sighed. "That means no trial?"

"It means Sabinus can judge my case himself."

"But his judgment is not going to be too hard, *ja*? You are a cousin of his wife."

I was also a cousin of Caligula Caesar, which meant that the governor might choose to dodge the political risk of judging me. As a citizen I had the right to be heard by Caesar, so I could simply be charged with treason and sent to Rome. The most likely punishment for a man of my rank would be revocation of citizenship and exile to some desolate end of the empire. I did not fear deportation, not if Aurima came with me. But the prospect of losing my Roman citizenship, my identity as one of those born to command the world—that was unbearable.

"Too soon to tell." I pretended to yawn. Whether it deceived her or not I did not know, for the yawn yielded to heavy weariness, and I slept.

Shouting.

Not inside the house. Coming through the garden window. Maybe a bear or an aurochs had escaped from its cage in the receiving yard?

The rioters.

58: IN A DARK CARRIAGE

I leaped out of bed. The room was dim, the lamp burned out.

Aurima clutched the coverlet over herself. "What is it?"

A shadow fell across the curtained doorway. Dio hissed, "Marcus, are you there?"

I swept back the curtain. "What is it?" I asked, low-voiced. The baby uttered a yawp, but did not rouse.

The lit sconce behind him obscured his face. "The governor's guards have come to take you to the camp."

"At this hour?" Black night filled the window. "Has the riot been suppressed?"

"I don't know. They say it's urgent. There's a carriage waiting in the courtyard."

Sabinus wanted to conceal my arrival at the camp. Not a good sign.

"Get ready to come with me," I said. "Cleon, too."

As soon as Dio was gone, Aurima slid out of bed. I put my hands on her shoulders and stopped her.

Despite the uncertainty of the governor's summons, the reassurance of her love had wrought new calmness in me. My heart still hurt, but fragments of it no longer stabbed and slashed like broken bones.

I kissed her brow, feeling armored in resolve like a man preparing for battle. "I will be back as soon as I can, *carissima.*"

She eyed me gravely, chin raised. "This time, I am coming with you."

"You and the baby are safer here." I did not want to worry her with a warning that Sabinus contemplated invading the Mark, since I was resolved to dissuade him.

"Husband, I am not going to be parted from you again. Wash your face, please, and finish dressing."

I began to object, then shut my mouth. She was a war chieftain's daughter, after all.

When we left the room, dressed in borrowed finery, I let her precede me with the child. Dio and Cleon fell in behind us.

Leonnatus waited in the atrium with his oldest son, who managed security for him. The trader's white brows were twisted, his long-nosed face taut with concern. "Tell me what I can do to help you, my friend."

His influence, though considerable, counted for little against Sabinus's authority. I cursed myself for failing to write a letter he could send to my mother. Yet there was one thing I could ask of him. I muttered in Greek, "If I am detained, will you see that Aurima returns to Bruna?"

"Of course," Leonnatus murmured. His son nodded.

Aurima swung around, cradling the infant. "What are you saying?"

"I said how beautiful you are, *mina dîsi*," I extemporized, knowing she deemed it impious to be called a goddess.

I could tell she did not believe me. But she only muttered, "Are you not lucky, then?" and walked on.

The carriage stood in the torchlit receiving yard, its ornate gilt and red paint dulled with dust, the three harnessed mules yawning. It was the very *carpentum* that had passed Boss and me on the road so long ago, when I was promising myself to bring back the lost Eagle with or without Ingiomar's help. A short distance away, half a dozen of the governor's bodyguards stood waiting beside their horses.

The experience of my senses told me it was well into the second watch, although not yet midnight. The late summons seemed more and more ominous.

Gratianus was in uniform now, helmet beneath his arm, his mail shirt glinting where the weapons belts had chafed it. "Lady Galla is returning to camp," he said. Firelight caught the planes of his face as he looked at Aurima, Dio, and Cleon. "My orders are to bring you with her. Alone."

"Is there still unrest in the camp?"

"None to speak of. The troops involved have been confined to quarters."

"Then my people are coming with me."

"I do not think that wise." His gaze held on the baby peeping from her blanket.

The carriage was large enough to seat four. I went to its side door, which stood ajar, and told Aurima, "Let me hold the baby while you step up."

Her eyes flickered in disquiet. I realized she had never been in a closed vehicle.

"Wait, I will pull you up." Dio mounted the folding step and ducked inside the carriage, clutching his satchel. "Oh," he exclaimed, "pardon me —"

"Hades' balls!" bit out a voice within the *carpentum*. "First murder and mutiny, now clerks and children. Get out, Eleutera!"

Galla's maid stumbled out of the carriage. Gratianus smiled grimly, fitting his black-and-white crested helmet over his ears. "Mount up!" he shouted.

Guards flung themselves on horseback, their striped crests swaying like sails. I paused for what might be a last look at freedom. At torchlight flickering redly on warehouse fronts; at Leonnatus standing on the top step of his house, arms folded, flanked by his three sons; at the servants watching silently; at the great, deep star-speckled sky. From his seat by the driver, Cleon saluted me with his stave.

The cab of the *carpentum* rocked on its suspension straps as I hoisted Aurima and the baby inside, then climbed in after them. Standing awkwardly crowded in the middle of the carriage, the two of us and Dio loomed over Galla, who was curled in a far corner. The painted walls and pillowed seats smelled of her expensive rose perfume.

"Well, this is cozy." The governor's wife smiled thinly, unfolding her legs to make room on the rear seat cushion.

I helped Aurima settle on the opposite bench and nodded for Dio to join her. Galla rearranged a shawl over herself as I sat down beside her. I said, "This is Dio, my secretary, and I am pleased to introduce my wife. Aurima, meet my cousin Cornelia Galla. Governor Sabinus is her husband."

"I am honored," Aurima said in her best emulation of well-bred Latin. Galla looked at her blankly, as if she had not expected to hear human speech.

When Gratianus shut the door, a ruddy glow from a small window on the other side of the carriage was all that defied the darkness. Before I could ask for lamps above the seats to be lit, he shouted, "Forward!" and the *carpentum* lurched ahead.

The thunder of hooves and squeal of oil-starved hubs made an excuse for muteness. However, we had scarcely wheeled out of Leonnatus's gates, leaving behind their vigilant torchlight, when I felt Galla's hand emerge from her shawl's wooly folds to touch my wrist. Staring at the swaddled baby, she whispered into my ear, "Is that . . . the barbarian child?"

I tugged my belt around so the longknife did not jab into my hip. Over the rumble of the carriage's ironshod wheels on paved road, I said, "Yes, that is our foster daughter."

Galla sensed the reproof. "I see." She withdrew into the corner.

Dark trees flickered past the small window. The night air smelled of cut hay and woodsmoke, with whiffs of leather and horse sweat when a guard cantered alongside.

Aurima gave a little cough. "What does 'munity' mean?"

"'Mutiny,'" I corrected. "It means rebellion. Disobedience."

"The soldiers have a rebellion? Why?"

Galla put in, "The legions are like an ill-tempered horse, my dear. Unless they are worked hard and fed regularly, they will bite and kick."

"But they are not beasts." The whites of Aurima's eyes gleamed as she looked at me. "What about the honor of Rome?"

"What about a centurion's stick?" Galla laughed. "That is what motivates them."

I did not like her cynicism. "Discontent breeds when the Republic is unsettled."

"As it is now, you mean." The lady's voice was light.

I glanced at her edgewise. Was she trying again to get me to declare for Lepidus? "The legions understand the need for control, and they are right to demand it. Mutiny is a failure of leadership."

"That is true," Aurima said vehemently. "They were cowards, those who did not punish the soldiers who killed my mother."

I caught the knife-flick of her glare at Galla, but the governor's wife did not acknowledge the insult to her husband. "You are right, Marcus Licinius. But you may not realize how things are in Rome. Caesar is still devastated by Drusilla's death. The Senate hesitates to carry out his wishes because they fear he may be possessed—by madness or brain fever; who knows? So he has come to believe they are against him."

"That has nothing to do with me." I turned my face away.

Pitching her voice so that only I could hear, she said, "Julia Agrippina thinks he still trusts you."

How could Caligula trust me, who had nearly died proving I loved someone else more than him? If Agrippina truly thought so, she must be as unbalanced as her brother.

I shook my head irritably. "I have already done more than you know for Rome. All I want now is to be left in peace."

Light flooded in from torches at the town's western gateway. Our cavalcade slowed, and a voice called a password. The top of an open gate rippled by as the wheels bumped over the stone threshold. A whip-crack, and the carriage sped up again.

At this hour the town should have been quiet, but the street echoed with shouts and curses at our racketing progress. Horses neighed in alarm. Wood smashed, which might have been a barricade being knocked aside.

I could see the trooper alongside more clearly: the thick vertical stripes of his horsehair crest, the circle of a bronze cloak pin, a scar on his cheek. "The moon rises," Aurima said. I saw, too, the pearl gleam of her beautiful breast as she suckled the infant.

One of the mules brayed. The carriage swerved and jerked to pass through gaps in stepping-stones that crossed to the municipal building. Dio grabbed a wall strap to steady himself. Cornelia Galla let herself be thrown against me.

Or perhaps it was not so willful, for moonglow showed me that her face was somber. "Well, cousin," I said, "perhaps it is time you told me what to expect. Am I to be flung to the rioters to feed their bad temper?"

Aurima and Dio stared at me. They did not know about soldiers assaulting me in the *taberna*, or my vicious reception at the camp from Festus and Licnos.

Galla said, "I know no more than you, Marcus Licinius." She straightened herself as much as the jolting carriage allowed. "But I owe it to your mother to observe."

She held my eyes. *To observe.* Did Sabinus plan on no one knowing what had become of me, taken away in the middle of the night?

Aurima was looking down at the baby in her lap. Her fingers kneaded a corner of the child's blanket, as if twisting a strand of yarn. I was reminded of how she had toyed with folds of her tunic while telling of her father's cruelty, after I had rescued her.

I tapped Dio's knee and beckoned him to take my place so I could sit beside her. "Little Misia grows used to her new mother, *ja*?" I offered, taking her hand in mine.

This tenderness won me a smile that tried to be cheerful. "Oh, my *frijdila*," I said softly. She leaned against me and we swayed together, shoulder to shoulder, as the rising moon animated the night.

Out past the eastern town gate. Into the sprawl of the camp followers' slum, reeking of smoke and ordure and spoiled fish. A commotion was raging there: women yelled and children wailed among the hovels. "Make way," someone bellowed.

I stood up, grabbing the wall strap for balance, and craned out of the window. A patrol was hauling someone out of a shack. As they shoved him toward a group of other dazed and disheveled men, a woman shrieked, "He has a pass until tomorrow!"

Suspension of leave was used only in an emergency. Had the mutiny flared up again? Were Germans massing to attack across the river, despite the hostage agreement?

"Husband," Aurima said, "I am not well inside me."

One look into her misery-stricken eyes, and I fumbled for my knife. Hammering the pommel on the front wall, I shouted, "Stop! Stop the carriage!"

My command went unnoticed over the thumping and swaying of the *carpentum*. Its speed did not slacken.

"Stop, driver!" Dio banged his fist against the side wall, with equally little effect.

Aurima put the back of her hand to her mouth. I was about to fling the door open, which would have made someone take heed even though we were moving too fast to jump, when Galla waved her hand out of the window. "Halt at once!" she ordered.

The driver hooted to his team, and the mules slowed. I plunged out before the wheels stopped rolling. Aurima thrust the squalling baby into my arms, half fell through the doorway, and was sick at the roadside.

We were no more than a spear-throw from the fortress's Left Gate. Gratianus's troops muddled around the stopped carriage. Torches burning at both gate towers spilled light onto a dozen cavalrymen spurting through the open gates toward us. The mules honked and tried to back away. Whinnying horses capered in the confusion.

"What—?" Gratianus demanded, before catching sight of Aurima on her knees.

Clutching the wriggling infant, I stooped to pull her loose palla out of harm's way. My borrowed mantle slid off my shoulder. "It was stupid to go at such a breakneck pace," I snapped.

Dio sacrificed his own dignity to salvage mine, tucking the baby under his arm like a second satchel. I was tidying myself when Cleon jogged up. "Is

Aurima all right? What happened?"

"Enough of this!" The governor's aide clearly knew he was losing control. "Get her back in the carriage, or I will have a hospital stretcher brought out."

"Back off, zebra bonnet." Cleon swung his stave under the nose of Gratianus's horse. The animal flung up its head and shied away.

The oncoming cavalry squadron had to stop short to avoid a collision. Its leader saluted Gratianus—"Centurion"—then frowned at me. "Tribune Aquilo?"

I moved to screen my indisposed wife. "Well met, Caturix. I see your rank was confirmed." The Fifth Gallica trooper whom I had promoted in battle now bore a double-feather crest on his helmet. "What has become of the disturbance in camp?"

"Resolved, sir. Prefect Lamia spoke to the men. And yes, thank you, sir." His curious troopers crowded in. I recognized most of them, who nodded to me. Certainly a less hostile greeting than I had expected.

In the corner of my eye I saw that Aurima had recovered. Gratianus must have noticed, too. "Clear the road, Decurion," he barked. "We are expected at headquarters."

Caturix sat immobile on his black horse. "Do you need assistance, Tribune?"

Cornelia Galla said tartly from the carriage doorway, "Are we stopping here for the night, Gratianus? Or do you mean to continue?"

"We are continuing now, my lady. Just as soon as everyone is ready."

I helped Aurima to her feet. With great composure she brushed dust and grass shreds from her tunic, then bent to pluck some sort of weed from the roadside. She chewed it to cleanse her mouth, spat it out, and rescued the baby from Dio.

"I am ready," she said resolutely.

Beyond the carriage and horsemen, the towers and rampart walks of the fortress were crowded with figures. The interlude had at least foiled Sabinus's attempt to smuggle me quietly into the camp.

It occurred to me that I should take advantage of the opportunity. I said, "As a matter of fact, Decurion, your help would be welcome."

59: MARCOMANNIA

Only a few lights burned in the corridors and rooms at headquarters, leaving shadows that engulfed doorways and hid swaths of floor. The second time Gratianus stubbed his toe on a broken tile, I said, "Let me lead." I knew the building's topography by heart.

"Fuck it." He stopped. We waited while the guard who had come with us returned to the rear door for a torch.

There ought to have been silence when the scrape of his boots died away, but a sound whispered through the building. It was not the soft fuming of our breath, nor yet the skitter of mice or squirrels' tiny claws. Were we not a thousand miles from the Mediterranean, I would have taken it for the sighing of a sea.

A chill ran up my arms. Perhaps I was possessed by the camp's strange unease. The long barracks blocks were dark, as they should be, but torches at the end of each century's row had showed too many armed soldiers patrolling the streets.

I had borrowed a horse from one of Caturix's troopers, leaving Aurima and the others to be delivered by carriage at a gentler pace than before. But Gratianus had ordered Caturix not to speak to me, so I knew no more about why I had been sent for than I did about why the Hispanians had erupted.

My muscles were tense, my mouth dry. At least I could confront the governor on my own. It would be several minutes before Galla's carriage caught up with us.

A trumpet sang out in the distance. The midnight watch change.

"We're wasting time." I cut ahead of Gratianus.

Light glowed from the atrium ahead. Two legionaries stood as usual beside the Eagle chapel; a couple of Sabinus's guards were posted inside the open front doors. They came to attention, weapons belts clinking and boots rasping, and saluted Gratianus.

A balding junior tribune popped out of the duty office. He stared. "Carinna?"

Praetorians on the steps of the outside portico spun around. Lamia's men: Battus and others. The prefect must be here, too.

A thread of words caught my ear. I ran up the steps at the side of the atrium.

"With Ironhand dead, who is there to challenge Vannius?" The muffled voice was Lamia's. "He will have an even tighter grip on the Marcomanni and Quadi."

"Breaking up their alliance will not solve—" Sabinus stopped. "Who's there?"

We had entered the anteroom of the Special Cohort offices. A lamp in a niche cast a tepid glow on grimy ocher walls, outlining a clerk's table and stool and, behind them, a gabled shrine housing a statuette of Victory. A door on the far side of the room led to what had been Glabrio's office, the source of the voices.

"Stay here." Gratianus gestured to the bench where informers and underlings usually waited. His knock on the inside door was answered by a grunt. A slab of brighter light fanned into the anteroom when he entered; then gloom fell again as the door shut.

I moved nearer to listen. "What took you so long?" the governor barked. "Is Aquilo here?" I missed Gratianus's lower-voiced answer. "Let him wait. Don't leave; the prefect and I are having a stimulating discussion."

I backed quietly away and shut the door by which we had entered. Skirting the creaky floorboards that I remembered, I edged around to the shrine where Victory extended her laurel wreath. Carefully I picked up the bronze statuette, set it on the floor, and leaned forward to look through the spyhole that her robes had hidden.

The three men were at the window end of the room, out of sight. My field of vision embraced a map of Pannonia and the Mark painted on the wall opposite me, its faded expanse updated with the blacker scribble of settlement names, new roads, and corrected watercourses. MARCOMANNIA had been scrawled in charcoal on the land north of the Danube. There was no mark on the wriggle of the Amber Road to show where Ingiomar's attacks had left Secundus, Licnos, and other Romans dead.

Lamia's voice was pitched so low that I would not have heard it without the peephole in the wall. "The old Princeps was afraid to trust the legions, so he kept them idle for over twenty years. But fighting is what they are trained for. Prepare them for war, promise them blood and booty—and, Governor, they will become yours."

His audacity amazed me. After the civil wars, all the legions had been brought under the Princeps' control. He paid them; he authorized their deployment; they swore obedience to him alone. Inviting a governor to usurp this authority was treason.

I wished I could see Sabinus's face. His reply, spoken over the sullen rumble of a distant thunderstorm, was slow and amused: "There is a bothersome little prerequisite for making war, Prefect: one needs approval from Caesar. And, of course, the Senate."

"We both know that a commander under attack is allowed to take immediate measures. As king of two Germanic nations, Vannius is a deadly threat. If we act now, before he has time to muster his men, we can take him down with one legion. When Caesar and the Senate see our success—*your* success, Governor—they will authorize deployment of the other Pannonian legions."

I heard the thump of feet, and a moment later Lamia strode to the wall map. His back was to me, so I saw only his silver hair and dark-striped mantle. "And then"—he swiped his hand across the bald swath north of the Danube—"we will annex Marcomannia, an unlimited source of furs for trade with the East, wild animals for the arena, and slaves for our mines, workshops, and homes." He turned toward Sabinus, and I heard a smirk in his voice. "Or soldiers, if they learn to follow orders."

His gesture had smeared some of the charcoal lettering, so it now read *MA NIA*. Appropriate, since annexing the Mark was a madman's fantasy. Even with three legions, trying to subdue the Marcomanni and Quadi in their own lands would be bloody and grueling. Anything other than complete success would lead to a political crisis in Rome that could spread throughout the world.

And though it was of little account in the tottering of an empire, a child some distance away from here would die—starved, smothered, or strangled—if Sabinus let Lamia persuade him to attack the Germans.

Hobnailed boots scraped on the stairs. Not Galla and my *familia*, obviously. I thrust Victory back into her shrine, and had thrown myself onto the bench by the time one of the troopers from downstairs pushed into the anteroom.

He peered at me. I nodded toward the inside office.

"Message from the duty officer, Centurion," he said when Gratianus opened the inner door. "Men are gathering in the assembly yard. Should he disperse them?"

"Gathering? At this hour?" Gratianus squinted past him, perhaps making sure I still waited in the anteroom. "How many? Why are they here?"

"About a score, sir. I don't know what they want."

"Go find out," he snapped. The trooper saluted and clumped away.

"Is Aquilo still there?" Sabinus called out. "Bring him in."

A six-branched candelabrum lit the long table that dominated Glabrio's office, now presumably Lamia's. The governor sat at one end beneath the shuttered window.

He gestured to a bench across from Lamia, saying something about getting to the bottom of the charges against me. I did not really listen. I was steeling myself to face the prefect and accuse him of deceit, incompetence, and treasonous ambition.

When I last saw him, Lamia had been haggard, unshaven, and as inflamed with spite as a rabid rat. His silver hair was sleekly combed now, his handsome face marred only by a scar on one temple that some might think added distinction.

I caught a flash of malevolence, or thought I did; his turn toward the candlelight made it hard to be sure. But then his eyes softened and his mouth bent into an apologetic curve of discomfort or embarrassment. Or pity.

"Aquilo," he said, "I am sorry, but the Germans have killed your child."

60: ODYSSEUS *POLYTROPOS*

The edges of the world vanished, and the narrow face turned to me became as featureless as a blank coin. Only his outline remained, bleached ash-pale as if in blinding sunlight.

My legs turned to sand. "No," I said. Whispered. I reached to steady myself on the table's edge, but missed and slumped onto the end of a bench.

An eternity passed before I became aware of his smirk. "Well, perhaps not yet," he said. He turned, all innocence, to Sabinus. "But who knows what those savages will do to a child begotten by an enemy?"

Insane rage burst through me. The anger of Thunraz, searing, sizzling, blinding. Strength flowed through my legs and back and arms. I roared. Fire and shadows leaped. Objects cascaded away. Cries. Clatters. A crash.

"Aquilo, sit down. Down, man!"

Someone tried to wrestle me. I was heaving the massive table with all my might toward Aelius Lamia. I was going to crush him against the wall like a bedbug. Going to see his guts spurt and blood spatter all over his fucking map of Marcomannia.

"Curse it, Aquilo! Calm yourself!"

Gratianus was pulling me backward. I was meant to control my fury. Did not want to. But slowly my sight cleared, and I saw Lamia had disappeared.

I stopped shoving. Sabinus edged around the shifted table to where the prefect had been and grasped a floundering arm. Lamia came up by awkward degrees, first thrusting against his toppled bench, then hoisting himself on the table's edge. He was red-faced and gape-mouthed, his hair and clothing rumpled.

As my breath slowed, I began to shake with the aftermath of anger. When I sat down, the table was a good three feet away from me.

A couple of troopers were summoned to restore it to its proper position. I took a great gulp of air, exhaled, and found my voice. "You will not learn the truth while this man is here, Governor. He lies as easily as others draw breath."

Lamia righted his bench, wincing. "Do you see ... what I was saying about his lack ... of self-discipline?" He was still winded.

"Compose yourselves, gentlemen," Sabinus said coldly. He signaled Gratianus to station himself against the wall near me. The troopers left.

Muttering under his breath, Lamia bent to pick up tablets and scrolls that had tumbled to the floor. I tried to suppress the thunder in my blood. "Have you decided against reprisals, sir?"

"I have decided nothing yet." The governor's gravelly voice was emotionless.

Lamia stood up. "We agree that Vannius cannot get away with killing Romans," he said, as if nothing had happened. "The legion is united on that. Cohort commanders, *auxilia* prefects, rank-and-file soldiers—everyone who knows what happened to my vexillation agrees that we must retaliate."

"Vannius had nothing to do with Inguiomerus's aggression," I countered.

"He is their king, is he not?" Lamia fired back.

"That does not mean he approved it. Or even knew about it."

"So you think we should let it go? You'll make excuses for anything they do, won't you—barbarian-fucker?"

Fury flashed through me again. I gripped the table's edge in both hands. It jolted, and fear slackened his face before he painted a triumphant sneer over it.

No. Do not reward his lack of honor.

Why did Sabinus not intervene? He sat at the table's end like a referee at a gladiatorial bout, letting us spar before him. A faint mumble of thunder almost sounded like the distant roar of an audience.

Lamia kept up the attack: "You fabricated this story of hostages to persuade us the Germans are no threat. Didn't you, Aquilo? You would never trade away your own brat."

My heart seemed to have crawled inside my skull, pounding so loudly that it almost smothered the sound of his voice. "The hostages we have exchanged are Inguiomerus's grandchildren, of the line of the Marcomanni king Maroboduus," I said as calmly as I could. "This is a formal agreement, one we must respect."

"What do you mean, 'we'? It is obvious that your loyalty is to the Germans. You'd like us to sit here, fat and stupid, while Vannius gathers his warriors to invade Pannonia. That would be well received in Rome, wouldn't it? That would add luster to the name of Calvisius Sabinus, eh, Governor?"

"Do not overstep yourself, Prefect," Sabinus said flintily.

His reproof helped my mind to clear, and I saw that I was not the prefect's only prey. He hoped to goad Sabinus into overreaching his authority, which would expose him to a charge of *laesa maiestas*. If he was found guilty, the glory for unmasking his treachery would be Lamia's. And Sabinus would be compelled for the sake of his family honor to commit suicide.

"Vannius is not planning to invade us," I said. "But if we attack the Mark, his warriors will fight. One legion cannot crush an army of men who ambush them from the trees and retreat along game trails. Certainly not this late in the year."

"It is barely September," scoffed Lamia, who must have thought military campaigns were like skirmishing with Cantabrian bandits.

"It snows here as early as November," I told him. "If you think a bloody forest war can be planned, fought, and won in sixty days, you are either a beetle-headed fool or a schemer intent on disgracing the governor."

"Next spring—"

I spoke over him: "Next year the legion will be fully occupied in recruitment, training, provisioning, and deployment for the northern campaign."

Before I could gauge Sabinus's reaction, another knock came at the door. The sudden draft as it opened made the candelabrum's flames flutter and stream. "Centurion, the crowd has grown," a soldier told Gratianus. "They want to see the governor."

"Raging Hercules!" Sabinus stood up, unlatched the shutters, and peered out. "You said you settled those Hispanians, Lamia."

"I did, Governor. Very firmly." The prefect rose to join him at the window.

Sabinus closed the shutters before he reached them. "Gratianus, go sort this out."

As the governor's aide and the soldier departed, Lamia strove to regain his dignity. "It does not surprise me that the men's discontent has spread. What better time to announce retributive measures, Governor"— he pointed at the map of Pannonia and the Mark—"and get them cheering about revenge and plunder?"

Sabinus sighed, rubbing his bare scalp. "I will decide that later. There is another matter to settle first." He looked at me.

My killing of Glabrio. Muscles tensed in my neck and shoulders.

"Stand aside, Gratianus," barked a woman's voice out by the stairway. Cornelia Galla swept in a moment later, her jewelry glittering in the candlelight. "Husband," she demanded, ignoring the rest of us, "what goes on with this midnight gathering in the assembly yard? Centurions as well as enlisted men, the duty officer says."

"My dear! They were not disrespectful to you, I hope."

"We entered from the back. But I saw them when I came into the atrium. Do you really think the main doors should be kept open?"

"Pay the men no heed. Gratianus is taking care of them."

I was on my feet, expecting Aurima, Dio, and Cleon to have accompanied her, but the governor's wife was alone. "Why are you here? Where is Aurima?"

Galla paused. Her makeup was worn, her clothing dusty and wrinkled. Frowning, she tucked a bloused swag of my tunic back under my belt. "Pull yourself together, cousin. She is nursing the baby downstairs, and the others are keeping watch."

Wishing she and the child were safe at Leonnatus's, I cursed my selfishness in having wanted her here with me. Being in the fortress must remind her of the disgraceful court-martial following her mother's murder. Had I brought her here only to have this visit end in a new calamity?

Galla went to the end of the table, where she gave Sabinus a cheek-kiss and Lamia greeted her with flustered effusion. I turned away to extract the thin flattened scroll she had casually inserted behind my belt.

The faintest whiff of sewage intruded on the room's aura of candle smoke. I sat down again and thumbed open the roll of papyrus beneath the table's edge. The creased sheet was about a handspan in width, lined with double rows of writing. Each upper line was in Latin, with a version beneath in encrypted gibberish. I cast my eyes over it swiftly.

D. AELIUS LAMIA, ACTING PREFECT, TO TRIBUNE L. FURIUS SAXA. EYES ONLY. Sir: Pursuant to your inquiry about provincial administration, I find G. Salvisius Sabinus to be a moderate and efficient governor, well served by his regional centurions. However, it may be desirable for the Pannonian legions to be commanded by a man who is more aggressive, or at least on less comfortable terms with Barbaricum. I am taking steps to generate material that might be used to prosecute the incumbent, should Caesar be so inclined. As to the capability of the legion commanders, perhaps

The papyrus had been torn off where the message continued. Dio must have judged this malicious excerpt of possible use, but how could it exonerate me of murder? I refolded the scroll and thrust it behind my belt buckle.

Lamia had pulled a writing tablet out of the assortment retrieved from the floor. He murmured to Sabinus, tapping a stylus on the tablet frame for emphasis. Galla seemed fully occupied in lighting new tapers to replace melted stubs in the candelabrum, but the flickering of her eyes betrayed her attentiveness.

"Marcus Licinius Aquilo." The governor thumped his fist to get my attention. He glanced at the tablet before him, eyes hidden beneath his crouching brows. "Prefect Lamia charges you with holding back troops who could have come to his aid during a barbarian attack, resulting in excessive casualties and enabling the enemy to seize him as a hostage. What do you say?"

"I deny it," I said. "He led an unnecessary sortie against a greater force of Inguiomerus's warriors. If I had thrown in the few troops left in camp, we would all have become casualties or captives."

"You incited the attack," Lamia snapped. "Hoping the barbarians would kill me, so you could take over my command and send more of my vexillation to their deaths."

"Wrong." I aimed my forefinger at him. "You took it on yourself to lead an undermanned column outside the defenses. Four brave men and I entered Inguiomerus's camp to save your life, you bumbling ingrate."

As I had guessed, he would have withstood a curse or an obscenity, but not a slur on his competence. He leaped up, his face in crimson contrast to his silver hair.

"Sit down, Prefect," Sabinus barked. "The risks Aquilo took in his rescue mission were confirmed by the quartermaster Aprilis. In fact, Aquilo nearly lost his own life. So I am dismissing the charge that he deliberately withheld support to let you die." He eyed Lamia. "Is that understood?"

Lamia swelled like a toad. "Governor, it is a mistake to dismiss my accusation. I am a regional prefect of the Praetorian Special Cohort."

"And I am a *legatus Augusti pro praetore*, so do not think you can piss farther than I can."

Galla reopened the shutters, perhaps to ease the tensions that heated the room. Cool and welcome air flowed in. The candle flames flared.

I said, "You are right to beware of this man, Governor. His intentions cannot be trusted. Or his honor." I reached to my belt for the encrypted message Dio had stolen.

"Who are you to speak of honor?" Lamia spat. "You destroyed a treaty by freeing your red-haired slut, and then killed the officer taking her back to Rome."

Sabinus held up his hand to silence us both. He flipped open a tablet and traced its contents with his finger, muttering to himself, then looked up. "Witnesses questioned by Centurion Gratianus said there was a great deal of confusion at the time of Glabrio's death. His men were defending themselves against a party of Quadi and a group of Marcomanni, who were also attacking each other. According to the senior surgeon of the Fifteenth, Aquilo had an unkempt beard and shaggy hair, and wore native clothing.

"So." He shut the tablet's leaves again. "It seems possible that Glabrio mistook Aquilo for a German and engaged with him." He looked at me. "Is that what happened?"

I withdrew my hand from the crushed paper at my waist. It was of no use now. Unwilling to lie outright, I said, "A man cannot be blamed for protecting himself."

Lamia burst out, "You assaulted him, Aquilo! I can prove it." His shadow lurched across the wall map as he pawed through scrolls on the table. "That bonecutter belongs to the cult of Mithras, the Parthians' so-called god of truth. When I asked him to swear by his god that Aquilo was innocent of attacking Glabrio, he refused.

"My secretary made these notes on the spot." He snatched up a sheet of papyrus and brandished it. "You cannot dismiss this signed statement, Governor. Aquilo was the assailant, not the victim. He deliberately murdered Vatia Glabrio."

Sabinus took the document and lifted it to catch the candles' fluttering light. Galla, behind him, craned over his shoulder.

Ah, Placidus: too honest a man to dissemble. I knew then that I was lost, but I could not let bloody disaster follow at my heels. "I urge you, Governor, do not let this matter overshadow the importance of peace with the

Marcomanni and Quadi. Your decision will affect the stability of our northeast frontier, perhaps for the next decade."

Lamia frothed with anger, spitting droplets like a sizzling griddle. "Do your barbarian friends really think swapping infants will let them escape Rome's vengeance?"

"I think you have been granted enough water, Aquilo," Sabinus said. He clambered to his feet with a grunt of weariness. "Gratianus will escort you to the vacant tribune's quarters. You will remain there under guard until a court-martial is convened."

"I have not finished, Gaius Calvisius," I said, surprising myself with the aristocratic intimacy to which I, alone of those in the room, was entitled.

Sabinus sank down, startled. Cornelia Galla touched his elbow, and he tipped his head to hear whatever she murmured to him.

"The issue is not revenge." I glanced at Lamia. "Nor is it conquest. It is honor." The mutter I had taken for a thunderstorm was louder now, and I lifted my voice to carry across the room. "The gods, or we ourselves, have chosen Rome to be a force for order in the world, to raise men and women of other nations from savagery."

I took a deep breath. "I have acted savagely, I admit, in repaying the treachery of men I trusted. I am not yet the man I want to be—a man of integrity who stands for truth and order, and against disorder and deceit."

"Another Mithras-worshiper," Lamia jeered.

"The Marcomanni and Quadi trust my word that we will not retaliate for Inguiomerus's madness," I said. "It is not because they credit my own honor. It is because they believe I represent the sacred honor of Rome."

Between the open shutters, across the unseen assembly yard, torchlight flared on the upper level of the headquarters gatehouse. Smoky candlelight danced around this room, too, on the tabletop and wall map, on the three faces turned toward me. Malice still animated Lamia's expression, although his smirk might have been palsied with faint unease. Galla studied me curiously. I could not read Sabinus's granite mask.

With no more to say, I sat. Gratianus would return at any moment to take me into custody. At least Aurima would be able to stay with me until my trial.

"Well, Aquilo." Sabinus heaved himself to his feet again. His brows were canted in regret, or perhaps sympathy. "Nicely said." A small smile without humor. "One would expect no less of Titus Carinna's son. But . . ." Shaking his head, he tapped the half-furled papyrus with its account of Placidus's refusal to lie for me.

"Better bar the door tonight, Aquilo," Lamia gloated. "The legion will not be happy to know you are back among them." He glanced toward the window. The diffuse mutter had become a jumble of men's voices, sullen and discontented. "It sounds like they have already found out."

"Come, Prefect, a little magnanimity," Galla said. "He did save your life."

"Pah! Inguiomerus would have freed me, Lady Galla; he knew who I was." He shrugged. "If you still hesitate to believe in Aquilo's perfidy, ask the men out there." He gestured toward the assembly yard. "Do not be surprised to hear them curse his name."

All my resolve to be a good man, to put aside revenge for conciliation, vanished. I rose up. "When the governor sees this, we will know better who can be trusted." I took the flattened scroll from behind my belt, flipped it open, and held it out to Sabinus. "This is the prefect's own copy of a message he sent to his master in Rome."

"How did you get this?" he demanded.

"I too have informers," I said.

The governor scowled, but took the scroll. As he tilted it toward the light, I watched his eyes flash from line to line.

"Aquilo, what did you give him?" Lamia blurted. His face was slack with stupefaction. He had gambled that I was bluffing about having stolen his correspondence.

Sabinus's fingers suddenly clenched on the papyrus. "'More aggressive, or at least on less comfortable terms with Barbaricum,'" he read aloud. "'Generate material that might be used to prosecute the incumbent'?" He glared at Lamia.

"What? No!" A sick understanding dawned in the prefect's eyes. "Governor, whatever you are reading must be a forgery."

Sabinus held the letter down beside the account of Placidus's interrogation and tipped the candelabrum to shed light on both documents. "The handwriting matches that of your secretary."

"Let me see." Lamia made a grab for the letter. Galla snatched at it too. The prefect's lunge knocked the teetering candelabrum out of Sabinus's hand. Galla screamed as it hit the table and burning candles jumped out of their sockets. Lamia flailed at himself, yelling: a taper had landed in the pouched curve of his mantle.

Light and shadows flew crazily around the room. I caught a rolling candle that spilled hot wax over my fingers. The door beside me swung open, and in the sudden current of air a bright flame spurted up from one of the papyri.

Galla held it, transfixed. Sabinus grabbed the blazing document away from her. As he swung around with it, a huge misshapen serpent of firelight lunged around the walls as if about to land upon us. Someone else shrieked.

I glimpsed the fiery paper flying out into the night. Then I was hugging Aurima in jittery darkness, lightened by a single candle someone had rescued. Her heart raced. The baby wailed in fright. "Hush, hush," I crooned to both of them. "All is well."

In truth, it was not. The message proving Lamia's duplicity had gone out the window in flames.

Aurima managed to calm Misia, cuddling her and patting her tiny back. We were buffeted once, then twice, by sweaty men shouldering past.

Gratianus now stood next to Sabinus and Galla, his crested helmet giving him the shadow of a colossus. Cleon had stationed himself between us and everyone else. "What's going on?" he demanded, gripping his cudgel in both hands.

Lamia stared at the window, as if fearing that his dangerous letter might swoop back inside. A wild hope sparked in me: perhaps it was not completely burned. If it had landed on the roof of the entrance portico, it might be salvageable. I released Aurima, rushed to the window, and hoisted my head and shoulders over the sill.

The assembly yard below teemed with men. Handheld torches bounced glints of light off sweating faces upturned to me. No, not to me; they were looking at the scrap of what had been papyrus, now flaring its last on the tiles of the portico roof. There was nothing left to retrieve.

The women's screams brought several of Gratianus's men bursting through the doorway, swords drawn. Aurima retreated to the far end of the room, where Cleon and Dio barricaded her and the child. Amid the commotion, Galla calmly relit candles and placed them in their holders.

"Silence!" Gratianus bellowed. Voices and motion stilled.

Sabinus said, "Prefect, send your supply officer to the legionary quartermaster by the start of the first watch, and draw provisions for a ten-day journey."

"A journey?" Lamia's voice was cautiously eager. "To where?"

"To any fucking place outside of my province." Sabinus spat the words over his uneven lower teeth. "If you and your men are still in Pannonia by the Ides, I will have a cohort from the nearest legion escort you to the border. You will not return without express authorization, in advance, from me. Is that clear?"

Lamia reared back. "You have no authority over the Praetorian Special Cohort."

Although Sabinus was shorter, fury made him formidable. "Within the boundaries of this province, I have the authority of Gaius Caesar Augustus Germanicus. Pack your baggage tomorrow and be gone with your troops by the next dawn."

Lamia seemed about to protest. The governor bellowed, "Go!"

The prefect looked around for support, but met only phlegmatic stares. "You will regret this, Sabinus." He headed for the door with as much dignity as a man in his situation could muster. "You too, Aquilo," he muttered, darting an evil glance at me before passing between Gratianus's two troopers.

Only then did shouting outside become noticeable. The crowd had grown impatient, chanting two syllables over and over that I could not make out.

Sabinus muttered something as Galla straightened his mantle and smoothed a crease in his tunic. He would not want to leave until the prefect and his guards were out of the way. I hoped he would wait as long to send me with Gratianus; it would be intolerable to give Lamia any satisfaction.

I thanked Dio for giving Galla the ill-fated copy of Lamia's message, and gestured Aurima and Cleon over to us. The background din was such that a whisper would not have been heard; even head to head, I had to speak up. "Listen: we are staying here in the fortress for a time. You can retrieve our things from Leonnatus's later today."

Aurima's eyes dilated in shock. She guessed at once, "He is going to judge you."

"For killing Bat-Ears?" Cleon screwed his face into an ugly scowl. "*Merda!* Marcus, I told you we shouldn't have stopped in Carnuntum."

"And I told you we could not outrun the law."

The clamor in the assembly yard intensified. A metallic din had joined the voices. Shouting and banging fell into rhythm together. *Crash. Crash. Crash.*

"Raging Hercules!" Sabinus stepped to the window again and leaned out over the sill. "Give me light, Gratianus!"

The clanging and shouting were drowned in a roar of acclaim. But when Gratianus held a flaring candle to illuminate Sabinus's face, the cheers died into a confused grumble.

The governor pulled back inside. Gratianus said something inaudible, pointing at me. Only then did I understand what the men were chanting above the clash of metal on metal: "Trib-une! Trib-une! Trib-une!"

If they had been goaded by Lamia's slanders, as he had predicted, I did not want to offer myself for their condemnation. I would leave headquarters by the back door, as I had entered it.

Gratianus beckoned to me. "Let them see you."

I held back. Aurima grasped my shoulder and touched her lips to my cheek. I breathed in baby milk, carriage leather, a hint of roses. "Show them you are a man of honor," she said.

With misgivings I walked toward the open shutters. The crash of iron on iron recalled the tumultuous battering of swords on shields, a prelude to battle. But that was impossible: no officer would let off-duty soldiers leave the barracks with their weapons.

The chaos sorted itself once more into a cadenced hammering and chants of "Trib-une! Trib-une!"

Well, Father, I have done my best.

I passed Sabinus and leaned out of the window with my hands on the sill.

They did not howl, hiss, or swipe their thumbs toward their throats. They cheered.

Voices roared, "Tribune!" up at me as soldiers crashed knives and spoons on pots and mess tins in clamorous salute. Among the crowd I spotted the quartermaster Aprilis, who had ridden with me to make peace with Ingiomar; Caturix, with the Gauls' *signifer* and others of our vexillation. And many others from the past whom I would never have expected to cheer for me: a couple of the narrow-stripe tribunes and even a few centurions—Festus, by everything holy!—legionaries and auxiliary soldiers and cavalrymen; clerks and orderlies and my former slave Baculus, manager of the junior officers' baths. I searched farther among the pumping fists and waving hardware, but had not found Placidus by the time Dio tapped me on the arm.

"Address them," he urged into my ear. "Make them speak for you."

He was right. Noise alone would not persuade Sabinus to acquit me.

I raised my arms for silence. It did not fall at once, but by degrees; too many of those assembled must have drunk a cup or three before their arrival. In lacunae of quiet I caught snatches of the governor's grumbling to his aide: "...humiliate me!...beyond belief that their officers..."

The right moment came to speak. Credit my rhetoric teacher. No, my father.

Do you practice your voice exercises daily, Marcus?

I shouted, "Comrades."

Another burst of acclamation. Heady stuff.

When the clamor ebbed, I said again, "Comrades! Let Governor Calvisius Sabinus witness your devotion to the Eagle of the Fifteenth."

I gestured to the governor, who leaned into the window. A cacophony of shouting overwhelmed the cheers. Forcing a smile, Sabinus lifted a hand in acknowledgment.

The chant rose again: "Trib-une, Trib-une."

Sabinus stepped aside, scowling. I took his place. "If I could," I shouted, "I would reward every officer and man here for his loyalty to Rome."

A bellow of acclaim from those who had missed the qualifier, or simply liked the sentiment. "But I have only praise to give," I went on. "No wealth remains to me—no house, no lands, no slaves, not even an altar on which to sacrifice to my family's spirits."

A murmurous hush settled upon the crowd. Every lowly recruit, even if he lacks two coppers to click together, has a shrine to his gods in his barracks.

I filled my lungs again. "That, because of my father's disloyalty to our *princeps*, Gaius Caesar Augustus." Overshadowed, for me, by his loyalty to Rome.

A few voices cheered reflexively at Caligula's name. Someone shouted, "Murderer!"

Behind me Dio muttered, "Marcus..." This was dangerous ground.

"Yet I myself am faithful to our Republic, to Caesar, the Senate, and the people. To my most holy *sacramentum!*"

A sustained roar of approval greeted this declaration. Nothing is more hallowed to a soldier, not even his Eagle, than his oath to Rome.

"Do I seek revenge? No! I desire Caesar's mercy. Nor do I seek revenge on the Germanic tribesmen we fought on the Amber Road. The madman who led them astray is dead." I thrust up my fist. "With this hand did I kill him."

Another roar.

"Now they, too, ask for mercy." I drew a long breath. "Will we refuse them, and unmake the *Pax Romana* that our brothers died for?"

"No!"

"Shall I be refused mercy, for striving to save those who relied on me?"

"No," they bellowed. "No!"

My throat was raw. "Mithras guide you, brothers," I rasped, "and the gods of Rome keep you safe." I raised my hands again in valedictory and stepped back.

"Trib-une! Trib-une! Trib-une!"

I turned in stunned gratification to Aurima, whose eyes shone in hope and anxiety. Beside her, Cleon wore a self-satisfied smirk. "Did you do this?" I asked him. My voice was ragged.

He shrugged, grinning. "Dio and me, we told some people. Caturix and his Gauls didn't like that you were in trouble for saving the vexillation. They told the guards coming off watch. We saw Aprilis on the way here. A few others."

I blinked at him and Dio. "My friends..." My voice gave out completely.

Sabinus seized my elbow. "You summoned them to embarrass me," he snarled. "You bribed them." His face was blood-red in the candlelight.

Mute, I could do no more than shake my head.

Gratianus answered for me: "Governor, I questioned some of the men. They support Aquilo, and object to turning him over to the Special Cohort."

"They object!" Sabinus snorted. "Do they take me for a weathervane, changing direction if they blow hard enough?"

Cornelia Galla placed a hand on her husband's gold cuff. If not for the noise from the assembly yard she would probably have whispered, but she had to lift her voice to be heard over it. "You know how sentimental they are," she said to him. "Let us not risk discontent." "Mutiny," the unspoken word, hung in the ill-lit room like Damocles's sword.

"Stay out of this, Galla!" Sabinus snapped. He poked his forefinger into my chest. "It was you, you vainglorious wretch, who endangered your troops in the first place." His eyes darted to Aurima. "By stealing the Germans' priestess and giving her a big belly."

Anger choked me. Before I could find speech, Aurima dived on him like a Fury. "No, it is you who endangered them," she shouted into his face. "You refused to see my father when he wanted justice for my mother's murder. You are the reason he turned against Rome. You are the reason he attacked the soldiers, the reason my husband was almost killed and my child is a hostage. It is you who made all this trouble!"

Sabinus said, "What nonsense, woman!" But his tone was unconvincing, and howls of fright from the baby nearly drowned out his words.

"Now you can make it good," she insisted. "You can give justice to my husband, and to my people who ask for peace."

I could not see her face, only his, as he confronted this implacable red-haired warrior-mother, as tall as he was. His eyes widened, then slitted in obstinacy.

"Governor," I said scratchily, "the men have asked you to show mercy."

His nostrils flared. In sudden dread I thought that the bull had been goaded too far; he was readying himself to gore me.

Aurima and I stood shoulder to shoulder, confronting him. The baby's squalls were dwindling into hiccups, and it was at last possible to be heard without shouting. But we had already said all that was important.

Sabinus picked up the topmost scroll before him as if to review Placidus's refusal to lie for me, then flipped it down unread. "You spoke of honor," he told me gruffly. He did not look at Aurima. "If I am questioned by Caesar, I must be able to say that I did not suppress evidence." He motioned to Gratianus; it was my turn to be sent away. "I am sorry."

Cornelia Galla said, "My dear, there is no evidence that Aquilo did wrong."

"The *medicus's* signed statement will be damning enough." He gazed somberly at the scattered reports on the table before him. "And the proof of that worm Lamia's treachery has gone up in smoke."

"No, dear, it was the *medicus's* statement that burned," she said demurely. "I don't suppose there will be time for the prefect to replace it before he leaves."

Sabinus lifted the top document again, glowered at it, then tossed it down and rummaged through the others. "Are you sure?" At last he swung around and stared at the window, perhaps trying to recall which scrap of blazing papyrus had sailed through it.

"Humph." He turned back to me. "It seems the evidence that you murdered Glabrio does not exist."

I dared to ask, "Then that charge too is dismissed?"

Once more he eyed the scrolls and tablets. "I do not see the copy you gave me of Lamia's message to Saxa. Did he steal it during the commotion?"

No answer. Evidently none of us had noticed. He cleared his throat. "Aquilo, do you have something else to use against him?"

I glanced at Dio. Grimacing, he tipped his head in a minute shrug that I took to mean "Nothing as good as that."

Sabinus gazed into the candlelight. Again he rubbed a hand over his bald scalp. I guessed what he was thinking: pardoning me might be disastrous. Without a hold over Lamia, how could he prevent the prefect from making trouble for him in Rome?

I drew a deep breath. Aurima's grip on my hand tightened.

Galla drew a thin flattened roll of papyrus from the neck of her stola. "By Juno," she said, wrinkling her nose, "this does stink! Licinius Dio, wherever did you keep it?"

She unrolled it daintily, using her fingernails. "'Decimus Aelius Lamia, Acting Prefect, to Tribune Lucius Furius Saxa.' This is what you are looking for, isn't it?"

She passed it to her husband. As he read it, his broad mouth curled triumphantly. With this document, he could not only protect himself but threaten Lamia's standing among Rome's Senators, magistrates, governors, and generals. Trusted by none of his betters, the Special Cohort prefect would know he could never advance to their level—a revenge more agonizing than anything physical I could have done to him.

When Sabinus looked up, he seemed surprised that we were still there. Galla moved closer to murmur in his ear. He nodded and handed the little scroll to Gratianus, who slid it carefully into his belt pouch. "Marcus Licinius Aquilo, the charge of wrongful death against you is dismissed for lack of evidence."

I managed to croak, "Thank you, Governor." Aurima slid her hand up my arm and pressed me against her. I felt the squeeze of Dio's fingers on one shoulder, Cleon's big hand on the other.

"What about the tribes?" I said.

Except for the outcry of jostling men below, there was silence. Moths fluttered soundlessly around the candelabrum.

Half a dozen heartbeats later Sabinus said, "I will invite Vannius to talk with me about peace. If he confirms what you have said, perhaps there is no need for reprisals."

"Bring him to the camp, Governor. Let him see there are no preparations for war."

"Yes, Tribune. I might have thought of that myself."

I tried for dignity, but could not manage it. Holding Aurima's face in both hands I kissed her soundly, not caring how ill-bred it was to display affection in public. "He is safe," she said with tears bright in her eyes, and I said it back to her. The distant shouts seemed to acclaim the relief coursing through us both.

Behind us the governor ordered, "Get rid of the men outside, Gratianus. Tell them their precious Aquilo is safe, and send them back to their barracks."

"But is this not an opportunity, Sabinus?" Galla interjected.

Their voices faded as I turned to my companions. Clasping Cleon's shoulders, I kissed him on both bristly cheeks like a dear friend. "I did not know you could unfailingly draw a crowd, Cunctator, even outside the arena."

He beamed broken-toothed, his hair thick with dust. "You're why they came, Marcus." He rolled his eyes at Dio. "Pen-Pusher helped. Sent a note to your surgeon pal."

"'Pen-Pusher'?" I shook my head. "No, Dio, the name you have earned is '*Polytropos.*' It is what Homer calls Odysseus," I told Cleon and Aurima. 'Wily.' 'Cunning.'"

To my surprise Dio hugged me, his satchel on its strap whacking my side. I leaned my head against his. We stood together, half brothers of different mothers.

He had sent a note to Placidus. I liked the thought that the crusty surgeon had rallied supporters for me, perhaps to make up for abetting Lamia.

"Well." Cleon rapped the butt of his cudgel on the floor. "Let's get going, then."

I turned to look at Galla. She was watching her husband step to the window, a tablet in his hand. "Cousin," I said raspily, "I am in your debt."

"Mine?" She raised her delicate brows. "I did nothing, Marcus Licinius. Sabinus is far too wise to be swayed by anyone else's views."

I met her knowing eyes. She reached up and straightened my torc so that the ends were centered. "One must help one's family, that's all."

Yells rose from the assembly yard as the governor leaned out of the window. "Soldiers!" he bellowed. "I am commending to the Senate and people of Rome Tribune *Ad Rem* Marcus Aquilo, who led his troops on the Amber Road with honor and courage."

I smiled. It was good to hear. And the burst of cheering indulged my pride.

Aurima nudged past me. The baby slept, exhausted, in the crook of her arm. "You did very much, Lady Galla," she said over the noise. "I think you are *polytropos*, too." She held out her free hand.

Galla looked startled at being offered a handclasp by another woman. She studied Aurima's face, and something changed in her cool eyes.

Her manicured fingers pressed Aurima's gently. "Take care of your little girl," she said, and smiled.

"Hear me now!" Sabinus shouted again. "To reward your steadfastness and bravery as guardians of the frontier, I will make a donative to each common soldier of two hundred denarii . . ."

The roar of acclaim was deafening. Augustus himself had left each legionary only three hundred in his will. And Sabinus was awarding this gift in his own name, which might not sit well with Caligula.

"May we borrow your carriage, cousin?" I asked Galla.

She waved her consent. Aurima with the baby, Dio, Cleon, and I tramped wearily down the torchlit stairs, leaving the governor and his shrewd wife to their intriguing.

61: ROMA AMOR

The stonecutter had done well in the few days he was given. A traditional relief of a legionary striking down a barbarian had been recut to show a gladiator in a *secutor*'s helmet attacking a *retiarius*. Beneath the image was incised an epitaph:

DM
CAPANEVSOLLIVS
SECHARENAEXXXVIIVICTOR
ROMACAPVAQVE
AETXXXIVNVCERNAT
FIDVSQADMOR
AMICISVIFECERVUNT

Pushing up the wide brim of my straw hat, I read it aloud to Aurima. "'To the gods and shades. Capaneus Ollius, secutor in the arena, thirty-seven times victor in Rome and Capua. Aged thirty-four, born in Nuceria.'" I paused. "Cleon thinks the age is right."

"Is there more?"

I cleared my throat. "'Faithful unto death. His friends made this.'"

"That is very nice." She studied the tombstone somberly. A breeze edged with autumn's first crispness fluttered the edge of the baby's swaddling.

Cleon was pouring wine into the small hole in the stone meant to convey it to Ollius's spirit. He had chosen a sunny spot for the tomb, just east of the camp amphitheater on the road to Portorium and the ferry crossing.

Dio jotted on his tablet at the roadside: more preparations to make, no doubt, or provisions to buy. Luckily, it had turned out that I was wealthier than I had thought; for Leonnatus had not only refused Lamia's demand to return the five thousand denarii paid to me, but had invested and nearly doubled it. He had sold me an amber drop of the hue Nina desired, and had overseen the silversmith who set it in a pendant.

Even after buying Ollius's tombstone and contributing to another for Secundus, I had been able to put substantial sums in accounts that Cleon and Dio could draw on in Narbo. As for the money plundered from Lamia's chest, I had wanted to use it to repay Silius, but was persuaded by Dio to keep it for the expenses of our move. Silius would not mind.

Glancing from Dio to stolid Zephyrus, who held the grazing donkey's rein, I missed Rufus's beacon of red-gold hair, his bright clever eyes, his hunter's lightfootedness. It was ironic that after vowing to reunite my *familia*, I had lost two of them. However, Leonnatus had agreed to find and negotiate purchases of the slaves sold at my father's death. He had already sold Zephyrus back to me to tend my horses, along with Zephyrus's wife, who would cook and help mind the child.

Our child . . .

My gaze was lost in the treetops that hid the Danube when Aurima hoisted the infant to face the tombstone. "Behold, Misia," she said in Germanic, "here is buried a man of honor who died for his *fraujaz*."

The baby mouthed an O, which made me smile. In Latin Aurima went on, "Capaneus Ollius, you guarded us well, and you saved my husband from the treachery of Berinhard. May you be welcome in the afterworld of brave men."

Her blessing put a seal on our informal ceremony. The remains of cakes and wine were gathered and loaded into the donkey's panniers. Concerned that the long walk from Leonnatus's had tired her, I offered her a hand in mounting the little beast.

She nestled the infant into her pouched shawl. "In a few days I will be weary of riding. I will walk."

"Take the hat, then." I swept it off and held it out to her.

"By the Goddess, no! Sabinus will be a bramble bush if you are recognized."

"Not *rubus*; 'red-faced' is *rubeus*," I corrected, although it was amusing to think of the governor sprouting thorns. One of the conditions he had insisted on was that I would avoid attention until leaving Carnuntum. Hence the hat.

It was barely a week since he had stood with Vannaz on the steps of the Temple of Augustus and Rome, surrounded by senior military officers and the king's escort, to announce that our peace treaty with the Marcomanni and Quadi had been reinforced by the giving of hostages. Already most of the *tabernae*, cookshops, brothels, and other establishments had reopened, and people who had fled the town were trundling sheepishly back with their mattresses, pots and pans, baskets and crates. A celebratory mood prevailed, as if it were Saturnalia.

I glanced down the road for traffic that might be a nuisance, such as a drove of pigs or a detachment returning from the quarries. Indeed, a couple of horsemen were coming from the ferry port, with several others riding in the dust behind them. One of the two in the lead wore a helmet with a black-and-white crest; the other was bareheaded.

Aurima waved. "Vangio!"

We had not seen him since leaving Grozhauga. The king's nephew separated from the troop and galloped toward us, blond hair flying. He flung himself off his horse and hugged her. Reaching to grasp his hand, I noted that his embrace would have been more ardent had she not pushed him back to protect the baby.

He was convoying Roman military equipment taken by Ingiomar, which Vannaz had returned as a sign of good will. "Even their god-charms," he said, sketching a small circle at his neck to denote a soldier's identification tag. "By now your Senate has approved the agreement between our peoples, *ja?*"

"They are certain to approve, but I have not heard yet," I said. He had an imprecise idea of the distance between Carnuntum and Rome.

"Vangio," Aurima broke in impatiently, "did you see my Beran? Is he well?"

His indulgent smile made his face even more dolphinlike. "I knew you were going to ask," he said in Germanic. "Helewidis says he is missing you but he is very well. And she hopes her Misia is the same."

Aurima talked for the next few minutes, loading him with messages. In that time the rest of the column caught up. Its helmeted leader was, as I had suspected, Sabinus's aide Gratianus.

He signaled for a halt. "Still here, eh?"

"Not for long." I flapped the dust away with my hat. "We are on our way to Gallia Narbonensis in a couple of days."

Vangio interrupted the flow of instructions for Helle. "You must come to the fortress with us, Aquilo."

When I told him I would not, he said, "Wait, then. Friduric sends you a present." He mounted again and rode back toward a string of ponies laden with bundles.

A present from Aurima's crippled brother, my son's new foster father? Would it be some insult, some token of gloating? *I have a boy now, and you do not . . .*

For distraction while we waited, I asked, "Any news of Prefect Lamia?"

Gratianus said solemnly, "I, too, will make you a gift, Aquilo." Leaning down to my level, he confided, "I found out why the Hispanians rioted. They heard a rumor that the Army would forbid worship of gods with two genders, which is a proclivity of theirs. Who do you suppose spread that false information?"

"The same prefect from Hispania who boasted about subduing their riot," I guessed.

He rewarded me with an angular smile. "An unfavorable report has been sent to his superior, the Guard co-commanders, and the Princeps." He straightened in his saddle.

"How unfortunate for him." I smiled too, thinking of the other purloined documents now stitched into our saddle pads and the bottom of the baby's basket.

Vangio cantered back, clutching a flat rectangular package wrapped in tanned deerskin. He jumped down and held it out to me. "Friduric says you must want this."

"Oh, no." Guessing the contents, I made a gesture of refusal with my free hand. "I thank Friduric, but no. Let it go to the governor with everything else."

He frowned. Well, let him be offended; I did not want the cursed thing.

Aurima was more sensitive to the possible affront, or perhaps merely curious. "Why do you not accept it, husband?" She took the package from Vangio and picked at the knotted thong binding it.

Useless to object now. Reluctantly I cut the tie for her. Seeing AMOR uppermost on the guard of my longknife, I flipped it over to show ROMA. As if I believed in omens.

Aurima unwrapped the deerskin. "What is— Oh! Oh, Austro guard me!"

Gratianus's horse shied at the suddenness with which she deflected Caligula's face away from her. The portrait would have flown from her hands into the dung-strewn road had I not grabbed it.

He glared up at me, his long flat brows nearly meeting in a glower of suspicion and threat, a contrast with the small smile on his lips. A ribboned wreath of laurel leaves hid the thinning hair.

The painting had surely been done before Drusilla's death. Were there lines under the gray eyes now, and grief in their depths? Was the sweet Julian mouth downturned in disillusion at the gods' cruelty?

"We cannot keep that," Aurima said in Germanic, her voice tremulous. "He is going to watch. Everywhere we go, he is knowing it."

"Do not worry, my heart." I rewrapped the portrait and put it in one of the panniers. I would give it to Leonnatus, who would put a frame on it and sell it to some devotee of our noble Princeps.

Dio tucked his tablet under his arm. "But, Aurima, we carry his picture all the time." He fished a coin from his belt wallet. "It is not him. It looks like him, you see, so people can tell this is a coin of Rome, which he rules."

She eyed the bronze *as*, as big around as a horse's nostril. "Is this a magic word, that does not end or begin?"

"No, it is just his name and titles. Not magic." He traced the abbreviations circling the rim. "C CAESAR AUG GERMANICUS: that is his name, Gaius Caesar Augustus Germanicus. PON M means he is Pontifex Maximus, the highest religious authority. And TR POT stands for 'tribunician power,' which means he has the highest political authority." He turned the coin in his fingers and put it away again.

"Germans are unused to lifelike portraits," I explained to Gratianus, who was looking on curiously.

His puzzlement evaporated. "Farewell, then." He waved his troop onward.

"The Goddess be with you, Aurima." Vangio kissed her hastily, nodded to me, and leaped on his pony to regain the lead.

We watched the rest of the cavalcade pass by: an honor guard of cavalry, a half dozen warriors who shouted merrily to Aurima without heed to their mission's solemnity, the pack ponies, and another score of horse soldiers bringing up the rear.

"Peace comes to the frontier," Dio said, half sardonically and half in resignation. He slipped the tablet into his satchel. "I must start back; there is still much to be done."

"We will all go," I said, clapping the straw hat on my head. We walked together on the stone road, our shadows flying like dark banners toward the forests of the Mark.

EPILOGUE

Leonnatus was sending a shipment of furs and amber to Narbonnese Gaul with us, or us with it, so experienced guides and armed guards would accompany us on the road. I had borrowed his office and was studying a map with our caravan's headman when someone in the arbor caught my eye, gliding past a small smoky fire of leaves and prunings.

The headman, turned away from the folding doors, did not notice. "Here," he said, tracking a line with his finger, "we descend from these little Alps, as they are called, and it is only a few more—" He stopped.

The figure in the arbor became Aurima. Her cheeks were still flushed from our walk to Ollius's tomb, and she wore the dusty-hemmed stola peeled off earlier for napping. In one hand she held a leather scroll case whose seal tightly bound its top and bottom. "Husband," she said, "a soldier has brought this. 'For Marcus Carinna,' he said."

Dio was teaching her the Greek alphabet, for that language is common in Mediterranean Gaul. I said, "Does the seal have a Greek lambda on it?" That would mean it was from Sabinus, now back in Poetovio. Some ancestor of his had adopted the shield symbol of the Spartans, reputed to be the Sabines' forefathers.

She peered at it and shook her head.

I looked up, frowning. "Does it have a head with two faces?" That was the seal of the Special Cohort, which Lamia would use. Or Saxa, his superior in Rome.

"No," Aurima said.

"Never mind, then." I turned back to the map. "I will look at it later."

"But this seal is very strange," she said. "On it is the same writing that is on Dio's coin." She peered closer at it. "'C CAESAR'—did he not say that means Caligula?"

For a moment I did not move. My eyes drifted from the map to the "R" on my left wrist that promised *I will return*. Then to the other scar that marked me as the father of a son who would grow up beyond the Roman frontier.

"What a pity," I said slowly. "For a letter to have come so far without reaching the right man."

Curiosity in Aurima's gray-green eyes melted into grave understanding. "I do not suppose Caesar wants the wrong man to read it."

"You are right." I rose. She smiled at me, scented with woodsmoke, sun-sweat, and sweetness. I twined my fingers with hers. "Come, *frijdila*. I know what we can do with it."

GLOSSARY

A
ad rem: for a specific event or thing
ala: a Roman auxiliary cavalry unit of 500 or 1000 men
amma (Germanic): grandmother
amor: love
ampulla: small glass container
ana morgan (Germanic): "Until tomorrow"
Andromeda: a maiden saved by Perseus from a sea monster
Antiope: an Amazon who sided with her husband against her sisters
appellatio: legal appeal
Arethusa: a sea nymph who fled her home to be a freshwater spring
armilla: arm-ring
as (plural **asses**): a bronze coin of low value
aureus: a gold coin worth 25 **denarii**
aurochs: a shaggy wild ox
Austro (Germanic): goddess of light
auxilia: auxiliary troops, part of the Roman Army

B
baltha (Germanic): brave
basia me: "Kiss me"
Belenos: Celtic sun god
beran (Germanic): bear
broodher (Germanic): brother
butyrum: butter

C
caestus: brass knuckles, sometimes with spikes
calo (plural **calones**): cavalry servant(s)
carissima: dearest (fem.)
carpentum: a covered traveling carriage for four people
cavere: to beware (imperative: **cavē**)
cella: the holy central space in a temple
centurion: commander of an Army unit of about 80 men
Cernunnos: a horned Celtic god, similar to Pan
clientes: dependants of a man of higher status (their patron)
congius: a Roman liquid measure, about 3¼ liters
cymbala: small cymbals with a chiming note

D

decurion: head of a cavalry squadron
delator: informer
denarius: a silver coin, worth about a day's wage for a skilled laborer
di manēs: gods and spirits
dolabra: pickax, mattock
dominus: master
dourateios hippos (Greek): wooden horse
driô (Germanic): three
dulthi (Germanic): festival
dumba (Germanic): idiot
duplicarius: second in command of a cavalry squadron
duumviri: a two-man board of elected town officials
dverga (Germanic): dwarf

E

edri (Germanic): intestines
eih (Germanic): oak tree
eironeia (Greek): irony
Epona: Celtic goddess of fertility, protector of equines
erlmann (Germanic): nobleman
evocatus: a legion veteran who has reenlisted

F

fader (Germanic): father
familia: all those a **paterfamilias** is responsible for, including slaves
fêla (Germanic): magic-woman, sorceress
fidelitas: the Roman virtue of faithfulness; loyalty to one's duty
fledarmûs (Germanic): bat
fluokhôn (Germanic): cursed
framea: heavy Germanic spear
fraujaz (Germanic): lord, chieftain
frijdila (Germanic): darling (fem.)
frijo (Germanic): husband
friund (Germanic): friend
frôda (Germanic): wise
fuir (Germanic): fire

G

garum: a favorite Roman condiment made of fermented fish guts
geist (Germanic): ghost
gladius: the legions' short stabbing sword
goukh (Germanic): bastard
Grozhauga (Germanic): Big Hill (Berinhard & Chlothar's stronghold)

H

haistra (Germanic): young oak tree
halla (Germanic): feasting hall
haljô (Germanic): hell, the underworld

Haljo Dunkara (Germanic): goddess of the underworld
haninnan (Germanic): hens
Hercules: a hero who took on 12 labors to expiate a fit of madness
heribanan (Germanic): a tribal call to war
hirsuti: hairy ones (pejorative term for Germans)
Hoheneih (Germanic): High Oak (Ingiomar's stronghold)
honestas: the Roman virtue of honor, respectability
hydra: a mythical giant water-snake with nine heads

I
Icarus: a boy who flew so close to the sun that his wings melted
Ides: the 13th of short months or 15th of long months
immo: "indeed" (reinforcing what has just been said)
imperator: supreme commander
imperium: power, dominion
invictus: unconquered
Ithaca: Odysseus's home, reached after 20 years of war and travails

J
ja (Germanic): yes
jawâra (Germanic): yes indeed

K
Kalends: the first day of the month
krig (Germanic): war
kuninga (Germanic): king

L
laesa maiestas: treason
lambda (Greek): the letter "L"
latifundium: a large estate worked by slaves
legatus legionis: military officer commanding a legion
legatus Augusti pro praetore: governor of a province where legions are posted
legion: an Army unit of about 5000 men
lemur: the restless spirit of an unburied person
ligula: small liquid measure; figuratively, "a drop"
lupa: whore (literally, she-wolf)

M
Mars: the Roman god of war
mavî (Germanic): maiden
Medea: a sorceress who punished her unfaithful husband by killing their children
medicus: surgeon or doctor
merda: shit
min fridu (Germanic): my love
min hersa (Germanic): my heart

mina dîsi (Germanic): my goddess
mirabile dictu: amazingly
mirmillo: gladiator fighting with a sword and shield
Mithras: a god linked with the sun, mankind's ally against evil
modicum: a little
modius: a unit of dry measurement, about two gallons
mola: mill
monstrum: monstrosity
mora (Germanic): bog
mulsum: wine mixed with honey
muot (Germanic): courage
muoter (Germanic): mother

N
nabja (Germanic): nose, beak
Nama Mithra (Persian): "Hail Mithras"
Nerthuz (Germanic): mother-goddess of Earth
nymphaeum: a room with a fountain, plants, and sculptures

O
Odysseus: a Greek king in *The Odyssey*, creator of the Trojan Horse
onager: a type of catapult whose swinging arm throws a heavy stone

P
paedagogus: an educated child-minder assigned to a well-born boy
Pannonia: a Roman province, now part of Austria and Czechia
papyrus (pl. **papyri**): writing paper made of plant material
paterfamilias: head of a **familia**, including its slaves and freedmen
pavor saltūs: terror of the forest
Pax Romana: the Roman Peace over its dominions
Perseus: mythological slayer of Medusa and savior of Andromeda
polytropos (Greek): many-changing, devious
posca: wine vinegar drunk by soldiers
post scriptum: an afterthought in a letter
prefect: a senior military or civil official with broad responsibility
Princeps: "First Chosen" (euphemism used by the Caesars)
Proserpina (aka **Persephone**): goddess of the cycle of life and death
pugio: soldier's longknife

R
res publica: the Roman state (see Historical and Other Notes)
retiarius: a gladiator fighting with net, trident, and dagger
reveniam: "I will return"
rhetor: a teacher of rhetoric (the art of arguing a case in law)
Roma Victrix: Victorious Rome
rôva (Germanic): "Be still"
rudra (Germanic): blood, red

S

sacellum: shrine at headquarters housing a legion's sacred insignia
sacramentum: soldiers' oath of allegiance to Rome and Caesar
salve lucrum: "Hail, profit!"
secutor: gladiator equipped with heavy armor and a visored helmet
sestertius: a bronze coin, about the cost of a liter of ordinary wine
signifer: military standard-bearer
signum: a unit military standard bearing images and medallions
skita (Germanic): shit
spatha: long Roman cavalry sword
sponsus, sponsa: fiancé, fiancée
SPQR (Senatus Populusque Romanus): Senate and People of Rome
stola: long sleeveless garment worn by women over a tunic
sudatorium: sweat-bath
svehra (Germanic): father-in-law
svert (Germanic): sword

T

taberna: tavern (the owner is a **tabernarius**)
tablinum: room in which a **paterfamilias** receives clients and guests
te amo: "I love you" (**te amo idem**: "I love you too")
tepidarium: warm room at the baths
Thunraz (Germanic): god of thunder
Tiwaz (Germanic): chief god of the sky, war, and law and order
tonstrix: hairdresser
tribune: an officer from a Senatorial family, second in authority to a legion commander (a broad-stripe tribune); or an officer from a lesser family, in charge of a cohort (a narrow-stripe tribune)
turma: a cavalry squadron of about 30 men
turpis: unclean, foul

U

umbo: the boss in the middle of a shield

V

vexillation: Army detachment sent on a mission
vexillum: military banner
Via Lactea: the Milky Way
vigiles: city watchmen/firemen
vikkan (Germanic): sorcerer
virtus: a Roman quality embracing honor, valor, and manliness
vis: strength
vivit post funera virtus: honor lives on after death
vulthu (Germanic): prestige, glory

W

wergelt (Germanic): compensation for having killed a man
Wodunaz (Germanic): the warriors' god

Z

zoubar (Germanic): magic

With appreciation for Old Germanic words to the 1909 *Wörterbuch der Indogermanischen Sprachen, dritte Teil: Wortschatz der Germanischen Spracheinheit*, by August Fick, Hjalmar Falk, and Alf Torp, published in digital form by the University of Pennsylvania Department of Linguistics. Any errors are mine.

HISTORICAL AND OTHER NOTES

Romans called Rome "the Republic" (*res publica,* or "the public entity"). In 38 AD Rome was still nominally headed by an elected leader, but Augustus's and Tiberius's designation of successors within the family meant it was becoming more of a monarchy than a republic.

Mithras, known as the Lord of Light, was identified with the sun. His role was to assist mankind in the global struggle between good and evil, a struggle which also took place within every man. Originating among Parthians in the East, Mithraism started to be adopted by Roman soldiers in the first century AD and eventually became widespread among the legions. The male-only cult had a military-like hierarchy among its brotherhood of devotees, who gathered regularly for ritual feasts.

The Council of Women, about which Aurima says, "There are many wise women ... It is not like the Senate of Rome, where men vote according to the side they are on," is my invention. However, "the matrilineal principle may have been in full force among at least some of the [Germanic] peoples ... and perhaps among a majority of them" (E.A. Thompson, *The Early Germans*), which suggests that women played an important role in certain tribes' decision-making. (Most of our information about early Germanic customs comes from Julius Caesar and Tacitus, who—being Roman men—weren't conditioned to look for, or give credit to, women's political contributions.)

The first military camp in Carnuntum was built around 6 AD, when Tiberius was preparing for an invasion of the Mark that didn't happen. Eight years later, the Fifteenth Legion Apollinaris was stationed there to guard this critical part of the Roman frontier.

Because Carnuntum was a stop on the Amber Road between the Baltic Sea and northern Italy, there was regular commercial traffic across the Danube. At the time of *Amber Road* (38 AD), it's likely that the river was traversed by a ferry docking at a customs port near Carnuntum, where tax would be levied on trade goods entering the Empire. Back then, the Danube flowed around many loops and islands, slowing the current enough for an oar-powered ferry to cross. (A pontoon bridge that appears on Marcus Aurelius's column in Rome was probably built expressly for his troops during the Marcomannic Wars of 166-177 AD. Then and earlier, the frontier would not have been secure enough to allow construction of a permanent Danube bridge.)

Ingiomar's intention to sacrifice his Roman captives to Tiwaz has a documented precedent. After a coalition of Germanic tribes annihilated Quinctilius Varus's three legions in 9 AD, an avenging Roman army reached the site to find ". . . human heads prominently nailed to trunks of trees. In the adjacent groves were the barbarous altars on which they had immolated tribunes and first-rank centurions." (Tacitus, *Annals* 1.61)

The Eagle standards of Varus's legions were captured during that massacre, a horrifying loss because they symbolized Rome's military strength. Two Eagles were regained in 14-15 AD by Germanicus Caesar. The third was not recovered until 41 AD.

The identifying marks tattooed on Marcus, Friduric, and their children may have been runes, reportedly developed by Germans in the first or second century AD.

If you'd like to quote some of Lamia's aphorisms in Latin, try these:

Bad beginnings lead to bad endings: *Mala principia malus finis.*

Deeds, not words: *Acta non verba.*

Everything has its price: *Omnia cum pretio.*

Forewarned is forearmed: *Praemonitus praemunitus.*

Fortune disdains the lazy: *Ignaviam fortuna repugnat.*

He who is given a gift cannot be choosy: *Ne eligat qui donum accipit.*

Like speaks to like: *Similis similibus.*

Where there's smoke, there's fire: *Ubi fumus, ibi ignis.*

Make haste slowly: *Festina lente.*

ABOUT THE AUTHOR

Sherry Christie

I work from a barn in a coastal Maine village, assisted by two cats and surrounded by Rome-related artifacts and pictures—great inspiration for *Roma Amor, Amber Road,* and other novels set in the world of the Caesars.

I've been a writer practically since I could pick up a pencil. After working for a magazine, I segued into advertising. That led to a freelance copywriting business and co-writing books on money psychology (with time off for long-distance sailing).

But historical fiction has always been my true literary love. I love to read (and write) novels that combine high-stakes suspense with unusual characters, extraordinary circumstances, romantic tension, and a splash of humor.

Have you signed up to stay in touch with the Roma Amor world? If not, please join the Readers Group at **roma-amor.com**. You'll receive exclusive newsletter updates, and qualify for a free e-novella right away.

In the meantime, thanks for reading *Amber Road*!

Photo credit: Deborah Bailey

ACKNOWLEDGMENTS

Spouses usually get thanked last in authors' acknowledgments, but mine deserves to be at the top of the list. Not only is Harry handsome, loving, and greathearted, but he's an ideal research partner—an enthusiastic photographer and off-the-beaten-path driver ("Wait, was that the turn for the Roman bridge?"). If Amber Road has a godfather, he's it.

I'm also deeply grateful to a cadre of friends and fellow writers who have cared, cheered, and critiqued over the years: Ruth Cash-Smith, Laurel Robinson, Fran Drabick, and Kelly Cunnane. Ruth was a beta reader, along with Carey Christie and Jenny Quinlan of Historical Editorial, saving my derrière by identifying story holes and other glitches. Roy Gott kept me from numerous errors of discontinuity and lack of context. Huge thanks to Cynthia Thayer, whose creative wisdom made our writing group better.

Laurel, who also runs Laurel Robinson Editorial Services, has been my awesome copyeditor for both *Roma Amor* and *Amber Road*, and Deborah Bailey of Barnstormer Design Group continues to be my brilliant web designer (www.roma-amor.com). I wouldn't be surprised if they can both walk on water. And Peter O'Connor of Bespoke Book Covers Ltd., my cover designer, must have some kind of ESP—no matter how rough a book description is, Peter always "gets it."

A tip of the cavalry helmet to Bill Altimari, author of the excellent *Legion* and *Horses on the Storm*, who graciously answered my horse questions, even the dumbest. ("Would two stallions be friends?")

Mille mercis to John Fanning and Kerry Eielson, founders of La Muse Artists and Writers Retreat in France; Alain Brichau, La Muse's new owner and *genius loci*; and the many friends I've made at La Muse while working on my fiction.

Thanks, too, to Jeff, Carol, Betsy, Laura, Helen, Aaron, Inge (my mapmaker!), Carey, Lysa, and Abby, as well as their partners who are all immensely likable people.

Last, I'd like to acknowledge our cats: Barney, Halsey, and the late lamented Sarge, who tried their utmost to help by sitting or lying on the keyboard.

And, of course . . .

Thank YOU!

Thank you for reading *Amber Road: A Novel of Love and Betrayal on the Roman Frontier* (Book 2 in the *Roma Amor* saga).

Are you willing to post a few comments to help other people looking for a good read? They (and I) would really appreciate it.

Just go to the *Amber Road* page on your favorite book-buying or book-reviewing website, then scroll to "Reader Reviews" to leave your feedback.

Thanks!

HAVE YOU READ BOOK 1?

Roma Amor: A Novel of Caligula's Rome

Here's a peek at how Marcus originally brought Aurima to Rome . . .

Chapter 1: Hostage

At first the girl was less trouble than I expected.

A glance back along the column showed me her coppery hair flashing now and then amid the mouse-colored cloaks of her warriors. At night she vanished silently into a tent with her women. Of course I posted a watch, even amid the placid fields and vineyards of Umbria, but she seemed resigned to captivity. The most bother I had was obtaining fresh meat every day for her and her little band of carnivores.

It was something of a letdown. After spitting murder on the battlefield, to have grown so tame! But such is the nature of barbarians: quick to violent emotion, lacking the self-control in which we Romans are trained.

"You look pleased with yourself, Tribune," said the centurion riding beside me. "A triumphal return, eh? Hostage and all."

He had put on his medals today, seven of them gleaming on the harness strapped across his chain mail. The legionaries had taken the covers off their wing-blazoned shields, and the cavalry horses sported amulets, ribbons, and gaudy tufts of wool on their manes and bridles. I wore my crested helmet and embossed breastplate, polished mirror-bright.

"Ready to parade before Caligula himself," I agreed.

"Gods grant him long life." The centurion slapped at a mosquito.

After days of rain the sun shone wanly, a luminous coin in a hazy sky. Crows jeered at the troops striding by, trailed by pack mules and baggage wagons. Muddy-legged slaves looked up from hoeing a field. Boys chased along, shrilling for a view of the soldiers' swords. The October afternoon smelled of wet pines and trampled leaves, turned earth and wood smoke.

My horse broke into a trot, sensing the journey's end. It was little more than a mile now to the Villa Publica, where I would relinquish my hostage and escort, hand in the dispatches I carried, strip off arms and armor, and reenter the sacred precinct of Rome as a private citizen.

I turned, splashing through puddles in the wheel-worn slabs of stone, and rode back past soldiers and troopers to the Germanic ponies. As usual, the six Marcomanni warriors gathered protectively around their young priestess. As usual, I tried to ignore her immodesty. Although her long skirts were decorous enough, seeing a girl astride a horse was still unsettling.

"We will reach the Field of Mars soon," I told her uncle Maelo, head of the tribespeople escorting her. He was a big hard-muscled man, with a thorn-bush of a beard and long tangled hair that a topknot kept out of his eyes. "Someone from the Palace will take charge of you there."

He was glowering at tombs under the trees. "In little houses of stone, how can spirits go to the gods?"

"That is why Romans keep them there, to frighten away enemies like us," the girl said in more fluent Latin. "Not so, Tribune?" She stared haughtily at me.

"Aurima." Maelo switched into their own language, which sounds like a dog growling. I had picked up enough of it to know he was telling her not to talk to me.

I said, "We Romans honor the spirits of our dead, priestess, and pray they will watch over the family."

Her uncle translated for the others. They shifted in their saddles, averting their eyes from the sepulchers on either side of the road.

I looked down at her from the back of my roan stallion, which stood a good two hands taller than her pony. Aurima wore her best for our arrival in Rome: silver banded her brow and swirled up her wrist. Her eyes were the pale green of *aminea* grapes, her sunburned nose as straight as a blade, her mouth wide but wintry. With her chin raised, the strong cheekbones and bold jaw betrayed her savage breeding. It was far too willful a face to ever be thought comely.

She turned away, her braid brushing the fallen hood of her blue cloak. I imagined for a moment that thick plait undone, her hair cascading in gleaming copper ripples down her bare shoulders . . .

Forget it, Carinna; she is not for you. In an hour—possibly two, allowing for administrative delays—I would be riding up to the doors of my family's house. No, I would stop first at the Spartan Baths for a sweat and a good scraping. And a girl, some agreeable wench who did not smell like a wet horse.

I was turning back toward the head of the column when Maelo said, "*Hvaz gebt?*"

Aurima sat up stiffly on her pony, her eyes fixed on a pilastered rotunda half hidden in a grove of cypress. She drew an amber pendant from under her tunic, and in a loud strained voice called out what could only be an incantation against spirits.

Dead leaves plastered the bronze doors of the tomb behind the cypresses, doors so black with age that they seemed to stand open on darkness. Yet I myself had shut and locked them three years earlier, after a last prayer in front of a shiny new urn. I still knew its inscription by heart, so much shorter than those of our distinguished ancestors in their niches: *Publius Licinius Carinna, son of Titus, grandson of Titus, whose life fell short of the honors to which his valor would have entitled him. Died at the age of twenty-two years.* The same age I was now.

The girl could not possibly know that. Until now, she had never been more than a few days' ride from the Danube. So the reason for her nervousness must be simpler: something in my demeanor, a gesture or glance of which I was unaware, had drawn her attention to my family's mausoleum on the Hill of Small Gardens.

A crow screeched from the tomb's conical roof. And a voice in my ear whispered: *Your turn, little brother.*

I whipped my head around so quickly that my helmet crest tugged at its lashings. No one was near enough to have spoken so softly to me.

Little brother?

By Mithras's Dog! What made me imagine ghostly whispers from a dead man? The Lord of Light had long since judged whether the good my brother had done in life outweighed the evil. His spirit was in paradise or hell, not here.

The Marcomanni rode past. Aurima turned and eyed me, clutching her amber talisman. "Mithras guard me," I muttered, and leaning over my horse's shoulder spat on the ground.

As I moved along the ranks, soldiers who had never seen any place larger than a legion camp yelled out, half joking: Would there really be black-skinned Pygmies? Camelopards as tall as a house? Sea battles in a giant pool? Hermaphrodites?

I laughed. They would find it all, I assured them, everything they could imagine, in Rome.

Roma Amor: A Novel of Caligula's Rome is available in print, ebook, and audiobook.

Made in the USA
Middletown, DE
07 October 2020